# The End of Paradise

## Craig Brown

New Generation Publishing

# Acknowledgments and Reflections

I have previous novels to my credit but this one has proved to be, as they say, a horse of a different colour. I needed to draw both inspiration and information from outside sources to bring what I hope is realism to certain chapters, and these areas of enlightenment must be acknowledged. Without them, there is no doubt that the story would have suffered because it would simply have been less believable.

First of all, I should mention my father, whose remarkable and unforgettable reminiscences from his years as Radio Officer in the Merchant Navy during World War 2 can never be erased from my mind. Dad is now – alas! – sailing the oceans in the sky, but he bequeathed me a wealth of memories which came flooding back to me as I planned the chapters featuring Stephen J. Kettering-Barclay. Very well, I admit I have freely embellished these tales – I am writing fiction, after all – but still the whole idea of this particular character arose from those marvellous latter-day conversations with Joseph Brown. It is important, however, for me to say – indeed, to emphasize – that my father's personality and private life are in no way represented in the fictional invention of Stephen Kettering-Barclay. They remain quite separate and different people, even though the war at sea connects them.

It is only sensible that an author portraying behaviour in a specific 'life zone' should ensure from the outset that he or she knows enough about the subject to paint an authentic and plausible picture of what the main character is experiencing. Failing that care and attention, you dig yourself into a dark hole and go blundering into greater and greater absurdity. Soon after I had started to describe the journey reluctantly embarked upon by Aisling McIver, it began to dawn on me that I was committed to exploring and detailing a lifestyle completely foreign to me, a folly which would surely result in Aisling's chapters emerging as two-dimensional and unconvincing. Determined to maintain direction, I spoke to a friend about this dilemma and it is fair to say, without a word of exaggeration, that a whole new world of knowledge and understanding was subsequently opened up to me. It is no longer a mere matter of acknowledging the help I received; I have to say a huge *Thank You* to all the people who gave so kindly and generously of their time in order to make sure that what I wrote of Aisling McIver's doubts and turmoils was as true to life as possible.

In this internet age, the popular wisdom is that by searching on-line you can soon become an expert on almost anything. This is not true. When I tried this approach in creating Aisling McIver, it took hardly any time at all for me to realise that merely reading about this particular 'industry' would be totally inadequate. I needed to find the right people and talk to them face-to-face. One helpful individual led me to another, and so on, and over a period of ten months I spent hours and hours – twenty hours, possibly – in conversation with people who were always pleased to talk to me, laugh with me, sometimes shed a few tears and always, *always*, share their experiences in absolute and engaging honesty. So for all the jugs of coffee, gallons of sparkling water and piles of sandwiches, not to mention the life stories, I extend my enormous gratitude to my lovely friend Natalie Keira Bealman, and to Sorcha McKinley, Ellen-Jane Aronson, Vivienne Brearley, Suzanne Catherton, Louisa Manning and Tara Wade. There are others I might mention, but they have not unreasonably asked to remain anonymous. They know who they are and I thank them nonetheless.

Finally, I promise that all the people inhabiting this book are pure inventions and not disguised images of real friends. The characters have lived inside my head for a year and now, at last, it is time to let them out.

CB

# Welcome to Paradise

The doorbell didn't work but, given a few weeks, Jack would see to it. Rome wasn't built in a day. The postman, rapping on the door with his knuckles, was delivering a card to Minnie Starling, a 'Good Luck' greeting from her parents to their daughter in her new home. Minnie had moved in yesterday.

"Nothing much happens round here," the postman told her. "This is a quiet area. You'll notice the difference after Mafeking Terrace."

"Ah well," Minnie said, evincing no interest in the assessment. She had things to do, boxes to unpack, vacuuming, curtains to hang, and that second-hand fridge could do with a clean.

The postman was essentially quite right, as postmen often are. *Nothing much happens round here.* That observation was made to the new occupant of number 33 in 1960, and now, more than half a century later, nothing much is happening in Paradise Park – or, for that matter, in the neighbouring thoroughfares of Paradise Walk or Paradise Row.

It's what Minnie's parents would have called 'a good class area'. The people living here are predominantly older, that is, they are what people in their twenties would call old; and in Paradise Park, there are very few householders in their twenties. In the Park there are sixty-five houses in less than half a mile of semi-rural road. Most people here are quite prosperous, but few are rich and many are not particularly successful or ambitious. Generally, they are comfortable and content. They rather like their lives the way they are. They are not apathetic, but they have reached an agreeable accommodation with the established order.

Nothing bad has ever happened in Paradise Park. No-one has been run over in the street, no-one has ever gone mad or flashed at children in the recreation ground or

3

stabbed their neighbour. It is demonstrably a decent sort of place. There is a calmness in the air.

By making this story ten times as long, we could peer through the windows of every house in the street and share a few bittersweet moments with all the people who live there. Well, obviously, that is not a good idea. That would be taking voyeurism too far. So what follows is what scientists or sociologists might call a sample study, a glimpse into the lives of seven of the residents of Paradise Park. They will be introduced, one by one, as the story unfolds.

Looking north, most of the houses in the road are on the right-hand side, leaving only a scattering of buildings on the left: a few houses, a water treatment plant, a newsagent's and the barns belonging to the farms which lie adjacent to the residential area. Until recently, Rani's Newsagent's offered paper deliveries to the Paradise homes, but the usual paper boy was Billy Smart from number 35, who proved increasingly unreliable, and so now people have to go to the shop in the morning. They frequently buy milk at the same time and perhaps a dusty, softening chocolate bar, a stale lemon roll, a pack of batteries, their potency rendered doubtful by the passage of time. At Rani's, time hangs grainily in the air like dust motes.

There is one local pub, The Rifleman, situated at the north end of Paradise Park, where the three Paradise roads interconnect. This is the venue for Minnie Starling's 100th birthday party, an occasion to which Minnie is keenly looking forward. All her friends and neighbours will be there to join her in her remarkable celebration. They are sure that this will be an evening to remember, and the redoubtable Mrs Starling is not about to disappoint them. While she has made many good friends over the decades, it is inevitable that Minnie has also inscribed in her mental black book the names of a select few people she feels entitled to dislike and to repay their inconstancy; for never let it be said that Minnie is not one to bear a grudge. As

4

time will shortly demonstrate, Minnie Starling grudges for England.

So let us walk the street, meet the people, pry unashamedly into their notably dysfunctional lives and then, on the 13<sup>th</sup> June, stroll along to the party. In an uncertain world, it can be said with confidence that the event will be unforgettable. Minnie is not one to let an opportunity pass her by, and she knows that, at 100 years of age, she has become untouchable, blameless and invisible. She has been born again.

# Chapter 1

## *Number 12: Mr and Mrs Clarnon*

Pat sat. To the casual passer-by, if they noticed him at all, it would surely appear unremarkable that Pat sat where he sat, upright at the steering wheel; he was simply an old man sitting in his car. To the locals and most certainly the neighbours, however, it probably seemed noteworthy and even a little eccentric that Patrick Clarnon not only spent each day perched in his elderly Morris Oxford, but also installed himself on the driver's side of the bench seat, where the wheel was merely an obstruction; for Pat was not going anywhere, not today or tomorrow or any other day.

Although Pat had chosen a long time ago to occupy this seat, rather than the more spacious passenger seat, feeling that here he retained some semblance of ergonomic control over his immediate environment, it was because of his son Ronan that the practice had been perpetuated. Ronan had helpfully fashioned for his father an airline-style folding tray with two angled metal clips, so positioned that they slotted neatly over the rim of the steering wheel. The tray could be flipped up out of the way against the wheel boss, or cranked down to form a horizontal platform above the user's lap. On the opposite side of the cabin, of course, there was nothing to attach it to. So this, day in and day out, in fair weather and foul, throughout the daylight hours, was where Pat sat.

Today was Monday, and on Monday it was baked beans. At 12.30 precisely the street door at number twelve opened and Martha Clarnon emerged, clutching a china plate upon which a half slice of buttered bread resided alongside a small bowl of Heinz beans decorated with a melting knob of butter, a fork protruding from the tawny mound. Martha stepped into the road and tapped on the car window with two knuckles.

Pat blinked, jolted and wound down the window halfway. Martha handed in the plate while her husband carefully lowered the plastic tray and pressed it until it locked securely flat. Neither of them spoke. When the plate was safely balanced, Pat wound the window back up, affording his wife the briefest of glances as she manoeuvred round the bonnet and disappeared indoors. He stirred the beans listlessly with the fork and licked his lips. Pat liked Mondays. It was always beans on Monday.

A few minutes later, his snack gone, he leaned over and placed the plate, bowl and fork on the floor in the adjacent footwell. Then he restored the tray to its upright position. Shortly, when she had finished the vacuuming, Martha would come out again, open the passenger door and retrieve the crockery for washing. On whichever day, whatever the lunch, this was how it worked.

Under his seat lay a grey plastic bottle, a male urinal. Pat reached down, felt for the bottle, took it out and looked at it, then decided he didn't want to go at the moment, so he replaced it under the seat and made himself comfortable once more. By the end of the day the bottle was usually full. When he went in at dusk, he would hand the receptacle to Martha so she could empty it down the toilet. That was how it worked.

As the afternoon wore on, the sky darkened and a thin drizzle hazed the windscreen. Pat waited until his view was almost totally obscured, before turning the ignition key and flicking the wipers on for a few seconds. The drizzle intensified until he could hear the *pinging* of raindrops on the metal roof. The Morris's interior cooled and grew earthily fragrant.

In the corner of his eye, a bobbing shape filled the rectangle of the passenger window. A woman, bent over, dressed in loose grey clothing, was mouthing at him out of an anxious face.

"Mr Clarnon, it's raining."

Pat shook his head. "I can't hear you through the glass," he groaned.

Mrs Stirrup from number four bustled round to the driver's door. Her raddled face was as grey as her clothes. She waved a forefinger to indicate that Pat should open the window.

The old man sighed and rolled his window down an inch.

"Mr Clarnon, it's pouring rain."

"I can see that," Pat said.

"Maybe you ought to go inside."

"I am inside."

"I mean, in the house."

"Why do I need to go in the house?"

"Because it's raining."

"Not in here it's not."

"It'll be damp. Your chest."

"What about my chest?"

"Breathing in this damp air," Mrs Stirrup explained.

"Yes, it's only damp because I've got the damned window open," said Pat.

"All this wet," Mrs Stirrup insisted.

Pat wound down the window another inch, rolling his eyes. "Mrs Stirrup, the only one of us getting wet is you, because you are standing in the rain. I, on the other hand, am perfectly dry, sitting here listening to you telling me I am about to get wet."

"It's just – I'm thinking about your chest."

Pat did not want women thinking about his chest, least of all Mrs Stirrup.

"Suppose I was sat here thinking about your chest," he submitted.

"Mr Clarnon!"

He wound the window right up and wiped the screen again. He stared straight ahead, and when he glanced to his right, his neighbour had gone.

The only trouble with sitting out here in the street was, you were exposed. People liked to interfere. That was the way of the world – people interfering. Pat preferred to be left in peace. That was why he sat in the car in the first place. You turned on the news in the evening, and all you got was international strife caused by people interfering. That was the world's problem in a single word: interference. He shifted in his seat, released a silent fart, eased its escape through the briefly opened window and sealed himself up again.

"Nothing wrong with my chest," he muttered. He allowed himself to conjure up a fleeting vision of Mrs Stirrup's chest, but the exercise did nothing for him. "Bloody woman!"

The rain was bouncing off the car bonnet now. The windows were starting to steam up. There was a cloth in the door pocket. He rummaged for it and wiped his side window and half the windscreen. When Martha came to collect the plate, he would tell her to bring out his umbrella, in case it was still raining when the time came for him to come in.

Something fizzing above his head drew his attention to the top of the windscreen. He lifted the hinge of the sun visor and found a large black fly skittering along the glass. Jabbing a finger sharply upwards, he felt the satisfying crunch of the gritty body as it smeared the window frame. Gripping the fly's wing between his fingernails, he dropped the dead intruder on to the discarded lunch plate. Pat was a little worried then, for a recent cut to his forefinger had barely healed, and he speculated apprehensively upon the possibility of some grim infection. He recalled the agonized Jeff Goldblum in Cronenberg's grisly movie and grappled briefly with the ghastly spectre of his own irreversible fusion, Patrick Clarnon rampaging through the streets, hairy arms akimbo and nose dangling, spewing froth over terrified pedestrians. He wiped his finger vigorously on his trousers.

Was school out already? Sauntering towards him, heedless of the rain, two navy-blazered adolescent girls, their short grey skirts revealing pale, stocky legs and rumpled socks. One worked her thick-lipped mouth, apparently chewing gum, while her companion used two downward-pointing fingers to grip a smouldering cigarette. Pat studied the girls discreetly from the corner of one eye, transferring his gaze to the rear view mirror as they passed.

"No better than they ought to be," he grumbled.

Half an hour later, the rain was still percussive on the car roof, when Martha Clarnon came out to retrieve Pat's plate. She opened the passenger door and bent to the floor.

"Might want my umbrella," Pat said.

"What?"

"If it's raining when I come in. Can you bring it out?"

"What, now?"

"Might as well. Don't leave the door open, rain's getting in."

"You want me to get soaked?"

"Umbrella. Just fetch the umbrella."

Martha slammed the door shut, muttering something he couldn't hear. He watched her go, holding the plate out in front of her as if to catch the rain.

She was a good woman, he thought, but sometimes…sometimes she could be quite unreasonable. You had to be tolerant, understanding. Yes, that was how it worked.

# Chapter 2

## *Number 15: Aisling McIver and Neamh*

"There, I've done it, so!" She thumped the stamp with the side of her fist. "Sure, let's hope it doesn't bounce, eh?" She picked up the envelope, as if weighing it, and dropped it back on the table. "It'll bounce, right? Of course it'll bounce."

Aislng was smiling thinly at the baby in the blue and yellow carrycot on the floor. The baby gazed up at her, one pink seashell of a curled fist waving, but offered no reply. Neamh was not yet two. Mercifully, she could neither understand nor judge.

Her mother kicked off her shoes disconsolately and stared at the baby. The baby peered up at Aisling. The mother sighed. The child gurgled and sneezed.

"You're probably wet," Aisling said quietly. "Well, so am I. I've a wet foot, from a hole in my shoe. Okay, so there you are, little one. D'you know how much is a pair of decent shoes nowadays, eh? It's nearly as much as is in that envelope, that's how much."

She bent down and picked up the left shoe and inspected the sole. The ragged hole hadn't quite gone through to the inside, but it was deep enough to let in water. She shook her head and tossed the shoe aside.

Neamh sneezed again.

"I hope you're not catching a cold, little one," Aisling murmured. "Guess we'll both be catching a cold when that cheque bounces. Am I right? Course I am. All I'm doing is, I'm showing willing, see. I'm paying them. That is, I'm sending them a payment. God help us. I'll get it sorted somehow, even if I have to hop on one leg."

She crouched at the carrycot, lifted the child out, shook her softly and put her down again, carefully adjusting the blanket.

"Your dad said he'd send us something more, but – well, it's like I'm waiting for a pig to go flying past the window. No, I won't pressure him. I want shut of him. Wait till you're a wee bit older, you'll understand."

A mouse-like squeak issued from the folds of the blanket.

"There, see. I knew you'd see it my way. Sure I did. You're a clever little mite."

She settled herself back on the upright chair by the table and kicked the damaged shoe away from her. "Bit of cardboard might do it for now, I reckon. So long as I don't go walking in any puddles." Screwing up her eyes, she glanced quickly round the room. "Let's hope they don't go cutting off the electric, that's all. When they get that rubber cheque. Suppose I can ask the social, if they do. It don't cost to ask."

There was a KitKat on the table. Aisling unwrapped the paper, broke off a finger and popped it in her mouth. "Well, there goes me lunch."

She stood up and crossed to the mirror over the fireplace. She stood stock-still, making faces. "So I've seen worse," she said. "You're no beauty, Aisling McIver, but maybe you're kind of a handsome woman." Reaching up with her palms, she primped her hair, turning her head to left and right, eyes fixed on her reflection. "Could use a bit of lippy, dare say. Got some somewhere." She slowly unbuttoned her blouse, tugging it down at the shoulders. "I always liked this bra. Lilac, I think you'd call it. Sort of elegant." She dredged up a laugh, but it was more of a snort. "Danny, he preferred what was inside. Most nights, he had his nose in there. And not just that. God knows how he ever got me pregnant."

She stood back and thought again about her hair. The natural colour was auburn, but a few weeks ago she'd had a woman round, friend of a friend, and sat patiently, a little apprehensively, while the visiting hairdresser cut, coloured and revitalized her hair, all for the gloriously unaffordable price of ninety pounds. The result had survived well, but there were time limits, and now she struggled to convince herself that her streaky style with its thinning blonde threads was merely contemporary. That was before she even began to think about the money.

She turned and looked down at the baby. "What do you think, Neamh? Does Mummy need her hair doing again? Could be it'll have to be that or the gas bill."

The intercom buzzed. She stepped to the doorway and pressed the button.

A thin electronic rattle gave way to a female voice. "Hi Aisling. It's Rona."

"Oh Rona. Come up."

She held the button until the downstairs latch clicked, then opened the door. Neamh clucked softly. "It's your Auntie Rona," Aisling whispered.

Rona Melville bustled in with her arms full of shopping and, bright-eyed, pecked Aisling on the cheek. Without waiting to be prompted, she unloaded her bags on the table, pulled off her coat and scarf and draped them over the back of a spare chair.

Aisling grinned. "Make yourself at home, Rona."

Her friend spun the chair round and sat down. "Got you some fruit from the market. Tons cheaper. There's satsumas, apples, bananas and some peaches. The peaches are quite ripe, so when you unpack them, be careful they don't bruise. Okay?"

"Thanks, dear. Love you."

"You're looking a bit pale. Not sleeping?"

"I'm all right, Rona. How much do I owe you?"

"What?"

"For the fruit."

"Ah, don't be silly. It wasn't much." She peered down into the cot. "And how is this little lady today?"

"Okay I think," Aisling said, gazing pensively at the bags on the table. There was a fruit bowl somewhere, except she'd need more than one. She had a colander, she could use that.

"Will you do something for me, Rona?" She picked up

the envelope from the table and held it out. "Will you post this for me when you're out?"

"Sure." Rona took the envelope and put it in her coat pocket.

"It's for the electric. They're not happy with me."

"Are they ever?" She puffed out her cheeks and gazed at the floor. "It's hard, I know."

Aisling said nothing, just shook her head, avoiding Rona's eyes.

Squinting into the shadow under the table, Rona asked, "Is that your shoe down there?"

"Whose else would it be?" Aisling retorted wearily.

"There's a big hole in it."

"So there is. I've a flat pair upstairs I can wear."

"And that makes it all right then?"

Aisling sat back in her chair and passed a hand feebly over her eyes. "Leave it be, Rona, please. It's just a shoe."

Rona blinked, chewing her top lip. That was the point; it wasn't just the shoe. It was everything about this gloomy room with its faded wallpaper peeling away from the ceiling. It was about the grubby carpet speckled with food spills and the net curtains turning yellow and the paperwork stacked beside the TV that looked suspiciously like unpaid bills. The shoe wasn't the disease; the shoe was a symptom.

"I should offer you a drink," Aisling said, in a small voice.

"In a minute. It's just – it's – "

"It's what, exactly?"

"Well, you know, sometimes I wonder how you're managing, Aisling. I worry sometimes." She nodded vaguely at the cot on the floor. "This tiny one, for instance."

"What about her?"

"Babies don't come free, Aisling. I mean, what do you do about food and all the other stuff? Clothes, too."

Aisling was perched bolt-upright on her chair now, eyes narrowed defiantly. "Rona Melville, I can't believe what I'm hearing. For Christ's sake! Are you suggesting I can't look after my child?"

"I'm suggesting no such thing," Rona said levelly, extending a placating hand in her friend's direction. "You're a model mother, anyone would know that."

"Thank you," Aisling snapped. "And your point is?"

"My point is, this is no time to be proud. If you need help."

"What d'you mean, help?"

She spread her hands. "Practical help. Money help. Living help."

Aisling subsided in her chair, eyes downcast, rotating a forefinger against her temple. At that moment, she loved Rona and disliked her, felt anger and relief at the same time. Damn you, Rona, she thought, and bless you too. Bless every interfering part of you.

"Put the kettle on," Rona said. "Before you do – can you tell me what they paid you at Beasley's?"

"What? Oh, I don't know. I can't rightly remember." She put her little finger in her mouth and chewed it thoughtfully. "I did four days a week. I think it was eight thousand a year."

Rona nodded. "Okay. Now make us some tea. I'll do a calculation."

"Hmm. You want some paper?"

"No, no. In my head."

In the kitchen, Aisling found two unchipped mugs, some teabags and a packet of malted milk biscuits. There was just enough milk. She put some biscuits on a plate, and leaned against the worktop for a moment to steady herself, counting slowly to twenty. Then she arranged everything on a plastic tray.

"Thanks, honey," Rona said brightly.

"Sugar lumps in the pot. Sorry I've no tongs."

"Pretentious," Rona pronounced, shaking her head.

They sat quietly, sipping their tea. Neamh squawked and kicked her feet. Rona smiled at her. A glass-fronted clock on the mantelpiece made a whirring noise and struck three, though it was not yet two o'clock. Rona looked solemnly at the clock and checked her watch.

"Well then," Aisling said, clasping her mug in both hands.

Rona stared at her, slowly nodding her head. "We can do something about this, you know."

"Such as?"

"Here's the deal. Call it a proposition."

"I'm listening."

Rona reached over and put her mug on the table. While Aisling was making the tea, she had thought of riffling through the papers by the TV to get an idea of her friend's indebtedness, but that seemed a scarcely justifiable intrusion. It could wait.

"Beasley's paid you eight grand a year for four days' work – yes?"

"Like I said, I think so."

"Aisling, you could be your own boss."

"What?"

"No-one to tell you what to do, nobody looking over your shoulder. You'd work from home, so no going out in the freezing cold and no getting trampled on by commuters. You'd be here with Neamh, so you wouldn't have to give your money away to a minder."

Aisling's face wore a mask of grim incomprehension. "I don't know what you're talking about," she said.

"You will do. You could still do a four-day week, no weekends, and restrict yourself to, oh, maybe just two hours a day."

Aisling's expression had shifted like a drifting cloud from incomprehension to exasperation. "So I'm doing eight hours a week, am I? What, am I stuffing envelopes?"

"Course not. I'd never suggest it." She took another sip of her tea and replaced the mug. "You'd be making the most of yourself, of what you've got."

"Rona, will you start making sense. This is some mad jape."

"No. I wouldn't come here to waste your time."

17

"Is that so?"

"You could buy all the shoes you wanted."

"Get to the point, Rona."

"If you did the eight hours, I'd reckon on forty thousand a year."

"Oh, you're crazy, Rona Melville! I can't sit here listening to this garbage." Her eyes flashed angrily and she gripped her hands tightly in her lap, as if to prevent herself from leaping from the chair in frustration.

"Well, maybe I didn't expect you to believe me. Not at first."

"Rona, if you could do that, sure, everybody'd be doing it."

"Yes, and a lot of people are. There's a girl I know, your age, drives around in a new Lexus."

"Forty thousand quid for doing next to nothing and not even stepping out the door?"

"That's about the long and short of it."

She straightened up. "I'm going to the loo, Rona. When I come back, you'd better start talking sense, or I'll be showing you the door. Okay?"

"Agreed. Take your time. Come back, sit down and listen carefully. Then I'll tell you how it works."

# Chapter 3

## *Number 22: Mr and Mrs Slocombe and Arthur*

It was one o'clock. Lunch-time. Hettie Slocombe was laying the table. The Slocombes always had lunch at one o'clock. They had no truck with the modern idea of dinner in the evening. You could have tea at five and maybe some soup for supper later, if you were still peckish. No use going to bed on an empty stomach. You'd only be up in the night, poking in the cupboard for a biscuit or a chocolate cupcake.

Hettie had draped a freshly laundered white cloth over the mahogany dining room table, to be overlaid with rectangular coloured tablemats depicting painted scenes of Victorian London, and finally the best silver cutlery from the walnut canteen that had been in the family since wartime. The plates she would bring in separately, once the food had been arranged on them.

Of course, Arthur would expect his lunch as well, but he wouldn't sit up to the table. She would see to him afterwards. She would find him something.

Today it was home-made fishcakes, croquette potatoes and peas. There was jam roly-poly with custard for pudding, but the roly-poly was out of a packet. That was all right; Alf wouldn't mind. She couldn't be cooking all morning.

When the table was set, Hettie stood for a moment and quietly surveyed her handiwork. Alf had always liked a nice table. He said it made all the difference. It showed that that touch of extra care had gone into the meal. Well, that was what Alf said, anyway. When he made the point, it left Hettie with a warm, self-satisfied smile.

She brought the plates in and placed hers on the Tower of London and Alf's on The Old Curiosity Shop. She sat down, smoothed her skirt under her, drew her chair a little closer to the table, picked up her knife and fork and began to eat.

"Yours'll be getting cold if you don't start, Alf," she told him.

She tucked in to the chunky fishcakes, made with fresh cod from Scrampton the Fishmonger in the High Street. The peas were from the garden, and she had shelled them straight into the pan. Hettie always added salt and a pinch of sugar.

"Come on, dear, it's your favourite."

She heard Arthur come in and sit in the armchair. "I'll get yours in a minute," she said, over her shoulder. She picked up a linen napkin, neatly folded into a triangle, shook it loose and dabbed at the corners of her mouth.

Evidently Alf was not very hungry today. This happened sometimes. You could never tell. He never said. She would leave his plate there, anyway. After all, he had always been a slow eater, a man who invariably chewed his food very thoroughly before swallowing it. Once, when their son Robert had come round for lunch, she explained to him that his dad always liked to masticate slowly while eating his meal, a disclosure which, for some reason she could not quite understand, had sent Robert into paroxysms of food-spattering laughter. Well, that was Robert; he was his own man.

"Will you be wanting pudding?" Hettie asked.

Alf didn't reply, but probably he was still thinking about his first course. It didn't do to rush him. Alf never did anything rapidly. She reflected that, in all their time together, she had never seen him hurry over a task or so much as walk down the road fast. Perhaps, she thought, to Alf, life was a long meal to be savoured, not bolted down.

Still, he didn't appear to be savouring this one. By now, surely, it must be almost cold. She reached across the table and gently pushed his plate an inch or two closer to him. "There," she said.

She heard Arthur shifting about in the armchair. "Just

be patient, Arthur. Yours is coming."

"Pardon. Did you say something, Alf?"

But Alf's only response was silence.

"Oh dear. I think it was next door's wireless I heard. They've got it right next to the wall."

"The fishcakes are nice, Alf." She sighed, dabbed her lips once more and stood up. "You wait there. I'll fetch you some roly-poly. It's proper custard."

She went into the kitchen, carrying her empty plate. Arthur jumped up to follow her, and she felt him behind her, bumping against her leg. "Learn some patience, Arthur Slocombe! I shall do yours in a minute."

For a moment she thought of giving her husband's neglected lunch to young Arthur, but she remembered he didn't like fish. There was nothing for it; the food would have to go in the bin. Rummaging in the basket under the sink, she took a handful of vegetables – carrots, lettuce and a head of broccoli, together with an apple – and chopped it all into a bowl with a fist of fibre pellets, then she put the bowl on the floor by the back door.

"There you are, Arthur. And see you eat every scrap."

The rabbit hopped across the floor, tail bobbing, and began snuffling in the bowl.

Hettie put out two portions of roly-poly and covered each liberally with custard. She took Alf's pudding into the front room and placed it on the coffee table with a spoon balanced on a coaster. He could sit comfortably and enjoy his pud while watching the television. He had always liked his sport. She turned the TV on and found some golf.

"Alf, I think it's the Open. Your favourite. I've put your roly-poly in here so you don't miss it."

Hettie would leave him there in peace for the afternoon. She didn't care much for golf, except that the golfers had kind faces and wore nice trousers. It was a civilized game, she thought. The men never fell over and pretended to be injured and they didn't spit on the grass. She wondered why Alf had never played golf.

When she had disposed of Alf's lunch, she went upstairs for a lie-down. It was cool in the bedroom and there were no cooking smells. It was as she kicked off her shoes that she remembered the slippers. "Silly me," she said to herself. So she went back downstairs and picked up Alf's slippers from under the coffee table, returning to the kitchen to pop them in the oven. Two minutes the right way up at gas mark three, then another two upside down. Arthur had disappeared, leaving a neat circle of dark droppings on the floor. Once the rubber soles smelled suitably warm, she lifted out the slippers and carried them through to the front room. She set them tidily by the armchair, smiling in calm satisfaction.

In the bedroom once more, she sat on the edge of the bed and applied some soft white cream to her face, massaging the moisture under her eyes and into the folds of her neck. Her gaze settled upon a framed photograph on the dressing table. Plucking a tissue from a floral box, she wiped her fingers before lifting the frame on to her lap. In the slightly faded photo, she and Alf, carelessly windblown, beamed at the camera against a backdrop of blue sky and whitecapped ocean. She turned the picture over. A scuffed label on the back read simply 'Us. Dorset 2004.' She closed her eyes and the memories came flooding back. The coastal path at Golden Cap. June, or was it July? A lady walking her dog had offered to take their photograph with Alf's camera. She stood on the dog's lead in case he escaped over the cliff. Kind of her. The sun was so warm on Hettie's bare back and shoulders, though a stiff breeze billowed off the sea, ruffling their hair into pale clouds. When the wind subsided, there was the distant susurration of the incoming tide as it breathed on the rocks below, and the yawping squeal of black-faced gulls swooping in over the crumpled tinfoil of the sunstruck waves. And there was Alf with his arm around her shoulders, loving and protective and so inseparably, irreplaceably a part of her. Summer 2004. That had been their last holiday together, barely five months before his cancer was diagnosed.

Hettie lay down with her head on the pillow, cradling the photo frame in both hands. Gently, she stroked Alf's grinning face with a trembling finger.

"Oh, my love," she whispered. "Oh, my dear love."

A tear slid from her cheek and tracked slowly down the glass.

# Chapter 4

## *Number 25: Miss Joan Descours*

Her colleagues at East Moulton College were sympathetically unanimous: Joan Descours was not traditionally beautiful, nor even notably attractive; but she was what might fairly be described as a handsome woman. With her long face, slender nose and prim mouth, the spontaneous impression gained from a first study of her features below the cheekbones was that Miss Descours' eyes were set uncommonly high in her head, an illusion accentuated by a low fringe that threatened to blend confusingly with her eyebrows.

"She has nice glossy hair," someone allowed.

"A pleasant, clean complexion," another pointed out.

"She always carries herself well," said an elderly female professor.

Doctor George Bramley thought Miss Descours had rather pert breasts, but a withering sense of professional decorum discouraged him from contributing this opinion.

"She's no oil painting," the bursar declared unkindly.

Joan Descours was one of the college's newer lecturers, tutoring students in $19^{th}$ and $20^{th}$ Century History. She was smartly-dressed, articulate and generally popular with her students, for she was unremittingly patient and exuded an air of friendly authority. She loved her work, frequently stayed late to finish marking papers and was not averse to offering private study at her home to those whose deliberations she felt deserved that extra attention. She drove to and from work in an aged Nissan Micra with the college's blue and white sticker in the rear window.

Today the college was closed. The entrance lobby and the dining hall were inaccessible to students as they were being used as a polling station for the local by-election. Everyone had a day off. However, that did not include

Joan Descours, for she had urgent work to do in supporting one of her young pupils, 17-year-old Barry Brown, who had been away ill and was behind with preparations for his end-of-term thesis and the accompanying presentation he would make to his peers as part of Miss Descours' carefully structured programme coupling academic achievement with confidence-building. Barry, small for his age, was a bright, willing lad, but a little withdrawn. It was part of Joan's master plan to educate the boy not merely in his chosen subject but also in the ways of the wider world. After all, he would have to live there.

In the brightly yellow-painted kitchen, she spread her files and papers on the table and opened her laptop. She made herself a mug of decaffeinated coffee and sat nursing the drink, examining her paperwork. Whilst wanting Barry to take the initiative in deciding how best he should formulate his thesis, she considered it her duty to point him in the right direction. It was like bringing up your own child, she thought: yes to guidance, no to indoctrination. As in the final oratory, it all came down to self-confidence, and that was something in which Barry Brown was conspicuously lacking.

The subject which Barry had asked to explore was America's involvement in the Second World War in the aftermath of the Japanese attack on Pearl Harbour.

"My grandad was in the war," he told Miss Descours, vaguely.

"But not in America or Japan, Barry?"

"Don't think so, Miss."

"Which service was he in?"

"Might have been on a ship, Miss."

"I see. Was he involved in the fighting?"

"Oh no, he had a good record, Miss."

And Joan Descours blinked, courteously suppressing a smile. "No, what I mean is…was he serving aboard a military vessel?"

"He had a uniform, Miss."

"A uniform. Right."

This, she decided, was an enquiry to be readdressed later.

Doctor Bramley had not entirely approved of his colleague's arrangement for private tutorial. "He's coming round to your house," you say.

"Indeed. On Thursday."

Bramley tugged nervously at his beard. "For study?"

"Of course, for study."

"Er…is that wise, Miss Descours?"

"It's very wise. The boy has only recently returned from a long period of absence. Some kind of colon problem, I believe. He has a lot of ground to make up, not to mention his anxiety over his future."

"And will there be other such visits?"

"I really can't say, George." She frowned irritably. "Is something the matter?"

"It's just – this presumably is unchaperoned?"

"George, this is the twenty-first century, for God's sake."

"Even so."

"Which of us needs the chaperone?"

"Oh, I – I'm sure neither of you does," he said, raising placating hands.

"Then you are flying in the face of your own argument," said Miss Descours defiantly.

George Bramley nodded, coughing quietly into his hand. "Yes, yes, probably," he muttered, "I suppose I'm a bit – could the word be *trepidatious*?"

Miss Descours sniffed. "I know of no such word," she said. "I think you must be losing your apples, Doctor Bramley," she adjudged, with uncharacteristic wit.

She was quite aware of the background to Bramley's aversion. Hardly a year ago mathematics teacher Jake Blanchard had been quietly dismissed after admitting to an inappropriate after-school relationship with a young boy, initiated on the pretext of essential pre-examination study. The incident had been skilfully handled and the college's reputation was never seriously compromised; but those on the inside still smarted from the awkwardness.

"George, are you alluding to that Blanchard man, by any chance?"

"To whom?"

"Come on, George."

Bramley wiped a despairing hand across his forehead. "Well, I hadn't forgotten that, yes. And, well, he was, you know, a highly-qualified, upstanding staff man."

Miss Descours speculated, with a confidence embellished by the student's more intimate revelations at interview, as to which part of Jake Blanchard had been upstanding at the time.

"That's sorted, George. It's dead and buried. The signs were there and we ignored them. It won't happen again."

Doctor Bramley offered her a patronizing smile. "I do hope not, my dear. It's just…"

"Just what? Don't you trust me, Doctor Bramley?"

"Oh, goodness, yes! Yes, of course."

"It doesn't sound much like it. Indeed, I can almost detect some vague insinuation lurking behind your unease." She stuffed a pile of papers hurriedly into her foolscap wallet and stood up.

"Miss Descours, I would certainly urge caution in this regard. That is my position."

"Hmm. I can do without your urges, Doctor Bramley." She elbowed him aside. "This conversation is at an end."

She hadn't seen Bramley since then. Stupid man. What was he a doctor of, anyway? In a briefly malicious moment, she dared to wonder whether he was contemptuous of Blanchard or merely jealous. You never could be sure. Joan Descours would keep her options open.

The bus stop was at the top of the road. Barry Brown would get off there and walk down, aiming for eleven o'clock. Miss Descours surveyed the table. She cleared a space for Barry to work in and filled a glass jug with orange squash, setting this refreshment to one side, with two tumblers. Perhaps he would like a little gentle background music; young people often worked that way nowadays, she knew. But what to play? She had some easy-listening CDs, they might serve the purpose, nothing too intrusive. Or there were classics, but Barry had never struck her as a Mozart man. God help her, he might want some ghastly pop racket. Popular music, was it? Well, it wasn't popular with her. Of course, she could remember when the groups came on dressed in suits and ties and somehow managed to sing their songs without near-naked women gyrating behind them. Those were the days, and you could even remember the tunes, catchy they were, and sing them to yourself afterwards. That was before music died and nobody noticed.

She decided to wait until Barry arrived and let him choose the music or reject the idea as a distraction. Reaching for a teacloth, she draped it over the open squash jug. Perhaps a plate of biscuits would be welcoming – or should she make some sandwiches? Still, he would no doubt have had breakfast, and it was too early for lunch. She told herself not to fuss.

The lad was punctual, ringing the doorbell at five to eleven.

"Right on time, Barry," she said, shouldering the door closed behind him.

The weekday buses were seldom reliable, she knew, so she wondered about Barry's punctuality. Had he arrived early and hung around until the agreed hour? It was raining and the boy looked flushed and dishevelled.

"Your hair looks wet, Barry."

"I'm all right."

"Do you want a towel?"

"Sorry, Miss?"

"For your hair."

"I'm all right."

At first she sat opposite him, then realized she would prefer to be able to see his work, so she moved her chair beside him, close enough, but not so near that her thigh might brush against his.

Barry had removed a laptop from the rain-pebbled

shoulder bag he had brought, and began setting it up on the table, his weather-blotched face a stern mask of concentration. After a minute or two he rubbed his hands on his trouser legs and glanced quickly at his tutor.

"Okay, Miss."

"Happy, Barry?"

"Yes, Miss."

Joan Decours focused on Barry's flickering laptop screen to avoid looking him in the eye, slowly, thoughtfully stroking her long nose. "Now let's set the scene," she said. "This has to be your own work, you understand, but I want to point you in what I see as the right direction."

"Yes, Miss."

"I think you could develop your narrative around four particular questions. First one: Why did the Japanese attack Pearl Harbour in the first place? What was their mid- or long-term strategy?"

"That's two questions, Miss."

"Call it two questions rolled into one, Barry."

"Yes, Miss."

"Okay. Second: Analyse the Americans' immediate reaction. Was their spontaneous outrage largely sparked by the attack itself, or were they equally incensed by the inept miscalculation surrounding the forewarning? Okay?"

"I think so, Miss."

"Good. Third: Less than four years later, the U.S. dropped atomic bombs on Hiroshima and Nagasaki. Do we see that as delayed retaliation, or as a means of ending the war in the East, thus saving the countless lives of an invasion force, or was it simply because they had a bomb and were desperately keen to see what it would do?"

Barry nodded, staring solemnly at the screen.

"Finally: What do we read into this from a moral standpoint? I don't mean just at that time, but also today, when a subsequent nuclear attack is an ever-present threat, and on a much broader scale."

"I understand, Miss."

"Yes. Only don't get too involved in the last question, or you'll find yourself drifting off into infinity. Keep it compact." She lifted some papers from an untidy heap and pulled out a paperback book. "Here, I got you this. Take it and let me have it back, whenever. You should find it helpful as well as thought-provoking."

Barry took the book and peered at it. "Thanks, Miss. Jonathan Schell, *The Fate of the Earth*." His lips carried on moving as he stared at the cover.

"No child this century should be allowed to grow up without reading that book, Barry. Always remember that."

"Thank you, Miss."

"Now, would you like a drink before you start work? There's tea or coffee if you'd rather. Oh." She raised a forefinger. "I meant to say. Toilet is upstairs and straight ahead. I - uh – I know you had a not very nice operation."

"I'm fine now, thanks, Miss Descours. P'raps I'll have a drink later."

"As you wish, Barry."

"Miss?"

"Yes, Barry?"

"I think your blouse is very nice, I mean, it looks good on you."

Joan Descours sat back and clasped her hands to her chest. "Well, thank you, Barry, for saying so." A slow warmth crept into her cheeks. "And now – let's get to work."

# Chapter 5

## *Number 12: The Clarnons*


Pat sat. Softly clearing his throat, he licked his lips and wiped them with a knuckle and the bony back of his forefinger, removing the small soup stains that had accumulated at the corners of his mouth. He burped, tasting the soup again, and patted his chest in the hope of assisting his digestion.

He stood up, tugging at the back of his shirt, stretching, gently groaning.

"Do you want the telly?" his wife enquired.

"No. I'm going back outside," he told her.

She laid her knitting in her lap and stared at him. "You've not long been in. You're not surely going to sit in that car again."

"Think I'll check the oil," he said. "Fetch me that rubber torch and a square of kitchen roll."

Martha got up and went to the kitchen, though not without wondering why. "Thought slavery had been abolished," she muttered. "Can't imagine why he needs to check the oil. He never drives anywhere."

The street was almost completely dark. There was no-one about. A tabby cat froze against the railings when it saw him and then bolted across the road.

Pat prised open the Morris's bonnet, switched on the torch and fumbled for the dipstick. He held the stick in the yellowish light, wiped the end, reinserted the spindly rod, pulled it back out and squinted at it. The oil looked rather black but the level was satisfactory. He replaced the stick and slammed the bonnet down, scrunching the dirty paper into a ball.

A nearby street lamp was illuminating the car's interior with pale amber panels. Pat thought it looked rather pleasant in there. Unlocking the driver's door, he slid on to the cold seat and shut himself in. "Might as well have a rest," he said.

He hunkered down in the seat, making himself comfortable. He turned the radio on. A band was playing a strident march. Pat smiled. He enjoyed a good, rousing march. He got his knees working, thumping his feet up and down on the floormat in time to the music. With all the noise in the car, it took him a few seconds to hear the tapping at the window.

Mrs Stirrup peered anxiously inside, one hand raised to her face to shield the reflection from the street lamp. "That you, Mr Clarnon?"

Pat rolled the window down an inch, grinding his teeth, and turned the music down. "Course it's me. Who else would it be?"

"It's dark, Mr Clarnon."

"I know it's dark. I can see it's dark."

"I just wondered what you was doing in the dark. I heard a bumping."

"I'm – I was marching, if it's any business of yours."

"Marching? You don't need a car to go marching." She straightened up and bent down again. "Where you marching to?"

"Nowhere," said Pat, gruffly.

"Ah, right. So you're in your car in the dark, marching to nowhere. You all right, Mr Clarnon?"

"Yes, I'm fine, thank you. Now if you don't mind –"

"Only you don't generally sit out here in the dark, as I remember."

"Is there a law against it?"

"No, Mr Clarnon, course there isn't. I just wondered, see."

"I came out to check the oil, if you must know."

"Check the oil? Can't have used much oil, you never go anywhere."

"I might just take a drive later," Pat said absurdly.

"Oh, right you are, then. You drive careful in all this dark."

Pat didn't hear this appeal, as he had wound the window up. He returned the radio volume to its original pitch and cocked his ear to the music. "*Washington Post,*" he said, with some satisfaction. His feet drummed rhythmically on the thin floor.

There was news on next. When they were both indoors in the evening, the Clarnons regularly sat and complained at the news together. Pat turned up the sound and waited patiently for something to fuel his indignation. There had been a slump on the Japanese stock market. Pat rolled his eyes, caring little for the Japanese, though he had never met one. Then, something about a daring rescue at sea. He scoffed unsympathetically, suspecting another halfwit trying to cross the Atlantic on a tea tray. Pat didn't much like the sea. He had been taken there as a child in 1953 and some of it had gone in his eyes, where it stung like red ants. The man blathered on. Someone had been stabbed in Croydon. Pat wondered by whose assessment this incident was classified as news. If they reported that no-one had recently been stabbed in Croydon, that could be newsworthy. He'd been to Croydon once, but had taken care to leave by four in the afternoon, before the stabbings began. The next item was interrupted by a knocking on the window.

Pat pressed the 'Off' button and turned to see Mrs Stirrup mouthing at him again. Did the woman never give up? She was holding what appeared, in the dim light, to be a brown paper bag. Sighing, he opened the window and gave Mrs Stirrup a weary stare.

Mrs Stirrup proffered the bag through the opening. "Something for the journey," she said.

"What? What journey?"

"Going for a drive, you said." She thrust the bag under his nose. "Some little fruit cakes. There's four, I made them in a bun tray."

"Oh, I see. Well, er…"

"Didn't know if Mrs Clarnon was coming with you. Just a little something. Only don't go eating them driving along. You stop in a lay-by and have a cake when you're peckish, then you go on to the next lay-by, or maybe the one after that, and pull in again and – "

"Yes, thank you, Mrs Stirrup, I get the general idea." He tried a smile, but it didn't come out quite right. "You're very kind."

She nodded and knocked the door frame, as if to suggest some form of farewell. Pat opened the bag and looked inside. He hadn't so much as seen a brown bag in ages. The cakes smelled good. He prodded one with his finger. It was still slightly warm. He folded the top of the bag over and pushed the cakes under the seat. They would do nicely in the morning. In the mirror he saw Mrs Stirrup walking briskly back to her house.

He wound the window up and sat thinking. Then he couldn't think of anything to think about, so he climbed out, locked the car and patted the door panel. "Goodnight," he said. The tabby cat scampered past with a dead mouse dangling from its mouth.

# Chapter 6

## *Number 15: Aisling McIver*

Aisling McIver looked at the baby. The baby looked at Aisling McIver. The baby said, "Cooo urrgh cooo gwaah guh." Her mother said, "Yes, Neamh, I know, I know. You and me, we have to deal with this."

She pulled her hard chair closer to the cot and tickled her daughter's sticky chin. Over her shoulder, she glanced at the flat grey slab amid the wreckage on the table. "What'll we say to your Auntie Rona, eh? I think we'll say a big thank you, don't you? Posh laptop for us. She says it's a spare from her work. God, I hope she didn't thieve it. No, surely not."

Aisling sat back, folded her arms and stretched out her feet until they rested either side of the cot. She stared intently at the dozing child. Tears warmed her eyes. She shook her head slowly from side to side, blinking back the teardrops, feeling a scalding in her throat.

"Rona's only trying to help us, see. Truth is, I don't much like the idea, but somehow – you and me – we have to make our way. I'd be doing this for both of us, Neamh, for our futures. Else, what futures would we have? Penny-pinching, scraping, going cap in hand to the social. You and me, we could have a little bit of money, maybe even a little bit to put by. Oh, don't you worry, little one, I'd see you were protected. Like, I wouldn't leave you in the same room if I was – well, you know. I'd not want you to have to look at that. You deserve better than that, my darling. I'm afraid it'd mean some guys coming in now and then, men you didn't know, but like I say, you wouldn't be seeing them, I'd make sure of that. And it wouldn't make one scrap of difference to the way your mammy loves you, not ever. Because I'd be doing this for you, more than for me. So really, I'd be doing it for love, the best kind. Oh, it's not that I want to do it, no, but sometimes you have to set your doubts and inhibitions aside." She chuckled, drawing her lips tight. "Dear me. 'Inhibitions', she says. Sure, that's an awful big word for a baby. What I mean is, if you feel guilty or unhappy about doing a thing, sometimes you just have to go ahead and do it anyway, else the outcome might be worse. We can't manage worse, Neamh. There's no room in our lives for worse. Oh, I could go back to Beasley's, yes. They'd have me back tomorrow, likely, but how would that help us? Tell me that. I'd earn my little pot of money and then I'd come home and give it all away to the – the whoever who was looking after you. Auntie Rona can't do it, not regular, and I'd be handing you over to a total stranger, to someone who didn't love you. And we'd still have nothing, the same nothing we have now. But. This is it, see, the big but. If I say yes to Rona and she shows me how to set this up, I can stay here with you and, if you don't mind occasionally a funny man comes in – well, not really a funny one, maybe even sometimes a nice one – then I'll get some decent money, see, and we'll share it and…" She lowered her head and began to cry. "Well, maybe, just maybe, we can get ourselves out of this fucking mess."

Swallowing the salt that trickled into her mouth, she knelt beside the cot and leaned in, her face next to Neamh's, and rested her nose gently against the peachy softness of the child's cheek, inhaling the creamy purity of each tiny breath.

"Mams are supposed to stay strong for when their babies cry," she said, her voice quavering. "And here's you lying there strong and silent and me weeping all over you. God, am I such a bad mother?"

She adjusted the baby's blanket to keep her warm. Tears spotted the edge of the cot. She stood up and went to the kitchen to make herself a mug of coffee and wipe her face with a sheet of paper from the roll. Cupping both hands, she splashed cold water on her cheeks and forehead. For a quiet moment, she leaned against the sink, eyes closed, steadying herself. When the kettle boiled, she mixed the coffee and carried her drink back to the living room.

"Reckon I ought to be playing with that computer, Neamh, eh? Get some practice in. I'm a bit rusty. It's a good one – Lenovo. Dear Rona. Funny, I asked her, did she ever do that stuff herself, with the guys, I mean. Only she seems so well-informed, more than you'd just get off the net. So she laughed and told me no, she has a friend who's a nurse at the Royal and this girl kind of supplements her income when she's off duty. Apparently she can double her salary that way. Well, good for her, I suppose, if it's your pocket money." Aisling sighed and tugged nervously at one earlobe with a puncture and no earring. "Course, I'd have to think it all through real careful, little one. Rona says to charge a hundred pounds an hour. Jesus, can you imagine it? Hundred pounds an hour! I'd be earning more'n the Prime Minister. I think maybe I'd make it just ninety to start with, so they think they'd be getting a bargain. Sort of undercut the competition. Be a bit shrewd, eh? One attraction is, there'd be hardly any overheads, just a few tissues and wipes, maybe the odd bottle of mineral water if they fancied a drink, some Durex obviously, they don't bring their own. Oh, and I'd have to set up some kind of calendar so they could see my availability. Then there's the hard part, deciding what exactly I'm to be offering. Remember, you're the driver, they're the passenger. Some stuff I just won't want to do, that's for sure. Have to make it clear in your 'Enjoys' list. Makes me smile, that does. Am I supposed to enjoy any of this? I mean, really *enjoy* it? Well, I guess I'd quite enjoy it when they pull the money out. And your mammy needs a picture, too, or could be three or four. Rona has a decent camera and she says she'll take care of it. Don't show them your face, she says, so either she'll decapitate me or I can turn my head away, no worries."

Aisling drained her coffee and seemed to slump in the

chair as if exhausted by the stark inevitability of what she was considering, the raw *unbelievability* of it. Shaking her head, she bent and lifted her daughter to her lap, carefully rearranging the child and her blanket into a single warm, moist, fragrant bundle which she could draw into herself and become one with her progeny and her future. For a moment, gazing down, she was overwhelmed by the immensity of the love consuming her. Neamh slept, cradled against her mother's breast, her face a perfect opening flower, yielding infinitesimally to the change of light. Aisling felt the tickle of tears tracking past her nose to drip thinly from her chin on to the small body beneath. With only the slightest of movements, she rocked the baby in part of a circle, just an inch or two each way, not to wake the child, to comfort and console herself.

"Rock-a-bye Baby, on the tree top... God love you. Your Auntie Rona's coming round tonight to help me set this up, get the show on the road. Dear Rona, she's quite matter-of-fact about it. Me, I'm still wanting to be convinced. Convinced about the rightness of it, I suppose. Me, I am Aisling Clare McIver and you, my little darling, are Neamh Anne McIver, and we are the whole world to each other and I don't want to be the *undoing* of any of that goodness, the spoiling of it. You have to understand, though. Yes, sure, if I had the money I would dump that old pushchair under the stairs and buy you a nice new one and do all kind of other stuff for you, sweet thing, some pretty clothes to wear in the summer when we go to the park, I've always fancied some cute red shoes for your little feet, and I don't mean from that rude man in the market, but I just need to know that you won't be thinking it's only about the money in the bank, the pennies in my purse. Oh no, dear God, no. I'd not demean myself for a balance sheet. This is about us sharing a proud life, my Neamh. It's about us holding our heads up in the future and walking with the all the powerful people and saying 'Let us by, we belong here, we are honourable, right through to our souls.' So there you are. God help us, little one, God help us."

# Chapter 7

## *Number 22: Mr and Mrs Slocombe*

Hettie woke with a start, jerking her leg, gasping. Arthur was nibbling her ankle. Sitting up, she waved him away and swung her legs clear of the small dark pellets he had left on the bedclothes. The window had turned grey with the fading daylight. She levered herself on to the edge of the bed, rubbing her neck to restore the circulation. She hadn't intended to sleep for so long. It was nearly six o'clock, and Alf would be worried about his tea. She had baked a batch of fruit scones this morning and there was Cornish clotted cream and strawberry jam. Pulling her slippers from under the bed, she stroked the back of her hair, steadied herself against the dressing table as she stood to cover her feet and went silently downstairs.

Alf must have fallen asleep in front of the TV, slumping down to invisibility in the armchair. Hettie leaned over him and plumped up his cushion. She glanced at the screen, sighing and shaking her head. The golf had finished and a brainless quiz show blared out, flashing lights, squawking klaxons and hysterical audience laughter. Alf's roly-poly congealed, untouched, beside him. Hettie changed the TV channel, stabbing the remote handset at the screen.

"I've got you the news, dear. You like to watch the news."

She stood behind the chair, watching the news over his head. A bridge had collapsed in America, pitching cars and a bus into the river. A black man had been stabbed in Croydon. A schoolgirl was mysteriously missing in Smethwick. In India, a train had come off the rails at high speed, careering into the undergrowth with spectacular casualties. Young people were interviewed, complaining of the impossibility of getting mortgages.

"I don't know why we watch the news," Hettie said. "They never put on anything cheerful. The news is just not entertaining any more. Don't they have any happy news? Where's all the happy things happening, that's what I'd like to know."

She carried the roly-poly to the kitchen and scooped it into the bin. From an airtight tin, she took two fruit scones and buttered them thinly, adding strawberry jam and a dollop of cream. She boiled the kettle and made a mug of tea with two sugars. Placing the snack on a tray, she took it through to her husband.

"Bit of tea for you, dear. I made the scones special."

Alf was still watching the news. Young men with hairy faces were rioting in Cairo. Farmers plodded through cow shit, grumbling about their subsidies. Men in identical grey suits sauntered down a street in Croydon, munching pies and dropping pastry down their fronts. In Stockwell, a bus had got itself wedged under a bridge, showering pedestrians with broken glass.

"Get the weather in a minute," Hettie said. "Probably be a tornado."

As evening dissolved into darkness, they slept for a while, Hettie in her recliner chair with Arthur on her lap, contentedly chewing her apron strings. Surfacing briefly from a dream, she imagined she heard Alf snoring, but it was only the fridge motor purring against the kitchen wall. She pressed the handset for one of her favourite 'soaps' and then dozed off again before she could absorb any of the action. Another hour passed. Arthur urinated on Hettie's apron and shuffled into a different position. The central heating clicked into stand-by, making the radiators gurgle.

It was nearly eleven thirty when Hettie woke up and tilted her chair upright. She swiped a hand irritably across her lap. "Get off me, Arthur Slocombe. You're heavy on my old legs."

Arthur hopped on to the floor and deposited a few moist droppings on the carpet, dark as chocolate beans.

41

Tottering wearily, Hettie fetched a brush and swept them into a folded newspaper.

"It's late, Alf. Time for bed."

Arthur bounded up the stairs but Alf didn't move. He was in no hurry. Upstairs, his wife selected a clean pair of pyjamas from his bottom drawer, candy-striped in maroon and white. Drawing back the bed covers, she carefully wrapped the striped jacket round a pillow turned lengthways and fastened the buttons, pulling the trouser legs down the length of the bed.

"Very smart, dear. I got them from Marks and Spencer's."

She slipped her nightie on and slid in beside him. The sheets felt cold against her bare legs. Arthur jumped on to the wicker chair by the window. Rolling on to her side, Hettie folded an arm around the softness of Alf's shoulders and inhaled the scent of him. She had always liked the smell of a man. Alf's usual smell was a blend of tobacco and lime with a hint of chocolate. The tobacco component was intriguing, as he had never been a smoker. On his birthday one year she had given him a pipe with a glossy walnut bowl and a pouch of pipe tobacco – *Old Klondike*, it was called – in the hope that he might fancy a puff now and then, for she rather enjoyed the thick, roasted fragrance of Mr Garfield's pipe, George Garfield being the man who came to do their plumbing and always worked with a smouldering briar protruding quite elegantly from his mouth. Alf, however, thought smoking was a grubby, slovenly habit and at once consigned his gift to the cupboard under the sideboard. Probably it was still there.

"You smell nice and clean, Alf. Nice and fresh. Mind you, I like a bit of a man-smell. If there's no smell, well, then there's – nothing. Now I don't care for sweat on your clothes, but on your body it's not so bad, or even better than not so bad. I like a man to smell like a man, like he's done manly things." She patted the yielding softness of his chest. "Just wait there a minute."

Hettie knelt on the stool at her dressing table and

fumbled in the dark for a bottle of perfume. She sprayed a thin jet on two fingers and stroked the wetness between her drooping breasts.

"I'm back, Alf. Can you notice anything different? It's Nina Ricci, *L'Air du Temps*. You gave it me, remember? It was always your favourite." She hugged him closer, tighter. "Do you like the smell of me, dear, hmm? You can smell me all you like. We can lie here and smell each other all through the darkness, yes. Why yes, I do believe I'm getting a bit of smell off you now, just a tang of something lemony, really quite nice."

An almost soundless bump told her that Arthur had hopped on to the bed. Hettie put out a hand for him. He snuggled up beside her, burying his nose in his paws.

"And there's you too, Arthur Slocombe, yes, I know. You don't like to be left out. You've got a different smell, of course. I'd say it was – let me think…damp straw and nuts and cabbage and a bit of wee-wee. You cuddle up close now and keep warm. We're three in a bed." She laughed quietly in the dark. "Young Robert said something about that, I don't remember exactly what it was. Apparently the youngsters nowadays like to be three in a bed sometimes. Well, it sounds a bit of a squash to me, seeing as most probably one of them's not generally a rabbit. And why would they want all to be cramped up in the same bed anyway? I don't know; young people, eh? Perhaps it's like when they used to see how many students they could squeeze in a telephone box or in a mini car. Maybe. I mean, you could have nine in a bed, going top and tail, but I doubt they'd get much sleep."

She turned on her back and gazed at the dimpled ceiling, irregularly lit by spillage from a street light through a chink in the curtains.

"That reminds me, dear. Robert telephoned. He's coming to visit at the weekend, with Alice and the grandkids. You'll like that, won't you? Course I know Ben and Ellie do run about and make a noise, but they're only young and children do that, it's only normal. I said we'd do them lunch, perhaps get a nice piece of beef. I might cheat a bit with the Yorkshires, they'll never know, just buy some of those *Aunt Bessie's*. I'll do roast potatoes in some goose fat, lovely. You can talk to Robert about golf, or there might be some athletics on. Oh dear, yes, Alice says Robert enjoys the women's athletics, says some of their bottoms should get a gold medal before they've even shot the gun. You notice they always have a man walking about behind the starting line when they're getting on their marks, well, Robert reckons he's the one has to award the gold medal for anatomy. Oh Robert! Yes, we'll have such a nice day!"

Arthur Slocombe crept down to the bottom of the bed, padded slowly in a circle like a dog and surreptitiously scattered a few moist surprises for the morning. Then he bum-shuffled a foot to the left and settled himself down. Hettie had provided an old foam-filled cushion for him on the wicker chair, but Arthur preferred the more comfortable bed. It was the perfect place to spend the night. The whole of number 22 was just right for Arthur, and that included his parents. Mr Slocombe didn't have much to say to him lately, but then he couldn't understand most of what the old man said anyway. There had never been fluid dialogue between them.

Arthur raised his haunches an inch or two and luxuriated in a goodnight widdle. The warmth permeated his back feet. He sank down into the duvet. All was right with his world.

# Chapter 8

## *Number 25: Miss Joan Descours*

Joan Descours returned from the kitchen with a Poole Pottery bowl containing two flavours of Pringles.

"In case you get hungry, Barry."

Pecking at the laptop keys, Barry Brown did not look up. "I'm not hungry, Miss."

"I said, in case you get hungry, Barry."

"Thank you, Miss."

She stood behind him with her hands on the back of the chair. "How are we getting on?"

"I'm doing all right, Miss."

She studied the way Barry's dark brown hair tapered neatly into a v-shape at the nape of his neck. His jaw-line and cheeks were pale and smooth and it appeared that he had not yet started shaving. The skin on his face looked soft and even slightly downy, and Joan wondered how it would feel to the touch. There was no sensation in all the world to compare with the flawlessly tactile smoothness of human skin.

"Is something wrong, Miss?"

"What? Oh no, nothing's wrong."

"Only you're standing behind me."

"Sorry. I'm putting you off."

"Just a bit, Miss."

A dining chair was set aside by the window and Joan Descours went to sit in it. She gazed into the garden, where small birds were fussing over the hanging feeder, occasionally jabbing at one another with their tiny beaks. Smiling, she turned back and allowed herself a lingering look at Barry's face in profile. The boy looked younger than his age, with his almost babyish face and long dark eyelashes. His dusky lips were set in a quivering pout of concentration and every now and then his tongue darted out to moisten them.

"Help yourself to orange, Barry."

"In a minute, Miss."

Barry had nice eyes and she wished he would look at her, just for a moment. He was a good pupil and she admitted to herself that, actually, she was quite fond of him. She hoped he was well looked after at home. She enjoyed being kind to boys like Barry.

"Would it help your concentration if I put some music on, Barry?"

"Some music, Miss?"

Barry still hadn't looked at her. His face was angled forward at the screen.

"Yes. I – er – I don't know what you'd like. I've got all sorts."

"Allsorts, Miss?"

"I mean, all sorts of music. Just tell me what you'd like."

"I like it quiet, Miss."

She sighed inaudibly. "Very well, Barry. Just – "

"Sorry, Miss?"

"Nothing, Barry."

She crossed to the table and poured herself some squash. The glass trembled slightly in her hand. She cast her eyes over the papers on the table but she didn't look at Barry Brown. For a while she felt safer holding the glass in both hands.

The funny thing was, she had known a man called Barry before. She frowned, searching her memory: what was his name? Barry…Barry Mackeson. They befriended each other briefly ten years ago. Barry Mackeson was not a teacher, but something to do with income tax; with taxation, anyway. Joan had met him at a university friend's party, where he had seemed kind and even mildly amusing. Tall and lean and touchingly unfashionable in his brown Oxfords and Cavalry Twills with fluff-speckled turn-ups, Barry kissed her a polite goodnight and asked for a date the following week, a request to which she had cautiously agreed. They had been together for six weeks. Mostly they went to weekend lunches or to the cinema, where Barry would choose seats near the back and gradually slide one arm around Joan's shoulders, hardly noticing how she stiffened unresponsively at his touch. In the fifth week, at his flat, they slept together for the first time, a somewhat bleak liaison when they confined themselves to unadventurous kissing, lasting long enough for the interaction to become more tedious than romantic. It was towards the end of a short night that Joan began to feel unwell and on edge, imminently to discover that her period had arrived, sending her scrambling in dry-mouthed panic from the bed to the bathroom, her embarrassment mercifully mitigated by the absence of any evidence on the sheets.

"I'm sorry, Barry," she told him, "I've timed this rather badly."

"I don't think I understand," was his response.

"Wrong time of the month, my dear."

"Oh, right. Oh dear."

"I am a woman, after all."

"Yes. Yes, I suppose so."

She hurried into her clothes, pulling on her coat with her hair still in disarray.

"Goodnight, Barry."

"Yes. I – er – I hope you'll be all right."

She stood in the open doorway, staring at him over her shoulder. "I'm not ill, Barry. It happens."

What did he mean – about her being a woman? *Yes, I suppose so.* She strode down the street in the darkness, repeating those words in her head. *Yes, I suppose so. Yes, I suppose so.* A few days later she rang to say it was over. She never saw him again.

Distracted by this solemn reverie, she hadn't heard the boy's appeal, but now he was gazing up at her, wide-eyed.

"Miss?"

"I'm sorry, Barry, I didn't hear you. I was in another place."

"Are you all right, Miss?"

"I'm fine, thank you. Did you want something?"

"Can I go to the toilet, please, Miss?"

"Of course. Upstairs and straight ahead."

Barry dragged back his chair and walked to the door.

"Can you manage, Barry?"

"Course, Miss."

She was concerned to hear him running up the stairs. The bathroom door banged shut. A rather long silence ensued. She thought of assessing the work he had done so far, but resisted the temptation; they would do this together. He had not asked for her help and might view her intervention as an intrusion, undermining his confidence. She wanted his approval.

Slowly, quietly, she climbed the stairs and stood at the bathroom door. Through the frosted glass panel, she could make out the boy seated on the lavatory, his white underpants round his ankles. The voyeurism excited and disturbed her. She closed her eyes and opened them again.

"Barry, is everything all right?"

"I won't be long, Miss."

"There's no hurry, Barry, no hurry at all."

"Actually, Miss…"

"Barry?"

"There's not much paper."

"Oh, right. Don't worry, I'll get you some more. Stay there."

Joan opened the cupboard on the landing and took out a toilet roll, placing it on the floor outside the door.

"Fresh one right outside, Barry."

"Thanks, Miss."

"Do you want it brought in?"

"No, Miss!"

"Then I'll be downstairs."

Joan Descours turned and stepped halfway down the stairs. Leaning back against the handrail, she looked in the mirror on the upper wall and saw Barry's reflection as he opened the bathroom door and shuffled awkwardly forward, clutching his dropped pants in one hand and reaching for the roll with the other. She saw the boy's anxious face. She saw the firm flexion in his hairless thighs and the moon-perfect curve of his pale buttocks. Closing her eyes one more, she gripped the banister rail fiercely in a shaking hand.

# Chapter 9

## *Number 30: Radio Officer Stephen J. Kettering-Barclay, Retired*

Mr Kettering-Barclay lowered his newspaper as the doorbell rang and looked at the clock. Surely his man was early. Fingering the adjustment on his metal leg, he stood up, teetered slightly, and tossed the paper into the armchair, before stomping to the door.

A stocky blonde woman in a green tunic stood on the step. "Mr Kettering-Barclay?"

He blinked, staring. "And you are?"

"I'm Janice Collins from South Central. All right if I come in?"

"Come in? I normally have Stuart."

"I know." She put one hand on the door. "May I?"

Kettering-Barclay curled his lip and stood aside, shivering lightly against the draught.

Janice Collins moved to the foot of the stairs and smiled pleasantly. "I'm sorry. I hope this will be all right for you. You see, unfortunately Stuart has met with an accident and at present the agency don't have another man available."

"An accident, you say?"

"Yes, he fell off his motorbike. Well, not fell off, but he was in a collision."

"I see. Dangerous things, motorbikes."

"Indeed. Mr Kettering-Barclay, do you mind a female carer?"

"Do I have a choice?"

Anticipating acceptance, Janice was pulling an apron and gloves from her bag. "SCCC can only send who they've got. But of course if – "

"No, no, no. I'm not bothered. I had a woman before Stuart – er, if you get my meaning."

The carer rubbed her hands briskly together and tugged her gloves on. "Very well, Mr Kettering-Barclay."

"Yes, I think you had better call me Stephen, or we shall be here all day."

"Fine, if that's okay. I'm Janice." She glanced up the staircase. "Can I do something for you now or should we go straight up. I see you have a stairlift."

"Wednesday," he said. "Stuart normally gives me a proper all-over wash on Wednesday."

"That's why I'm here, Mr Ket – Stephen. Do you have a bath?"

"No, not a bath. I don't have a bath."

"Ah. You haven't got a bath?"

"Yes, there's a bath in the bathroom."

Janice screwed up her eyes in confusion. "I thought you said there wasn't one."

"I have got a bath upstairs. Only I don't get in it."

"You don't – why don't you get in it?"

Stephen sighed, swaying on his bad leg. "Stuart understands the position."

"Yes, well, I'm afraid Stuart isn't here, Stephen, so you'll have to explain it to me."

"It's really quite simple…Janice."

"So – so are you telling me Stuart gives you a complete wash but doesn't put you in the bath?"

"That is correct. Is he going to be all right?"

"He's in hospital. We can't say. Don't worry, I can look after you."

Stephen Kettering-Barclay shuffled past her and sat on the stairlift. "We can go up. I expect you're busy."

Janice Collins picked up her bag and followed the lift up the stairs. "Nice house," she pronounced.

A wooden chair, appearing rather battle-scarred, stood in the middle of the bathroom floor, and the old man sat on it and rubbed his knees. The gaseous squeak of a fart escaped into the room.

"Sorry, my dear."

"No problem at all. Now then."

"I can undress myself. Stuart normally hangs my clothes over the edge of the bath."

Janice scratched pensively at the back of her neck. "But he doesn't put you in the bath, no?"

"No."

"The thing is, Stephen…how shall I put this? You are – forgive me – a little too fragrant, presumably for the simple want of a bath. So why don't we just slide you down in some nice warm water and I'll get you –"

"No bath!" The old man thumped a fist on his good leg as spit flew from his mouth.

Janice sensed that this was not a moment to become overly assertive, though she could not relinquish the opportunity to remind Mr Kettering-Barclay of her social authority. There had to be good cause for her to relent. She sat carefully on the bath rim and leaned towards her client, hands clasped between her legs.

"Stephen, what's the matter? Why don't you want to get in the bath?"

"That's my business."

"Do you want me to wash you?"

"I do. That's what Stuart does."

"Stephen, will you tell me why Stuart doesn't put you in the bath?"

"Because. Because I can't…" His eyes clouded over and brimmed with tears. "Stuart understands."

"Stephen, is it you don't want to undress for me, is that it?"

"No. No, it's not that." He rocked to and fro in the chair, slapping his thighs. "What the hell! Let's get on with it. Best get it over with."

Janice nodded and stood up. "Right, if you start getting undressed, I'll run you a nice warm bath." She opened a cabinet on the wall and rummaged inside. "There's some Radox in here, I'll pour some in, help to relax you."

While the bath water ran, she helped to support Stephen as he laboriously removed his clothes. A mat of black hair covered much of his thin body and, naked, he exuded a sour smell of stale sweat. His long, skeletal feet were streaked with grey grime, the heels scabbed and yellow.

"How long is it since you had a bath, Stephen?" she asked peevishly.

"Don't remember, don't keep on." He laid his clothes on the chair and propped his prosthesis against the sink pedestal. His chin dropped. "Bloody woman," he muttered.

Janice was small but strong and had little trouble in manoeuvring him into the steaming bathtub. It was a matter of balance, not strength. The frothy water surged around him, instantly drawing opacity from the dirty body. She reached down gently and massaged the pink knob of his stump.

"Soon have you all clean and fresh," she said brightly.

Kneeling on the floor, she gripped the bath edge with one hand and reached in to soap the old man's limbs with the other. "There you are, there, there," she said.

Stephen snorted and threw back his head. "Don't come any closer!"

"Pardon?"

"You. Take your hands off the side, you'll tip us over."

"It's all right, Stephen, I'm being careful."

"You're not getting in." His eyes glazed angrily. "There's no room."

"Oh you. What are you like?" she scowled, chuckling nervously.

"I told you. Keep away. This boat's full. Wait in the water."

Janice moved back, a brandished sponge dripping water down her arm. "Stephen, listen to me, you're safe, you're in the bath."

Stephen was plunging around in the scummy water, lifting his bottom into the air. "Go back!" he shrieked. "Get away from us!"

"Stephen!"

"Warning you. You'll sink us. Find another boat."

The alarmed carer leaned forward and placed a hand firmly on Stephen Kettering-Barclay's swarthy shoulder.

She didn't see his other shoulder rotating towards her, nor the piston-drive of his right arm as it pumped into her face, the bunched white fist smashing between her eyes, propelling her flat to the floor, blood springing from her nose like a fat red spider.

# Chapter 10

## *Number 12: Mr and Mrs Clarnon*

Pat sat. He had turned the armchair to face the window and appeared relaxed, but the glaze and focus of his eyes suggested that he was staring at the glass rather than through it.

Martha came in from the kitchen and peered at him. "You not in the car this morning?"

"Plenty time," Pat said, not looking at her.

"You feeling all right?"

"Fine. Matter of fact, I thought I might go for a run."

Martha stopped wiping her hands on the tea towel she was holding and brought the cloth up to dab her face. "Go for a run? What, in your shorts?"

"No, no. A run in the car. Got petrol in."

"Am I hearing right? Starting the engine and driving the car on the road?" She shook her head. "What's the world coming to?"

Pat decided to ignore the sarcasm. He sat up in the chair and fixed his wife with a wide-eyed smile. "Tell you what – you could come with me."

"Oh. Where would we go?"

"Well, to the country."

"The country? What country?"

"This country. I mean the countryside."

Martha perched sideways on the arm of the other chair and fanned her face with the tea towel. This was an unprecedented departure; if, indeed, there was to be a departure. Patrick would be sacrificing his secure position at the kerb, a rectangle of the planet upon which the sun never shone, to go jousting with the traffic on the way to nowhere in particular. Could he even be trusted to steer the thing? That he had proposed such an event, without exhaustive preamble, beggared belief.

"The man did say it would be a nice day," she allowed.

"Man? What man?"

"On the radio. The weather man."

"Depends where he meant."

"All over. An area of high pressure moving eastwards from the Azores. That's what he said."

Pat pursed his lips, squinting at the sky through the parted curtains. Cumulo nimbus. What he really wanted was high cirrus. Still, it was early yet; maybe later. It would take a while to get going. Martha would have to put her face on. Six days out of seven, he was married to a woman with no face. Then she would want to put stuff on her hair and comb and brush it, peering doubtfully in the mirror, as if the woman in the reflection were nothing to do with her. Outdoor shoes in assorted colours would be lined up and surveyed, though most of the time they would be in the car and nobody could see her feet. That must be what they meant by *motoring trials.*

"Tell you what!" There was something almost conspiratorial in her smile. "We could take a picnic!"

"I suppose," he said guardedly.

"Yes. I've got bananas and apples. Make some ham and pickle sandwiches and a couple of hard-boiled eggs. Some of those little pork pies you like. There's a bit of that fruit cake left, could have a chunk of cheese with it."

"Steady on!"

Pat had led a life of frugality and had conditioned himself to avoid the pain of disappointment by embracing the concept of minimal expectation. He saw he would have to caution Martha against the perils of excess.

"Could go to the forest," he suggested. "Spring flowers'll be out."

"I've got that nice wicker picnic basket, the one Robert and Alice gave us last Christmas."

"Aha. Just some fruit and sarnies, eh?"

"And a flask of sweet tea."

She disappeared into the kitchen and made housewife noises, humming tunelessly over a percussion of clattering

56

and chopping. Breakfast was hardly done, and the day felt good already. Old Pat, well, he wasn't such a miserable old stick, not all the time, anyway. She leaned against the worktop, shut her eyes momentarily and imagined the blur of the hedgerows streaming past the window, the bright sun dancing in her eyes and that sickly-sweet aroma of the Morris's exhaust filtering in through the dashboard. She put two extra eggs in the pan and found a giant bar of Dairy Milk at the back of the cupboard for dessert. After all, this kind of thing didn't happen very often.

After they had watched the breakfast news and Pat had unearthed his dog-eared road atlas from the bottom of the wardrobe, Martha followed him out to the car and stowed the hamper in the boot. Sitting primly upright next to her husband, she cast her eyes loftily along the house fronts, behind which she managed to convince herself there were many faceless people going nowhere.

"So where's our destination?" she enquired.

"Ashdown Forest suit you?" He handed her the road atlas. "Lunch on the heath. Wild flowers, butterflies, maybe a lizard or two."

"It'll be just grand," Martha assented.

"Be nice to get out for some fresh air. Bit of a ramble, perhaps."

"Get some sun on our faces."

"Stretch our weary legs."

"Clear out our lungs."

"Let's go."

Pat turned the ignition key. From under the bonnet came the wail of a small animal being tortured. He stopped, sniffed and tried again. The engine rocked and squealed but made not even a pretence of firing.

"Won't it start?" asked Martha, superfluously.

"It's cold," Pat said.

"Cold? Course it's bloody cold, it hasn't been turned on since last year." She stuffed the atlas under the seat. "You could look under the bonnet."

Pat got out and propped the bonnet open. There was

nothing to see except an engine. He wondered about the carburettor, or perhaps it was the spark plugs or the electrics. It could be anything. He knew nothing, except how to drive it. The problem could be anywhere and it meant they were going nowhere. He slammed the bonnet and got back inside.

"Is it the engine?" Martha asked.

"Course it's the engine. It's the engine makes it go."

"Well, it's not making us go. There is an engine in there, I take it."

"Don't be bloody ridiculous."

They sat silently, staring ahead through the windscreen, grinding their dentures. A low-flying pigeon on an early bombing raid dropped a grey-green device on the Oxford's windscreen wipers. Martha solemnly observed this unsavoury assault but said nothing about it.

"You could call the AA," she said, after a while.

"I'm not in the AA."

"Right."

"Turn the news on," said Pat.

"We just listened to the news indoors."

"Something else might have happened."

Martha fiddled with the radio. There was a news round-up. A black man had been shot outside a petrol station in Croydon. A baby had been found dead under bushes in Cleethorpes. Energy prices were expected to rise.

"That's just awful," Martha said.

"Poor little mite," said Pat.

"I meant about the bills."

Pat drew a deep breath and let it out slowly. "I spy with my little eye…"

"Oh, for goodness' sake!"

"…something beginning with – "

Martha yanked the door open.

"Where are you going?"

"Fetch my book from the boot."

She went to the back of the car, retrieved her paperback and slumped back in her seat, crossly slapping the book.

"Any good?" Pat enquired agreeably.

"Philippa Gregory. It's about the wives of Henry the Eighth." She pulled out the bookmark and raised her reading glasses from the chain round her neck. "Why don't you try it again?"

"What?"

"The car. The engine."

Sighing, Pat churned the engine, with no effect. The starter protested with a loud squawk.

"Best leave it," he said. "Don't want to flatten the battery."

Martha threw back her head and laughed, a harsh cackle. "You're mad! We're obviously not going anywhere, so it hardly matters whether the battery's flat or not."

"Woman's logic," Pat growled darkly. Then he offered her what he hoped was a kindly smile. "You can go inside if you like. I'll call you if it starts."

"No, no. We can sit a while. We don't spend that much time together."

"We sleep together."

"Well, I should hope so. Who else would you be sleeping with?"

"I was talking about marital harmony, not sex."

Martha hunched her shoulders stiffly. "I certainly don't want to sit out here talking about sex. Get enough of that on the news."

Pat closed his eyes and rested while his wife read about Henry the Eighth. The radio news gave way to a breeze of melodic strings and in this reverie he felt himself wafting towards sleep behind the flickering red field of his eyelids. Only his occasional stuttering snore interrupted the silence. It was the clang of a dustbin lid as the refuse men came up the street that jarred him back to bleary-eyed reality. For a moment he sat blinking, screwing up his eyes, trying to remember where he was and why. Next to him, Martha slumped with her chin in her throat, glasses dangling from her ear, a drool of saliva seeping from her

59

lips. Her book lay tented on the floor, buckled against her ankle.

Pat wiped his eyes with his fingers and looked at his dozing wife. Though they were supposed to be going out, she had not bothered, after all, to apply anything to her pallid face and her puffy lips were grey and bloodless. She was looking her age, he thought. To think he had once dreamed of getting her into bed and slobbering over her open mouth. As for her breasts, they had started their inexorable journey towards her pants, her once-tight cleavage become a broad, barren gully landmarked with white bones.

A bin lid crashed to the pavement. Martha opened her eyes and jolted upright. "Ooh, what was that?"

"Dustbin lid," Pat told her.

Martha wiped her chin with her sleeve. "How long was I asleep?"

"Don't know, I was asleep."

She picked up her book and folded the pages flat. "Think there's a play on," she said, twiddling the radio knob.

"A mystery, maybe."

"Yes, well, it's a mystery why we're sat out here."

"I told you, go in if you want."

"After I've listened to my play."

Pat worked his lips, wrinkled his nose and ground his teeth. His feet were cold and he stamped them on the floor. He could do with going to the toilet, but he didn't fancy using the plastic urinal with Martha perched next to him. Some things were private. In any case, it was years since she had set eyes on his old man. You never knew what her reaction might be. Women, you could never predict them.

"We can hear the play and then –"

"Shush!"

Martha turned up the sound and settled into her seat with her eyes closed. The play lasted for an hour. Pat listened for a few minutes and then grew bored. He tried to go back to sleep but couldn't get comfortable. He worried about his bladder. With a furtive glance at his wife, engrossed in the play with her eyes shut, he reached under the seat, found the urinal bottle and, twisting his torso away from her, quietly unzipped himself. Maddeningly, it seemed to take an age for his tawny flow to run dry, but finally he was able to cap and hide the bottle and awkwardly adjust his clothes, revelling in the relief. Tugging a handkerchief from his pocket, he wiped his hands and mopped a sweat of anxiety from his brow. A fitful sleep overcame him then, and when he once again became aware of his surroundings, a draught from the partly open passenger door swept over him and he heard Martha opening the boot.

"What are you looking for?" he called.

She didn't reply, but hurried back, carrying the hamper.

"What's the time?" Pat asked wearily.

"Time? It's time for our lunch." She flung open the wicker lid. "Move closer."

He slid towards her and she spread a gingham cloth neatly over their legs. The gear lever protruded between Pat's thighs like a bulbous erection. Martha poured two plastic cups of steaming tea and passed one to her companion. They munched sandwiches and dropped crumbs down their fronts. Conversation was at once redundant and impossible.

They both had hard-boiled eggs gob-stopping their mouths when Mrs Stirrup knocked on the window. Pat sighed, averting his eyes, though not without reflecting how it would have appeared if their neighbour had looked in on his toilet arrangements.

"Put your window down," Martha said, almost choking. "What does she want?"

"How should I know?" he snarled, opening an inch of window.

"Mrs Clarnon! And how are you?"

"Yes, I'm – we're having our lunch."

"Lunch, is it? Funny place to have it."

"Do you want something, Mrs Stirrup?" Martha asked

briskly.

"No, nothing special. Looks like a picnic."

"Feels like an intrusion," Pat said, under his breath.

Martha dug her elbow into his ribs.

"Mrs Stirrup gazed briefly up the road and crouched by the door again. "You could go off somewhere while the sun's shining."

Martha smiled charmlessly, brandishing a peeled banana. "Yes, they do say the Ashdown Forest is nice at this time of year."

Pat rolled the window up. It was time for Martha to go in, take half the picnic and her acidic remarks with her. Enough was enough. Besides, a pungent fragrance informed him that the urinal bottle was leaking on to the floor.

# Chapter 11

## *Number 15: Aisling McIver*

Tallboy70 was his nickname. When he booked to see her he gave his own name as Donald, but she kept an open mind about that. It wasn't important, anyway, except that it would be awkward not to call him something when he arrived.

She had registered herself as Irish Willow. Rona, who had suggested the name, had taken eight photographs for the website gallery, pictures with good resolution but conspicuously excluding Aisling's full face and displaying her figure rather than her naked body.

"You have to be careful," Rona warned her. "No real names and shield your face. You never know who's peeking. People you know put two and two together, they might get four."

It had taken an evening and countless glasses of red wine for the pair of them to decide upon the definitive list of Irish Willow's services. At one point she had broken down in tears, shaking her head in unhappy confusion.

"I'm just not sure I can do this, Rona. I don't know as I even want to do it."

Rona did not see this vacillation as a trigger for sympathy. "Up to you, honey. We've done the groundwork. Now it's your call."

Another brimming glass of Merlot would seal the arrangement. This, Aisling knew, was no time to be faint-hearted.

"I won't be doing anything – well, perverted."

"Fine. No need to. They ask for that, you show them the door. You've not offered it, so they've no right to expect it."

"Do I give them the money back?"

"Sure, why not? There'll be others."

"Rona, is this safe?"

"Safe? What's safe? Look, you're not walking the streets. You're not under the finger of anyone else."

Despite these jagged misgivings, she had slept soundly that night, warm, light-headed, grape-drugged.

Donald was due at noon. Before then she had changed Neamh, fed her and laid her down warmly, snuggled up with a woolly toy dog.

"You sleep now, Neamh. Your mammy's got a job to do. Nothing for you to worry about."

Afterwards, she would remember Donald only for his black moustache, his stubby fingers, less than clean, and how he never smiled at her, not once. She was ready fifteen minutes early, hovering by the window to look for a man coming up the path, clenching her fists to quell the shaking in her hands.

She had asked Rona what she should wear. "Lord, don't tell me I have to open the door stark naked!"

"Not advisable. Most men will find that disconcerting."

"Do I build up slowly, is that it?"

"Common sense, Aisling, common sense. You've some nice clothes, so put them on. Believe me, you'll know when to start undressing. It'll come naturally."

The trouble was, to Aisling, none of this behaviour seemed anything other than completely unnatural. She'd had only two serious boyfriends, and just one of them had seen her unclothed body. Her mother had seen it, of course, but that hardly counted. The idea of a total stranger, a man she had never seen before and might never see again, strolling in the door and running his lascivious gaze over her private parts, was a scenario she struggled to accommodate, even as the footsteps sounded on the stairs.

She released the downstairs lock promptly to prevent him ringing the bell and opened the flat door at his approach. "So you're Donald," she said.

Donald nodded and looked at her expressionlessly, unbuttoning his coat. Aisling tried a tight-lipped smile, but it wasn't reflected in her eyes. She wore a close-fitting black bra and matching lace panties, with dark stockings, stilettos to enhance her height and a turquoise cotton dressing gown over the top. In the mirror, on the way to the door, she stared at herself in mindless amazement.

The man pulled a wad of notes from his pocket. "Count it."

She flipped the notes over in trembling fingers. "Ninety. That's right."

"Okay. What do I call you?"

"You can call me Willow, if you like." She put the money in her dressing gown pocket. "Can I get you a drink of anything?"

"No. Are you Irish, then?"

"Sure, is that a problem?"

"No."

"Shall I hang your coat up for you, Donald?"

Donald shook his head and draped the coat over the back of a chair, then he stood, arms hanging, and stared at her gloomily. Aisling pondered his taciturnity, wondering if he was nervous. Should she confide to him that he was her first client? Though that disclosure might mitigate his unease – for it occurred to her that he, too, could be a novice – there was also the risk that by confessing her inexperience she might simply render herself vulnerable.

Neamh stirred in her cot, but the man seemed not to notice. Aisling's mouth was dry, but she was reluctant to leave Donald alone in the room while she went to the kitchen for a glass of water.

"Well now. Shall we go upstairs?" she asked him.

"Lead the way."

He followed her up, stumbling slightly as he reached the last step. She drew the curtains halfway across and turned the light on. Mostly they liked to see what they were doing. Sex was visual as well as tactile.

Aisling took off her dressing gown and placed it on the bedside chair. What now? Should she do a twirl? "Am I fine?"

"Very nice," Donald said.

"So what would you like today?"

"What?"

"What can I do for you?"

"Oh. Perhaps a massage," he replied.

She kept a straight face but could have smiled with relief. For ten minutes, maybe fifteen, she could satisfy this man with minimal touching of the intimate parts of his body. It wouldn't be so bad. She thought of the tea caddy downstairs where she would put the ninety pounds. She thought of a decent pushchair for her baby. How much was a new one, anyway? No matter, there would be other visitors on other days.

"Take everything off?" Donald asked.

"Yes. Lie face down on the bed." She had spread a towel over the duvet. "Make yourself comfortable."

She went into the bathroom while he undressed. "Would you prefer oil or powder?" she called to him.

"Talcum," he said, his voice muffled by the pillow.

He was quite a hirsute man. His shoulders, back and buttocks were swarthy with dark hair. Aisling looked at him and sighed. She wished, just for this first time, she had asked Rona to stay in the house. She would ring her tonight, for sure. Approaching the bed, she unclasped her bra and tossed it on top of her dressing gown. Her breasts were not large, but today, in this room, with this man, they somehow felt heavy and unusually sensitive. Placing one knee on the side of the bed, she patted powder on the man's back and rubbed it in. He sighed and raised both arms so they rested on the pillow beside his head. Aisling massaged him firmly but gently, starting at his shoulders and working down either side of his spine, kneading the knots with the heels of her hands, round and round, up and down, applying a little more pressure when he didn't flinch, squeezing the malleable flesh of his buttocks until the colour changed.

"Are you all right, Donald?" she asked, in a small voice.

"I'm good," he murmured.

Rona had told her, they always liked the next two parts. Don't forget them. She brought herself up on to the bed, balancing carefully as the mattress depressed, and knelt astride his legs, reaching up for his shoulders once more, so that her breasts brushed the length of his back. Donald moved but said nothing. His body hair pricked at her nipples. Then she put four fingers of each hand inside his upper thighs and very softly drew them apart, just by an inch or two. Her right hand burrowed into the space she had created and caressed Donald's scrotum and his lengthening penis. His exhaling breath boomed in the folds of the pillow.

She had left her wristwatch on and flicked a glance at it. The time was passing slowly. She would give his talc-slicked back another good rub, leaning into the task, expending energy.

"Are you enjoying this, Donald?"

Donald said something, but she couldn't hear what it was. She spent a few minutes more on his back and between his thighs, feeling her hands beginning to tingle and ache a little.

"Would you like to turn over now?" she suggested, stepping to the floor.

When he rolled over on to his back, Aisling could see that her ministrations had excited him, for all his sullenness. She ignored this response for a moment and carried on with the massage, working down the flanks of his body and his parted thighs. After a while she came round to the other side of the bed and stood beside him, gently flexing her hands.

The man looked at her solemnly and pointed at her panties.

"What? Oh, okay. If that's what you want."

She stood back and quickly peeled off her panties. She kicked off her shoes as well, standing there naked but for her stockings. She resumed the massage, sliding down to his ankles and feet. It was when she straightened up by his heaving chest that she felt his two fingers thrusting inside her. This would happen, she knew. If she just let it be, she probably wouldn't have to have sex with him. So long as his nails didn't scratch her. Anxious now to bring the session to its natural conclusion, she parted her legs a little and leaned towards him, reaching for his erection. After all, despite her misgivings, the hour would end prematurely.

She wiped him with a Kleenex and handed him the pack. He lay there, staring at the ceiling, breathing deeply, his shaggy chest rising and falling like a bellows.

She took her dressing gown into the bathroom. "I'll let you get dressed," she said.

When she came out, he was ready, standing by the door.

"Are you all right now, Donald?"

"Thanks."

"Well, don't forget your coat."

He went downstairs in front of her. She wondered about the goodbye. Really, she didn't want to have to kiss his moustache. Donald pulled his coat on and took a bunch of keys from his pocket. Mercifully, he reached for her hand.

"Thank you, Willow."

She closed the door behind him and leaned heavily against it. Parting the folds of her dressing gown, she touched herself with quivering fingers. Slowly at first, and then more rapidly, she climbed the stairs and hurried to the bathroom. The shower ran hot in seconds. Before she could even remove her stockings, Aisling bowed her head, thrust out her chin and vomited copiously over her feet.

# Chapter 12

## *Number 33: Mrs Minnie Starling and Darling*

It was not a new smell. It had been there for ages. Minnie couldn't say exactly, when Roland James asked her for its history, but she knew it seemed like a very long time, and it was gradually getting worse. In any case, she reasoned, the age of the smell surely had little relevance. It was a bad smell, and it was there, inside her airing cupboard, and she wanted rid of it.

"So you don't know how long?" Roland James stepped back from the airing cupboard and carelessly shoved Minnie's towels and bed linen back into place. "I mean, is it days or weeks or what?"

"I told you, I can't say. It's there now, that's all that matters."

Roland James wrinkled his nose and scratched the side of his head. He hated problems like this one, where you couldn't get to the bottom of anything. Where was he supposed to start? There was a ragged hole in the cupboard wall, at the back, dark and fist-sized. Maybe the smell was coming from there. He agreed there was a smell, though he couldn't say what it was, sort of an oily smell. The hole ought to be blocked up; that would be the logical first step.

Minnie Starling's house was one of four in the street not owner-occupied. She had lived at number 33 since 1960, the year her husband died. Her grandson Charlie came to stay with her from time to time, but mostly it was a rather lonely place, just her and Darling, her ginger tom. At her advanced age, it was both inevitable and essential that, living alone, Minnie had social service carers in to see to her four times a day. Even with this level of support, it was remarkable that Minnie managed as she did, for she was soon to celebrate her 100th birthday.

Mr James was the landlord. The street's four rented

properties all belonged to him. He couldn't have been described as a rich man, though many people in the street thought he must be. People believed that if you owned property, you must be prosperous, whereas the truth was that all too often it was the properties you owned that drained your resources and made you no better off than anyone else.

"Was there something else?" he enquired cautiously.

"Yes. That gutter's still drooping over the bedroom window. It spills water when it rains." She ground her teeth at him. "I told you."

"So you did, so you did." He helped her on to the stairlift and slowly followed her downstairs. "I'll get Raj to look at it."

At the foot of the staircase, Minnie made no attempt to dismount, but sat staring at him. "It's not looking at it wants. It wants repairing."

"Yes, yes. Raj will do it."

"I told you week before last. He didn't come then. All down the window, it leaks."

"I probably forgot to tell him. I'll get him round sharpish. And he can do that hole in the cupboard."

It was Minnie's recollection that Roland James never did anything 'sharpish' and neither did his workman, Raj. Their attitude to maintenance was distinctly weary and the standard of workmanship was at best rudimentary.

"A hole, you said."

"Yes, Mrs Starling. There's a hole behind your airing cupboard."

"Well, I don't like that Raj." She held out an arm and he helped her up. "He's Indian, for a start."

"He can't help that, Mrs Starling."

"He smells of curry," Minnie added.

"Hmm. One smell after another." Roland James picked up his clipboard and headed for the door. "Your cat's clawing the curtains."

"Darling, stop that!"

When she had heard the front door bang, Minnie took

her stick and went to inspect the tear in the curtains. There was hardly anything to see. Darling was lying on top of the sofa backrest, slyly watching the departing landlord through the window. Good riddance, she thought. She wasn't sure which of them was worse, Roland James or Raj. Last winter's burst pipe that sent water cascading on to her bed; the skittering roof tiles the wind blew into the garden; the kitchen cupboard door left hanging loose on its broken hinges; not to mention the detached guttering... these faults she had dutifully reported to the landlord as soon as they became apparent, but someone in the office merely grunted down the phone and a fruitless silence would ensue. The roof tiles still had not been replaced, and the cupboard door had fallen off again within a week of Raj repairing it. These were operators who had converted inefficiency into an art form.

Charlie was coming to see her tomorrow. Minnie looked forward to his visit. He didn't come very often and DIY was not his strong point, but at least he took an interest and tried to be supportive. She would ask him what he thought about the smell in the bathroom. She would tell him to stand halfway up the stairs and say whether he could smell it from there. The smell was getting worse.

She crept to the back door and let Darling into the garden. He scampered on to the lawn and suddenly dropped to a stealthy crouch, facing the low picket fence at the boundary with a patch of woodland. A spark of light revealed a blue tit perched on a wooden spar, below which Darling slowly, artfully eased himself into a position of fatal access. The tiny bird flapped its wings but stayed on its perch, viewing the garden over the cat's head. Minnie watched with a comprehending smile. It took perhaps one second. Darling sprang upwards at a perfectly calculated angle and, with one flailing paw, punched the blue tit from the fence. The cat nosed the dead bundle and turned it over on the grass, mewing softly.

Minnie stabbed her stick at the floor, licking her lips.

"I'd like to do that to Mr James," she said.

# Chapter 13

## *Number 35: Mrs Leila Smart and Billy Smart*

Leila Smart leaned against the doorpost and cast her eyes around her son's room. She frowned, not in disapproval but to register a kind of weary disappointment. The room was not exactly untidy, but it was cluttered and unclean, and the musty warmth carried the smell of inadequate ventilation and neglect, a sourness redolent of damp straw, old newspapers and animal urine. It was not a pleasant place.

Leila could not remember when she was last in this room, but it was a long time ago, probably a month or six weeks. It was Billy's den, his private retreat, and a mildly overheated space he shared with his animals, friends with whom he had nurtured a kind of wordless communion, an unwitting compensation for his apparent inability to achieve a meaningful relationship with his few human acquaintances.

When people asked politely of Mrs Smart the precise nature of her son's condition, she replied only that she didn't really know what the problem was. The doctor was uncertain, she said. A specialist had been consulted, but his findings had been vague and thinly documented. She had searched on-line for information, tapping brief descriptions of Billy's behaviour into Google to see what enlightenment or guidance might be delivered on-screen. The exercise had resulted in frustration and confusion and a futile sense of having spent hours going nowhere.

"My brother-in-law, he said something about what they call Logan's Syndrome," Mrs Stirrrup up the road had told her, in the paper shop.

Leila Smart went home and typed the name into her computer, but nothing that came out made any sense. Little that happened in Billy's room made any sense to her, except that it seemed to keep the boy in reasonable balance, which was all that she could ask or expect. He loved his animals, and their undemanding calmness pacified him. For most of the time, that was enough.

Billy was lying on his back on the bed with his eyes closed. He was fully dressed, including his outdoor shoes. The only sound, or sounds, came from the various tanks and cages arranged around the room, rectangular refuges populated by a family of small creatures, some eating, some sleeping, some scrabbling unproductively in their own dirt.

"Billy," Leila called softly, "can you hear me?"

The gentle, almost imperceptible rise and fall of Billy's chest suggested sleep, but a twitching in his hands indicated to Leila that he was merely at rest. She waited. In one hand she held a small parcel, while she moved her free hand, Carex-scented from the kitchen, to cover her nose, shielding her senses from the foulness that threatened to envelope her.

"Something came in the post for you, Billy."

"Eh? What?"

Her gaze roamed around the walls. A tan-coloured rat wrinkled its nose at her, as though she were the source of the bad smell. Two guinea pigs shared a stale apple, burbling softly. A budgerigar, immaculate in blue, white and black, twittered brightly as it hopped from one leg to the other on its crusted perch. Two newts lazily straddled each other, half submerged in filthy water. A tortoise sat motionless under the bed. In a cage on the window ledge, four white mice scuttled to and fro, apparently busy with their housekeeping.

"Billy, you ought to open a window in here."

"Mmm?"

She jumped, gasping, as something punted her in the cheek, a blunt, rubbery nudge. Denzil, Billy's West African python, lay coiled on top of the wardrobe behind the door, and slid forward to introduce himself. Kiss kiss.

She shrank away, clutching her chest. "Billy, for

Christ's sake!"

Billy rolled over to face her, blinking the mist from his eyes. "Wassup, Mum?"

"How long have you had that thing?"

"What thing?"

"Bloody snake!"

"It's a python, it won't bite you."

Denzil leered at her from the top of the wardrobe, chiselled head swinging in space.

Leila threw the parcel on to the bed. "Your mail. And get this room aired."

Billy swung his legs to the floor and picked up the package. "Food supplement for Molly," he explained.

"Molly?"

He pointed to the snuffling rat. "Molly."

His mother shook her head, retreating into the corridor. She felt sick. Dirt, smells, a snake sizing her up with its cold, unseeing eyes.

"Close my door, Mum!"

Leila shut the door and briefly propped herself against it with one arm. Billy had made a facsimile of a coloured poster from a magazine and stuck it on the door: the A4 copy advertised Billy Smart's Circus.

Inevitably, she worried about Billy. She knew he wasn't quite right. Physically he was okay, though it would be good if he washed more often, but there was something going on in his head – or maybe there was nothing going on in his head. That could be the problem. She worried about that and about his sullen preoccupation with the animals. She wished he had some decent friends or, even better, a girlfriend. Now he was old enough, he had a part-time job at the fish and chip shop in the High Street, *In Cod We Trust*. It wasn't the best job in the world, but it might just be the best job in Billy's world. At least it brought him a bit of money and got him out of the house. She didn't like him coming home reeking of fat and fish, but he always smelt of something unpleasant, anyway. Unexpectedly, he'd got a car out of it. That was another worry. He hadn't passed his test yet, but as the chip shop was only minutes away he had taken to driving there and back with no L-plates. One of the chaps at the shop had offered him the car, an old Vauxhall, for a knock-down price, and Billy had done the deal with uncharacteristic alacrity. It was a time-worn barge of a car and, with its fat tyres and lowered suspension, it looked as if it had been sat on by an elephant.

Damned snake. She went to the bathroom and washed her face, shuddering. What would Roger have made of all this? Three years now since the break-up. Probably Roger would have done exactly nothing; he couldn't manage his son, anyway. Roger could barely manage Roger. Some men were so feckless. You couldn't believe it. The only thing worse was the daft women who found these losers attractive. Still, she didn't want Billy to grow up a loser.

She sat on the edge of the bath, drying her face. "Billy, Billy, Billy," she murmured to herself. She kept her teeth tightly clenched. She would not cry.

# Chapter 14

## *Number 30: Stephen J. Kettering-Barclay*

She had swept the man's clothes off the chair on to the floor. Now Janice Collins sat there leaning forward with one hand clamped over her bleeding nose. Blood ran down her wrist, darkening the sleeve of her uniform. She had pulled the bath plug out and thrown her client a towel, which he had draped over his bony shoulders. With the water gone, he sat shivering in the scum-fringed bathtub.

"Stephen, why – why did you do that?" She licked blood from her lips. "Tell me."

He glanced at her, then stared at the floor. "I'm sorry. I didn't mean to hurt you."

"Stephen, it wasn't an accident."

"I didn't know what I was doing." He looked at her again, more critically. "Have I broken your nose?"

She lifted her messy hand away and inspected it. "I don't think so."

"I – I am truly sorry."

"Whatever were you thinking, Stephen?"

"I said, I don't know."

She took a face flannel from the wash basin and wiped her nose and mouth. "We'd best get you out of there," she said, "before you catch cold."

Struggling against shock and the pain in her nose, Janice helped Mr Kettering-Barclay on to the floor and sat him on the chair. She dried him carefully and began replacing his clothes.

"These aren't very clean," she said. "I can't go fetching new ones now. I'll try to come back."

"I'm really sorry, nurse."

"Janice. I'm not a nurse."

"You're as kind as a nurse."

"I'm doing my job, that's all."

"What can we do about your nose?"

"Have you a medicine cabinet?"

"Over the sink."

"Right. I'll find something in a minute. Don't worry about it."

She eased him on to the stairlift. He sat there, staring at her mournfully. "I'm a bad man," he said.

"No. But we need to get to the bottom of this – don't you think?"

She went downstairs in front of him and helped him dismount at the hallway. "Poor old man," she thought.

He sat in the armchair with the newspaper in his lap. His white hair was damp and tangled. They had forgotten his shoes, left in the bathroom.

"Suppose you're going to report me," he said quietly.

"Well, I'll have to make some kind of report, yes, but I won't be incriminating you."

"How do you mean?"

"I'll say I had a fall – my fault."

"You'll lie to your employer?"

"Like I say, I'll take care of it, Stephen."

"You're a good woman."

"Hmm. This good woman's going up to mend her face. Don't move till I get back."

Janice returned to the bathroom and found some antiseptic wipes in the medicine cabinet. Gingerly, she inserted a little finger in each nostril, bringing out a smear of rusty blood. She cleaned the bath and perched on the rim, attending to her bruised face. By now she had stopped shaking, though she was unhappy at the thought of meeting her next client with blood on her uniform. Perhaps she could keep her jacket on to cover it.

Stephen was sitting stiffly in his chair, clutching his paper but not reading it. His eyes were glassy and unfocused. She asked him if she could come back later and find him some fresh clothes.

"Wouldn't bother. Hardly been washed."

"Well, that's your own fault."

The old man sighed and slapped the newspaper on his thigh. Janice didn't want to give up on him.

"Look, I've two cancellations this evening. Why don't I come back about five and get you changed. Then we can have a cup of tea and you can tell me what's going on with you. How does that sound?"

He gazed at her with tears gleaming in his eyes. Biting his lower lip, he nodded and fought for the vestige of a smile.

Stuart was in hospital. She thought she might visit him, though she didn't know the man well. Aside from a courteous check on his condition, she could ask him about Mr Kettering-Barclay. Ought the client to be left on his own? Were agency callers safe in his presence? Janice was not permanently assigned to him, neither was she his social worker or psychiatrist; but a natural and instinctive concern for the welfare of others, particularly those to whom she had been granted professional access, impelled her to investigate this unhappy gentleman's background. There was work to be done here.

When she returned at the end of her shift, Stephen was watching a television quiz show. She stood gazing at the screen over his shoulder as he pointed crossly at a woman contestant.

"Where do they get these people, eh? This one thinks Stockholm's in Scotland."

Janice smiled sympathetically, shaking her head. Her eyes travelled from the TV screen to roam around the rather dingy room, settling upon the elderly, undusted sideboard with its tired cargo of willow-pattern plates, old newspapers and empty vases. Three framed photographs drew her attention. In one, a blonde woman, gap-toothed but with a winning smile, sat in a canvas chair in the sun. In another, the same woman, dressed in shorts and T-shirt, posed proudly beside a duo-tone MG Magnette, a black mongrel at her feet. The third picture, monochrome, showed a weather-scarred ship, apparently out at sea, dark smoke curling from two funnels. Janice craned her neck to read the inscription beneath the photo: S.S. *Daedalus 1942.*

"That your wife in the photos, Stephen?" she asked chirpily.

Mr Kettering-Barclay slowly turned to look at the sideboard. "Oh. Yes, yes, that's Marjorie. Lovely lass. Lost her four years back."

"Ah, I see. She has a happy face."

The old man puckered his lips and nodded reflectively.

"You don't have the dog any more?"

"No. He died a year after Marjorie. Shame. Still, I couldn't look after a dog now."

"They're good company. We have a little terrier, Starbuck."

He reached for the remote control and turned the television off. "You said about changing my clothes."

"I'll help you, yes."

"I put some out. Front bedroom, on the bed. Bring them down, I don't want to go up again." He stood up, wiping his hands on his trousers. "I'm tired."

She fetched the clean clothes, pulled the curtains and changed Stephen like a child. His legs were stick-like and his upper body appeared almost cadaverous. She wondered about his diet and if he got enough to eat. Probably Stuart could enlighten her about that, too.

When he was back in the armchair, she moved to the sideboard and picked up the photograph of S.S. Daedalus. There were two lifeboats visible, hanging above the deck. The sea looked calm.

She held the photo towards Stephen's chair. "Were you on this ship?"

He peered at her and then at the picture. "What? Oh yes. The Daedalus. For fourteen months I was First Radio Officer. She was a fine ship. 9,220 tons."

"I see. Merchant Navy, then."

"Aha. Twelve years at sea. Went to all corners of the globe."

Janice put the picture back, pulled out a wooden chair and sat down. She thought about the incident in the bath.

She remembered the boat.

"Was – did you have a bad time in the war, Stephen?"

"No-one had a good time in the war," he replied.

"No. No, I suppose not. If you weren't in it, you can't begin to imagine."

"Of course." He was staring straight ahead, gripping the wings of the chair. "I wasn't afraid, you know. Well, maybe once."

"Stephen, forgive me for asking, but is that how you lost your leg?"

"Blast shrapnel. Damned thing still hurts, even though they cut it off."

"Dear me. A bomb?"

"Torpedo."

"I see. And that was on the Daedalus?"

He nodded. "Coming back from Shanghai, August '42." He smacked the sides of the chair with both hands, as if that might clear his head and help him to remember. "Don't rightly recall what we'd loaded. Light machinery of some sort, I think."

"Surely the Germans didn't get as far as Shanghai?"

"No, no. Japanese submarine on the way home. Single torpedo amidships."

"And you were injured in the explosion?"

"I was, together with several of my shipmates. We had five killed and twelve injured."

"Out of…?"

"About a hundred."

"But you survived. And your shipmates, what happened to them?"

Stephen sighed and shook his head. "We lost nearly half. We didn't have the time, you see. She went down by the bow in ten minutes and the best we could do was launch three boats out of four. So many men went in the water, others were stuck on board as she sank."

Closing her eyes, Janice struggled to imagine the scene, the raucous shouts, the jabbering panic, the groaning of the vessel as it listed in its death throes. Then she envisioned

81

the boats, and it began to form itself into some vague, almost ethereal sense, as a positive slowly prints into relief out of a dark negative. Boats. All they had now. Boats.

"You were lucky to get in a boat with your leg, surely."

"Yes, I was. I tried to get to the radio room to send a Mayday, but I couldn't make it. Blood was pouring out of me. I got someone to fetch my portable so I could transmit from the deck. I got off a position and then we all abandoned. They virtually threw me in a boat, lifted me up in their arms."

"Brave spirits," Janice said.

Stephen made a strange, guttural noise and twisted round to face her, anguish pulsing in his eyes. "It wasn't enough. There weren't enough damned boats."

"What happened, Stephen?"

"Ship's medic trussed up my leg just before we got off, or I'd have bled to death. God bless him. Lots of wounded, not just me, and there was a lot of blood in the water, people splashing about, yelling. Course, Pacific Ocean in summer, the sea was quite warm, and soon they came looking for us, sharks, bloody great things nearly as big as a boat, might have been great whites, I don't know, and next you knew, blokes were screaming for their lives, mad with terror."

"Did they try to get in your boat, Stephen? Is that what – "

"Course they did, poor buggers! Can you blame them? What choice did they have? Drown or be eaten alive."

"Your boat – was it full?"

"Overloaded. If the sea hadn't been calm, we'd have been swamped."

"Oh God."

"I remember one man, think he was a stoker, he grabbed hold of the side of our boat, nearly tipped us over. No-one had the strength, maybe the will, to haul him in. No room, anyway." His eyes blazed, ignited by the searing memory. "No bloody room!"

"What happened to him, Stephen?"

"I – I killed him."

"What happened, Stephen? What did you do?"

"I balled my fist and punched him hard in the face, all the strength I had. He let go and fell backwards and he went down and – and I never saw him again."

"Jesus, Stephen," Janice whispered.

"That wasn't the end of it. There's more." He squeezed his hands together, both arms shaking. "Some other fellow took his place, same trick. I thought, well, this boat's going over, we'll all drown, or worse. So I grabbed an oar and, so help me, I smacked him over the head, everyone shouting at me to stop, I bashed him over the head with the blade of that oar, made him let go."

"And he drowned?"

"No, I wish he had. He'd have wished the same. Sometimes drowning's beautiful, merciful. So along comes this bleedin' shark, you should have seen the size of it, scooped him up in its mouth like it was feeding time at the zoo. We watched him taken, nothing we could do about it, nothing. That shark, it went racing off in a circle, then it came back and – and for a second I thought it had picked up some red seaweed, streaming out along its side, and then when it went roaring past I could see all that man had left was his head and torso, and the seaweed trailing behind was his spewing intestines, like a red octopus on the water, and you know, you know, that poor chap with his smacked, split head, he stared up at me with these terrible wild eyes, like he was begging me to know why I'd done this to him, when all he'd done was ask to be saved, same as us. All he wanted was a chance."

Tipping the chair over in her desolate haste, Janice went to him and draped her arms around his heaving shoulders, nuzzling the white barbs on his cheeks. Only the old man's wrenching sobs disturbed the silence, as his carer held him close and rocked with him while he wept.

# Chapter 15

## *Number 22: Mr and Mrs Slocombe*

Hettie Slocombe woke up in the dark and wondered what the time was. She stretched her legs across the bed to relieve the pressure of Arthur sitting on her feet. To see the clock, she switched on the bedside lamp, screwing up her tired eyes. It was ten past two. Instinctively, she patted the sheet beside her, feeling its coldness. Alf was not there. Wheezing at the effort, she dragged her legs out of bed and slowly burrowed her feet into a pair of fur-lined slippers.

"Alf! Are you in the bathroom? Is it your prostate?"

Alf did not reply. At the foot of the bed, Arthur curled a paw over his eyes to shield them from the light.

"Alf!"

Hettie crept from the room, touching the walls to steady herself. When she clicked the landing light switch, a millisecond flash of light was snuffed out in a hollow *pop* as the bulb burst, plunging her back into darkness.

"Damn!"

With one hand on the banister rail, she inched her way to the bathroom door and pushed it open. Nothing. No-one.

"Alf, dear!"

Hettie should have turned on the bathroom light, but in her sleep-befuddled state this logical action did not occur to her, and so she turned left and moved to the head of the stairs, reaching for the newel post. She knew what Alf would like, bless him.

"It's all right, dear. I shall go down and make you a nice hot chocolate. You know how you love it, so soothing when you can't sleep."

If Alf had got up, so had Arthur, hopping along the landing in the dark. Nervously, in animation virtually suspended, Hettie stood poised with a thumping heart in her dry mouth, measuring her body weight against the fickleness of gravity, one foot hovering above the first stair in a freeze-frame of impossible balance. It was precisely as she allowed that foot its slow descent to the carpeted step beneath, that Arthur, with a careless flip of his hind quarters, did the same. The rest was inevitable. Hettie's invisibly planted foot found not the flat security of the rectangular platform, but the rounded, yielding hump of Arthur's back, whereupon the rabbit, yelping, skipped away, and the old lady's quiet accommodation with gravity was hopelessly compromised. The inertia of silence was instantly transformed into a whirling helter-skelter of percussive noise.

With breathless suddenness, she was riding, unharnessed, on the big wheel. Black and grey shadows rotated past her, each one dealing her a sickening blow on the head or shoulder or back, until the street light filtering through the glass panel in the front door granted the scene a dim illumination as silence returned, mercifully accompanied by retardation. The big wheel braked to a standstill.

Several minutes passed. Curiously, she was unable to work out which way up she was or in which direction she was facing. What little light she could see might be coming from anywhere. Instant death, however, seemed to have been avoided. Pain, yes, there was pain, but it was not unbearable, and for some strange reason she could not be sure from where the separate messages of pain were coming. Her left arm felt numb, so she left it where it lay and tried to move her right leg, buckled against the wall, only to find, as she shifted her position, that her arm was in protest after all, sending a shockwave knifing through her shoulder. She thought better of it and decided to remain quite still and hope she didn't wet herself. By abandoning all thought of movement, she soon found a new peace and sense of security, reasoning that the accident had now happened and thus she had been transported out of potential danger into a realm of repose, a place where consequential safety had been benevolently vouchsafed. If she stayed where she lay, something moderately good would surely happen next.

It occurred to her that Alf would be wondering what had happened to his hot drink. Poor Alf. Stunned and breathless, she could not call out to him. A crunching sound from the kitchen told her that Arthur was snacking on his nuggets, oblivious to the crisis unfolding a few yards away.

*Move, Hettie,* she told herself. *You have to move. You cannot lie here till daylight.* With ponderous, almost fearful caution, she extended her arms until her fingers found a rounded ledge which she realized must be the front edge of the bottom stair. Biting her top lip against the surge of pain in her left arm, she managed to ease her body from its contorted resting place and slide down, snake-like, on to the hall floor, until only her ankles lay upon the last step. When she could feel the cool floor under the palms of her hands, she lay still for a minute, maybe two, renewing her meagre strength. Then, with one last aching heave of protesting shoulders and legs, she fought her shocked weariness to roll over and slump against the wall, helpless as a broken doll. Her heartbeats thumped in her head, a dull pounding at her temples.

"I'm so sorry, Alf," she whispered.

Now there was pain and fear and confusion and darkness and nothing else. She wondered why he did not come to see to her. What had happened to love? Of course, if he was ill…

Arthur came bouncing from the kitchen. She felt him nestle between her legs. Dear Arthur. She reached out a trembling hand to stroke his head between the ears. The phone was too far away to reach. She could whisper but not cry out. It was dark and she was cold. She kissed her fingers and rubbed them on Arthur's ears. Propped against the wall like a puppet thrown there, she closed her eyes and thought about what it would feel like to die. Hettie's chin dropped as she prepared for sleep. She waited.

# Chapter 16

## *Number 25: Joan Descours*

Joan Descours studied her reflection in the lounge mirror. What she saw did not please her. "Joan," she admonished herself quietly, "you are not a pretty woman. Your face is too long – or perhaps it is your head that's too long. When you laugh, on the rare occasions when you have something to laugh about, you resemble a horse ready to whinny. Sometimes I wonder if you were the last of the batch, and God, having miscalculated the amount of material required, decided to avoid wastage by using up all that he had left on your one slab of a head. Just don't laugh, that's all, or they'll stick you in a stable."

Barry Brown's footsteps sounded on the stairs. Joan returned to the kitchen table and pulled Barry's chair out for him. A sheepish smile coloured the boy's cheeks as he sat down, tapping the laptop keys to bring the display back to life.

"Sorry about that, Miss," he said.

"Nothing to be sorry about, Barry. Nothing at all."

"I left your bathroom all clean, Miss."

"I'm sure you did, Barry. Now are you quite sure you're all right?"

"All right, Miss?"

"To continue, I mean."

"Oh yes, Miss. Another ten minutes and I shall be done."

"Just take your time, Barry. Speed is not important."

She backed into the corner by the fridge, folded her arms and stood gazing at this vaguely elegant young man. Why did God do this, she asked herself. He made people like Joan Margaret Descours, gave them horses' faces and stuck their eyes in the wrong place, and with the next saintly breath he created beautiful beings like Barry

Brown, blessed them with pearlescent skin the colour of milkshake and eyes as bright and clear as pebbles washed by the sea. If you painted Barry Brown ascending to Heaven, you would change nothing about his face, embellish not a line or contour. This boy would shortly become a handsome man, poised, polite, charming in his delicate innocence. Women who looked like horses would stand no chance.

Barry seemed to have lost concentration. His head darted back and forth between the screen and his mentor, and his eyes flickered under furrowed brows. "Please, Miss," he blurted.

"What is it, Barry?"

"Sorry, I can't concentrate, Miss."

"What's the matter?"

"It's you, Miss. You're staring at me."

"Am I? Yes, I suppose I am. I'm putting you off, aren't I?"

"Sort of, Miss."

"Thoughtless of me. Tell you what, I bought some sausage rolls – from the baker's, not the supermarket – and I think I'll pop them in the oven for us. Then I shall go next door and wait. How does that sound?"

"Go next door, Miss?"

"I mean, in the next room. I'll come out when the food's done. Yes?"

"That's nice, Miss."

Joan set the snack to warm in the oven and moved to the lounge, leaving the door ajar. She considered examining herself in the mirror once more, but resisted the temptation; nothing would have changed. She would still be Joan Margaret Descours, aged 48, plain, erect, slightly haughty of bearing, beginning to feel, around the feathery, fragile edges of her conscience, a curious, vestigial longing for something she was too afraid to confront. She sat at the polished dining table and clasped her hands on the veneer. She gripped them tightly to stop them shaking.

Reminiscing, she thought of Barry Mackeson, though

really there was no good reason to recall him. He wasn't a bad man; or was he a man at all? That one night, under the pointless privacy of the duvet, he had caressed her shoulder, kneading the bone with his fingertips, while they kissed and breathed moistly in each other's faces. Moments ago, from her voyeuristic position on the stairs, she had learned more of Barry Brown's pale young physique, gleaned from that fleeting glimpse, than she had ever known of her erstwhile boyfriend's unaccessed body. Yet here, too, was an ill-advised, unsafe recollection.

A small voice drifted from the kitchen. "A hot smell in here, Miss."

"Coming, Barry."

They cleared two spaces on the table and ate quietly, pausing now and then to wipe their fingers. In a somewhat feminine gesture, Barry repeatedly used his thumb and forefinger to pinch the crumbs from the corners of his lips, licking the pinkish flesh to remove the flaky residue. Joan watched the boy's mouth in this small work. Her own tongue, she thought, would accomplish the task as well, erasing every last speck of pastry in an undisguised kiss, the brush of her lips, feather-light, tasting the sweetness, worlds compressed into seconds.

"These are really good, Miss."

"Glad you like them, Barry." She cocked her head to one side. "Barry?"

"Yes, Miss?"

"Barry, I was thinking. While we're in the house, why don't you call me Joan? I mean, we can use each other's names, can't we?"

"I don't know, Miss."

"Don't know what, Barry? Don't know if we can use our names or don't know if you want to do it?"

"I'm – I suppose, Miss."

"Very well. Of course, when we're in the classroom you should call me Miss or Miss Descours, but here in the privacy of my house I think it would be perfectly all right for you to call me by my name – don't you?"

"If you like, Miss."

"Well, I rather think it's a matter of what we both like. More relaxing, perhaps."

"All right, Miss."

"So you'll try it then?"

"Yes, Miss."

"No, Barry. Try saying 'Yes, Joan'."

"All right – Joan."

She nodded, smiled and gazed at the boy's slightly blush-pinked face. "You've a crumb on your chin, Barry."

Barry quickly brushed two fingers across his chin. "Sorry, Miss."

"It's nothing to apologise for, Barry. I've probably got crumbs on my chin – have I?"

He peered seriously at Joan Descours' chin. "Not that I can see, Miss."

"Not that I can see, *Joan*," she reminded him.

"Oh. Yes, Miss."

Joan Descours smiled a little sadly and shook her head at the small wonder of it.

# Chapter 17

## *Number 15: Aisling McIver*

Rona bustled in, throwing her bag on the cluttered table. "Hi there, Irish Willow! So what's new?" She fixed her friend with a mock-serious frown. "You look a bit pale."

Aisling waved a dismissive hand. "I'm okay. That name…"

"What's wrong with it?"

"Makes me sound like a bloody race horse."

"Better that than an old nag. Could call you Dobbin."

"Thanks."

Rona sighed, grabbed a chair and sat down heavily. "Did he come, that – Donald, was it? By that I mean, did he arrive, whether he actually came or not. If you get my –"

"Yes, okay, thanks, Rona, I think I understand."

Rona stared at her, thoughtfully sucking her teeth. Aisling didn't look well. Was that consequence or coincidence? "Do you want to tell me about it?"

Aisling slowly shook her head, staring bleakly at the floor. "Rona, am I supposed to enjoy this?"

Silence intervened, mitigated only by the baby's gentle clucking in the corner. Rona gathered her thoughts, reluctant to look at her friend while unformed doubts assailed them both. She had known Aisling for ten years and throughout that time she had struggled to convince the girl of her own worth. While she could advise and support her, it was another matter to make her believe in herself. She remembered the movie, *Fantastic Voyage*. If only she could crawl inside Aisling's head with a surgical bag and daringly adjust that miraculous mechanism.

"Aisling, listen."

"Oh, I'm listening."

"First, you have to give it a chance. You should know that. I take it you didn't get on with Donald. He's upset you?"

"He didn't upset me. Probably I upset myself. Donald, he had all the charisma of a potato."

"That's not what it's about, honey. It's not about personality." She leaned towards Aisling's face, steely-eyed. "It's about making money out of a man's weakness. You have the upper hand. Go with it."

Aisling nodded, working her lips in a wetted circle. "I remembered the preliminaries you told me. Except I forgot to ask him to wash his hands."

She shrugged. "So you'll remember it next time."

"I guess so. I have to get used to it."

"In any job, Aisling – I'm sure you had all this at Beasley's – there's days when it just feels wrong and you want out of there and go home. Yes?"

"Yes."

"The way I see it is, you could be working in a shop and all the time there's people coming in and picking stuff up and putting it down and fiddling with this and that, poking and prodding, seeing if they think it's any good. Well, you know how it works. If you're an escort, my dear, point is, you *are* the shop. A man comes in and he looks and feels and probes and fingers, and you, the merchandise is you. So like when you were in the shoe shop or the newsagent's, and some days you couldn't wait to shut the place up and leave, okay, now you've had quite enough of being handled goods and you want it to stop. That's what this is, Aisling, that's what they're buying with the money. They're paying for pieces of you."

Aisling rubbed her eyes and blinked until her vision cleared. "Well, I'll stick with it. I have to, don't I?"

"Did anyone else contact you?"

"Yes, they did. For tomorrow. There's Martyn at lunch-time and Roy in the evening. They sounded all right on the phone. Roy could be an older guy. He's coming at six."

"Good. Be pleased when it's older guys. They're generally polite and grateful and don't hassle you. The younger ones – remind me what we put down about minimum age."

"What?"

"In your Profile. We stipulated a minimum age."

"Oh, right. Thirty-five, wasn't it?"

"That's good. In any case, it's a waste of time looking out for handsome, debonair young men, they're mostly spoken for. If you look like you're straight out of a magazine ad, you've got a girlfriend you can shag any time, or there's even your girlfriend's girlfriend. So why would you pay for it?"

"Oh, I'm not bothered what they look like, Rona. So long as they don't make me feel abused. Still…"

"Still what?"

"It's just – do you think I'm pretty enough for this?"

Rona burst out laughing. "Oh, Aisling, Aisling! Most of them would do it with a bag over your head. It's your body they're interested in, not your face. They're not looking to marry you, for God's sake!"

"Ah, that's a blessing," she said acidly.

"Glad we've sorted that one." Rona stood up and gazed about the room. "Can I make us a drink now?"

"Sure. Coffee would be nice."

"Your man Roy. Six o'clock you said?"

"He's coming after work. Probably all hot and sweaty."

"So make him use the shower first. Do you still have your box room?"

"Course."

"Then I shall be hiding in there. Don't worry, he won't know. But I'll keep my ear to the door. For your peace of mind, honey."

At last Aisling managed a smile. "God bless you," she murmured.

# Chapter 18

## *Number 33: Minnie Starling*

Charlie Dixon hovered on the middle tread, one foot nonchalantly balanced on the stairlift rail. "From about here, Gran?"

His grandmother peered up at him from the hall, gently prodding the floor with her stick. "Yes. What can you smell?"

"Nothing much." Charlie wrinkled his nose obligingly. "A bit musty, maybe. Could just be damp."

"It's not damp. Nothing's damp."

"Whatever you say, Gran. I'll go on up."

He opened the airing cupboard door and sniffed inside. There were black smears on some of the towels and that ugly hole in the wall was shedding plaster, as if it had recently been inexpertly patched up. There was a smell of oily decay.

"What do you think?" Minnie called.

"Don't know, it's a bit odd. Those black marks."

"It's not a rat, is it?"

"A rat? What, in the airing cupboard? Rats are after food."

"I hope it's not a rat," Minnie grumbled.

"Who mended this hole?"

Flakes of grey plaster littered the woodwork and discoloured the linen. Most of the towels would need another wash.

"That Indian chap. He did that and the gutter by the bedroom."

Charlie went into Minnie's bedroom and looked through the window. Two lengths of black plastic guttering slanted downwards against the glass in a truncated V-shape, the broken bracket still attached to one dangling tube.

"Have you seen this gutter, Gran?" he yelled.

"It broke this morning. I heard it go."

Charlie sighed and shook his head. She was an old lady trying to cope on her own, for God's sake. Did nobody care any more? *Don't worry about it, she'll be dead soon. The house'll be renovated before we let it to a new tenant. We don't need to impress anyone.*

"Charlie!"

"Hello."

"Charlie, are you in the bedroom?"

"I am. What is it, Gran?"

He heard her stick knocking against the banisters. "Something I can't reach. On that shelf, top of the wardrobe, there's a black cardboard box with tape round it. Bring it down to me, please."

He found the box, peered again at the hanging gutter and came downstairs. Minnie took the box and put it on the table next to a vase of dead flowers. The box, he remembered, used to belong to his grandfather. One day, as he walked into the room, the old man was sitting in a chair with his pipe in his mouth, wheezing with the effort of wrapping brown tape around the box to secure the lid. He had resisted the temptation to ask what the box contained.

"Grandad had that box, didn't he?" he said.

"He did. Now you're going to ask me what's in it."

"Is it something valuable – old and valuable?"

"Who's to say what's valuable and what isn't?" Minnie replied.

"Is it some kind of family heirloom, perhaps?"

"Perhaps."

"So what is it?"

Minnie lifted the box, shook it gently and replaced it on the table. "None of your business," she said.

Charlie looked grimly at the dead flowers. There was nothing more depressing in a room than dead flowers. The stagnant water smelled of sick.

"You could do something useful, make us a cup of tea,"

Minnie said. "I've got Jammy Dodgers," she added, making it sound like a disease.

"Right you are. Have you got the number of that man's office, the landlord?"

"Card on the kitchen wall next to the calendar. I keep ringing him."

"Gran, he's hopeless. So's his sidekick. They need their heads smacking."

Minnie subsided backwards into her chair, prodding her stick at the floor between her feet. "I blame that Roland James. If he will insist on employing workmen who can't do a proper job. Call himself a manager. He's about as much use as a chocolate frying pan."

Charlie picked up the flower vase and carried it to the kitchen. "I meant to tell you," he called through, "that Mrs Stirrup caught me as I was coming in and gave me an envelope. I put it in the car."

"Ah, I know what that'll be. I had one on the doormat. It's a party invitation."

"Party? Whose party?"

"Mine, of course. When I'm a hundred."

He came to the doorway and stared at her. "You what? You got an invitation to your own birthday party?"

"It's meant to be a surprise. If I didn't turn up, that'd be the surprise. So they sent me a card."

"And who's 'they'?"

"Are you making that tea?"

"In a minute. Is this your neighbours getting together?"

"Oh, I don't know, Charlie," she said wearily. "Still, be nice to have a bit of a party. Last party I went to was the Coronation, when we were all in the street and it rained and all the sausage rolls got soggy. Well, you wouldn't remember that."

"Probably because I wasn't alive, Gran."

"Ah, that's my boy. You always had an excuse."

Charlie made tea and biscuits and read the party invitation which his grandmother had propped on the mantelpiece. The event was at The Rifleman in ten days' time, starting at half past six, thoughtfully obviating the need for the elderly guest of honour to stay out late. He made a mental note to bring his camera. Returning to the kitchen, he telephoned the estate office to speak to Roland James, but his call went to the answerphone, and he left a message for Mr James to ring his mobile as a matter of urgency. He had little confidence that his enquiry would elicit any response. Probably he would gain nothing but that brief burst of Vivaldi before the machine cut in.

He went back upstairs and sniffed the bathroom air again. Minnie's cat followed him and jumped lightly into the airing cupboard, settling himself on a pile of folded sheets, where he lay loosely curled, purring softly as the warmth enveloped him.

It could have been his imagination, but he thought he heard something rustling on the other side of the wall.

# Chapter 19

## *Number 22: Mr and Mrs Slocombe*

Hettie hadn't heard the doorbell but her eyes flickered open when she heard the rattle of the letterbox. In a jab of daylight, the postman's eyeballs appeared like two boiled sweets about to be pushed through the slot. Hettie sat slumped against the wall, massaging her left arm, idly wondering why the floor under her felt wet.

"Mrs Slocombe, can you hear me? It's Joe, the postman."

Hettie groaned and, with a valiant effort, managed to raise her left leg a few inches off the floor.

The postman's eyes swivelled to the right. "Mrs Slocombe! Are you hurt?"

"Joe, I can't move. I'm all banged up."

"Can you let me in, Mrs Slocombe?"

Hettie groaned again, only louder this time. "Course I can't. I'm stuck here."

Joe sighed and gave the door a useless shove. "Is there someone can help?" he shouted. "Can I ring someone?"

"I think – yes, number twelve." She winced, catching her breath. "Mrs Clarnon's got a key."

The letterbox clanked shut. Arthur Slocombe hopped towards her and paused to deposit a clutch of dark droppings on the doormat. There was something cold and wet under Hettie's thigh. She closed her eyes and the hallway seemed to reel about her, as if she were falling from a ferris wheel.

A draught of cold air hit her as the front door opened and two figures stood silhouetted against the light. The postman wore a baffled expression and Martha Clarnon wore a sky-blue jumpsuit.

"Hettie, what's happened?"

"Oh, it's you. You look like you come by parachute."

"I run up the road with Joe." Cursing, she stepped in the rabbit's mess. "Tell me what to do."

"My arm," Hettie said.

"I'll be off then," the postman said.

The two paramedics, brisk in their kindly efficiency, arrived within ten minutes. Suki, small-boned and compact, was accompanied by Stan, tall and gangling, and as they bent over the crumpled Hettie they appeared, in their green overalls, as stick insects quietly feeding. Suki asked Mrs Clarnon to find them some clean clothes to replace the old lady's urine-soaked nightdress. Martha came down with a pink cotton skirt and a shapeless blue T-shirt, and a red blanket completed the ensemble as they carried the patient to the ambulance.

"Sorry about the wee," Hettie said to Suki.

"That's quite all right, dear. It's all in a day's work to us. Pee, poo, blood, vomit. Tell you the truth, I scarcely notice it."

"Years since I've been in an ambulance." Hettie gazed around at the stacked equipment with sudden alertness. "Will we be having sirens and a blue light?"

"I don't think that'll be necessary," Stan replied. "You just hold on tight and talk to Suki."

Hettie smiled. "Bless you," she said. Then she sneezed and wet herself.

Lying on her back in the emergency bay, the curtain open, she felt exposed and ridiculous. A Chinese doctor, fiddling with his stethoscope, came to stare at her, then went away again. An hour later, she had been X-rayed and the same doctor wandered back.

"You have fractured your lower left arm," he told her sternly. His manner seemed accusatory.

"I fell down the stairs," Hettie said.

"You must be careful. We keep you in overnight for observation. Plaster and sling."

Hettie blinked back her tears.

Five miles away, Martha Clarnon gave up watching for a returning ambulance and put her coat on. She stepped outside and motioned to Pat to wind down the car window. On the radio a comedian was telling jokes, accompanied by gales of cacophonous laughter.

"Where you going?" Pat asked.

"The hospital."

"Are you ill?"

"Course I'm not ill. If I was ill, I'd be going to the doctor's."

"So are you going to the doctor's?"

Martha rolled her eyes. "It's not me that's ill, it's Mrs Slocombe."

"Why don't she go to the hospital, then?"

"She already has. I called the ambulance."

"So she's all right, then?"

"I don't know. That's what I want to find out."

Pat frowned and shuffled his feet on the pedals, trying to make sense of this conversation. He was missing some good jokes here.

"I'll get the bus," Martha told him. "I'll take her in some things."

At Saint Peter's, Martha met a nurse in the Acute Medical Unit. The nurse's badge said Stacey Maxwell. Stacey had a blue wave in her hair and a ring in her nose.

"I'm Hettie's neighbour," Martha explained, dropping a bag on Hettie's bed.

"We'll monitor her overnight," the nurse said, "and hopefully send her home tomorrow. She's going to the Plaster Room shortly."

They discussed the patient's domestic arrangements. Nurse Maxwell asked about Hettie's husband.

"I'm afraid he's not well," Hettie said.

"He's expired," Martha elaborated.

The nurse nodded sympathetically. "Is there anyone else at home?"

"There's Arthur," Hettie replied.

"Arthur. I see. And is he – capable?"

"Capable of being a rabbit," said Martha.

Stacey Maxwell glanced from Martha to Hettie and

back again. Sometimes she wondered whether, for her, this was really the right profession.

# Chapter 20

## *Number 35: Mrs Leila Smart and Billy Smart*

Dawn light filtered through the curtains, but the sleeping Billy Smart did not stir. The animals, time-programmed in their tiny brains, snuffled and shuffled in their cages, but Billy did not stir. Beyond the window, in the back alley, a motorbike engine coughed and revved, but Billy did not stir. Billy, flat on his back in bed, snored and dreamed. The motorcycle roared like a wild beast, accelerating over the rough track towards the road. Ten minutes passed. Billy dribbled down his cheek on to the pillow. Another half-hour passed. Billy sleepily crossed one ankle over the other and rubbed them together to soothe an itch. He slid his feet apart and brought them together again. He did this twice more, then he blinked, opening his eyes, squinting at the ceiling. Billy stirred, lifting his head, propping his weight on his elbows. He was awake.

Something was wrong. Something was different. Something was missing. He peered down the bed to his covered feet. There was nothing to be seen except the rumpled duvet. No Denzil. For as long as he could remember, Denzil had spent the night coiled at the bottom of the bed, resting on Billy's feet. Billy was accustomed to the pressure, aware of it as a kind of reassurance. As a cold-blooded creature, Denzil could not keep Billy's feet warm, but his sinuous weight seemed to lock the boy's legs in place, locating him securely on the mattress. But this morning there was no Denzil.

Billy rolled over and eased his legs to the floor. His left heel grazed the shell of the snoozing tortoise under the bed. A rat chattered at him, nibbling the cage bars. Breakfast was late today. Billy cast his eyes around the room, but there was nothing amiss, nothing unusual that he could see, except that there was no python to be seen anywhere. This unnerved him. This was not good.

His mother tapped on the door. "Billy, are you awake?"

"Huh?"

"Billy, have you seen the time? I thought you were doing the shop lunch-time today."

"Yes."

Gingerly, Leila Smart opened the door and peered round it. "Well, it's gone ten. You need to get up and washed and dressed. You need to get moving."

Billy, stiff-necked from sleep, rolled his head from side to side. "Slight problem," he said.

"Are you not well?"

"No."

"You're not well?"

"No. I'm all right. It's – it's Denzil."

Leila screwed up her eyes as if in pain. "The snake's ill?"

"No. It's not that."

"So what is it? What's this problem?"

Billy spread his hands uselessly. "He's gone. I don't know where he is."

"Gone? What do you mean, gone?"

"Gone from the bed. No sign of him."

"Have you got up and looked? Have you?"

"Not yet."

His mother clenched a fist round the edge of the door and pressed her eyes against her fingers. "Billy, get dressed. Search this room. Find the snake. Don't ask me to help you."

She shut the door. The room's thick animal stink hung in her nostrils, layered her throat. Her son lived in a pig-sty; all it lacked was a pig. He lived in dirt, ate in dirt, slept in dirt, stank of dirt. Her son was an animal.

Now that his mother had gone, Billy sat naked on the edge of the untidy bed. He scratched his armpits and then, parting his legs, he scratched the cleft between his scrotum and his thigh, rubbing the warm grease into his fingertips. There was half an hour before he needed to leave for the

103

chip shop; half an hour to find Denzil. He pulled on sweat pants and a T-shirt and stumbled round the room. He peered under the bed, checked that there was no loose floorboard and opened the wardrobe in case the python had fallen from its habitual resting place on top and landed inside. Of the four-foot reptile, there was no sign.

They were both in the room, he remembered it now. That was three, maybe four, years ago. They were arguing. He had returned from the pet shop with a glass container of newts, his mother confronting him on the stairs with an expression of tired outrage, and he shouldered his way past her without looking her in the eye.

Leila Smart shouted after him. "This is my house, Billy. It's not a zoo."

When Roger Smart came in from work, she told him of the latest arrivals. He shrugged in aimless despair, drifting his gaze across the floor. "Leave the boy be, Leila. He's doing no harm."

She followed him to Billy's room. His dad did not openly encourage the boy's hobby, but neither did he demonstrate any disapproval. Leila bristled, feeling isolated. Billy responded to the tainted atmosphere by keeping his ambitions to himself. At first he paid for the animals with his pocket money, later buying new friends and improved accommodation for them with his shop wages. Amid the sighing and grumbling, he came to believe that only his animals showed him any unconditional affection. They were beautiful in their simplicity.

Somewhere to hang his clothes, that's what he needed. The old wardrobe stood gathering dust in the spare room, unused rolls of wallpaper lying forgotten inside it. Before the wardrobe was heaved in for Billy, there was a blank wall beside the door and, where it turned in a right-angle, an alcove fitted with three bookshelves. Billy had few books. He wasn't a reader. There was a world atlas, a *Guinness Book of Records,* some comic annuals and a small collection of handbooks from the pet shop. He enjoyed the pet books and read them from cover to cover.

"Dad, can I have that brown wardrobe in here?"

Leila ground her teeth. "You're not going to put animals in it."

"For my clothes!"

His mother slapped her sides in unreasoning frustration. "At the rate you're going, there'll be no room left for anything except cages."

"Leila, you're being ridiculous!"

Billy couldn't recall exactly how the arguments had gone after that. Their raised voices became shouts and then screams of senseless anger. He cradled the tank of newts in his arms and slid it on to the window sill, secretly wishing he had never bought the newts, never walked into the pet shop. He could just have gone for a ride on his bike.

For a fleeting moment, he thought his dad was about to strike his mum, his face red with rage, a trembling fist balled at his chin, his words tumbling out in a spray of spit.

"Dad, no, it's all right, please!"

Roger Smart stomped round the room like a demented robot, while his wife covered her eyes with her hands.

It was a single swift blow, an arcing right-handed punch that made his knuckles crack audibly as the descending fist smashed into the wall, toppling the books, scattering plaster. Dad had broken two fingers. The hospital's orthopaedic team repaired the fingers, but Roger never repaired the hole in the wall. Billy put some books in front of it. With the arrival of the wardrobe, the damage was obscured and soon forgotten.

Until today. Until maybe. Until just possibly. Billy took a torch from the ledge above the bed and moved to the blocked bookshelves. He pushed some books aside and found the ragged hole, slightly larger than the size of his father's fist. From the top of the wardrobe to the hole below was a drop of about six inches. He thought for a moment. He thought about curiosity and locomotion. Craning his neck into the gap between the corner of the wardrobe and the middle bookshelf, he shone the torch into the dark hole and waited for his eyes to focus.

Out of the dusty darkness, unblinking, a cold, opalescent eye stared back at him.

# Chapter 21

## *Number 30: Stephen J. Kettering-Barclay*

He went to the fridge, took out a beer and cracked the tab. Even the smell of it was good. Returning to the armchair, he drank from the can, gasped at the sudden, bitter chill and wiped the back of his hand across his wet lips. That woman, Janice, had put the photograph back in the wrong place, so it seemed to wedge in the corner of his eye. Funny, he thought, Stuart had been coming for over a year and he had never mentioned the picture, yet Janice had noticed it straight away.

He tilted the can again and shook it to judge how much was left. Half full. The misplaced picture irritated him, so he got up and moved it back where it belonged. His other hand fell naturally to the left-hand drawer, which he drew open. A scuffed canteen of tarnished silver cutlery lay on top of an unsealed manila envelope, the gum on the flap long since dried and darkened. He tipped the envelope and the heaviest of its contents, a dark blue wallet, slid into the drawer.

"Not seen you for many, many years," he whispered.

In the armchair, he took another mouthful of beer, placed the can carefully on the floor and examined the wallet. *Continuous Certificate of Discharge.* He flipped to the page for 1942 and read the faded fountain pen entries. Halfway down: 'S.S. Daedalus. Master, George Tilley. 25th August 1942. Vessel Sunk.' That was all it said, all there was room for, all that Merchant Navy procedure required.

If only it had been that simple, that devoid of conscience or consequence. Tilley he remembered, hardly a leader of men, but a good man nonetheless, riding to the bottom with his ship. Though he fought against the impulse, he remembered, for the second time that day, the death-mask faces of the men he drove from the lifeboat to meet their end with the sharks or the deep. Then his heart lurched with a wrenched beat as he remembered the cook, Glaister.

Before the sharks arrived in their foaming, iridescent scores, snouts thrusting out of the rust-coloured water, they had already dragged Glaister into the boat. The first shark had seized him as he dangled over the side, and clamped its jaws around the man's leg. Someone beat it off, but in those few seconds Glaister's fate was sealed. They lay him, half-sitting, at the prow of the boat, shoeless, his left leg torn off below the knee, the splintered bones splayed like mashed timber.

"Is the doc here?" someone called.

"Not in this boat," came the answer.

Glaister howled in agony. Blood pumped from his shattered leg, darkening the soaked boards. A man at the stern ripped off his shirt and passed it forward to be used as a bandage or a tourniquet. The sounds were of tearing cloth, choking sailors, thrashing sharks, the screaming cook.

Glaister fought to make sense of his pain by speaking through it, describing it, articulating the help he craved, but his words spluttered out of him in a mad torrent from foam-flecked lips, his eyes saucering with terror. Glaister had forgotten language, reduced to primal noise.

"For God's sake, do something!" the shirtless man cried.

But there was nothing anyone could do, except stare at Glaister and try not to stare at Glaister, pretend Glaister was not there. Inside Glaister, Glaister was not there any more.

"Hoo me!" the cook bawled.

Stephen was near him now, reaching for his arm. "Tell us, Glaister! Tell us what to do!"

"Hoo me!"

"I can't – "

A man was being sick over the side, turning to wipe his

mouth. "He's saying, 'Shoot me!'"

Someone's legs thumped wildly on the bottom of the boat. "My God!"

"Hoo me!"

Stephen slitted his eyes and stared through the huddled men. "Does any – has anyone got a gun?"

No-one replied, just a few shook their heads. They were sailors, not soldiers.

Glaister arched his back, banging his hands on the boards. "I seh – seh hoo me!"

There was blood in his mouth now, scarlet ribbons on his chin. The man who had interpreted was vomiting again, not bothering to lean from the boat. No-one looked at him. The boat rocked as the sharks circled, plunging in their blood-crazed madness.

When Stephen had disposed of the invading crew members, they rowed away, sweating oily rivulets under a soaring sun. A few sharks tracked them, cruising lazily around the boat, but they lost interest and dived out of sight.

His blast-peppered leg was hurting now and the foot was numb. The man next to him nudged him, pointing to Stephen's bloodstained trouser-leg. He helped Stephen pull up the tattered fabric for inspection. A dark starburst of embedded metal shards spiked the weeping flesh beneath the hasty dressing.

"I'm all right, mate," Stephen said. "Cook's worse than me."

"Yeah. I'm Bascombe, by the way," the man told him.

"Pleased to meet you, Bascombe. Shame about the circumstances."

Bascombe shouted for the binoculars hanging from another man's neck. He scanned the shimmering sea to the horizon. All he could see was water and sunlight under a cerulean sky.

"Don't understand. The other boats…where's the doc?"

Bascombe looked at Glaister, his cloth-wrapped stump oozing blood on to the floor. The cook seemed to be unconscious, lying still at last. A man facing them leaned over and placed two fingers on the side of Glaister's neck, his eyes roaming the sea as he waited.

"Faint pulse," the man said. He shuffled forward and balanced on his knees close to Stephen and Bascombe. "Are we going to let him die?"

"Better than letting him live," Stephen said. "Don't you think?"

The men huddled close, thinking about this dark responsibility. For several minutes, they did not speak, but each man's thoughts were well known to the others. They did not need to talk about them. What they had to do was what was right, and that was beyond doubt.

"Gangrene soon," said Bascombe, shaking his head. "We could be out here for days."

Stephen sighed and nodded. The cook was out of it for now; but when he woke up…? He was a small man, and the three of them would be enough. It would not take long.

The man who had joined them spat on his hands and rubbed them together. "Come on, lads, let's do this. You with me?"

No-one wasted breath on a reply. Four hands reached under the slumped body while Stephen steadied him, and they turned him on his face. Grunting, cursing, biting their salty lips, they heaved Glaister on to the side of the boat, shoved him forward and grabbed his right foot. The shock of the water on the cook's face as he slipped down brought him round, and he coughed and spluttered, crying out, and Bascombe let go of the foot, pitching the man down into the green swell, and he seemed to hang there, bubbles gurgling from his mouth, until Stephen fetched an oar and pressed the blade on the back of his neck to drive him down, and they leaned back then and let him go, spinning down with his legs trailing like a diver, visible for a few seconds, perhaps for fifteen feet in the sun-bright water, and all of a sudden he was not there any more, just a blood-streak in the froth.

Stephen hauled the oar in. "Let's get out of here," he said.

# Chapter 22

## *Number 15: Aisling McIver*

Rona arrived at five-thirty. She pulled out a hard chair, dropped her handbag under it and sat yawning, running both hands through her hair. "How're you doing, kiddo?"

"Yeah, good," Aisling replied flatly.

Rona nodded at the cluttered table. "Can I say something?"

"Course."

"Can you get this stuff cleared up? It makes the place look untidy. People need to know you're making an effort."

"I suppose. I'll see to it."

"These guys, they like to come into a welcoming environment. This room is a tip."

"The bedroom's neat and tidy, Rona."

"But they have to walk through here to get there. It's a small gesture, Aisling."

"I said, I'll do it."

"Half an hour till your man gets here." She stood up. "Have you any sparkling water?"

"In the fridge."

"I'll get us two glasses. Make a start on that bloody table."

In the kitchen Rona poured two flutes of sparkling water, topped up the levels as the bubbles subsided and then, deciding that the glasses were too full to carry, sipped a small mouthful from each one. She studied the calendar on the wall, red question marks scrawled at yesterday's and today's dates and another for two days ahead. Her phone rang in her pocket and she spoke briefly to her hairdresser Miguel, while in the background to her conversation she heard thumping noises from the next room as Aisling busied herself at the paper-strewn table.

She carried the drinks in and handed one to her friend. "Cheers! Hey, you've made a difference, Irish Willow!"

"Most of it's gone in the cupboard under the stairs. I'll sort it properly later."

"Promise?"

"Promise."

"Pay some bills, Aisling. Before you buy anything, pay some of your debts. You'll feel better." She drained half of her water. "Your morning man come?"

"Martyn? Yes, he did."

"And?"

"He was a bit strange. He rang to say he'd be late."

"That's polite, not strange."

"No, I don't mean that. I mean he was an odd sort of chap."

"Odd, how?"

"Well, while I was waiting, Neamh started whining, so I took the opportunity to feed her, quieten her."

Rona toyed with her glass, studying Aisling in silence.

"So, anyway, when he came in, I had no bra on, because of Neamh, just that green and blue kaftan over me. He apologized again and I said something like, not to worry, I'd been feeding the baby meantime. He asked how old she was, I told him, and so he asked, did I feed her myself."

Rona nodded and finished her drink.

"I told him, yes, I believed in breast feeding. 'That would be nice,' he said, and he smiled at me in a funny kind of way. Sort of sly, you know. Oh, not nasty sly, but kind of – secretive."

"Young mothers," Rona said. "It happens."

"I didn't realise that." She drank some water and sighed. "We went upstairs and sat on the side of the bed and he dropped his trousers round his ankles. Then he just – he put his head under my robe and suckled me like a baby, and all the time he was playing with himself, just quite content, you know, quite happy. Way before time, he was finished. I didn't have to do anything, not really. He never asked me to. Next I knew, he was tidying himself up, ready to go." She shook her head. "Tell you the truth, I felt a bit sorry for him."

Rona put her empty flute on the table. "Well, there you are, then. No pain, plenty gain."

"Maybe. I hope they don't ask me for adult baby minding."

"Doesn't matter. You've not stipulated that, so you just say no."

"Funny guy," Aisling said. "He never really looked at me, not at my face."

"Finish your water. I'll fetch us another."

"Have we time?"

"Sure. I'll take mine up to the box room if your man shows. Roy, is it?"

"I think. Calls himself Bubbleboy." She glanced at the clock. "Get a drink if you want one. I'm going to get changed."

Rona refilled her glass and went up to the box room. A canvas chair lay folded against the wall, and she opened it, pulled the door an inch ajar and sat down to wait. Aisling was moving about in the bedroom, opening drawers and cupboards, and she hurried downstairs when the door buzzer sounded. After a brief exchange of voices, she and Bubbleboy came slowly up the stairs, talking quietly, the man chuckling nervously at something Aisling had said. They went into the bedroom and their voices fell to a whisper.

Only now did Rona wonder about the nature of her presence. Was this intended as security, or merely voyeurism? She suddenly felt uncomfortable, dishonest. Roy did not deserve to be spied on. Eavesdropping seemed a poor fit in the scheme of things. She would not do this again.

They were very quiet in the other room. A quarter of an hour passed. She shifted awkwardly in the uncomfortable chair, taking care to make no sound. Somebody dropped something on the floor – a shoe, perhaps? – and the man coughed and cleared his throat.

At first she thought it might be Aisling in trouble, upset or in pain, but then she realized that the timbre of the mewling sound could not be Aisling's voice; what she heard was unmistakably a weeping man, a man in distress. Roy was crying. Aisling's voice, soft and gentle, briefly overlaid the hollow whimpers, but soon a thin tissue of breathless moaning filtered from the room, and Rona pressed her fingers over her ears, eyes closed, waiting for the sad music to stop. Finally, as she feared she must press still harder to obliterate the sound or hum quietly to herself to smother it, she heard a single wail of release, as of a pain purged, a demon exorcised. She sat back in the chair, arms hanging at her sides, breathing deeply, waiting for footsteps.

The main door clicked shut and she moved to the window, watching Bubbleboy walk unsteadily down the street, dabbing his eyes with a handkerchief. With his blond hair and pale face, he looked a little like Michael Caine, she thought. Bubbleboy. Blubberboy. She folded the chair and replaced it by the wall.

Aisling was sitting at the table, hands interlocked around a mug of coffee. "Hi. I made you one, too."

They sat side by side. Neamh squeaked and fidgeted but did not wake. Aisling had pulled a dressing gown on, loosely tied at the waist, her breasts visible at the parting.

"So, was that grief or ecstasy?" Rona enquired cautiously.

"For who?"

"For him. Did he have problems, issues?"

Aisling lifted her mug and gazed abstractedly at the wall. "He's a security guard, works alone most of the time. He talked in whispers, like a child with a secret. Not married, parents dead. All he wanted – he just wanted someone to hold him for a while. I don't know, someone to pretend to love him, I suppose."

"Sometimes that's all they need."

"I almost felt guilty I'd taken the money."

115

"Don't be. You gave him what he wanted, something he couldn't get from anyone else. It doesn't always have to be just about sex."

She turned to look directly at Rona. "All these weak, inadequate men. I didn't – I thought they'd come in full of themselves, slapping down the cash and hustling me out of my clothes."

"You want aggression?"

"No, of course not. I'm just surprised, that's all, surprised and, well, sort of humbled, in a way. I seem to be so much more powerful than they are."

"You're learning fast, kiddo."

"Do you know, he put his arms round my shoulders and let me hold him, and apart from that, he never touched me. I was naked, Rona, and he never touched me."

"And you?"

"What?"

"Did you touch him – Blubberboy?"

Aisling put her mug down hard, so that it splashed on the table. "Don't you be calling him that, Rona. You hear me?"

"Okay, okay." She raised both hands to her face, defensively. "I'm sorry. I guess I'm misjudging him."

"I think you're misjudging me."

Rona drank, rested and licked her lips. She looked sideways at Aisling, respecting her, loving her. She had to know this could still be a hard road. You never knew who was about to come through the door. You couldn't trust them, not even the friendly ones. You took them on trust, but you couldn't trust them. The system didn't allow it. Inside the system, you were always one step away from being a victim. You relied on your intuition, because that was all you had. They paid you for taking a risk. It was a dangerous profession.

She reached out and stroked her friend's brow. "Are you quite all right, my darling?"

"I'll manage. Don't you go worrying about me."

"The way I see it, Aisling, is…these guys, they come in

116

out of the dark and you switch on a light for them, just for an hour or so. Happy sunshine. Then the time's up and they crawl back into their dark holes, kind of festering till the next time. You're a bit of a life-saver, Aisling. Only don't go getting a conscience about it. Take the happy money. Be proud. It could just be, you're all they've got."

Two visitors came on Thursday and, somewhat reluctantly, she accepted one more on Saturday. The first two, in their thirties, were her youngest clients yet; one handicapped by a starkly non-participatory detachment, as though Aisling were merely a picture in a magazine; the second man nervous and demonstrably inexperienced. Saturday's caller, nicknamed Gordon55 - presumably either his age or his birth year – was older and gentlemanly, unfortunately overdosed on an after-shave which pervaded the room for an hour afterwards.

With Gordon55 gone and the bedroom aired, she took the money she had slipped beneath a framed photograph of Neamh and went to the tea caddy. She removed all the ten- and twenty-pound notes, turned them round the same way and smoothed them out in her hand, before folding them neatly and replacing them in the tin. She had £540.

Neamh lay in her cot by the window, chuffing and kicking her feet. Aisling smiled, gazing at the milky-lipped child.

"More than five hundred pounds, Neamh. D'you hear me? Your mammy's going to pay some bills and then you shall have a new pushchair. That's a promise."

She was getting more used to it now. Already she had refined her welcome, keen to put her clients at their ease. She looked each visitor in the eye with an open smile, asked him how he was feeling today and took his coat, if he wore one. Then she offered him a hot or cold drink and a shower. Most declined the shower, but she liked them to wash their hands, as Rona had recommended. When the client undressed, she hung his top and trousers on a hanger and put it on the hook on the back of the bedroom door.

There was now a bedside lamp at either side of the bed, and she played soft music from a meditation CD to provide a relaxing background. A scented candle glimmered on her dressing table.

She was careful to wear no lipstick or perfume. If the man was married, he would not want to carry any red marks or unfamiliar scent home to his wife. Aisling did not otherwise concern herself with matters of fidelity. The client had made his decision and his choice, and at that point in the transaction, hers was a passive role.

With a slow-burn of inner strength, she learned to face each new day with calm anticipation.

# Chapter 23

## *Number 12: Mr and Mrs Clarnon*

Pat sat. Staring through the grimy windscreen, he saw Martha plodding up the road towards him, carrying a plastic bag. Approaching the car, she motioned to him to open the window.

"Where you been?" Pat asked her.

"I told you. To see Hettie."

"Oh, right. She okay?"

"Of course she's not okay. She's in hospital with a broken arm."

"They keeping her in, then?"

"Yes. Look, I can't stay bent down like this. Can you open the door?"

Pat leaned across and unlocked the passenger door. Martha climbed in and put her bag on the floor. She pulled a tissue from her sleeve and began mopping her face. Pat wound the window up again.

"The Social's involved now," Martha said. "They're not happy about her being on her own, specially now she's handicapped. Probably keep her in till something can be arranged."

Pat nodded non-committally. "What's in the bag?"

"I thought you most likely hadn't eaten anything."

"I had a Mars bar from the glovebox."

"Is that all?"

"Nothing else in there."

"You can't feed yourself out of a glovebox. We've got food in the house."

"I'm not in the house."

Martha sighed. "I got us some sandwiches from the hospital shop." She rummaged in the bag. "There's cheese and pickle or something called BLT. That's with bacon in."

"I'll have the cheese. You didn't buy a drink?"

"I'll do you one later." She ripped open both packets and gave Pat the folded bag to protect his trousers. "They seem quite worried."

"What about?"

"About her. She's not right, is she? Twice she asked me to go and get Alf's tea ready."

Pat lifted the top of his sandwich and peered inside it. "I wonder what'll happen when that rabbit dies."

"She'll find him his very own place in the garden with a little grave, some flowers and a headstone."

"Or maybe in the casserole pot," Pat suggested. "I used to like a rabbit stew."

"You're all heart, you." Some scraps of bacon dropped down her front and she brushed them on to the floor. "Anyway, I was going to ask you."

"Ask me what?"

"Even if they get care for her, whoever comes can't be there all the time. I thought perhaps I ought to make the effort, go round in the afternoon, three or four times a week. You know, make her a cup of tea, bit of a chat. I don't like the idea of her spending all day talking to a rabbit and a dead man. It's not healthy."

"I don't know," Pat said.

"Don't know? What is it you don't know? You mean, you don't know if she needs it or you don't know if you want me to do it?"

"I just don't know."

They finished their sandwiches and wiped their mouths. Pat reached for the radio knob. Soft music filtered into the car.

"What are you putting on?"

"It's 'Desert Island Discs'," he told her.

"Right. Living with you is a bit like being on a desert island. I'm stranded on my own."

"You can sit with me. Plenty extra seats."

"Hmm." She took the empty bag from his lap and screwed it up. "So is it all right about Hettie?"

120

"Sounds like you've made your mind up."

"It'd be neighbourly."

The music stopped and a man's voice intervened. An old van rumbled past and backfired, making them jump. Mrs Stirrup walked by and waggled her fingers at them. The music resumed, and they settled back in their seats.

"Who is this?" Martha enquired.

"Think it might be Mozart."

"No, no, I mean on the programme – the castaway."

"Not sure. The paper said Sir Nicholas somebody-or-other. Politician."

"Huh. Ought to put all the politicians on a desert island." She glanced over and patted his thigh. "Would you like to be on a desert island?"

"What, with you?"

"No. On the programme you have to be on your own. You'd be alone on a desert island."

"I don't know. No food and the works of Shakespeare. That's all you get, apart from your music."

"Plenty room to do your marching, Pat. Could go marching all over the island. You could be your own little army."

"They let you have one luxury. I would ask for a boat. How come no-one ever asks for a boat?"

"Suppose that would be cheating," Martha suggested. "You'd sail away and you wouldn't need your eight records. Then that'd be the end of the series."

"Course, if there was hula girls…"

"What, on the island?" She chuckled. "An old man marching up and down. I doubt they'd be much bothered."

"Ah, but if I was the only man there. They'd be gagging for it." He gazed at the sky, smiling. "We could repopulate the island."

"Perish the thought. An island full of Pat Clarnon clones. Have to find a lot of washed-up scrap metal so they could all build cars to sit in."

"So – uh? When you going round, then?"

"To Hettie's?"

121

"Yes, to Hettie and the rabbit."

"That reminds me. I've got to go over and feed Arthur. Think I'll do it now." She opened the door and dangled one leg out. "You, you could march smartly in the house and make us some lunch."

Sir Nicholas' next choice was Wagner, *Siegfried's Funeral March,* but although he liked the sombre melody, Pat found it too slow to march to. Instead, he conducted the orchestra with a stiffened forefinger, nodding his chin in time to the music.

As the piece was aborted, he saw a blue van coming up the road, a smart Mercedes with bold yellow lettering emblazoned on its side panels: *HomeTech Moto – A Garage on your Drive.* The van pulled up outside the paper shop, and Pat fumbled in the glovebox for a ballpoint pen. He wrote the phone number on the back of his hand, a barely legible blue smudge.

Perfect, he thought. Surely this operator could get the old Morris working again. It was Martha's birthday in a few days' time, and he would drive her out to the country for a celebratory pub lunch, chugging along the lanes with Vivaldi inside the car and birdsong in the hedgerows. He imagined a table for two by an inglenook fireplace, a fruity bottle of Californian Grenache, perhaps a lobster salad or a medium ribeye with garlic bread, blueberry ice-cream and coffee to finish.

Or would they offer a fine, full-bodied rabbit stew?

# Chapter 24

## *Number 25: Joan Descours*

The printer chattered and buzzed, finally spooling out four close-typed pages of A4. Joan collected the documents and took them to her seat by the window. Barry remained at the laptop, pecking abstractedly at the keys. For several minutes neither of them spoke.

The boy, squeezing his fingers, regarded her nervously from the corner of his eye. She sat with pursed lips, eyebrows raised. Finally she shuffled the sheets back into sequence and laid them carefully in her lap.

"Is it all right, Miss?"

"Joan," she prompted him.

"Oh yes. Is it all right, do you think?"

"Say my name."

"Will it be all right, Joan?"

She swung round in the chair and stared at him. "No, as a matter of fact, it's not all right."

"Oh." In a single breath, Barry evinced dismay, indignation and disappointment. "What don't you like about it?"

Joan waved the sheets in front of her face like a fan. "Nothing, Barry, nothing at all."

"I don't understand, Miss…Joan."

"I'm sorry, Barry. I suppose I'm teasing you. Very unfair of me. You see, you asked me if what you had written was all right. I said no, for the simple reason that it is substantially better than all right."

"Joan?"

"Barry, this is a very fine piece of work. I would not damn it with faint praise by describing it as all right. Do you understand me?"

The boy allowed himself a relieved smile. "Yes. I mean, thank you, Joan."

"It's me who should be thanking you, Barry, for rewarding my efforts by delivering such a well-thought, conscientious essay. I'm gratified and impressed."

Barry nodded, eyes downcast, and appeared to squirm awkwardly in the chair. A rosy flush bloomed in his cheeks.

"You have covered all the aspects of the subject I outlined to you and your responses are mature and soundly reasoned," Joan told him. "Your narrative is well-constructed and your command of written English is excellent. This is a superior student work."

At last he turned to face her. "Thank you. That's kind of you." He shuffled forward, winced and shifted his position. "You've helped me a lot."

"Kindness has nothing to do with it, Barry. I do my job, that's all. At times like this, I feel – fulfilled."

"But I do appreciate your support – Joan."

"I'm sure you do." She leaned towards him intently. "Barry, is something the matter?"

"No, I'm okay, Miss."

"Joan."

"It's just – I think I may need to go upstairs again, if you don't mind."

"Yes, I see you looking a bit uncomfortable. What can we do for you?"

Barry stood up, holding the back of the chair. "Will you excuse me a moment, Miss?"

"Joan."

"Joan."

"Are you on medication, Barry? I meant to ask."

"Yes. Just one tablet a day."

"And have you taken that tablet today?"

"Oh yes. I mustn't forget."

"Is it to calm things down? I mean – was it something like colitis you had?"

"Similar, Joan."

"Oh dear. That can be very unpleasant, very debilitating."

124

"But I'm getting better all the time, Joan. Normally I - "

"Normally you do what, Barry? Tell me."

"Take my medication when I get up. And have a warm bath."

"I expect you find that soothing, Barry."

"Yes."

"I'm a little concerned about the 'normally', Barry, that's all."

Barry gripped the chair back, rocking it back and forth on its legs.

"Don't do that, Barry, you'll break it."

"Sorry. I really do have to go up."

"Of course. Come on, let's go."

She followed him upstairs and ushered him into the bathroom. He stood in the middle of the floor, suddenly ungainly, as if uncertain what to do next. Joan put a hand on his shoulder and turned him to face her. In the gleam of his eyes there was an incipient tearfulness and his body trembled to her touch.

"Barry, did you not have your bath this morning?"

"Yes. Well, no, actually. I didn't know how long it would take me to get here, so I just had a quick shower."

"I see. That was silly, wasn't it."

He shrugged, looking away from her. "I suppose."

"No wonder you're uncomfortable." She clapped her hands together. "Right, I'll leave you now and I shall put my bedroom chair on the landing. My dressing gown is on the back of the door – see – and when you've finished you are to put that on and come out and sit, while I run you a nice warm bath. Understood?"

Barry nodded once and, where the light fell upon his averted face, she saw a single tear trickle down his cheek. "Why are you being kind to me?" he asked, and his voice was little more than a whisper.

Again, she squeezed his shoulder. "Kindness, Barry, should be a default, not a virtue. You don't need a reason to be kind. You need an excuse to be unkind. It's called humanity."

He opened his mouth to respond, but nothing came out, no words, just the tiniest gasp of grateful comprehension. Then he went into the bathroom and closed the door, and Joan brought a cushioned chair from the bedroom, placed it against the wall and sat down to wait. After a while she heard a tearing of paper and the rush of the flushed lavatory, the bump of bare feet moving and the busy splash of the boy washing his hands.

The door opened and he stood there, embarrassed, in Joan Descours' pink dressing gown.

"Hardly your colour," she observed, "but we can't have you catching your death. What would your mother say?"

"She'd wonder why I was standing in your house with no clothes on," Barry said, nervously.

"No cause for her to know," Joan reassured him. "Now then." She stood up. "You wait here and I will call you when your bath is ready."

She ran the bath a third full and swished the water to check the temperature. From a bottle on the shelf above she poured a generous measure of fragrant green gel, until the lightly steaming water was the colour of the sea, and soon her flurrying hands had masked the aquamarine beneath a silvery carpet of foam.

"You can come in now," she called to him.

Barry stood in the middle of the floor, toying with the sash of the dressing gown. He looked at her, blankly. She gazed back at him. Even in an absurdly unsuitable gown, he was a good-looking boy, she thought. She glanced at the pale pink V of his chest where the cloth parted and at his white feet and ankles. He didn't move, just stood there, planted, staring at her. She stepped towards him, brushing her wet hands. There was a strange taste in her mouth.

"Barry, do you want me to – "

"No, no," he blurted, "I can do it. I can get in okay." Lowering his head, he loosened the sash, and his lips moved rapidly, as if he were talking soundlessly to himself. "It's all right, you know."

Joan walked past him, touching his arm with trailing

fingertips. Her tongue felt like a dry leaf trapped in her mouth. "Leave the door. I'll get you a towel."

She went to the cupboard opposite the stairs, selected a large dark green towel – acceptably masculine, she reflected – and tapped her knuckles on the door. "Are you decent?"

Even as the words left her lips, she wondered at their banal absurdity. Of course the boy was decent. He was a decent person. His clothes, her dressing gown, were a mere artifice, a collection of woven fibres; yet they were considered decent, whereas the youthful body underneath could be labelled improper, unclean. No naked body could be indecent.

If Barry had replied, she didn't hear him. She walked in and hung the towel on the rail. Barry was in the bath, gently soaping himself with a sponge. His wet shoulders shone glassily under the light.

"Brought you a nice fresh, fluffy towel," Joan said.

"Thanks."

She approached the bath. The bubbles covered him just above the navel. His elbows skimmed the froth. He looked at her, his eyes softening in a quick, uncertain smile. A blob of foam sparkled in his hair.

"Do you want anything, Barry? Anything more?"

He shook his head.

"I could do your back for you."

He made no reply, just carried on sponging his legs under the water.

"Hand me the sponge, Barry."

He stopped washing and seemed to freeze for a few seconds, before passing her the dripping sponge. Joan dipped it in the foam and, kneeling beside the bath, began to massage soapy water over the boy's arched back, starting at the shoulder-blades and then, with slow, circular motions, working down to left and right towards the base of his spine. A perfect back, she thought. One little brown mole – she imagined a tiny cocopop – glistened above the cleft of his buttocks, but otherwise, as her sliding fingers traced the hard nubs of his vertebrae, Barry Brown's glossy white back was a thing of sculpted beauty, perhaps the trunk of a small tree cast in ivory.

She squeezed out the sponge and returned it to him. "All done. All nice and clean."

"Thanks, Miss."

"Thanks, Joan."

"Yes, thanks, Joan."

She swished her hands in the water next to his thigh. "Is this warm enough for you?"

"Yes. Yes, Joan."

Leaning forward, she rebalanced herself against the bath rim and, with a trembling hand, reached under Barry's ribs and traced her middle finger down, down, until she felt the soft dimple of his navel. For a moment she left her finger in that small burrow, feeling the warmth.

"What are you doing, Joan?"

"Nothing, Barry, nothing for you to worry about."

Just a few more inches, maybe, she knew. Already one or two coiled hairs. She closed her eyes, her head angled back to face the ceiling. But no, not this, not now, not today, not in this place. Please, not yet. Please. Dear God, no.

Silently, she stood up and walked quickly from the room.

# Chapter 25

## *Number 33: Minnie Starling*

Roland James reintroduced Raj to the hole. Raj stared blankly at the hole. The hole stared back at Raj with scarcely less expression.

"So what do you think, Raj?"

Raj peered more closely at the hole. "It's quite a big hole," he said.

"It seems to me," Roland James intoned levelly, "that we have, so to speak, been here before."

"Indeed we have, Mr James, on several occasions."

"Yes, I was speaking figuratively, Raj."

"Mr James?"

"What I am getting at, Raj, is that, to the best of my knowledge, you have previously repaired this hole, yet here it is, as large as ever, if not larger." He turned and looked his man squarely in the eye. "How do you account for that?"

Raj put one finger in the hole and promptly withdrew it. "Possibly shoddy materials, Mr James."

"Indeed? Then what do you think of the novel idea of employing non-shoddy materials? Eh, Raj?"

"We could try," Raj said brightly.

"Hmm. You see, in my gospel, when we have a problem like this, we can keep attempting to solve it, but the better way is to get rid of the problem altogether, once and for all. Problem-solving is an imperfect art, Raj. Problem removal is the preferable alternative."

"Yes, Mr James," said Raj, looking slightly bewildered.

"It's a bit like dentistry. You can plug the problem tooth with amalgam, or you can pull it out." James flung his hands wide. "Gone for ever."

"But we cannot pull out the hole, Mr James. We cannot – "

"No, I know that. But surely we can – that is, you can – effect a permanent repair, by taking a little more time and using the best available fixative."

"Then we fix it, Mr James."

"Excellent. So when can you do it?"

"It's quite a big hole," Raj said, rocking his head from side to side. "Maybe tomorrow after lunch I could do it. Or maybe during my lunch."

"Yes, I think after would be better. Otherwise – that's how Man created the Austin Allegro."

"Sorry, Mr James?"

"Never mind. I'll spare you the history lesson," he said, under his breath. He narrowed his eyes and tried to see inside the hole. "You know, I'm sure there's a speck of light in there."

"A light, Mr James?"

"Just a tiny speck." He drew back. "The thing is, we don't know whether this is our hole going forwards, or" – he tapped on the wall – "if it's their hole coming backwards. Is it our hole or their hole?"

"Then perhaps we should ask next door, Mr James. What do you think?"

Roland James sighed and wiped his brow. "I don't own their house, Raj. I really think it would be most expedient if you were to block up this hole and leave it at that. If they've got a hole in their wall, that's their problem."

"Ah yes, Mr James. So I will undertake the work tomorrow. Very good."

"I sincerely hope it will be, Raj." Stepping back, he picked up his clipboard from the floor. "You can close the door now."

As they reached the head of the stairs, James grabbed Raj's arm. "What are we doing about the gutter? She'll ask about the gutter."

"The gutter?"

"Yes, the gutter. We looked at it when we arrived – remember?"

"Ah yes. The gutter is loose."

"Loose? Raj, my boy, the gutter is fucking falling off and liable to clout somebody on the head. You told me you'd sorted it."

Raj rolled his eyes wildly. "Mr James, lots of rain this winter, rain and wind."

"I'm not looking for the cause, Raj, what I want is a solution. The gutter is dangerous." He jabbed a menacing finger at a point between Raj's eyes. "Put it this way, my boy: if I get sued, you get the chop."

"A chop, Mr James?"

"Yes, my friend, a very large chop. A chop you will have great difficulty in digesting."

Raj smiled obligingly. "Thank you, Mr James."

"The gutter has to carry the rainwater away, you see. It should not fall down because of it. That is akin to the wheels of your car becoming unscrewed when they go round. Am I making myself understood?"

"Oh yes, Mr James. The car wheels."

"The – yes, quite. I'm told it rains a lot in Poona, Raj. Their guttering, I believe, does not fall off."

"I have not been to Poona, sir."

"Really? Well now. I dare say they mend it *soona* in *Poona*, eh? What d'you think?"

He waited patiently, but in vain, for Raj to appreciate the joke. He heard Minnie moving around downstairs, hitting the furniture with her stick. Time was getting on. He had a meeting with the Council at twelve. Things needed to get done. He had to rely on people, but it was a risky business.

Minnie Starling, leaning against the doorpost, met them at the kitchen. "Shall I make you men some tea?"

"Be nice," James said. "Raj, put the kettle on."

Raj went into the kitchen. Minnie curled her lip. She didn't want the cups smelling of curry.

"Raj is coming back tomorrow," James informed her, smiling pleasantly.

Minnie crept to the living room and, carefully reversing into her chair, slowly subsided on to the faded floral cushions, where she sat with her stick between her legs, her chin balanced on the gnarled hands that grasped the handle.

"I hear you're having a party," Roland James said, perkily.

"I am. Have they invited you?"

"Me and Raj."

He could hear Raj muttering in the kitchen. He wondered if Raj knew how to make tea. Still, tea came from India. Surely he must know how to make tea.

"You all right there, Raj?" he called.

"Yes, I am doing in the pot."

Minnie blinked impassively.

"He's doing in the pot," James repeated.

Minnie sighed.

"Fancy," James murmured. "A hundred years old. What an achievement." He shook his head. "I doubt I'll live that long."

Minnie raised her chin from her clasped hands and fixed the landlord with a solemn stare. "You certainly won't," she said. "Trust me, I know about these things."

A thin chill seeped through Roland James's heart, the faintest tremor of unease, the thread of a fault-line in the bedrock of his confidence.

# Chapter 26

## *Number 22: Mr and Mrs Slocombe*

Janice Collins did not think of herself as a vain person, but early that morning she had met her reflection in the bathroom mirror with more than a little dismay. A glance at her face told her instantly that Mr Kettering-Barclay's punch, after some misleading delay, had brought a distinctly unflattering reddish-mauve bruise to the cheekbone beside her nose, together with a distracting tenderness.

"Bugger!" she hissed, a curse directed more at the forces of nature than at the perpetrator of the assault.

Carefully, for to exert pressure on the discolouration was really quite painful, she massaged some creamy oil into the blemish, and then applied a few dabs of talcum powder to the area, hoping by this ruse to disguise the unsightly inflammation. The outcome of these deliberations was, to say the least, unsatisfactory, for the woman staring back at Janice from the mirror resembled a clown whose make-up procedure had been rudely interrupted. She wiped her face clean with a wet flannel and searched unsuccessfully for an oversized pair of dark glasses.

Hettie Slocombe was peering at Janice over the rim of her teacup, while she rested her plastered arm, temporarily freed from its sling, on the hump of her abdomen.

"You make a nice cup of tea," Hettie said. "What happened to your face?"

Janice gingerly touched the bruise with a fingertip. "Promise you won't say."

"Say what?"

"I got smacked. That man at number thirty."

"What? Were you looking after him?"

"Trying to."

Hettie put her cup down and rubbed her chin thoughtfully. "Thirty. Is that the old chap with one leg?"

"One and a half legs," Janice emended.

"Huh. I hope you gave his good leg a kicking."

"Then I'd have lost my job. Retaliation is not an option."

They drank their tea. Janice had already explained to Hettie that the agency would sanction a daily morning and evening care visit while her arm healed, allowing half an hour each time. In practice, she warned, it was common for thirty minutes to shrink to twenty, in order that the day's schedule and its travel implications could be accommodated. In social care, time warps were an inescapable phenomenon.

"Does your arm hurt?" Janice asked.

"Not too much. It's more the bruises." She sat up straighter in the chair, wincing. "They told me I was lucky."

"And you've plenty of pain-killers?"

"Oh yes, dear."

"That's good, Mrs Slocombe."

"Please, call me Hettie."

"All right then, Hettie. Is everything within easy reach for you?"

"I can manage. Or I can always ask Alf."

"Alf?"

"My husband."

Janice frowned, passing a hand over her brow. "But you're widowed, surely?"

"In a manner of speaking."

The carer nodded slowly, studying the carpet in peevish confusion. "So – so where is Alf right now, Hettie? Hmm?"

"Oh, I don't know, dear. He could be in the shed."

"In the shed," Janice repeated, tonelessly. "In the shed. I see."

Hettie leaned forward with intense deliberation and seemed almost to plunge herself into Janice Collins's eyes.

"But you don't, do you, dear? You don't see at all. When it comes down to it, dear, you're no different to all the others. You think I'm a bit of a loony, a poor old lovelorn biddy quietly gone crazy. Well, I tell you, I'm not a mad woman. My Alf, bless him, he got cancer and that did for him, did for him in ways you can't begin to imagine. Now I'm left here without him sat opposite me – but you just think about it, dear, I never told you he was dead. I never told anyone he was dead."

Janice stared at Hettie, open-mouthed. "Mrs Slocombe, I – I really don't understand. Tell me again – where is your husband?"

Hettie sighed and slowly replaced her arm in the sling. "I don't rightly know," she said wearily. "He might be in the shed, like I said."

Janice stroked the bruise at the side of her nose, as if the pulse of pain might jolt her back to what she conceived as reality. "You dead husband is in the shed? Is that what you're telling me?"

"It's you as told me he was dead, dear."

Arthur Slocombe bounded into the room and hopped on to Janice's lap.

"Oh, my goodness!"

"It's only a rabbit, dear. He won't hurt you." She bent over and stroked Arthur's head between the ears. "Will you, Arthur?"

"He's your pet?" asked Janice, shrinking back in the chair.

"He's my little boy," said Hettie, proudly.

Hettie's little boy shuffled his feet judiciously and supplied Janice with an aromatic sample of his inner workings, darkening her uniform apron in a symbolic territorial affection.

"Pat his bottom and he'll jump off," Hettie advised.

Janice patted the rabbit's bottom. Then she looked at her watch. Hopefully the stain would dry out in the open air.

"I shall be back at six this evening," she said, reaching

for her bag. "Would you like me to get you any shopping?"

"Oh no, dear. The boy from the mini-market delivers. I give him a list and he brings the next lot, see."

"Ah, you have a system."

"I have an absent husband and a broken arm," Hettie said tersely. "Can you let yourself out? I need to do the breakfasts."

"Of course. What does Mr Slocombe like for breakfast?"

"I make him an egg with toast."

"And – and does he eat it?"

"Sometimes," said Hettie, defensively. "Sometimes he does, sometimes he doesn't. It all depends."

Janice was moving towards the door, leaving her apron on in case the fresh air might neutralize the wet patch.

"Depends on what, Hettie?"

"On whether he's here or not."

The cool air felt soothing on her face. She heard the front door click shut behind her and Hettie Slocombe calling out in the hallway, her voice cracking into falsetto. Janice thought she might have been addressing the rabbit, but she made out the word 'egg' and all doubt was removed.

Through a gap in the hedge she could see round the corner into the side of the garden. The sun blinked brightly on the shed window. She hesitated and peered to the right, craning her neck round the foliage. The shed door was ajar, and as she watched, a hand slid out and pulled it shut.

# Chapter 27

## *Number 35: Mrs Leila Smart and Billy Smart*

Billy sat on the edge of the bed with his head in his hands, staring grimly at the carpet. He wasn't sure what to do; that is, he had not the slightest idea what to do. His reasonable experience of pythons did not extend to knowing how to coax them out of holes. How could he go off to work, leaving Denzil lying in the wall? He doubted that, having crawled forward into the restricted space, the snake would have room to turn round and come out again. Snakes did not travel in reverse. With neither food nor water, Denzil would die, and before long there would be putrefaction, maggots, the stink of rotting flesh. Billy would spend his days and nights alone with a decomposing reptile.

His mother rapped on the door. "Get a move on, Billy!"

"I can't."

Slowly, by just a few inches, Leila eased the door open and peered round it. "Billy, you're going to be late."

"I found Denzil."

"Oh. That's good. Where was he?"

"You mean – where is he?"

"What?"

"Denzil. He's in the wall. I can't think how to get him out."

"What do you mean, he's in the wall?"

Billy stood up, still stark naked, and flung a hand towards the bookshelves. "The hole Dad made when he got mad."

Leila closed her eyes and ground her teeth together. "Shit!"

"Come in and see if you like, Mum."

She drew back. "Thank you, I am not about to put my face next to a hole with a snake in it."

"He won't hurt you," Billy said plaintively.

"You and your bloody animals."

Billy hopped desperately from one foot to the other, making his penis swing. "What're we going to do, Mum?"

"Well, you can start by putting some clothes on. My son's jumping about naked and there's a python in the wall. I can't be doing with this."

Down in the kitchen, she tried to pacify herself by rearranging the contents of the cupboards, checking the 'Use By' dates and amassing a collection of packets and bottles to be thrown out. At least she was doing something useful. At times like these she almost wished Roger was still with her, not that he would have been particularly constructive, but she could have discussed the latest predicament with him and used him as a sounding board for any ideas she might summon to mind. This was not something she could do with Billy; problem-solving was not one of his strengths. One thing was certain: the boy was going to be late for work again.

Against her better judgment, she thought about the man at the pet shop. When Denzil had first arrived, Billy had been too squeamish to feed him live mice, and he just refused to take any interest in dead ones. Until Billy could force himself to overcome this aversion, they had asked Mr Rabinowitz to come round and do the gruesome deed after he had shut the shop, handing him a bottle of wine for his trouble. It did not take long for Leila to intuit that the swarthy little man's willingness to help owed rather less to his concern for the snake than to an unwholesome fondness for rubbing Mrs Smart's bottom as he passed around and behind her, issuing perfunctory and unconvincing apologies at each furtive caress. She told herself he was a mucky little Jew, and one without whom they would have a dead snake in the house. Now the prospect had revisited them.

She picked up the phone.

"Hello, yes, good morning, *Creature Comforts.*"

"Is that Mr Rabinowitz?"

"Rabinowitz, yes, speaking."

"Mr Rabinowitz, this is Leila Smart, Billy Smart's mother. You probably remember me."

After the briefest of hesitations: "Ah yes, of course. Dear Mrs Leila Smart." He cleared his throat and gasped appreciatively. "What is it I can do for you?"

She was careful, as she explained what had happened, not to sound unduly anxious or upset, suspecting that to betray her true concern would be to engage Mr Rabinowitz's sympathy, when all she needed was his advice.

"This I think could be a problem," he said, his voice rasping down the line.

"It is a problem. It's a problem right now."

"Indeed. But for you – "

"Mr Rabinowitz, do you think if we were to put a mouse in the hole…"

"A mouse?"

"If you could bring a mouse."

"You are talking of a – a lure? Mrs Smart, my dear, I do not think this would work. Even if the python took the mouse, he probably would not come out. However…"

"Mr Rabinowitz?"

"In my lunch-hour, I will come. But I will not bring no mouse."

She went back to Billy's room and told him to get dressed. Then she rang the chip shop and told them apologetically that Billy was ill and would not be in today. Waiting for the man from the pet shop, she changed into an old pair of shapeless trousers and buttoned her blouse up to the neck. This was not a time to take further risks.

Mr Rabinowitz came in like a Dickensian doctor, wearing wire-rimmed spectacles balanced on the tip of his nose and carrying a small black bag. She let him go in front of her as they climbed the stairs. Billy, half-dressed, showed him the hole in the wall. He grunted, unclipped his bag and extracted a flexible probe with a torch on the end.

Billy reached for his mother's hand.

"It's all right, Billy," she said quietly.

Mr Rabinowitz crouched awkwardly, peering into the hole, manipulating the light. "Hmm. A hole," he murmured. "A hole, but no python."

"He was in there," Billy said. "I shone my torch and saw him."

"This is maybe." Mr Rabinowitz nodded, knocking his head on the wall. "But here and now, at this moment, there is nothing to see." He stood back and switched off the torch. "But…"

"But what?" Leila Smart spread her hands in frustration.

"But I see another hole, a hole which is at the other end. You understand?"

"You mean – "

"I mean, dear lady who is smelling nicely of soap, your son's snake is gone up the hole and gone out the hole. He is a gone snake."

Leila clasped a hand to the side of her face and, behind closed eyes, considered the enormity of this event. Of all the animals that might conceivably escape from the room, Denzil was certainly the most alarming, even if he was not necessarily the hardest to recapture. Snakes, inevitably, carried with them an undesirable emotional baggage and, in captivity, seldom found favour outside their normal domain.

Billy, wearing one sock and a baffled expression, stood staring at the hole and at Mr Rabinowitz. "What do we do, Mum?"

Mr Rabinowitz slid an arm around Mrs Smart's shoulders. "You are upset, of course. Is not a nice thing." His mottled cheek, roughly shaven, moved closer to her neck. "I give you little hug."

"Has Denzil gone next door, then?" Billy's voice was hardly more than a squeak.

"Is logical," said Mr Rabinowitz, kneading Leila's shoulder.

She squirmed away from him, making a chopping

140

motion with her hands. "The lady next door is nearly one hundred. If she sees a snake coming down the stairs towards her…"

"So we go next door and hope to intercept." He picked up his bag. "We go now."

"She'll want to know why we're there. If we tell her there's a python in her house, she could die of fright."

Mr Rabinowitz widened his eyes and emitted a bleat of derisive laughter. "Dear lady, if she encounters the snake in surprise, same result – no? I think we must get to the snake before the snake gets to the old lady." He placed a hand on Leila's back to turn her towards the door. "And we do not have much time."

Leila turned and snapped at Billy. "You're coming with us! Get a top on and some shoes. Pray to God we find him before Mrs Starling does." She opened the bedroom door. "So how do we smuggle him out?"

"Dear Mrs Leila Smart, I do not walk past old lady with python curled round my neck. No, is all right, in my bag I have cloth bag folded up. If she queries, we tell her – I do not know yet what we tell her, only we do not say is bloody great python."

Billy, wriggling about on the bed, pulled on some clothes. He followed his mother and Mr Rabinowitz out of the room. They were halfway down the stairs when they heard the screaming start.

# Chapter 28

## *Number 33: Minnie Starling*

Darling Starling was no different from cats the world over. He loved to curl up snugly in a soft, warm place and go to sleep. It only had to be a brief nap; a few hours would do. He could always come back and have a few more. At night the kitchen floor, next to the range cooker, was often the warmest area in the house, and Darling liked to sleep in his basket, comfortably installed in the space between the cooker and the washing machine. After breakfast, this hideaway gradually cooled, and the cat padded quietly upstairs and sprang lithely into the bathroom airing cupboard, where the boiler ticked and thrummed, issuing a constant, gentle heat. Here Darling could settle himself, paws protruding sideways, in a nest of fluffy towels, burying his nose in the feather-soft folds, hardly noticing the occasional draught from the hole in the wall beside the boiler. It was a good place to be, warm and quiet and safe.

Safety, of course, can be compromised, often by a change of circumstance. If Darling possessed any concept of circumstance, it was constrained by natural biological limits, unkindly exempting him from any useful appreciation of consequence or implication, for these are human faculties, not widely distributed to animals. Darling had once briefly observed the hole in the wall and then forgotten it, because it was just a hole. It was not something with which he considered he should concern himself. He had disposed of the hole by choosing to ignore it. When, today, his attention was drawn to the hole, it was already too late to make allowance for it. The hole was quivering. It was making a noise, a kind of rustling sound. In that small fragment of time, Darling needed to comprehend either the probable consequence of the disturbance or its implication, in order to take the appropriate action, but Darling, remember, was a cat, factory-fitted with a feline brain. Darling would have been well advised to vacate the airing cupboard immediately, but instead he hunkered down, ears pricked, and froze in his nest, languidly regarding the dark hole through slitted eyes.

It was many weeks since Denzil had moved so fast. Whether Denzil saw Darling before Darling noticed Denzil, or the other way about, was as uncertain as it was immaterial. The certainty was that once the python had encountered his furry companion, who had neglected to escape when the opportunity first arose, the cat's fate was sealed. With a plaster-spraying lunge, the snake powered half its length from the hole and seized Darling's head in its jaws. The cat could only find breath for a yelp of shock before a terrible darkness engulfed him. Mucus dripped from Denzil's greedily articulating mouth as he convulsed, rested and convulsed again, drawing in his prey, all the while encircling the shuddering body in a rubbery spiral of iridescent coils. As the last feeble whisper of air was squeezed from Darling's body, he oozed a trickle of excrement on to the towels, and lay still, imprisoned like a grotesque pig-in-a-blanket in the muscular web that Denzil had spun for him.

In the kitchen below, Minnie Starling was searching for a tea towel. When she found the drawer empty, she remembered that Charlie had taken the laundered towels upstairs to hang over a wooden bar in the airing cupboard, telling her that they were still damp. She clambered aboard the stairlift and ascended to the bathroom, sure that by now the cloths would be dry.

"I know he means well," she said to herself as the whining lift rose, "but he could have saved me a journey."

Moments later, she dismounted, planted her stick firmly on the landing carpet, and pushed open the bathroom door.

In the creatures' brief struggle, some towels and pillowcases had spilled on to the floor. Minnie cursed as the rubber tip of her stick skidded on the fabric, almost toppling her over. She steadied herself, bending from the waist, and caught her breath, before she turned.

A huge, gasping inhalation contorted her face, shrinking her lips back over her dentures and saucering her eyes until the whites threatened to explode. From the snake's slavering jaws, Darling's hind legs and tail hung motionless, the thigh-bones already compressed by the fierce pressure of constriction.

Minnie retched, choking, and a great blast of air billowed out of her, rattling her frail body, until the scream came, high-pitched at first, and then, upon its repeat, in a shuddering guttural roar that filled the room.

Leila Smart ignored the puny plastic bell-push and banged violently on the front door with the side of her fist. Her son kicked the door until she told him to stop.

"We go round the back!" Mr Rabinowitz commanded.

They clattered through the back door, leaving it wide open, and rushed up the stairs. Minnie Starling was lying on her side on the landing, her stick fallen out of reach. A thin drool seeped from her lips, wetting her chin. A smell of urine hung in the air.

Billy sat on the stairlift with his hand over his mouth, staring wide-eyed at Minnie's crumpled form, while Leila took the old lady in her arms and tried to ease her upright. In the bathroom, Mr Rabinowitz stood with both hands pressed to his chest, watching the closing seconds of the ingestion. He heard a muffled pop as the cat's bones snapped.

"Lordy-Lord!" he intoned in a trembling breath.

Minnie sat propped against the wall, legs splayed, her head cradled in Leila's shoulder. Her eyes were empty, without focus, but she glared grimly at Billy Smart sitting opposite her, and Billy stared back at the old lady with tears in his eyes. The only sound to break the silence was a faint rustling from the bathroom cupboard as Denzil inched his engorged bulk towards the side wall.

"Circus Boy," Minnie muttered.

"I'm Billy from next door," Billy whimpered.

"I know who you are, Circus Boy. I know where you live."

Leila stroked Minnie's stringy grey hair and touched the back of her hand to the old lady's cheek. "Best not talk, Mrs Starling. You've had a fright."

"Circus Boy," Minnie said. "I didn't know they had snakes in the circus."

Mr Rabinowitz unfolded his cloth bag and measured Denzil with his eyes. If this worked, he would need help.

"I'm- I'm really sorry," said Billy.

"Darling was my darling," Minnie said.

"I don't want you to hate me," Billy told her. "I'll hate it if you hate me."

Leila gave her a hug. "Shall we get you an ambulance, hmm?"

"An ambulance? What do I want an ambulance for?"

"You've had a terrible shock, Mrs Starling."

Billy wiped his eyes and forced a smile.

Minnie leaned away from Leila's enfolding arm and returned Billy's smile, but there was no smiling in her eyes, only a thin crease in her grey lips, and then the lightness slipped away like a picture falling from the wall.

"We are very sorry," Leila said. "We will make it up to you somehow. Yes, we will."

"Circus Boy. I might have known."

Mr Rabinowitz was in the doorway. "I must ring the shop. Edward is there. Edward must come now, to help me with this damned snake. On my own, I cannot do."

"Do what you like," Leila said, not looking at him.

Mr Rabinowitz closed the bathroom door and went downstairs. They heard him speaking on his phone.

"Don't cry, Circus Boy," Minnie said. "Crying won't help. Crying won't bring my Darling back."

She leaned her head back against the wall and closed her eyes. "There now, I've gone and wet myself." She sighed. "I'm an old woman and I'm nearly dead and my cat's eaten and I've got wet pants."

Leila kissed Minnie's sunken cheek. "Don't worry.

We'll make it all right again. You'll see."

"Oh, is that so? What is it you're going to do for me, eh? Buy me a new cat and change my knickers? Then life will be perfect once again, just perfect."

"My mum'll look after you," Billy cried, swinging his legs to and fro. Tears ran down his face and collected on his quivering lips.

Minnie wiped her runny nose with the palm of her hand, then she clamped the same hand over her eyes and rested in the darkness.

"I'm not really a circus boy," Billy told her, "not a real circus boy. I mean, I can't do trapeziums and stuff. It's mainly animals I like. I like to talk to them and smell them. I wake up in the dark and hear them doing things, moving about and that. Even with my eyes shut, I can sort of see them. Denzil, he sleeps on my bed and I like the weight of him, all comfy, like, on my legs. I've got newts and they smell like the sea. You can come and see my animals if you like, Mrs Starling. Mum would make you a cup of tea and you could have one of her jam tarts she makes, they're really nice, not like the ones you get in the box and you can't get them out of the foil. We're gonna be kind to you, Mrs Starling, because you're very old and I know I've sort of done a bad thing and you've not got a cat any more and I like animals so I can understand, see, how you must be all sad. If I do ever get a circus, Mrs Starling, I'm going to tell them to send you a free ticket so you can come and sit in the best seat and watch all the animals and the clowns and the ladies with short skirts on the trapezium, sometimes they have a big net underneath, case they fall and it's high. Have you ever been to the circus, Mrs Starling, when you weren't so old?"

"Hush, Billy, hush," his mother said, stroking Minnie's hair.

The old lady uncovered her eyes and impaled the boy with a steely stare. She tugged at her skirt and licked her crinkled lips until they gleamed like two grey worms. Her tongue flicked out and hung extended for a moment, as

146

though drawing inspiration from the air.

"Oh yes, I've been to the circus. Oh yes. I remember more than fifty years ago, Circus Boy. We were in America. Detroit, it was. Way up on the high wire were the Flying Wallendas. You should have seen them, they were so brave. They had this spectacular act, Circus Boy. A seven-man pyramid, balanced on the wire. But that night, one man faltered. Perhaps he lost his nerve, I don't know. And you know what happened? The whole pyramid collapsed like a pack of cards and the Wallendas crashed to the ground, hurtling through space. No net, you see. They didn't use a net, the Wallendas. Anyway, two of them were killed and another two were seriously injured, one left a paraplegic."

Billy sucked in his breath and bit his lip. "That's just so frightening. That's like in the films."

"Real life, Circus Boy, real life. And then real death."

Mr Rabinowitz trudged up the stairs, clutching his phone. "So Edward, he is coming soon, to help with the – the – er…" Stepping over Leila Smart's legs, he rested a hirsute hand on her exposed shoulder, a forefinger teasing her bra strap. "Edward is very strong."

Minnie sat on the landing, leaning against the wall. Leila sat next to Minnie. Billy sat on the stairlift. Mr Rabinowitz sat on the edge of the bath, gazing out through the open door. Denzil sat in the airing cupboard, unable to move. The cat sat in Denzil.

A few miles away, Roland James sat in his office, talking to Raj on the phone, asking him why he had not gone round to number 33 to repair the hole. "We don't want any trouble," he said.

Leila put her arm round Minnie's shoulders. "Are you quite sure you don't want me to get you an ambulance?"

"I told you, I don't need an ambulance. I'm not ill."

"I can smell wee," Billy said.

Leila nodded, eyes downcast. "Be quiet, Billy."

Minnie stretched and yawned. "Would someone tell me what we're waiting for?" She began to cry. "Please, will

147

someone just tell me what's happening?"

"Don't cry, Mrs Starling," Billy said. "My mum, she said she'll make it right for you."

Mr Rabinowitz's hand appeared round the door frame, shaking a box of tissues. "For the lady."

Leila dabbed Minnie's eyes and wrapped a tissue round the old lady's reddening nose so that she could have a thorough blow. Then she held out the scrunched paper to Mr Rabinowitz for him to place in the lavatory.

Minnie studied the young man on the lift seat with a purposeful concentration, as though seeing him for the first time. "Stand up, Circus Boy, and let me have a good look at you."

Billy rose nervously to his feet, still holding on to the arm of the stairlift.

"Hmm. How old are you, boy?"

"Eighteen," Billy said.

"Eighteen. Well, you're not a bad boy. Let's say, you and me, we're both victims of circumstance; that's Minnie Starling's verdict. As for my poor Darling, I will return a verdict of misadventure." She nodded in apparent satisfaction. "And now…tell me, Billy Smart the Circus Boy, are you coming to my party?"

"I hope so."

"Make sure you do. I'll have a surprise for you."

"You mean, like a present?"

"Not exactly. But something rather special, something you wouldn't be expecting."

"Say thank you, Billy," Leila said.

"I haven't got my surprise yet," Billy countered.

Minnie folded her hands in her lap and looked strangely content. "Sit very still and close your eyes and you will get a big surprise. That's how it goes. Then everything will be all right."

"I'm looking forward to the party," said Billy.

"It'll be a night to remember," Minnie assured him. "Now then…come here and kneel down so I can reach you."

Billy came closer and sank awkwardly to his knees. Minnie took both his hands in hers and began reciting: "*Sit* quite *still* and *close* your *eyes* and *you* will *get* a *big* sur*prise*." And with each emphasized word she squeezed Billy's hands tightly, eight fist-clenches of impressive strength. "There now. Enough."

Billy stood up and scooted backwards on to the lift seat, smiling vacantly.

"I think we should all go downstairs and have some tea," Minnie proposed. "I only came up here for a tea towel. Fetch me a clean one, Circus Boy."

Mr Rabinowitz handed Billy a tea towel and Billy gave it to Minnie Starling. She rode downstairs with the towel in her lap, Billy and Leila following her. Mr Rabinowitz stayed in the bathroom.

"I'll put the kettle on," Leila said.

A few minutes later, the doorbell rang. Leila opened the door and met large Edward from the pet shop.

Minnie stared at the stranger. "Who's this fat man coming in my house?"

"I am Edward from the pet shop," said Edward from the pet shop.

Edward laboured up the stairs, squeezing noisily past the stairlift. Mr Rabinowitz said hello to him and, ushering him into the bathroom, closed the door.

Leila Smart smiled pleasantly at Minnie Starling. "How do you like your tea?" she enquired.

# Chapter 29

## *Number 30: Stephen J. Kettering-Barclay*

Stephen woke up at five o'clock in the morning, rolled over to face the window and lay wondering about the curtains. The old red ones had darkened the room effectively, making it easier for him to sleep, and they were thick enough to keep the cold out, but they had been fitted years ago and looked shabby. The man from Tunstall's in Market Street had been very helpful. His lady assistant had brought round a catalogue for Stephen to browse through, with the promise that a new pair of curtains in any colour he fancied could be supplied and hung within a fortnight. Stephen thought the turquoise would be suitable – calm and restful, a peaceful colour.

That was what he thought then. Now, this morning, with the sun already tilting at the window, he was not so sure. The turquoise curtains were thinner than the old pair and filtered the daylight into a dim green haze, as if the bedroom were his cabin aboard a ship that had sunk to the bottom of the sea. Too many of his friends and shipmates had taken up residence on the sea-bed, some of them sent there by his own hand, and the prospect of waking each morning to be reminded of their fates was distinctly unappealing. Perhaps he should have chosen the blue ones, after all. The sea was often blue, of course, but usually not at the bottom. There, miles down, after the stricken electric green, it was black, hideously black, populated by skeletons, and some of the bone men owed their dark destiny to Stephen Kettering-Barclay, who lived up in the sun and struggled to forgive himself and to forget all that the sea had made him do. He wondered about ringing Tunstall's and asking them to remove the turquoise curtains and bring the blue ones instead.

He heaved his legs out of bed and, fumble-fingered,

attached his prosthesis. Grasping the bed footboard for support, he stomped to the window and drew back the curtains. The road was patched with damp from overnight rain, but the sun was rising, glancing off house windows in spears of white light. Just as he was registering the absence of humanity, the clean symmetry of the deserted street, a car engine reverberated to his right, and an open-topped BMW driven by a woman with billowing black hair roared past. The speeding car's throaty exhaust seemed to echo off the silent buildings, while the driver's windblown hair streamed behind her like dark smoke. It was early, he thought, for such self-exposure, but the woman was surely an extrovert, for only people who liked to be seen drove convertibles. *Hey, look at me, aren't you impressed? Am I not an achiever?*

Something clicked in his mind, a thought-pebble rolling, locking into a suddenly-illuminated hollow. Francine, he remembered Francine. Francine had the same hair as the BMW woman, thick and black and fashionably unruly. That was – what?- thirty years ago. She used to come to the house to cut his hair and, sometimes, his toenails as well. There were only five to cut, of course. Francine's hair was so thick and dark, she would wear a plastic comb in it and lose the accessory for an hour in the depths of the dense waves.

"This is ridiculous, it's got to be in here somewhere."

Stephen had a full head of hair then, steely-grey and left over his collar at the back, in the style of someone he had observed on the television and adjudged to be fashionable. He always instructed Francine to leave his hair long at the back. She trimmed his toenails and, curiously, attended to the cleanliness of his stump, removing his appendage to wipe the folds of the rounded end. She would massage the bony calf in both hands in a manner vaguely suggestive of masturbation, while Stephen reclined with his eyes closed. She had a lovely touch. Ah, Francine!

He tried to recall how old she was. Fifty, maybe – a

151

young-looking fifty. She was what you might call a handsome woman, not beautiful or overtly attractive, but possessed of a poise and confidence that some might interpret as arrogance, but which he found indefinably arresting.

Which was why he had invited her to dinner. For hours beforehand he had gone *clonk clonk clonking* round the kitchen and the dining room, preparing the meal, checking the oven, setting the table, selecting the right wine. Overbalancing once, he had dropped a plate and smashed it, cursing then as he knelt precariously on the floor to collect the pieces, sweating helplessly into a clean shirt. But the dinner, yes, had been a success, and after they had embarked upon the third bottle of Rioja and chuckled their way from the disordered table to the leather sofa, Francine had allowed him to kiss her for the first time and, a little later, trace a trembling finger down the tight slot of her cleavage.

Well, it hadn't lasted. That is, it lasted about four months. She used to cut his toenails as he sat on the edge of the bed, and when the job was done he would pull back the covers and invite her to lie next to him, and they would laugh and lightly misbehave with their clothes on, but for Stephen it was never enough, never near enough, never sweet enough. Still, he enjoyed the feel of her cool fingers on his warm toes.

She met someone else at her bridge club. That was the trouble. That was the end of it, or the beginning of the end of it. Francine Kessler. She came to dinner in a sleeveless summer dress and he glimpsed coiled hairs when she put her arms up. He liked that, sensing it as a kind of proclamation of freedom of the flesh. If only she had allowed him a little more of that delicious freedom.

"Will you still come and do my hair?"

"If you want."

"I want."

"Then I'll come."

"So who's this other chap? What's his name?"

"What's it to you?"

"I was only asking."

"Well, don't."

"I suppose he's got two legs."

"You know, it's a funny thing, as a matter of fact he has."

"Do you cut his hair? Do you touch his toes?"

"No. I don't see him for that."

"What do you see him for?"

"None of your business."

Despite the sardonic exchange, they had parted on good terms. After two more haircuts, it all became too much, and he asked her not to visit him again. A clean break, that was what was needed, even if it was not what he really, truly desired. He had never made love to her, not once. It happened that way, the way of not happening.

Over a breakfast of buttered muffins, Stephen was visited by a simmering unease. Absurdly, the spectre of the woman in the open car was beginning to disturb him. If only she had not put him in mind of Francine. He sat sipping tea from his favourite mug, decorated with the Merchant Navy crest, and the silver BMW raced through his head, east to west and back again, exhaust barking, the woman's hair rippling on the wind. *Damn you, whoever you are,* he thought.

Janice should be here by now. She was half an hour late. Janice was all right, though it would be good to have Stuart back, because Stuart understood him. Still, for as long as they sent Janice round, he had the brief company of a kind woman, a healthy ingredient missing for too long from the tedious menu of his sedentary life. He was ninety years old and handicapped by a damaged leg, yet a nagging physical desire had not deserted him, and sometimes, some days, he felt it as a taunt, a vaguely pleasurable ache that would not be appeased and would not go away. If he intimated any such need to Janice, he would only scare her, and the agency would find him another man or send along a battleaxe.

153

He wondered. He gazed at the table top until his eyes lost focus. The woman in the BMW careered through the kitchen at breakneck speed. Stephen believed he could smell her flying hair. The image spun around his head like an angry wasp as he stood running hot water into the sink, and he realized that he was troubled.

He seldom used the laptop. If asked, he would have said that it was not 'his thing'. Now, nervously, hesitantly, he cleared a space on the table, wiped the surface with a damp cloth and opened the computer lid. For a few moments he sat staring at the keys, trying to remember what to do with them. His password was on a scrap of paper taped to the bottom of the machine. The battery was almost flat, so he had to find the power cord and plug it in. On the screen, a fuzzy picture of the Daedalus appeared, patched with ikons for which he had long ceased to have any use. At least finding *Google* was easy. Soon Stephen was up and running, prodding the keyboard with one gnarled finger. He winced as a sharp pain coursed through his bad leg. Perhaps, he thought, this was a warning.

He went to the first site offered. One would probably be as good as another. His right hand was shaking now, obstructing him from striking the right keys. He told himself this was crazy, he was a lunatic, a pathetic old man, submitting to a sad, weary desperation.

He filled the boxes, giving his name and his age, admitting only to being eighty. Even that could be prohibitive, he suspected. He made up a nickname to disguise himself. Finally he entered the postcode of the area within whose radius he sought friendship. Slowly at first, and then more rapidly, opportunities blinked on to the screen. Feeling slightly sick, he licked his lips, flexed his fingers and leaned back.

It was not a random choice. The girl lived in the same town and her location map reinforced her accessibility. He studied her profiled facilities in case his age might prove a deterrent, but she claimed to welcome disabled clients, a concession which heartened him, even as he told himself that, in fairness, he would have to disclose his physical deficiency before the meeting. Getting to her would be a problem, of course. Perhaps she would come to him, although she had not specified Outcalls. To Stephen, the money was irrelevant, and if necessary he would pay for a taxi for her, provided to do so did not entail a lengthy journey. He could not recall ever having travelled by taxi himself, but perhaps this once…

He moistened his dry mouth with the cooling dregs of his tea, then he reached for the phone. It was early, but he feared that, if he waited, his fragile resolve would desert him.

She answered at the third ring, in a softly lilting voice that simply said, "Hello."

Stephen swallowed and cleared his throat. "Good morning. Am I speaking to Irish Willow?"

# Chapter 30

## *Number 15: Aisling McIver*

Rona lifted the paper tag attached to the pushchair frame and looked impressed. "Mamas & Papas. £329. Wow! And I just love those Formula One wheels!"

"It was in the sale," Aisling told her. "I thought the red and silver looked grand."

"She's a lucky young girl, your daughter." She placed a hand on her friend's shoulder. "And I'm glad you can do this now. It's great for both of you."

Aisling nodded, looking mildly embarrassed. She still wasn't used to this profligacy. Sometimes spending the money felt worse than the method of obtaining it.

Rona pulled out a chair and sat at the table. "Nice and tidy here. No piles of paper. Does that mean you've paid all those bills?"

"Sure, I've settled most of them."

"Good. Just make sure you – "

"Rona, will you leave it, please. Look, I'm real grateful to you for your help and advice, course I am, but don't try to run my life, okay. Things are coming along just fine, that's all you need to know."

"Okay, okay." Rona raised her hands apologetically. "I was only – yeah, right, I understand."

They drank coffee from brand-new mugs, without looking at each other. Neamh snoozed with smears of mother's milk crusting on her chin.

"So you're keeping busy?" Rona enquired.

"Yes, I am. So far I've no-one today, nobody on-line, anyway." She turned and patted Rona's arm. "Here, I must tell you about the guy came yesterday evening. He was just so – so – I don't know."

"Weird?"

"Intense, I'd say."

156

"Old? Young?"

"About forty. Clean-cut. Nice after-shave. Polite."

"Doesn't sound intense."

"No, well…you see, he rang back half an hour before time and asked me, did I have any running gear."

"Running gear? Was he going to fuck you or race you?"

"Well, I did wonder. Then he said for me to run round the block a few times and get myself all hot, because what he really liked was a sweaty woman."

Rona laughed, spilling her drink. "That's magic. And did you?"

"The neighbours would've thought I was mad. And I couldn't leave Neamh, could I? So anyway, there's that old exercise bike upstairs, the one I had before Neamh came along, so I pulled on some jog pants and went pedalling nineteen to the dozen, Jesus, like I was in the Tour de bloody-France, working up a real old lather, I can tell you."

Rona grinned, shaking her head. "Brilliant! Did it work?"

"Oh, I think it did. Yes, I think so." She seemed sombre for a moment, reflective. "The thing is, you know, I always like to be clean and fresh for them, I think that's important. I mean, I expect the same of them."

"It's what you should do, yes."

"So here's this – this LennySoulman – that's what he was calling himself – striding in, wanting me to be dripping perspiration and smelling rank. I mean, Rona, I'm not saying I don't get it, there's all sorts out there, God, I know that, but I just couldn't get comfortable with him, cos I wasn't comfortable with myself – does that make sense?"

Rona smiled and pulled a sympathetic face. Whatever you said about Aisling McIver, she was deeply conscientious, there was no argument about it. A girl couldn't ask for a truer, more dependable friend.

"I'm with you, Aisling. Go on."

"Well, we went up and my clothes, they were damned-near sticking to me. He started rubbing them with his fingers, didn't even ask me to take them off at first. Then I had my top off, and this Lenny guy, he was all for sniffing my bloody armpits, licking the damned grease out of them, going at it like there was no tomorrow. No talking, just this kind of snorting, like some kind of animal. When I finally got my pants off, he was as sweaty as me, he was – "

"Yes, actually, for once, I'm not sure I want to know any more, Aisling. He was okay, though? I mean, he didn't try any rough stuff or hurt you? You got the cash?"

"Obviously. He said he'd like to come again – to come back, I mean. He didn't ask to fuck me. You know, it's surprising how often they don't. Just so long as they get to the finish, they're happy."

"Hmm. Was he married?"

"I think so. He wore a wedding ring."

"Well, the straight stuff, they get that from their wives, don't they? They don't need to pay for it. It's something different they want, that's where the adrenalin comes from."

In recent days Aisling believed she had acquired a reasonable knowledge of what she cautiously construed as her new role in society; but she also had the wit to realise that there remained much to learn about an intriguing pastime that, whilst enticingly lucrative, was at times tinged with a certain darkness. As she took her baby on to her knee, unfastened her blouse and eased Neamh's little head towards her nipple, she could not help but reflect upon who else had put his lips there, suckling greedily as his face mashed her breasts. Back home, the old home, in Ireland, her mother probably thought that Aisling still worked at Beasley's, doing the filing, producing meaningless spreadsheets and queuing solemnly for ghastly coffee from the drinks machine, Beasley's, where human contact meant the occasional 'Good morning' smile or a dry peck on the cheek when someone had the courage to resign. Someone like Aisling McIver, for that matter.

Molly McIver was a God-respecting woman, slender of mind and body, who would surely look upon her daughter's new-found profession with a disdain scarcely distinguishable from revulsion, brought up as she was to regard even a sleeveless dress as a sexual invitation.

"So which is it I am, Neamh, eh? Am I an entrepreneur or some kind of whore?"

Neamh smiled and showed her pink gums and brandished a curled fist, fragrant as a seashell.

"You see, Neamh, your mammy's doing this as best she can. Your Auntie Rona tells me I'll get to enjoy it, not just the money, but the – the social intercourse, though I think she was maybe joking when she put it that way. Well, dear one, I can't say as I've had one I enjoyed yet, them with their hairy bodies and crumpled clothes and their sticky old mouths trying to swallow you like you was some lump of meat and them starving half to death. Me, I'm waiting for that sweet, kind, respectful gentleman to walk in the door, a man who has even the slightest concept of what a woman likes, besides just getting her legs open. Where's all the decent guys who only need to spend an hour in a bubble where they can love and be loved in a way they've forgotten. Show me that God-forsaken man, Neamh, and I promise you I'll welcome him with open arms and hope to see him again. Oh surely, yes."

It was early in the morning, Neamh freshly bathed and tidied, when the phone rang. Aisling looked at the clock and pulled a face. Maybe it was a wrong number.

"Good morning. Am I speaking to Irish Willow?"

"You are, yes."

By the voice, he sounded old, but possibly polite.

"I've seen your – your advertisement on the website. Your profile, is it?"

"My profile, yes."

"Quite. I was wondering…I have a false leg, that is, the lower part of it. I would quite like to meet you, though, if it could be possible."

"Possible? How d'you mean, possible? Is it you're

159

disabled?"

"Oh, I'm not disabled. I can get around with a stick. I'm not helpless."

"I see."

"Could you come to me, to my house?"

"Well, I don't offer Outcalls. They're not convenient for me."

"I would pay for your taxi or your petrol."

"I don't drive. Like I said, I don't do Outcalls."

"Oh, very well."

"If you're happy to pay for a taxi, can you not come to me?"

She heard him sigh. She waited. No-one had ever called her so early in the morning. Fancy, a one-legged man. She wondered how old he was.

"I expect I can manage that, yes. Where are you exactly?"

"I don't do 'exactly' till you're in the neighbourhood. Have you a mobile?"

"I do. If I can find it."

"When are you wanting to come?"

"Tomorrow at two o'clock. That would be nice."

Aisling gave him her postcode. A small whooping sound came down the line, as though someone had pinched him.

"Is that all right?" she asked.

"Why, yes. You see, your postcode, it's the same as mine."

"Is that so? Well then, maybe you won't be needing the taxi. I should say, though…I do have some steps up to the first floor and stairs to the bedroom. Can you manage that, now?"

"I can do stairs if I'm given time, if I take it slow."

"Okay, my dear. Why don't we call it an hour and a quarter, to accommodate your bad leg? How would that be?"

"You're very kind."

"So you ring me at five to two and I'll give you the

house number."

"I – I understand."

"Now listen, dear. What is it you like?"

"Pardon?"

"Is there something in particular you're looking for when we meet? Sure, I always like to ask that."

The silence her question evoked lasted so long, she wondered if the man had reconsidered and rung off; but his breathing rustled in her ear, a slow, rhythmic panting. His voice, when at last he spoke again, was but a muffled croak.

"I'm looking for forgiveness," he said.

# Chapter 31

## *Number 12: Mr and Mrs Clarnon*

The blue *HomeTech Moto* van pulled up across the front of Pat's Morris, its nose projecting into the road, and the driver in blue overalls jumped out, brushing his hands together.

"You're blocking the road," said Pat.

"Wide enough," the man said. The embossed lettering over his top pocket read 'Dave'.

Pat shrugged.

Dave stood working his lips into a ragged circle as he stared at the crippled car. "Can you open the bonnet?"

Pat released the bonnet and propped it open. Dave pulled a rag from his side pocket, laid it considerately over the front wing and rested one hand on it as he surveyed the engine bay. After a while it occurred to Pat that, standing there with his head bowed, the mechanic had in fact shifted his gaze and was now looking glumly at his boots.

"Mr Carroll, is it?"

"Clarnon. Patrick Clarnon."

"Hmm. Mr Clarnon, when was this vehicle last serviced?"

Pat curled his lip and flung out his hands. "Couldn't rightly say. It's got an MOT."

"What, out of a cracker?" He fingered his nose dubiously. "This car's got cobwebs hanging off the engine."

"Would they stop it going?" Pat ventured.

"No, but it does suggest inattention." He unscrewed the radiator cap, peered inside and screwed it back on. Standing back, he studied the car distastefully, then he stepped forward and slammed the bonnet down.

"You haven't done anything," Pat complained.

"Workshop job. We need to get this vehicle off the road

162

and start going through all the components, one by one – battery, spark plugs, fuel pump, electrics. Copy?"

"On your van it says, 'A garage on your drive'. I didn't know you had a workshop."

"Course I got a workshop. Modern, fully-equipped facility." He pulled a phone from his pocket. "Need a breakdown truck."

"Sounds like this is going to cost me," Pat said.

"Damned right it is. You want the vehicle running or don't you?"

"I wouldn't have called you, otherwise."

Dave was listening on the phone, shaking his head. Pat began to experience an unpleasant sinking feeling, as if his breakfast was making a premature bid for freedom.

"Ronnie, it's Dave. Clapped-out Morris Oxford. Need the pickup, soon as you can." He listened, nodded and shut the phone down. "Twenty minutes. Copy?"

Pat copied. He copied the pound signs piling up in his head, the unaccustomed reliance on a stranger's skill and honesty and also the fact that he would have nowhere comfortable to sit for the rest of the day. Not that Martha was particularly sympathetic, as she sat facing her husband in the matching armchair.

"Seems funny to see you sat there in the daylight."

"Funny? What's funny about it?"

"P'raps you should have got him to unscrew the seat from the car before he drove it away. You could have sat on the kerb."

"Yes, Martha."

"I remember when we was little, me brother and me. Dad got us one of them red and yellow plastic steering wheels kids used to have when they went out, you know, you stuck one end on the dashboard thingy and pretended to steer like a grown-up."

"What about them?"

"Well, if you had one now, you could pull a chair up in front of you, stick the little wheel on the back of it and make like you was still sat in your car. Be brilliant."

"Be ridiculous," Pat growled.

"Suit yourself. I was just saying…"

"I heard you."

"Well, you don't have to looks so grumpy about it. It was your idea to get the man in. Then, if he does a good job – bingo! – we can go for our picnic."

"We already ate the picnic, remember."

"I can do us another. We just need a car that goes."

And before the dusk, viewed through a chink in the curtains, a golden dawn of improbable reality, as Dave the mechanic, expressionless at the wheel, brought FRK 154 back to the Clarnons' front door under her own modest power. Pat stepped out to greet the car like an old friend, though not without trepidation. Even the bodywork was shiny now, the soggy tyres inflated, the windows sparkling in the last of the sun. Good work had plainly been done, and good work habitually involved good money.

"Documentation," Dave said, handing Pat the car key and a sheaf of papers clipped together.

"Come inside," said Pat, "the wife's made jam tarts."

They sat at the table, dropping crumbs on the paperwork. Martha stood behind them, one hand resting on Pat's shoulder. The tea was tepid and milky.

"Everything all right, then?" Pat asked, in a small voice.

"Invoice and a detailed worksheet," Dave indicated, separating the pages. "Plus we did an MOT and a road test. It's all there."

"We're grateful to you," Martha said. Pat peered at her over his shoulder.

"Suppose you want some money," Pat said, removing the cap from a ballpoint. He picked up the invoice and held it up to the light. His eyes flickered wildly.

"Cheque or cash." Dave gazed round the room, as if reluctant to witness Pat's discomfiture. "Lot of work."

"Blimey! I didn't pay that much for the car in the first place." He shook the invoice and turned it over and back again, as though that might favourably alter the figures.

"It's a fair price, Mr Clarnon. Car's nearly as good as new. Plenty life in that old engine."

"That's because he never drives it anywhere," Martha explained.

Pat gulped the last of his tea. "I'll give you a cheque. Biggest cheque I've ever written."

"Copy," said Dave.

With a shaking, ponderous hand, Pat wrote a cheque for £625.50.

Dave was examining the worksheet. It didn't do to look directly at a man in torment. "Five hours' labour, new battery, four spark plugs, radiator flush and antifreeze, oil change – old stuff came out like bitumen – oil filter, fan belt, starter motor, two tyres, carburettor wash-out and MOT." He slapped the sheet back on the table. "Cheap at the price."

"And it goes?" Martha said.

"Course it goes. I drove it here, didn't I?"

Pat slid the cheque across the table. "It's okay, it won't bounce."

"I know where you live," Dave reminded him, standing up. "Thanks for the tarts, Missis."

While Martha showed Dave to the door, Pat sat staring in mournful bewilderment at the cheque stub. "I've bought my own car all over again," he muttered. He put his chequebook back in the dresser drawer and went outside to sit in the reincarnated Morris. The interior smelled of polish and strawberries, the unfamiliar sweetness issuing from a scented deodorizer dangling from the mirror. The garage's treatment of the leather seat had made it alarmingly slippery, and with each twitch of his hips Pat felt as if, at any moment, he might be sent spinning into the footwell. He patted the steering wheel affectionately and a slow smile crept over his face.

Martha yanked open the passenger door and slid next to him. "Here we are again, two peas in a tin pod," she declared.

"Copy," said Pat.

"You can stop that, Patrick Clarnon."

"Right you are. What's for tea?"

"Tea's in the afternoon. We had tea. Next is dinner."

"What's for dinner?"

"I was thinking." She grabbed the deodorizer, sniffed it and pulled a disapproving face. "The man on the telly said sunshine all day tomorrow. We could have that picnic, go to the forest."

"Might give this seat a wash-down, sliding everywhere."

"How many hard-boiled eggs, d'you think?"

"Steering wheel's slippery an' all."

"I've got plenty salad stuff."

"I see they didn't put any petrol in."

"We could have French sticks from the baker's."

"Reckon these tyres are pumped up a bit hard."

"Get a few choc bars from the paper shop."

"They've mucked up my radio station."

"Or we could have some nice tinned salmon. That always goes nice in a sandwich."

"Think they've swapped these mats over."

"Do you like anchovies? I never can remember."

"This seat adjustment's all to cock."

"Shall I use butter or that soft spread?"

"Suppose I ought to look under the bonnet."

"There's loads of those sweet little tomatoes in the fridge."

"Some smudges on that side window."

"Bunch of bananas, they're always handy."

"Hope he's checked all the lights work. Suppose he must have, gave me an MOT."

"Shall I buy us a chicken?"

"Gear lever knob's slippery, an' all."

"Think I'll just get some drumsticks."

"Clutch pedal feels a bit stiff."

"What do you fancy to drink?"

"He never mentioned the brakes."

"I'll do us a Thermos of tea and a bottle of Lucozade."

Pat turned and stared at her. "Lucozade makes me blow off," he said.

The elderly Morris burbled along, smooth and willing, gently surprising its occupants. Behind his slightly sweat-glazed forehead, Pat felt a curious buzzing, like an effervescence in his brain, for many years had passed since he last ventured on to the open road and the experience at once excited and intimidated him. The sun glanced in silver shards off the polished bonnet, and he silently reprimanded himself for forgetting his sunglasses. Though his eyes were good for his age, Pat's view of the road ahead was compromised by a tendency to focus a mere few metres beyond the end of the bonnet, a habit which restricted his speed as much as did his nervousness at the wheel.

"You looking at the road signs?" Martha asked, apprehensively.

"I'm looking at the road. You have to keep your eyes on the road."

"You can go a bit faster. There's people behind."

"I'm not one of them racing drivers."

Martha sighed and searched for a tissue in her handbag. It was good to be out in the country, lovely to see the blue sky and the puffy white clouds and the green fields. As the car trundled by, it was like watching a nature film, a constantly changing panorama of bright colours and shifting light, scenes revealing golden crops bending in the breeze, quiet cows patched black and white like demonstration Rorschach tests, dusty tractors sun-bleached in open barns, plump travellers in T-shirts at wooden pub tables lifting mugs of honey-hued beer.

"We're only doing thirty, Pat."

"Doesn't matter. Soon be there, don't you worry."

"Must be nice to be driving again."

"Tell the truth, I'm a bit rusty."

Martha resumed her survey of the slowly passing countryside. Pat did not notice the view. He was concentrating on the white line in the middle of the road and the grass-bordered bends. Pat did not see the grazing cows or the trickling streams beneath hump-backed bridges or the reds and blues and greens of hanging baskets outside white-walled inns. He saw the quick glint of sunlight on the Morris's nose and the way the grey ribbon of the road threaded underneath him, making his eyes smart.

Pat did not notice the sign that warned of a dangerous bend. Neither did he judge how the car was veering to the right as he failed to follow the tightening curve. When the tanker hurtled towards them, he could not see how swiftly the driving cab's square metal bulk loomed large and impossible until it filled the old car's windscreen.

Pat heard Martha's wordless high-pitched scream, heard it for a second. In the next second her voice was obliterated by a greater scream of tearing steel and shattering glass, and Pat's vision was filled to bloody bursting with a folding cliff of screeching metal exploding into his face. Then, after all that terrible noise, all that mad dance of blinding black light, came silence and a red haze and awful darkness.

# Chapter 32

## *Number 25: Joan Descours*

Joan sat at the kitchen table, clasping her face in her shaking hands. Licking her lips, she tilted her head backwards and forwards, stretching the muscles in her neck. She took a deep breath, held it and released the air slowly through her mouth. Her heart was thumping rapidly and she felt a dampness under her arms. With her middle fingers, she massaged the thin skin at the corners of her eyes in a rotational motion, distorting her vision.

Above, she heard Barry Brown moving about in the bathroom. There was the sound of water running away, then a perfunctory splashing. It was warm in the room, and Joan unfastened two buttons on her blouse and then did them up again. She sat back in the chair and watched the doorway. On her tongue lay the acrid taste of anxiety.

Barry came in fully dressed, carrying his shoes. His hair was tousled and a pink blush bloomed in his cheeks.

"Are your shoes not comfortable?" Joan asked him.

"Got to lace them up," he said. "I'll do it down here."

He pulled out a chair and sat next to her. He looked at his paperwork but didn't touch it. Joan listened to the clock ticking behind her back.

"Was your bath to your liking, Barry?"

"Yes thank you, Miss."

"Yes thank you, *Joan*."

"Yes. Sorry."

She moved to get up, then sat down again. She could feel the warmth coming off the boy's softened body.

"Do you feel a bit more comfy now – now that you've relaxed in the warm water?"

Barry nodded. His discarded shoes were under the table. He smelled of soap and talcum powder.

"Well, I think we've done enough work for today, don't

you, Barry?"

"Do you want me to go – Joan?"

"No. I would like you to stay a while. We can tidy up, then we can have some coffee and we can talk – if you'd like."

"Talk about what, Miss?"

"Joan!"

"Sorry."

"Don't keep being sorry, Barry. There's really nothing to be sorry about."

Barry nodded.

"Are your parents expecting you home, Barry? At any particular time, I mean."

"Not really."

She smiled and touched his arm. "I was meaning to ask you – do you have a girlfriend, Barry?"

Barry looked at her in apparent puzzlement. "A girlfriend?"

"Yes, Barry. You know what a girlfriend is."

He absently picked up some sheets of paper and put them down again. "Not at the moment, I don't."

"Right. In the past, perhaps."

"About a year ago, I had a girl called Robyn."

"That's a nice name. And was she pretty, Barry, hmm?"

"I don't know, Joan."

"You don't – Barry, you must remember if she was pretty. You must know what she looked like."

"I did like her. She was funny."

Joan tugged surreptitiously at the fabric in her armpits. There was a residual wetness there. "I'll make us a drink," she said.

Barry raised each foot to the chair and tied his shoelaces, then he wandered into the living room and combed his damp hair in the mirror. Moving to the glass-fronted bookcase, he stood with his head on one side, studying the titles on the spines of the tightly-packed books. He liked houses with lots of books, felt their presence reassuring, just as he liked mirrors and paintings and perhaps a cat or dog, though he had seen neither at Miss Descours'. There was a keyhole in the cabinet door, but it opened easily to his touch, and he ran his fingers down the hardback spines and was pleased at the feel of the bindings and the dark smell of the covers. Engrossed in this tactile appreciation, he didn't hear Joan Descours come in to stand behind him.

"There you are, Barry. I've made us a little something."

"Oh." He turned with a start. "I was just – "

"Looking at the books. That's good. Look at any you want. If that's your pleasure, it's mine as well."

"Thank you."

"In the kitchen, Barry, I've brought us a – well, it's not really a lunch, but I thought we should have something to eat."

Joan had laid raffia mats on the table and placed sunflower-pattern plates of poached eggs and cherry tomatoes on toasted wholemeal bread. In the light from the window, the egg yolks shone a vivid tawny yellow.

Barry sat down, smiling. "You're very kind, Joan."

"Got to look after you," she said.

"This is nice."

"Nothing special. I get my eggs from the farm up the road, lovely rich yolks."

He was concentrating on the food, tucking in enthusiastically with his head down. She watched him eat, seeing the oily shine on his lips and the red curl of a stray fragment of tomato adhering to the corner of his mouth. Barry had a nice mouth, she thought. A thin shank of his dampened hair curled upwards at the back, and she wanted to reach out and brush it down, letting her fingers linger on the softness there. He was a good-looking boy, but not exactly masculine, almost pretty from a profiled angle. As she studied him, she carelessly laid down her fork and lifted one hand to apply a little gentle pressure through the material covering her right breast.

"Joan."

Quickly, she dropped her hand and pretended to carry on eating. "What is it, Barry?"

"I was meaning to ask you…"

"Ask me what?"

"I was wondering – umm – what perfume you use."

"Perfume, Barry? I haven't put any on."

"No, but when you do. There must be one you really like."

"Oh. Well, I suppose I'm a bit of a traditionalist when it comes to…I like Elizabeth Arden, and I also rather like Chanel Number 5. That's been around a long time." She speared a tomato, popped it in her mouth and put down her fork. "Why do you ask, Barry?"

"It's just…you're being very kind to me, and I thought I could buy you a sort of present."

"A present – whatever for?"

"For helping me."

Joan wiped her lips with a paper napkin and peered at the boy's reddening face. "Barry, I'm a teacher and you're my pupil. It's my job to help you."

"Even so."

"Barry, it's a very kind thought. Don't think I don't appreciate it."

"Nina Ricci," Barry said thoughtfully. "I've heard of that."

She lowered her head and affected a stern expression. "Now don't you go spending your money on me. It's absolutely not necessary, or appropriate."

"I've got money," Barry said. "I'd like to – "

"Barry! Look, I'm very flattered; but I think it would be best if we talked about something else, don't you?"

"But I like nice scents."

"Scents are what you get off animals, Barry."

Barry thought about this. They finished their food. Joan took the plates away and stood by the sink for a while, fiddling with her blouse buttons. She could feel Barry's eyes on her back. When she had slid the plates into soapy water, she came to stand behind him, resting her hands on the back of his chair.

"So – uh – do you put on after-shave, Barry?"

"Not usually, Miss."

"Not usually, *Joan.*"

"Yes. I mean, no. See, I only need to shave twice a week."

"You're very smooth-skinned." Holding her breath, she ran her hand over the upturned flag of hair at the nape of his neck, flattening it. "There. Some hair sticking up."

"Oh. Thank you."

She remembered, in the bath, the little hairs below his navel, where her fingers had played. "Oh, Barry," she whispered.

"What's wrong, Joan?"

"Nothing. Nothing's wrong. Don't worry."

A wave of fear surged in her stomach, filling her mouth with a flood of sourness. Gripping the chair more tightly, she leaned over until her nose nestled close to Barry's ear. Her tongue flicked out to moisten her lips. Barry stared straight ahead, unmoving. Very slowly, she turned her face to one side and placed her hands on the boy's shoulders, feeling the smell and the warmth of him. Her mouth hovered scarcely a breath away from his cheek. She squeezed his shoulders fiercely, drawing him back towards her.

Barry turned and let his eyes swim into hers. His face was paler now, emotionless, immobile.

Joan reached for him with her parted mouth and sealed a warm kiss upon his dry lips.

# Chapter 33

## *Number 22: Mr and Mrs Slocombe*

"I could come in by the back door," Janice said to herself. "It wouldn't matter." The reason, of course, had nothing to do with convenience. There was something odd about Hettie Slocombe, an irregularity that went beyond her eccentric references to her absent husband. Janice had known the lady only a day or two, but already she wondered if Hettie was lamenting Alf's death or the indisputable fact that he wasn't there. What if the old lady had immersed herself in the culture of mourning to deflect the attention of others from a more unpalatable reality? Janice understood that, to make herself into a convincing widow, Hettie Slocombe was wise enough to know that she must practise her ultimate grief constantly, day in, day out, until it became second-nature. She would have to believe what she needed others to believe.

Janice pushed open the side gate. A late evening sun bathed the garden in a translucent wash of buttery light. The green lawn held a tincture of blue and the bright flowers she remembered from the morning now furled their petals towards pastel sleep. She approached the shed, treading carefully on the edge of the lawn to silence her footsteps as she followed the curve of the gravel path. The wooden flanks of the structure glowed tawny-red in the lowering sun. She hesitated, drew breath and tried the door. It was unlocked. Janice hooked one finger round the edge, pulled the door towards her and peered inside.

Large as the shed appeared from the garden, Janice could not resist a gasp of amazement as she cast her eyes around the huge interior. This was the size of a small holiday chalet and equipped for the same creature comforts, bright and clean and freshly painted, with light spilling in through three windows at the back and sides.

Letting the door swing shut behind her, she slowly paced out the length of the wooden floor, judging it to be twenty-five feet by perhaps ten feet wide. Turquoise rugs were scattered on the floor and each window was draped with a pale green curtain decorated with a butterfly print, the insects depicted in yellow, blue and gold, wings outstretched in flight. The workbench beneath the left-hand window had been skilfully adapted to suit a domestic purpose, with a square washbasin fed from a plastic water tank below and a neat hob connected to a gas bottle. A microwave stood adjacent to the hob, together with a bread bin and a knife rack. The only item obviously missing was a washing machine. Under the end window she saw a table and two chairs and, above them, a television bracketed to the wall. On a high shelf opposite the kitchen range, above the window, three framed photographs were on display and, beneath them, a wide single bed spread with a patchwork duvet occupied the space at centre-right. What resembled a tall cupboard abutted the bed-head and, opening the door, Janice found a portable toilet with its waste pipe dug into the ground. Between the cubicle and the end wall, a two-seater sofa completed the furnishings.

She picked up one of the photographs. A lean man with thinning grey hair stood with his arm round a blonde woman wearing sunglasses and a toothy grin. The woman had a striped holdall over her shoulder and the man, instead of copying her smile, looked nervous and awkward. They appeared to be at the sea-shore. Janice put the picture back on the shelf and checked her wristwatch. Mrs Slocombe would be wondering where she was. Closing the shed door behind her, she walked across the flagstones to the back door and quietly let herself in.

Hettie was sitting at the kitchen table, munching toast. She had a dressing gown on over her clothes.

"Oh, I wondered who it was," she said, looking up. "Didn't expect you round the back."

"I hope you don't mind. I just – well, I'm not sure why I came this way."

"Makes no difference. Saves me opening the front door."

Janice sat down and put her bag on the table. "Lovely evening. I was just taking a look at your garden."

Hettie shrugged. "I don't go out there much. There's a man comes round."

"A man?"

"To do the garden. The grass and that."

Janice nodded. Glancing round the room, she noticed a framed photo on top of the fridge, two people sitting on a stone wall, smiling at the camera. The woman wore a large sunhat, but even with the shadow on her face, it was clearly Hettie Slocombe. The man next to her, hands clasped sheepishly in his lap, looked relaxed and cheerful, and his happy disposition could not disguise the fact that he was the same gentleman who appeared ill at ease in the picture in the shed. Janice found herself staring at the photograph, trying to work out what had happened here.

"You could make us some tea," Hettie suggested.

Janice filled the kettle and set it to boil. Hettie shifted in her chair and rested her broken arm on the table.

"Mugs or cups?" Janice asked.

"Whatever you like." Hettie looked weary. "Mugs is less washing up."

When the tea was made, Janice sat facing her client, fingers interlocked round her mug. She lowered her head and looked Hettie Slocombe squarely in the eye. A touch grimly, Hettie stared back at her.

"Are you all right, Mrs Slocombe? You look unhappy."

"What's to be happy about?"

"Something's wrong?"

"You could say. I had some very bad news. It was on the local radio."

"Oh dear. Do you want to - ?"

"My dear friends went out for the day – Mr and Mrs Clarnon. They had a car crash. Both killed."

"Oh my God! Yes, come to think of it, I believe I did hear something."

"Pat Clarnon, he hardly ever drove that car." She shook her head and tears welled in her eyes. "We used to laugh at him, sat by the kerb all day. First time in years he goes out…"

"Did you know them well, for a long time?"

"Long as I've been here." She drank some tea and gazed forlornly into the mug. "Pat and my Alf, they used to go to the bowls club together. Well, that was a long time ago."

Janice looked again at the photograph on the fridge. "Is that Alf in that photo?"

Hettie glanced quickly over her shoulder. "That's him."

Janice sipped some more tea and searched Hettie's face again. "Mrs Slocombe, I – well, I was in your shed."

"What? It's not my shed." She sat upright in her chair. "What are you doing in the shed. You're supposed to be my carer."

"I know, yes, of course. I'm sorry, I was curious, that's all."

"You're curious all right."

"In your shed – in the shed there's a picture of Alf with a blonde woman."

"Hmm. You've been having a good nose around."

"Is there someone living in the shed, Mrs Slocombe?"

"What's it to you?"

"I just wondered. I mean, it's not really a shed at all, is it? Not on the inside."

Hettie finished her tea and banged the mug down on the table. "So what exactly are you, Miss Nosy-Parker? Are you the police or the social services or the inland revenue, eh?"

"I'm Janice Collins from the care agency, here to look after you while your arm heals. I'm nothing more."

"Honest?"

"Honest."

For a while they sat quietly, inspecting the table-top. Arthur hopped in and nuzzled Janice's ankle, leaving a small chocolate gift at her feet.

Hettie stretched out her arms and yawned. "You going to help me get me nightie on, then?"

"Of course. That's what I'm here for."

"Really? I thought you was doing some kind of survey."

"Mrs Slocombe, please."

"Nightie's over the banisters. I'll get undressed down here."

Janice fetched the nightdress, untied Hettie's dressing gown and eased her out of her clothes, folding them into a neat pile on the kitchen table. She carefully released the broken arm from its sling while she fitted the nightdress, then repositioned it and adjusted the straps.

"You're very gentle," Hettie said, offering her a withering smile. She looked at the clock. "Expect you'll have another lady waiting."

"I can be a bit late. You never answered my question."

"Oh, and what question was that?"

"I asked you if there was somebody living in your shed."

"And what business is that of yours?"

"None, I suppose. Let's just say, I'm allergic to secrets."

"Secrets?"

Janice rested a hand over her eyes and spoke from beneath it. "Mrs Slocombe, your husband Alf, he isn't dead, is he?"

"I never told you he was," Hettie said.

"I thought – lots of people think – he died of cancer."

"Well, they can think what they like."

"I think – I think Alf is very much alive and – *installed* in your shed with a blonde woman of unknown identity. Now I know that sounds completely mad, but that is my suspicion, and maybe even my conclusion. Mrs Slocombe?"

"Proper little detective, aren't you?" She sighed, shook her head and gazed out at the gathering dusk. "You're gonna be real late."

"Pardon?"

"You'd better put the kettle on again. We'll have a fresh cup in the front room, sat in comfy chairs. You're a decent sort, Janice Collins. I'll tell you how it happened. I'll tell you the whole story, though, God help me, you'll never believe it."

# Chapter 34

*Number 35: Mrs Leila Smart and Billy Smart*

Billy's mother tapped her knuckles on the bedroom door and waited. She never liked to barge in unannounced; it was Billy's private room, after all. With teenage boys, you couldn't imagine what they might be getting up to, although her son had never, to her knowledge, had a girl in there. Once, before the room was full of animals, she had gone in there to clean, and found the dressing table mirror propped against the wardrobe, leading her to conclude that Billy had used it to look in as he jerked off. Well, there was nothing wrong with that; it showed he was, at least in some respects, just a normal boy.

"Hello."

"Billy, what are you doing? Have you seen the time?"

"I know the time."

"Billy – I'm opening the door. All right?"

The door clicked open and through the gap came Billy's face and a strong smell of animals.

"Why aren't you at the shop?"

"Because I went there this morning and they sacked me."

"Oh, Billy."

"Mr Wu, he said I was late."

"Were you late?"

"Ten minutes. And I was late yesterday. I didn't go in yesterday cos of Denzil escaping." He opened the door wider and stood back. "Mr Wu said I was unreliable. Mr Wu said, he said it didn't matter how well you did your job, if you didn't turn up, you were useless."

"I have warned you before about being late. Lateness, Billy, marks you out as slovenly and unprofessional."

"It's only a chip shop, Mum."

"That's got nothing to do with it." She stepped into the

room and, wrinkling her nose, peered around the walls and shabby furniture. "Where's that snake?"

"I put him in the wardrobe."

Leila shuddered. "You've got your clean clothes in there."

"He won't hurt them. He's fat now. He's asleep."

She sighed helplessly. "Is that a rat under your bed?"

Billy looked behind him. "It's Montgomery."

"So why is he not in his cage?"

"I was cleaning him out."

"I see." She held a hand over her nose. "Billy, what are you going to do? You've got that old car to pay for, and there's animal food."

"It's all right, Mum. I'll think of something."

He would, of course; but his mother knew perfectly well that the process would be ultimately fruitless, for Billy's thinking embraced nothing of consequence, logic or practical use, being restricted generally to animals, cars and how to avoid getting up in the morning. That was how he was wired. It was not that he was a bad boy; he was gentle, kind-hearted and did not race the streets in dubious company. Yet, in a cunning world, Billy suffered by not being clever. He possessed nothing of guile or ambition, and he would surely be left standing meekly on the world's street corner while the fast movers passed him by.

Leila Smart could not help but wonder if Billy's indolence meant that, somehow, somewhere, she had gone wrong. Were Billy's faults her own fault? This train of thought led her, inevitably, to question her wisdom in dismissing Roger from her life – and from her son's life also. Roger had been unintelligent, boorish and occasionally violent, but he cared for his son and managed to develop a frail rapport with the boy in his adolescence, a vehicle for meaningful growth which the Smarts' separation had prematurely removed from the domestic orbit. If it was painful now for Leila to reflect upon what she suspected had been her peremptory carelessness, it was a natural response as well, a mental sore at which she picked and probed until her eyes simmered with self-doubt.

Downstairs, she studied herself in the living room mirror, pouting her lips, primping her hair and angling her head this way and that to catch the most favourable light. At the age of forty-one, she had mellowed into a good-looking, if not conspicuously attractive, mature woman, whose disinclination to bother with make-up, despite the tiniest suggestion of crow's feet beside her hazel eyes, seemed in no important way to compromise her facial freshness. The last time she had applied colour to her face – the lightest brush of bubble gum blusher from The Body Shop on her cheeks and cheekbones, a trace of coral lipstick, a dab of iridescent mauve on her eyelids – was on the evening of the supermarket's Christmas party, soon after she had started work there. By then she had been divorced from Roger for nearly two years, trying daily to convince herself that she enjoyed the freedom that came tainted with regret.

Along the bottom of the mirror, if she gently hoisted them upwards, Leila could see the rise of her breasts, features largely obscured by a woollen roll-neck jumper. She was satisfied that they had not sagged more than an imperceptible half-inch in recent years, and her figure remained toned and well-balanced. As if to confirm these convictions, she dragged up the hem of the jumper to expose her bra and armpits, and jiggled herself almost playfully from side to side, defying her montage to unseat itself.

The supermarket customer service job, entailing shifts of eight till three and three till ten, brought her less money than Roger had earned at the builder's, but the people were pleasant to work with and the store was near enough for her to ride there on her bike. In winter she left earlier and walked, or sometimes got a lift. At the Christmas dinner and dance she had drunk a little more than she was used to, and one of the trainee managers from a neighbouring store had offered to drive her home, a gesture she was too unfocused to turn down. The man's name, she recalled, was Pierre Rondeau, and he was ten years her junior. She naturally presumed he was French, though he spoke English with no discernible accent. In the freezing cold car, Leila quickly found reason to re-examine her rashness in accepting help from this stranger, but it was too late to decline, with the engine running and two plumes of breath fogging the windscreen. Even in her somewhat befuddled state, Leila soon determined that it was taking Mr Rondeau longer to drive her home than the journey normally lasted when she walked it, which was not a good sign, except perhaps for Mr Rondeau, who pulled into an industrial park, switched off the engine and applied first the handbrake and then a generous quota of his Gallic charms.

"Leila Smart, you are a very attractive woman. I need to know you a little better."

Leila was confused. Surprising herself, she found this young man's attentions quite flattering, and no-one had touched her in this way since Roger's departure. When he reached under her coat and fiddled with her bra, she felt more concerned for the expensive garment than for her sexual safety, and she did not struggle. This apparent compliance was, of course, a mistake, for it encouraged her companion to believe that she was a willing participant. What else would he think? He even had the temerity to switch on the internal light to see and appreciate what he was doing, and Leila still visualized, in a flash of memory, the scarlet stripe of her skimpy panties as Pierre's strangely warm hand burrowed inside and made her wet.

"Leila Smart, you are lovely, lovely. Oh my God, Leila Smart!"

"Pierre, please, what if a policeman comes?"

"Then I tell him, I was here first," he said, only vaguely considering whether she would appreciate the joke.

She did not see Pierre Rondeau again. For that matter, although not specifically to avoid him, she did not go to the staff Christmas party again, either.

Making her jump, Billy's face loomed behind her in the mirror, and she clapped a hand to her chest in surprise. "Oh, Billy!"

"Sorry, Mum."

"Creeping up like that."

"You were like miles away. Mum, I had this idea."

"Go on then."

"Mrs Starling…p'raps I should get her a present and take it round. To show I'm sorry."

She turned to face him. "Billy, that is possibly the worst idea you have ever had. As a gesture, it would be completely inadequate."

"Do you think so?"

"I know so. Mrs Starling may be old, but she's not daft. She would simply conclude you were trying to worm your way back into her affections. 'Sorry I killed your beloved cat, here's a box of chocolates.' Do you not see how insincere that would look?"

"But I was thinking of something better than a box of chocolates."

"No, Billy. This is not the way to do it."

"And it wasn't me killed her cat, it was Den –"

"Billy, you can't blame the snake! It was your responsibility to make sure accidents like that couldn't happen. You got it wrong, Billy, totally wrong. You're careless and irresponsible."

Billy slumped heavily on to the sofa and sat hunched like a sack of potatoes. Leila gazed at him, grinding her teeth. She felt sorry for him, but she dared to feel sorry for herself as well. The boy was a liability, a passenger. He would never amount to anything except an obstruction. In that fusty room, he was just one more animal.

"Okay, Billy, I tell you what we'll do." She sat down beside him and laid a hand lightly on his knee. "We've an invite to Mrs Starling's birthday party. So we'll go along and between us we'll give her a nice birthday present and a card. But we won't mention the cat. There's no need to mention the cat."

"I told her I was sorry," Billy said.

"She heard you," Leila said coldly.

Billy leaned against her, snuggling his face into her neck. "I love you, Mum," he said.

"I know you do, Billy, I know you do."

# Chapter 35

## *Number 15: Aisling McIver Entertaining Stephen J. Kettering-Barclay*

She was worried about the old man. Over the phone, he had sounded rather breathless. She wondered about the steps to the first floor and then the stairs afterwards. Rona had amended the Profile to include 'Disabled Clients' , for it stood to reason that there would be older, less able men out there whose needs could not be satisfied by family or friends. Perhaps it would be prudent to ask Rona for her definition of 'Disabled'. Then, of course, a bizarre multitude of deficiencies suggested themselves. There was no lift, so a wheelchair-bound person could not possibly get up to the flat. Still, the old guy had not mentioned a wheelchair.

"Sure, Neamh darling, your mammy's getting herself proper stressed about this. What d'you think, eh? Should I go down and meet this man at the street door, help him up the steps? No, I don't know either. Then there's the stairs to the bedroom, when he's already gasping. What if he has a seizure or a heart attack or God knows what? I mean, is he able to, you know, manage himself, if you see what I'm getting at? Jesus, is he all right, is he senile or demented? I was going to give him the extra time for a round hundred pounds, but maybe that's not kind, no maybe not, so let's say it's the usual ninety and I'll not go ripping off an old pensioner. God, d'you think he'll want me to kiss him? You know, Rona said she heard of a girl doing the business and an old guy turned up with a colostomy bag. Jesus Christ Almighty! Neamh, am I even right to be getting into this stuff? I mean, yes, I like the money, sure I do, but sometimes I get scared, not knowing from one day to the next what's going to walk through the door. Sometimes I just get – scared."

She went upstairs and tidied the bed and laid a clean towel over the duvet. As Rona pointed out, the last thing you'd want is brown streaks on your bedclothes from when they were grunting and grinding on their backs. You had to think of all this stuff. She reached into the bedside drawer and took out a few condoms, though it was surprising how often she didn't need them, if they weren't looking for that at all. So long as they got the happy ending, that was all that mattered, and they would roll on to the floor with a sheepish smile and fumble for their socks, give their hair a quick swish in the mirror, stumble about getting their clothes on and mumble a few platitudes as they made for the door. Some of them only asked for half an hour, so she charged them fifty pounds, and they always seemed content. Even the others, the ones who paid for the full hour, often finished well before their time, and she'd offer them a drink, maybe a bit of a chat, to make up the minutes, but usually they just wanted out of there now the urge was gone. She could understand how it was.

She checked on Neamh again, but she was asleep on her back, blowing tiny bubbles from the corner of her mouth. She was such a good little mite. As much as possible, Aisling wanted the money to go to Neamh, to give her the best chance in life, to keep her safe. As soon as the child was old enough to comprehend what was happening around her, Aisling would stop all this and think of another way to sustain the pair of them. She wouldn't have Neamh wondering who were all these strange men coming to the house. By then, that many years down the road, there would be enough in the bank to fall back on, some security and no debts to worry over.

Before the old man, she had an 11 o'clock appointment and ought to be getting herself ready. He'd sounded pleasant over the phone, mature, though she hadn't asked his age. She seldom did. He showed up on the e-mail as RobRoy 51 and he specifically asked her to leave her normal clothes on at the start. She was happy to wear whatever they requested, if there was any preference at all, although she politely refused to dress up as a schoolgirl, feeling that was a move into the tawdry. Neither did she do leather, as it was too uncomfortable. The morning sessions always surprised her, for she imagined sex as an appetite that gradually developed during the day until reaching its peak in the afternoon or evening, and the notion of a quenchable desire arising so early seemed starkly improbable.

RobRoy rang at five to eleven to ask directions. She smoothed down her hair, gave Neamh a soft teddy and let him in.

"Good morning, Willow," he said, shaking her hand with a quick, firm grip. His confident smile focused on her eyes.

"Hi there. So are you Scottish?"

"No, why?"

"Rob Roy. I thought maybe – "

"Oh, I see. No, my name is Robert Roy Jamieson. Simple as that."

"And are you fifty-one?"

"'Fraid not." He laughed abruptly. "I was born in fifty-one. Here, present for you." He gave her a wad of folded notes. "Formalities over."

"Thank you. Can I get you a drink?"

"Still mineral water would be nice. Am I to call you Willow?"

"If you like. You don't need to call me anything."

"No. No, I suppose not."

She fetched his water and one for herself. She liked to do that, drink with the client. It seemed more friendly, somehow. You had to put them at their ease. Very often the men were nervous, insecure, out of their depth in an alien environment. Sometimes the anxiety was so pronounced, they couldn't do it at all, fumbling their way to a disappointed, unconsummated exit. Aisling regretted the failures, but she viewed them as the clients' inadequacies, not hers. She gave the time and had the money. That was all the rule book said.

She noticed RobRoy's hand shaking as he drank. "Take your time," she said.

"Very cold," he said.

"What?"

"The water. Cold from the fridge."

"Oh, right. For a moment there I thought you meant me."

"No, no." That brief chuckle again. "You're – well, you're rather lovely, actually."

"You don't know me."

"I'm a good judge of character." He put his empty glass on the table. "Shall we go upstairs? I mean, if you're ready."

She found herself liking this man already. He didn't look his age, though his fair hair, greying at the temples, had all but abandoned the crown of his head, leaving the merest froth of colourless tendrils. Meticulously clean-shaven, his face exuded a lemony tang of subtle aftershave, the skin pink and creaseless. RobRoy had looked after himself.

And he was courteous and gentle. A gentleman. A gentle man.

"Shall I take my things off then?" she asked him, patting the side of the bed for him to sit next to her.

"Let me. I like to do this."

His fingers trembled as he unfastened her buttons, but she pretended not to notice. The clasps on her bra were a slight problem, so she lifted her arms in case that helped, and soon he was loosening her and she felt her breasts falling free.

"You must tell me what you like," she said.

"We can talk a little, Willow. I like to do that." He cupped her left breast in his warm palm. "We've an hour. That's plenty time."

"I think you're a nice man," she said. "Nicer than most."

"So do you see a lot of people?"

"What's a lot? I see who I want to. I wouldn't say a

189

lot." She lay down and touched his chest through his shirt. "How about you?"

"Me?" He shook his head a little sadly. "My wife died. I miss her, that's all. Sometimes I have to do this. You understand? Call it companionable sex."

In years long gone by, he had, she realized, been something of a redhead, as evidenced by the russet tinge retained in his pubic hair, stubbornly, secretly defying the onset of the ashen colour of old age. Smiling privately, she admired him there.

Even inside her, he loved to talk. While Aisling lay back, watching his hovering face, he asked her about her baby and how long she had been away from Ireland and if she had a good man in her life to care for her. He spoke of the death of his wife from a brain tumour a year ago and of the places they once visited together before her illness, and Aisling's eyes followed the track of a tear down his cheek, slowly propelled by memory. He loved music, he told her, and described the symphonies of Carl Nielsen, sound-pictures of summer days and brief storms, and he asked her if she liked to read any of the great Irish writers whose novels it was a privilege to experience.

At the end, she sat on the edge of the bed, watching him dress, allowing herself a small smile as he pulled on his Mr Men socks, bent over with his back turned, in case she thought him funny.

"Can I see you again?" he asked her, and he clasped her face in both his hands.

"Sure, you'd be more than welcome. Bless you."

He kissed her softly on the lips and she closed her eyes and let him linger there for more than just a moment. When he had gone down into the street and she was soaping herself in the shower, she was careful not to let the water wash her face, not to rinse away that sweet man.

Puffy-skinned, herb-scented, she went to Neamh and picked her up, and there on the cot cover was a ten-pound note, surely a parting gift for this little one. She reflected anew on the kindness of strangers.

"Neamh McIver, you're a lucky babe." She lowered her face to the warm bundle. "I think it's changing you need. Sure, you're a bit ripe and no mistake. Let's get you fresh again, shall we? Your mam's got another gentleman coming at two o'clock. He'll be smelling you through the door."

To her dismay, she found herself wishing the old man – Seadog he'd called himself – would not arrive. She would miss the money, but something about the booking disquieted her. An old man with part of his leg gone…probably done his best for his country in the war, perhaps earned some medals, a citation for bravery, with the sun going down on his life, all alone in the world, counting the days. *Come on, Aisling, give the guy a chance, all he wants is to buy a little glimpse of happiness.*

She put on a new set of underwear, an orange and black bra with matching high-cut knickers, and tied a modest dressing gown over the top. She looked at herself in the mirror, parting the dressing gown and closing it again.

"Jesus, Neamh, d'you think I'll be sending his blood pressure through the roof!"

She sat down to wait. "Neamh, should I take this off, d'you think, and just wear some ordinary clothes?" She shook her head, laughing. "Forget the robe, underneath your mam's done up like a whore. Christ, will you look at these pants, and me sat here with half me bits hanging out!"

The doorbell rang.

"Who is it?"

"It's me. It's Mister…Seadog."

She pressed the buzzer. "You can come up. Can you do the stairs?"

He didn't reply. She opened the door a few inches and heard his trudging footsteps coming nearer. More than a minute passed. A pale, thin face, lightly pebbled with perspiration, appeared from the dusty gloom.

Aisling stood back, forcing a smile, clutching the wings of the robe together. "Good afternoon. Come on in."

Mr Kettering-Barclay shuffled into the room and turned to left and right, as if uncertain where he was supposed to go. His breath rattled in his throat and he avoided meeting Aisling's anxious gaze.

"Here, sit down, why don't you." She pulled back a chair. "Can I get you something to drink?"

"Hmm, what?"

"I'm asking you if you'd like a drink."

Seadog slumped into the chair and sat capsized like an abandoned dummy, his eyes glazed.

"I could make you some tea," Aisling offered.

The old man glanced at her and nodded. Beads of sweat glistened on his forehead.

"You sit there and get your breath," she told him. "I'm making us a nice cup of tea. Do you take sugar?"

"What?"

"In your tea – do you take sugar?"

"Please. One lump."

"It'll be a spoon. You rest now."

In the kitchen, she stared grimly at the boiling kettle. This man worried her. She had checked his website status, and he claimed to be eighty. He looked more than that, she thought. Was he an old eighty, or maybe a young one hundred? The kettle boiled and spat, and she ground her teeth and spoke in a dark undertone to the hissing jug, cautious lest Seadog should hear her – or was he out of range from deafness? – to articulate the brooding clouds of her doubts.

"Aisling, my dear, are you okay to do this? He's not paid you yet, remember. Can he do the stairs? Can he do anything? For God's sake, should he be here? Rona, I must get Rona to put an age limit on my Profile. I guess I don't do old, if truth be known. Oh yes, and there's another thing: the old chap smells. Jeez, so how do I tell him that? Can I lie next to him, when he's nothing on, me in my best seductive underwear, and him reeking of stale tomato soup? God, if I'm doing this stuff, well, this is the arse end of it, and no mistake. Well, here goes, I'll bring his tea, do it in a cup and saucer, then he can have a spoon, they often like the spoon, and the way I see it, by the time he's had his tea and caught his breath and climbed those stairs and got himself undressed and made up his mind what it is he wants, okay, there won't exactly be too much time left anyway – except of course I did offer him the extra quarter-hour, more fool me. May I forgive myself."

She put her tea in a mug, his in a cup and saucer and set them on a tray with a few biscuits. Bending carefully, so her body did not slide into view, she laid the tray on the table in front of him.

"Tea. I've put sugar in. Have yourself a biscuit."

"Thank you." He glared at the table-top.

"Mister – uh – is there something you've forgotten to give me?"

"Beg your pardon?"

"You're supposed to settle up – before we do anything."

"Do I not pay at the end?"

"Sure, you're not here for a haircut. It's normal you give me the money first."

He reached into his trouser pocket and withdrew a ragged fistful of notes, which he dropped on the table. "Take what you want."

"Thanks." She counted out ninety pounds and pushed the remainder back towards him. "Put that away or it'll blow on the floor."

The smell was bad. Make a virtue of it, she thought, tell him he's to have a nice shower, take his time, then he'll be drying himself and soon it'll all be over, hardly anything of it left. He'd still have to get dressed and stagger downstairs again, after all. It could even end up easy money. *Aisling, you are borderline immoral.*

"Now, Seadog, I'm afraid I have to ask you something."

For the first time, he turned to look at her, squinting to focus his rheumy eyes, tugging out a crumpled handkerchief to dab his wet lips. For a moment, as his eyes

193

fixed hers, she forgot the odour and found herself wondering where this man was coming from and what his expectations might be. It came to her that probably he would not ask for very much, nor demand from her more than the briefest glimpse of transient pleasure.

"My friend," she said quietly, "I think you are not looking after yourself."

"So what are you asking me?" he said, wiping his eyes.

"You – you seem a tad unfresh. Do you understand me? Before we get a little more friendly, I really think you ought to have a bath or a shower. Please. I can come up and help you if you'd like."

"I see. It may be my clothes."

"Whatever. You'll be taking them off, surely."

"Yes." He nodded agreeably. "Yes, of course. Forgive me, I believe there's holes in my socks."

"Ah well, we won't be worrying about that. Now, what do you say?"

"No bath. A shower, perhaps. But I can't stand – my leg, you see."

"Of course. Shall I help you with the stairs?"

"That would be kind." He eased himself up from the chair, wincing, and balanced with one hand on the table. "I wondered what kind of a woman you would be. I'm all right now."

Aisling climbed behind him to the top of the stairs and led him into the bathroom with one hand on his back. She sat him on a wicker chair and turned to adjust the shower temperature. "Wait here," she told him.

From a cupboard on the landing she took a small wooden stool and, returning, placed it in the bath beneath the shower head. Stephen Kettering-Barclay was slowly, laboriously loosening his clothes, revealing white slashes of his scrawny body. His lips quivered, as if he were talking to himself.

"Should I help you undress?"

"I can manage. I'm not helpless."

"I know. I know you aren't helpless."

"To get in the bath. You can help me with that."

"How did you lose your leg, Seadog?"

"In the war. It was injured and became infected."

"I see. I'm sorry."

"Yes." He nodded reflectively. "Everyone's sorry. Everyone who wasn't there."

"Just tell me when you're ready. I'll look after you."

Aisling waited while Seadog unfastened his prosthesis and handed it to her, and she placed it carefully under the washbasin without looking at it. Then she took his arm and helped him over the rim of the bath, supporting his back while he lowered his sunken buttocks on to the wooden stool.

"There now." She squeezed his shoulder, feeling the thin blades of his bones. "That wasn't so bad, was it?"

The old man stared straight ahead, covering his private parts with his hands.

"Now don't you mind about that, I've seen it all before, Seadog."

"I haven't seen you before," he said.

She turned aside, her throat catching at the smell coming off him. *Come on, Aisling, just imagine he's a baby, a big baby. You can stand the smell of babies. Just baby him.*

She reached over his head and turned on the shower. "So – uh – you said something about being forgiven – remember? On the phone."

"Did I?"

"That's what you said."

He moved his hands and gripped the sides of the bath. The water coursed over his head and shoulders. She saw that he wasn't aroused.

"Not now," he said. "I can't tell you now."

"Then when you're ready. Sure, I'm a good listener."

"You're a good woman," he said, his voice breaking. "You're such a good woman."

She took a soft-bristled brush and cleaned his back and chest, rubbing until the flesh glowed pink. The water ran from him the colour of coffee.

"It's not too hot for you?"

"It's good, very good," he replied, with his eyes closed. "You can – please can you touch me?"

"Well, it's only what you've paid for."

She picked up the sponge and began soaping him vigorously between the legs.

Seadog tipped back his head and his mouth gaped open. His hands tightened their grip on the bath sides until the knuckles seemed they would burst through the skin.

A mewling cry came out of him. A baby's cry.

The water splashed over his upturned face and, mingling with the steaming river, the tears streamed down his cheeks like rain.

# Chapter 36

## *Number 33: Minnie Starling*

Minnie reached under the bedside table, picked up the black cardboard box and rested it on her lap. The brown tape had been wound round it for years and air had seeped under it, loosening the bond. When she slid a skinny finger under a dry corner, the seal began to unravel, and it was an easy matter to strip away the tape and remove the lid. Two balls of scrunched up newspaper hid the contents from view. She took the paper out and dropped it on the bedclothes. Yes, the thing she wanted was still there, together with an old mustard tin which rattled when she shook it. She prised the lid off the tin and saw that it was half-full, which she knew would be more than adequate. She would only need a few. Sighing in satisfaction, she rolled over and slid out of bed, wrapping the box and its contents in the duvet. Later, she would find a safe place for it all. A broad smile creased her pallid face.

That awful young man was coming at ten, or so he said. Raj must have another name, but she didn't know it. Probably it was Patel, because nearly all Indians were called Patel. Translated into English, Patel meant Smith. So she started to get dressed, as the clock showed half past eight. She thought about having a wash, but the she hadn't been anywhere to get dirty, and ever since the dreadful incident with the snake in the airing cupboard, she could hardly bring herself to stand naked in the bathroom, not while that gaping hole yawned darkly at her from the back wall. Presumably the boy only had the one snake, the one that would now be too fat to fit through the hole. He had various other pets, of course, and she speculated as to the likelihood of a veritable avalanche of animals scampering in a torrent through the wall, reminiscent of scenes from *Willard* or *The Company of Wolves*.

That old cardboard box could go. She opened her handbag and put the contents inside it, emptying the mustard tin into an envelope. Minnie never went anywhere without her handbag, so she would certainly have it with her at the party. That would work perfectly. People at parties liked surprises. Well, she would present them all with a huge surprise, one they would always remember. It was funny, really; at a birthday party it was usual for whoever was celebrating the birthday to receive a surprise, whereas on this occasion it was Minnie herself, the birthday girl, who was set to deliver the biggest surprise of all.

She slid on to the Stannah and cruised down to the kitchen. She made herself a soft-boiled egg with bread and butter – toast was tastier, but hard on her gums – and as she was scooping the last wisps of white from the shell, the telephone rang.

"Gran, it's me, Charlie."

"I'm just finishing my breakfast, Charlie."

"Gran, listen, I've got a mate near you, he's a plasterer. He's willing to come out and mend that hole for – well, it's not much money."

"Thank you, Charlie, but I don't want to pay any money."

"I'll pay it, Gran."

"No, Charlie. We shouldn't have to pay. Anyway, that Raj is coming this morning to put it right. I'm waiting for him."

Charlie was silent for a moment. "Can you trust him, Gran?"

"No, of course I can't trust him. We both know that perfectly well. He can't be trusted to arrive when he says or to do a good job when he gets here. But the point is, it's his responsibility to do the work and charge me nothing."

"My man's a good tradesman, Gran. It won't cost you anything."

"Charlie, look, I don't want Raj or Roland James let off the hook – understand? They've got to do this and make sure it's a proper job. I don't want to tell them it's all right and they don't have to worry. Why should I smooth the way for them?"

This time Charlie was quiet for so long, Minnie thought he had rung off; but after what seemed like an age, she realized she could hear his breathing on the line, as he struggled to control his frustration. Her grandson was a kindly man, but he invariably tended to solve these problems by taking the easy way out of them. Sometimes it was best to stand your ground.

"You still there, Charlie?"

"I'm here, Gran. So what time's he coming?"

"Ten o'clock, Mr James said."

Charlie blew a noisy breath, hissing through his teeth. "All right. Gran, will you please ring me if he hasn't shown by eleven. Will you do that?"

"Yes, Charlie. Now, let me wash up."

It was nearly eleven o'clock when Raj arrived, carrying his tools in a large cardboard box with *Heinz Baked Beans* printed in red on the outside. Minnie rode up to the top landing behind him and sat peering in at the bathroom door.

"Mrs Starling, your big hole will now be sorted," he said, clattering his equipment on to the floor.

"Sorted? I rather hoped you were going to repair it."

"Ah, repair it, yes. This is good. And I am sorry."

"Sorry for what?"

"For the terrible thing that has happened. Oh dear. Mr James, he is telling me about the cobra that has come through the wall."

"Is he now? If it was a cobra, we wouldn't be having this conversation."

"Yes. No. A snake from next house." He began pulling all the sheets and towels from the cupboard. "But I am here now, Mrs Starling. I will do you a good job and the hole, it will be gone."

"After the horse has bolted," Minnie muttered.

"You have a horse?"

"Raj, my friend, if I had a horse, most of it would fit through that hole. So get on with it."

"Yes, and when the job is done, I will be taking a look at your falling down gutter."

"Yes, well, many people have taken a look at it. What it needs is for someone to mend it."

"Mend it, yes. This is right. Everything we will do."

Minnie watched Raj kneeling on the floor, minutely inspecting his tools. Somewhat to her surprise, she found herself feeling sorry for him. All he needed, probably, was management guidance and a decent wage. He needed putting out of his misery.

"Raj, I hope you and Mr James are coming to my party."

"Oh yes. We will not want to miss this great occasion. Mr James, he has shown me the invitation. We are very excited." The whites of his eyes sparked in the light from the window. "I am wearing my new shoes – for the dancing."

"Hmm. I don't think I shall be doing much dancing," Minnie said. "Not at a hundred."

"There is to be a band?"

"A motley assemblage of musicians," she said, under her breath.

"A motley?"

"Never mind, Raj. Just fill that bloody hole."

As she rode downstairs, the lift juddered and squeaked, and she made a mental note to tell Charlie so that he could arrange a service visit. The house had no ground floor toilet, and for Minnie easy access to the upstairs bathroom was essential. Her grandson had suggested a commode, but this seemed to her an insanitary solution and, in any case, she would still have to go up eventually to empty it. She imagined herself riding up the staircase with a smelly pan of poo balanced on her lap; and after that she would have to lurch into the bathroom with her stick in one hand and the container in the other. It didn't bear thinking about.

Fixed to the fridge door with a *Beautiful Bournemouth* magnet, the Residents' Association birthday party invitation flyer caught her attention, and she plucked it free, sat down at the table and reached for her glasses.

*Dear Friend*

*Our most senior friend and neighbour, **Minnie Roseanne Starling**, will celebrate her 100th birthday on Saturday, 13th June, 2015.*

*Minnie has lived at number 33, Paradise Walk for more than half her life and in that time she has earned the affection and respect of so many people in the local community.*

*It is with this distinction in mind that the Paradise Residents' Association, comprising the member residents of Paradise Park and Paradise Walk, unanimously decided at a recent meeting to acknowledge the occasion of her centenary by organizing a special birthday party for Minnie, to which as many as possible of her family, friends and neighbours will be invited.*

*Your receipt of this letter indicates that your presence at the event is sincerely welcomed. If you are able to attend, kindly bring this invitation with you.*

*The party will take place at The Rifleman public house at the junction of Paradise Walk with Paradise Park, from 6.30pm until late on the Saturday of Minnie's birthday. A private room has been set aside for party-goers.*

*Children will be most welcome provided they are accompanied by a parent or suitable adult.*

*If you have a gift for Mrs Starling, you may bring it to the party.*

*Thanks to the generosity of the Residents' Association Committee and the Parish Council, it has been possible to meet the costs of providing food and soft drinks out of allocated funds, but please note that, to defray expenses, there will be a non-obligatory collection during the evening for those who may wish to contribute.*

*Music will be provided by the Albert Thirlwell combo.*

*The bar will be open from 6.30 until 11.00pm and alcoholic drinks will be available at normal prices.*

*We look forward to the pleasure of your company.*

*Arthur J. Setright*
*On behalf of the Paradise Residents' Association*

Minnie put the letter under a pot of marmalade and dialled Charlie's number to tell him Raj had arrived.

"About time. Make sure he does the job properly."

"How will I know that?"

"Take a look before you let him go. Ring me if you aren't happy."

"Yes, Charlie."

"You want me to come round?"

"No. Here, I was reading that invitation again. It says music will be provided by Albert Thirlwell."

"Do you know who he is?"

"Course I do. I'm amazed he's still going. Albert Thirlwell played his clarinet at our street party when I was in Mafeking Terrace. That was Her Majesty's Coronation day."

She heard her grandson chuckling.

"I mean, that was more than sixty years ago. He must be nearly as old as me."

"I wonder who else is in this combo."

"I bet you Teddy Baverstock's in it. Him and Albert

were mates. Teddy played the violin, when he was sober enough to hold it the right way up." A sigh of cooing laughter rippled out of her. "Old Teddy, he was – well, I tell you, he was older than Albert."

"Great days, eh, Gran?"

"Yes, right. Look, I'd better let you go. Just wanted to tell you the Indian's arrived. I'll go back up in a minute and check on him."

Putting the phone down, she squinted across the floor and saw Darling's food bowl still on its paper by the back door. She sighed and shook her head. Tears blurred her eyes. Rising slowly to her feet, she went to pick up the bowl and placed it in the sink, filling it with warm water.

"Poor Darling," she said. "You've come to a bad end, the worst sort. But don't you worry, there'll be payment made, I shall see to that. Because it wasn't an accident, you see, no, it was down to neglect. Neglect is deliberate. Neglect has to be paid for."

A thump and a loud crash interrupted her monologue. She leaned on her stick and laboured to the stairlift. "I'm coming up," she called.

Raj met her at the top of the stairs. There was white dust on his face. "Ah, Missis. Everything is fine," he said, waving his hands.

"What was that noise?"

"I am only dropping something. Your wall – well, I am doing it."

"Doing what, exactly?"

"I am repairing."

"You sure you know what you're doing?"

"Yes, I am repairing."

"Perhaps I should take a look."

Raj shook his head and dust fell out of his hair. "Is nothing to see. Everything is fine. I have a plan."

Minnie nodded her head, smiling craftily. "Oh, so do I," she said, "so do I."

# Chapter 37

## *Number 25: Joan Descours*

"It's no trouble, no trouble at all," she assured him. "You look tired, Barry – and there aren't so many buses in the afternoon."

"You're quite sure?" The boy was adjusting the strap of his laptop bag on his shoulder. "It's very kind of you."

"Nonsense. Come on, my car's just up the road."

He seemed to have trouble in belting himself in, and Joan leaned across him to pull the straps into place, brushing her arm over his lap. "There. Tight enough?"

"Thanks." He looked down. "My feet are on something."

"Oh. Plastic sandwich box. Ignore it. Sorry, this old car is a bit of a tip. I just can't afford a new one."

"Maybe they ought to pay you more. You're a brilliant teacher."

She smiled and patted his leg. "And you're kind."

"It's you that's kind," he said. "It's you that's helping me."

She rolled down the window to let some heat out of the car. The engine started with a clatter and they pulled out behind a large, gaudily-painted truck. A minute later the truck braked and turned through the open gates of the recreation ground. The vehicle's exhaust fumes billowed into the car, to be swiftly overwhelmed by a mingled aroma of toffee and warm oil.

"Fairground," Barry said.

"So it is." She braked to a standstill. "Shall we go in? I love a fair."

Barry sucked in his cheeks impishly. "Did you say love affair?"

She grinned, slapping his thigh. "You know what I said, Barry Brown."

204

"Okay. But I think they're still setting it up. Those tents are collapsed, look."

Joan parked by the entrance and switched off the engine. Barry released his belt, picked up the sandwich box and dropped it on the back seat. Joan turned towards him and squeezed his shoulder. They could hear the engine ticking as it cooled. Metallic music churned from a merry-go-round in the distance.

He looked at her out of the corner of his eye. He could feel himself gradually discerning her wavelength. It scared him a little, but it was like being frightened and excited at the same time, the kind of sensation he knew from walking to the edge of a high building and experiencing a tightening in his core on looking down, yet wanting to go back again, wanting to do it again, the pain thing, because the badness of it felt good. He wondered what would happen if he touched her.

"So did you mind what I did back there – in the house?" She spoke staring ahead through the windscreen. "When I – you know."

"What do you mean, Joan?"

"Oh, I think you know what I mean, Barry. When I kissed you." She glanced at him quickly. "Don't tell me you've forgotten it."

He felt himself blushing, and when he tried to suppress the reaction, that only made it worse, until his face swarmed with heat. "Course I didn't mind," he said, playing with his fingers.

"That's all right, then. I shouldn't have done it, of course."

He knew she was waiting for him to contradict her, to say he'd liked it. He licked his lips and quietly inspected his fingernails. What would it feel like, he wondered, if he touched her. He wanted to touch her, but he didn't want to want to touch her. He was not quite sure, but he thought she wanted him to touch her. When she had touched him, in the car or in the house, it was only a fleeting moment of respectful warmth, but probably there was something else there, just under the surface, like a veil you had to lift aside, as lightly as anything, and just let it happen then, just go with it and not think about it.

"Some of it's open," she said. "Let's take a look – yes?"

"If you like."

"I'll buy you a toffee apple. Do they still do toffee apples?"

"Don't think they count as one of your five a day."

She laughed, tossing her head. "You're funny."

He waited while she put his laptop in the boot and locked the car, fiddling with the key, frowning. A breeze danced across the open space, briefly lifting Joan's patchwork skirt to expose her knees. "Come on." She took his hand as they walked.

A small blue tent, hardly larger than a wigwam, stood beside the path with its entrance flap pinned back. The cardboard sign read: 'Meet Griselda, the Bearded Woman'. Barry bent down and peered inside, Joan crouching next to him. A wizened man with a moustache sat in the gloom on a wooden chair, smoking a cigarette. They turned away.

"Bearded woman not arrived yet," Joan said.

"Maybe that is the bearded woman."

She laughed, clutching his arm.

The dodgems had still to be assembled, cables snaking over square holes in the floor. They stood gazing at the painted framework, and a man with a ponytail told them the cars would not be running until the evening.

Barry pointed to the hoop-la stall. "Over there. I'll win you a prize."

With his last hoop, he won her a glass jar of liquorice allsorts. They shared them as they strolled.

"Look!" She waved a hand at the big wheel, slowly turning against the trees, its few occupants dark specks scratching the sky. "Let's ride. It'll be worth it for the view."

She fumbled in her purse and paid the bored man at the

kiosk, who extended a perfunctory helping hand as they shuffled sideways into the seat.

The fairground music faded to a tinny whisper as the wheel began its climb, the gondola rocking slightly in the wind. It was colder above the ground, and Joan pressed against him, rubbing arms. He felt the pressure of her thigh, compressing his, the soft warmth of it.

"Not much room in these things," she called, slitting her eyes in the breeze.

Barry angled his thigh so that it felt welded to hers. Up here, in the silence under the big sky, he felt curiously detached from the earth below, enclosed in a microcosm of the real world, their own small bubble where nothing mattered or counted and what they had left behind was suddenly without consequence. He tried, half-heartedly, to admire the view, maybe look out for his house beyond the fields, but all he could think of now was being up in this swinging cradle with Joan Descours leaning against him, the air currents flapping her skirt next to his hand, and no-one here to see them in this quiet, private place.

She grabbed his arm, pointing. "Look! I can see Paradise Park! There's my house with the lily pads in the pond!"

Barry Brown ground his teeth tightly together and, when the wind lifted the hem of Joan's skirt, he put his hand there and slid it just a few inches along her thigh.

"Hey, what are you doing?" She moved her leg away. "Did I say you could do that?"

He looked up into her face to see if she was angry, but she was smirking and there was a playful light in her eyes.

"I'm sorry," he said.

She sucked in her cheeks. "Bet you're not."

"Are you cross with me, Joan? Have I spoilt it?"

She sniffed, turning her head away. "Oh, I think I can forgive you," she said. Her heart was beating wildly. She let her leg fall back on him.

The gondola was at its highest point, its rotational movement scarcely noticeable.

"I knew I should have worn trousers," she said. "In this wind."

Barry twisted his head round to see the other cars, then leaned forward to look at those below. Nearly all of them were empty. He and Joan were almost alone on the wheel. When he sat back and stared up at the clouds, a strange, disorientating vertigo unsettled him, and he gripped the bar ahead of his chest, harder and harder, until his hands grew pale. It was while he was watching the colour drain from the backs of his hands that he felt the whole structure judder and wobble.

"What was that?" Joan asked, raising a hand to her mouth.

"I don't know. We've stopped. The wheel's stopped."

"I hope not, Barry."

"I'm telling you, it's stopped."

"Shit!"

The sun had gone behind a bank of grey cloud and the wind was keener now, thrashing their faces. The buffeting wind was the only sound that reached them, a pulsating percussion circling their heads.

"Barry, I really don't want to be stuck up here."

He thought of reminding her that it had been her idea to get on in the first place, but that might antagonize her and it would achieve nothing. Worse, it could precipitate ill-feeling, and this was no place to have an argument.

"Barry, would it embarrass you if I asked you to put your arms round me? I am actually quite cold."

He managed to squirm round in the chair to face her legs. Miss Descours had rather nice legs, he thought. He remembered touching her left leg, the silky sheen of her stocking under his fingers. It would have been nice to go all the way up, not so much to feel anything, but just to find out how much she would let him do, to see if she liked him enough to allow it to happen.

"Did you hear me, Barry?"

He folded himself to the right and wrapped both arms round Joan's shoulders, his nose brushing her cheek. She had a sweetish smell, a bit like apples. They sat quite still. Her left thigh pressed hard against him. The wind whipped their hair into crazy spirals.

A faint voice drifted from below.

"There's a man," Joan said, craning her neck. "I think he's got a megaphone."

"This is weird," said Barry.

"This is ridiculous," Joan said. "Hold me tighter, I'm freezing."

"I can't move any more, I'll fall out."

The man lifted the megaphone, hollering at the sky.

"Can you hear what he's saying?" Her lips moistened his ear. "This wind's carrying it away."

"Wait," he told her. "Don't talk, listen."

The man walked away from the kiosk, taking up a new position. The sun glided from the dark cloud and glinted on the metal trumpet raised in his fist. Fractured words drifted upwards, distorted by distance and by the eddying breeze.

"Is he calling to us?" Joan asked.

Barry was surprised to find himself irritated by her enquiry. Who else would the man be shouting at? The machinery had broken, so obviously he had to make urgent contact with the passengers. There could be no doubt whom he was addressing.

"He's trying to reassure us," Barry said. "We need to hear him."

It was the man with the ponytail. From high above a bald spot showed on the crown of his head, resembling a white pimple, a defect which had not been noticeable at ground level.

"I could catch pneumonia up here," Joan announced.

"They'll get us down soon. We just have to – shush!"

The megaphone was pointing straight at them, its mouth a black hole completely obscuring the man's face.

"Can you hear me on the wheel? Can you hear me?" The words rang with a metallic anguish. "We are working to repair the fault. Please sit still and remain calm." The next few words were scattered on the breeze, but Barry heard something about "…hot drinks when you return."

He let go of her and eased himself back in the chair. She reached for his hand and was surprised and comforted by its unexpected warmth.

"We must be mad," she said. "I was giving you a lift home and we've ended up marooned a hundred feet in the air."

He squeezed her hand.

"Will they send a helicopter, do you think?" She shook her head. "I've never been in a helicopter. Or perhaps they'll bring a crane."

"Might have to get the fire brigade," he said. "Except I don't know if their ladder'll reach."

"Hmm. Let's hope we don't have to leap into a blanket."

The idea made him laugh, and the cold air scratched his throat, sending him into a spasm of coughing. He slipped his arm round her shoulders and hugged her against him. The weight of her felt good, very good. He thought of touching her again, but probably she wouldn't want that if she was so cold. In his mind's eye he saw the places where he would like to touch her, and he hoped it would not be long before he could make those imaginary places real. His anticipation raged like a sickness.

The man below was yelling again, but they couldn't hear what he said. Workmen in grubby overalls were scurrying to and fro, some of them carrying toolboxes. A group of visitors approached the kiosk and the megaphone man waved them away. The wheel jolted violently, but it did not rotate.

"We could be up here all day," Joan said. "What do we do if we want to go to the toilet?"

"Just do it. Abandon your pride."

"I've never wee'd in mid-air."

Barry glanced around him. "There's about six people on this thing. Pity we can't orchestrate it: when I raise my hand, all pee at once."

"I reckon you're a bit kinky, Barry Brown." She raised her head, shielding her eyes with a flattened hand. "Oh, I can see my car."

Repeated clanging blows, metal on metal, reverberated through the structure, followed by a raucous yell. The chair shuddered again, and the wheel began to move.

Joan grabbed the bar with both hands. "Thank God!"

Slowly, inexorably, the ground swung up to meet them. Workmen's upturned faces loomed towards them, pale and dirt-grimed. The wheel rumbled and trembled, but it kept on rolling.

"Warmer down here," Joan said, brushing the hair from her face.

Barry imagined he was an astronaut coming in to land. His relief was tainted with a mist of disappointment, for he felt that he had not savoured their isolation to the full. Up in the sky, alone with Joan Descours, he had been gifted a few precious minutes in a secret place, huddled close to her, private and unseen, and although she had challenged his first advance, he could have persisted, in the knowledge that the fragile environment they shared would also serve as their protection. Joan could not have offered any strenuous resistance, trapped at that height, and even a cry of protest would have been lost on the wind. He doubted, in any case, that she would have rejected him. She was fond of him, he was sure of that, and earlier in the day she had made the opening moves. She had tested him, and it seemed to him that he had not risen to the task. A ball of sullen despair lay heavily in his stomach.

Ponytail extended a tattooed arm to help them down. "Sorry about that. Drive belt failed. Can we get you a hot drink, no charge?"

"Thank you," Joan said archly, "I just want to get out of here."

In the car she held her hands out in front of her, opening and closing the fingers. "Numb. Ridiculous."

"You all right to drive?"

"Can you drive, Barry?"

"No."

"Well then."

At the gates, he looked left, but Joan turned right.

"Going the wrong way," he told her.

"No I'm not, my dear. I may be going to the wrong house, but I'm going the right way. I'm going the rightest way I know."

# Chapter 38

## *Number 22: Mr and Mrs Slocombe*

"Myeloma," Hettie said. "It's a form of bone cancer."

Janice Collins nodded. "Yes, I know."

"Oh. Well, I suppose you would, being in your line of work."

They drank milky tea from bone china cups with fragile handles too small to fit their fingers through. A matching plate with scalloped borders carried a selection of chocolate biscuits.

"At first, you see, we thought he'd strained himself in the garden. He liked his gardening. He'd wake me in the night, groaning with this awful back pain. Eventually I got him to see the doctor. He advised some tests, I don't know, some sort of tests."

"Did they refer him?"

"Yes, to Saint Peter's. More tests."

Janice massaged her temples and took a chocolate finger.

"I think, with myeloma, you often get periods of remission."

"Yes," said Hettie, frostily, "unfortunately you do."

"Why unfortunately?"

"Why? Because if he'd just felt sick and poorly all the time, most likely none of this would ever have happened."

"None of what, exactly?"

Hettie waved a hand in the general direction of the shed. "This. Shacking up in a shed."

"So – forgive me – where does this blonde woman come in?"

Wetting her lips with more tea, Hettie hunched her shoulders and shifted awkwardly in her chair. "It got so he couldn't manage. I mean, he couldn't get himself dressed or wash himself. Some mornings he was doubled up with the pain. I told the doctor, the one who'd got him the consultation, and he contacted the social services. Next I knew, these two women were coming round, twice a day."

"Not from our agency?"

"No. It was Silver Angels."

Janice wiped the chocolate from her mouth with her fingertips.

"Well, one was black, usually a bit sweaty. Their faces get very shiny, don't they? The other – well, I didn't take to her at all. A bit too familiar by half. Called me Hettie soon as she came in the door, kept patting my arm. Whenever she helped Alf off with his clothes, she was making this silly cooing noise, like he was a blinkin' baby. Course, Alf, he lapped it up, didn't he? Men! Brassy blonde undressing him."

"But that was what she was employed to do, Mrs Slocombe."

"It was the way she did it I didn't like. Sort of – sensuous, like."

"Are you sure you didn't imagine that?"

"No, dear, I observed it. I sat there with my eyes open and I saw what was going on."

"I see. And what was going on?"

"Enticement, that was going on."

Janice cast her eyes around the ceiling in a process of assimilation. "This is just so hard to believe. This woman – what's her name?"

"Gloria. Gloria Glenister."

"Gloria. Well, I don't know her. But she must have proper qualifications."

"I never said she didn't, dear."

"Is she – was she experienced?"

"In a number of fields hereabouts," Hettie said acidly.

"Maybe she took a shine to your husband and was just being a little over-attentive."

"Oh, it was more than a shine," Hettie said. "As was to be proved."

"Meaning?"

"Meaning the bleedin' obvious. Meaning three-dimensional technicolor. Go on, have another digestive."

Janice took a biscuit, broke it in half and inserted the fragment thoughtfully into her mouth. "Are you saying you found them in a compromising position?"

"If you want to put it that way. It started with Arthur."

"Who's Arthur?"

"My rabbit."

"Oh yes. Where is Arthur?"

Hettie looked vaguely round the room. "He'll be hopping about somewhere."

"So what did Arthur have to do with it?"

"He got something wrong with his foot. It wouldn't get better, so I booked him into the vet. You have to make an appointment. The only slot they had was about the time Alf's evening carer was due. He was in a bit of remission then, so they cut him back to the one woman, mostly blondie. Anyway, off I went, plenty of time, I'm not one to be late, and when I got to the surgery, people were all standing outside. Evidently they'd just had a flood, water pouring through the ceiling. There was even a fire engine standing by, not that the firemen seemed to be doing much. Well, they couldn't see any animals, could they? The girl came out with her whatsit – her computer – and sat on the step and rebooked everybody for another day. The water was even running down the steps, so she was sitting in a puddle. So all I could do was pick up me rabbit and go home."

"I see. And did you surprise them, is that what you're telling me?"

"On the sofa. On our sofa. Alf, he was starkers, her, she was sprawled on top of him with all her credentials hanging out. Not a pretty sight, I can tell you."

"Hmm. Arthur has a lot to answer for."

"Yes. Funny how it all comes down to a rabbit's foot. More tea, dear?"

Janice waited, resting her head in her hands, while Hettie Slocombe stood up to boil the kettle again.

"I'm sorry, Hettie." She shook her head, chiding herself. "You're in a sling. Let me do that."

Hettie smiled thinly and sat down. In the kitchen, Janice found clean cups and saucers and caught sight of her reflection in the darkening window. She turned to confront herself, surprised at the clarity of the image. "You've been doing this job for seven years, Janice. Tell me if you've ever heard a more bizarre story. I don't get this, I can't fathom it at all."

"Who are you talking to, dear?"

"No-one. Bringing it in a moment."

They sipped fresh tea, eyes downcast, each waiting for the other to resume the conversation. Arthur skipped into the room and sat nibbling the carpet. They each took a chocolate finger.

"Hettie, what I don't quite understand is why Alf is in the shed. I mean – well, don't you think that's a bit odd?"

"Odd in what way, dear?"

"After the – the incident, you threw him out?"

"Not immediately. I gave him notice."

"That seems a bit harsh. He was a sick man."

"A bit harsh," Hettie repeated slowly. "He's waited till I'm out of the house, then he's made time with the carer. I'd say that was a bit harsh, wouldn't you?"

"Didn't you want to discuss it – the situation?"

"Yes, we did. The discussion simply revealed how long they'd been playing around."

"And did you complain to the agency about her, this Gloria?"

Hettie cocked her head to one side and looked thoughtful. "Matter of fact, I don't recall I did. I just told the woman I wasn't having her back. Yes, I warned her if she ever came back in the house, I'd report her to her employer. Next I knew, she'd gone and resigned."

"But – living in a shed. Living in your shed."

"Oh, like I told you, it's not my shed, dear."

"Couldn't they have gone to her place, moved in together?"

216

"Not once she'd resigned. Silver Angels is big round here, see, and they have a kind of flats or dormitory thing for regular staff. Gloria lived in there. So, no job, no accommodation." She dipped a chocolate finger in her teacup and solemnly watched the coating run off. "Course, neither of them had the money to buy anything round here. Out of the question."

"I see."

"I was always telling him that shed was ridiculous, taking up half the garden. More like a holiday chalet."

"So he moved her in there and…"

"And that's how we ended up, my dear."

"But surely – doesn't everyone think he's dead?"

"Some of them may do. Doesn't matter, does it? I'm not claiming death benefit or anything."

"What if he needs to go out, maybe to the shops?"

"Go out to the shops, dear? He's not well, he can't go walking round no shops. That blondie, she does all that kind of stuff. He's happy sitting in there with his telly, waited on by a bit of blonde skirt twenty years his junior. He'll die in there, of course, but he'll die happy."

Janice locked the back door and helped Hettie up to the bedroom. Arthur followed them, bounding up the stairs like a miniature kangaroo. It was getting late, but the carer had no other clients to visit that evening, and her time was her own. Crossing the room, she moved to draw the curtains, pausing to look down at the shed, where a dimly-lit window now glowed in the gloom. Alf Slocombe's arm swung briefly across the glass.

"Time you were going, dear." Hettie sat on the edge of the bed, rubbing her injured arm. "Help me get me legs in and then I'll just have the bedside light."

"Hettie."

"Yes, dear."

"Do you miss him? I mean, you must see him coming and going."

"I thought I'd made it clear, dear. There's no coming and going. And he's not about to come knocking for a cup

217

of sugar."

"Around the house, you must miss him."

Hettie sighed, tilting her head from side to side, scratching her nose, and when she took her finger away, a single tear rolled down her cheek. "Course I do. Course I miss him. He was the love of my life."

"You – you never had children?"

"No, dear, we had a rabbit."

Janice considered this a poor substitute, but she felt it imprudent to say so.

"Oh, case you're wondering, there was never anything wrong with that part of our relationship. The physical, I mean. My Alf, he was quite a physical man, see."

Janice nodded, chewing her lip. "Yes. And now he's getting physical with a blonde woman in the shed."

"That's about the long and the short of it, dear."

"It's an extraordinary story, Hettie. I'd call it a quiet tragedy."

"Oh, don't let's dramatise it, dear. Come on, do my legs."

She lifted Hettie's legs carefully into bed and stood gazing down at her. "Do you have any idea how long he has left?"

"Not really. He could go on for years, or he could drop down dead tomorrow."

"Then you'd have his fancy woman living on your property."

"That's right, dear. I'd have a blonde tart stuck in my garden shed and me sleeping upstairs with a rabbit. It's a queer old life."

Arthur hopped onto the bed and scrabbled himself a nest against the footboard.

"You know, dear, I've come to a conclusion. Well, a suspicion, anyway." She squeezed her shoulders into the pillows. "Seems to me, it's like driving a car."

"How do you mean, Hettie?"

"Well, life is like, they give you a car with no petrol gauge, see. You don't know how far you can go, and when you're stuttering to a halt, that's the first you know about everything shutting down. You just keep on driving, mile after mile after mile, until one day it all goes quiet. The juice runs out." She jabbed a thumb over her shoulder towards the shed. "Let's hope his juice hasn't run out, eh?"

Janice widened her eyes and smiled, and soon the smile spilled over into laughter, and her mirth became infectious, bringing bright tears coursing down Hettie's cheeks as the two women bumped heads and shared their gentle amusement. In Hettie Slocombe's eyes glimmered a kind of sorrowful resignation, a questing for all that might have been.

# Chapter 39

## *Mr and Mrs Clarnon*

They sat together on a green-painted, weather-scarred metal bench beneath an overhanging tree where the slope of the cemetery rose to afford a broad view of the ranks of headstones and the green and yellow fields beyond. Mrs Stirrup sat close to one arm of the seat, leaving a three-foot space between her and Hettie Slocombe at the opposite end. A lilting breeze stirred the dark branches of the tree shading them. Hettie's sling lay discarded in her lap.

"Nice here," said Mrs Stirrup.

"Oh, I always enjoy a cemetery," Hettie agreed.

"Shouldn't you be looking after your arm?" asked Mrs Stirrup.

"I am looking after it. I'm letting it breathe."

"You don't breathe through your arms."

"I'm just resting my shoulder."

Mrs Stirrup looked down the slope and trained her eyes on the freshly-dug plot where Pat Clarnon and his wife were laid to rest. "I'm glad we made the effort," she said.

"Yes. I was thinking – it's funny."

"What's funny about it?"

"All the furniture and knick-knacks they had in that house. We all accumulate so many possessions, don't we? Now look. All they've got apart from a box each is that scruffy wooden cross stuck in the mud."

"They've got each other," Mrs Stirrup said. "That's all that matters now."

"Is someone going to see about a proper headstone?" Hettie asked her.

"Hard to say. There's no children, far as I'm aware."

"No, well, he was sat in that car all the time, wasn't he?"

"Pardon?"

"You know what I mean, love."

"But he didn't sleep in the car," Mrs Stirrup said.

"I never said he did."

Hettie Slocombe lifted the sling to her nose and sniffed it. "This thing could do with a wash."

"Were you at the funeral, Mrs Slocombe?"

"Yes. Very tasteful. Martha came to see me in the hospital when I broke my arm. It was the least I could do to pay my respects."

Mrs Stirrup nodded and yawned. Hettie gave her sling another good sniffing and put it down again.

"Should have brought a flask of tea," Mrs Stirrup said.

"It's not a picnic."

"All the people that come here…you'd think they'd have a little café."

"You'll be wanting a bouncy castle next."

"Just some tea would be nice."

Hettie yawned, massaging her injured arm. Bending, she inspected the mud on her shoes.

"I suppose it's a bit ironic, when you think about it," said Mrs Stirrup. "Every day I used to walk past him sat in that car, and her indoors on her own. Alive but separated. Now they're dead, they're together at last."

"It's a funny old world," Hettie mused, "even when you're not in it any more."

Mrs Stirrup brushed leaves from her skirt. "We could walk," she said. "There's a tea shop in the main road. Here, did I see you leaving fruit on the grave?"

"Yes, I put some nice red apples."

"Oh. I just left a bunch of flowers."

"Whenever I went in the Clarnons' front room, they had this big fruit bowl on the table, piled with these gorgeous shiny red apples, looked like bowling balls. I saw they had some in the paper shop, he got them from the Farmers' Market."

"I see," Mrs Stirrup said dubiously. "Me, I like to leave some flowers."

"You can't eat flowers," Hettie said.

"You can't eat apples if you're dead."

"Well, we don't know, do we."

"Your apples will turn to mush."

"Your flowers will wither and blow away."

They stood up and walked. Hettie stuffed her sling in her pocket. The path ran steeply downhill, and they trudged along leaning backwards to compensate for the incline. An elderly groundsman in a yellow tabard grunted at them as he jabbed at the earth with a spade.

"Give me your hand a minute," Hettie said to Mrs Stirrup.

"Don't go getting soppy."

"It's just, I wouldn't want to fall over."

"Oh, right."

They walked on, hand in lightly clasped hand.

"Mrs Slocombe, did you wear black at the funeral?"

"I did not. Funerals are depressing enough without dressing to be morbid. I went in a blue and yellow dress with a yellow scarf and blue shoes."

"Perfect."

"Wearing black, it's like you're trying to remind everybody how awful it all is. At my funeral, I don't want anyone wearing black. I shall tell them that beforehand. Then, if they turn up in black, it'll be disrespectful."

Mrs Stirrup stopped to read the inscription on a recent headstone. "You know, sometimes I think there aren't any dead people in a graveyard."

"Sorry, dear?"

"You notice, they've all gone to rest or fell asleep. This one, look, he's five and he's gone to play in Heaven."

"Well, they can hardly put 'dropped down dead', can they?"

"They can say he died. They can dispense with the euphemism."

Hettie pulled a face and gripped her companion's wrist. "So what do you want on your gravestone?"

"I'm not dead."

"But when you are – dead."

"I won't be reading it. They can put what they like."

"Still, it's nice to have something complimentary."

"Huh. A bit late for compliments. Me, I'd rather have the compliments while I was still alive. Reckon I'd be sticking my head up and saying, 'Now they tell me!'"

Hettie sighed. Her arm was beginning to ache and there was a pebble in her shoe. "I think I want the toilet," she said.

"No toilet here, dear."

"There's one in the tea shop. Come on."

Supporting each other on the sloping path, they walked slowly towards the iron gates, the sun warming the back of their necks. At the exit, Hettie hesitated, gazing back up the hill at the stone forest of petrified memorials.

"I still can't take it in," she said. "That they should both have gone so suddenly. It makes it seem so violent."

"Best that way. There's no bereavement and no grief."

"I'm grieving," Hettie said.

"For them, I mean. All they have now is quiet togetherness. What more could they ask? It's the perfect end."

Leaning on the gatepost, Hettie considered the pragmatism. The pain of death came from knowing about it. The dead were spared that knowledge. Before they were born, the world was in darkness, its revolutions and consequences unknown to them. Now the light had been extinguished once more, and the old order was restored. To perceive such departures as tragedy was purely sentimental. All we could ever expect was that blink of light.

Mrs Stirrup laid a consoling hand on Hettie's shoulder. "I'll buy you a cup of tea and a toasted teacake," she said. "In Margery's."

"Their teacakes are to die for," Hettie declared. "Oh. Perhaps that's an inappropriate observation." They pushed the gate shut behind them. "I was just thinking, it's funny in a way, I never really got to know you, before this."

"Ah, right. Call it a friendship forged in the crucible of

death."

"Well, that sounds rather sinister. I'm not sure I like that description."

Mrs Stirrup shrugged, stamping the dirt from her shoes. "Feel free to supply an alternative. Are you ready?"

"For what?"

"To seal this new-found friendship over a table in Margery's window. We can look out and see life going on and forget anything was ever any different."

For a moment Hettie walked looking backwards, as though something or someone were pursuing her. "Do you think they'll be all right in there?" she asked peevishly.

"Of course. They've got each other."

"I can't help it, I'm sad for them."

"Watch where you're going or you'll break something else. No tears, no sadness. Maybe we should feel jealous."

"How do you work that out?"

Mrs Stirrup waved her arms at the scenery. "All this, all the garbage, everything – they're out of it. I could do with that."

"I can still see that stick stuck in the ground."

"Don't worry about that. I'll get on to the Residents' Association, see about getting a proper gravestone, then everyone can come and visit."

Hettie stopped and hoisted her arm back in the sling. "Look at me, I'm a daft old woman with one arm."

"No you're not. You're someone who cares. Give yourself a chance."

"I'm glad we came. Aren't you?"

Mrs Stirrup placed a hand in the small of Hettie's back. "Walk. Margery'll be shutting. We'll miss our tea. Stop your fretting."

The afternoon sun painted their shadows on the pavement like pale ghosts escaping.

# Chapter 40

## *Number 35: Mrs Leila Smart and Billy Smart*

Billy's mother tapped on the door and opened it a few inches, instantly inhaling the fetid odours of perspiration, urine and soiled straw. She clamped a hand over her nose, preferring the smell of chopped onions impregnating the flesh of her palm.

Billy sat naked on the edge of the bed, Denzil coiled next to him. The cat appeared partly digested, its grotesque hummock now reduced to an elasticated distension of the tan-coloured markings on the snake's body.

Struggling against a wave of revulsion, Leila tilted her face through the gap in the doorway. "Billy, what are you doing?"

"What does it look like I'm doing?"

"Billy, it's ten-fifteen. You need to wash, dress and get moving."

"Move to where?"

"God, this room! You're not a child any more. Look at you! Stark naked with a bloody snake. It's like a scene from a Gothic horror movie."

"Mum!"

"Billy, you need to clean this room and leave the window open. And you can't sit around all day talking to animals. There's a world out there."

"Mum, I lost my job, remember. There's nothing to go out for."

"Yes, Billy, there is. You should go out and get another job, not shut yourself away in here." She tossed a piece of paper on to the floor. "You get dressed and you ring that number. Vacancy at the waterworks. They want a filing clerk, ten till four. If there's a form, I'll help you fill it in."

Billy slid off the bed, glum-faced, and picked up the scrap of paper. Denzil watched him, forked tongue flickering in and out. A brown rat scampered across the window sill and disappeared under the bed.

"Can't you ring them, Mum?" Billy held the paper under his nose. "I'm not much good on the phone."

"You're not much good anywhere. Just explain to me what you're going to do for money, Billy. There's that old car outside and this – this menagerie inside. It all costs money, Billy. It all has to be sorted."

"How did you know about the job, Mum?"

"Notice in the newsagent's window."

"What shall I say to them?"

"Tell them you're interested in – Billy, for Christ's sake! Don't be so damned feckless! I want to see you downstairs and on that phone."

The door slammed. Billy perched on the bed again, scratching his scrotum as he studied the slip of paper. Next to the phone number was a name: Miss Palmerston. Denzil hissed quietly and urinated on the bedclothes. Billy imagined Miss Palmerston. He had seen people walking in and out of the water company, but he had never seen anyone attractive. Probably Miss Palmerston was old, over thirty, with crimped hair and a brooch pinned to her cardigan. She would look askance at him, her eyes filled with a toxic blend of incomprehension and disapproval, because mostly that was how old people looked at you.

Apart from the incident with Denzil, Billy was good with his animals. He understood them and they understood him. They didn't tell him what to do, because they knew he was in charge of them. Even if they could talk, they wouldn't tell him what to do – like people did. Mr Wu at the chip shop was always giving him orders, telling him he hadn't done something right, and so Billy wasn't that upset about being sacked, except he would miss the money. Even if he went for an interview with Miss Palmerston and got the job, he could see himself regretting the move, for it would mean commitment and discipline and routine and strangers telling him what to do. Still, at least he wouldn't come home reeking of chip fat or raw fish. Everyone on

Mr Wu's staff had to wear a silly hat; probably at the water place he wouldn't have to go about in a silly hat. Maybe he would ring the number and hear what Miss Palmerston sounded like. Then Mum would be pleased, for a while, anyway. He didn't like it when she told him off. If he spoke to the lady and didn't like how she sounded, he could always say something to her that would discourage her from considering him, and then he could tell his mum he had tried and unfortunately failed.

Leila Smart, loading the washing machine, turned as her son pulled out a kitchen chair. "You're up at last. Did you do that room?"

"I'll do it later. Maybe I'll ring that number."

She drew herself up and stared at him. "Really?"

"Yes, Mum. Only can I have some breakfast first?"

"No, do it now, while you're thinking about it." She handed him the phone. "I'll stay in the room, just pretend I'm not here."

"So what do I say?"

"Just tell them you've seen the advertisement and you'd like to know more about the vacancy. Take it from there."

"But I didn't actually see it – the advertisement."

"Billy, they won't know that. That's irrelevant. Ask this Miss Palmerston for some more information, only don't start by asking her about the money. Whatever they're paying, it's more than you're getting now."

"I could tell her I live nearby. So she'd think I'd be reliable."

Leila sighed, averting her eyes. Billy, she knew, would never be reliable. Billy didn't have a reliable bone in his body. You could always rely on Billy to be unreliable.

"Okay. If that comes up. If they offer to send you an application form, say you'll go in and collect it. Show you're keen, but not desperate." She sat down, supporting her face in upraised fists. "Do you understand me, Billy?"

"I think so."

"And if she asks you something you're not sure about,

take a deep breath before you answer, to think about it, and ask her to make it clearer if you need to. Don't blurt out something daft."

"What if she asks about where I worked before?"

"Then tell her. Don't go into a long rigmarole, just answer the question."

"Supposing they want – "

"Billy, don't! Just ring the number. Be focused. Then at least we know you've tried." She stood up and opened the cupboard under the sink. "I'm making you some breakfast. Now ring Miss Palmerston."

He waited, hearing his own heartbeat, while the receptionist connected him. Miss Palmerston sounded younger than he had anticipated, leading him to suppose that she was selective rather than elderly. She asked his age and full name.

"Wait a minute…aren't you the young man whose snake ate Mrs Starling's cat? It was in the Gazette."

"That was an accident," Billy said.

"It may have been for you, for the snake it was deliberate."

Billy swallowed and felt sweat gathering around the handset. "Does that mean you don't want me to apply?"

Leila, standing opposite him, hissed, "Don't say that!"

"Mr Smart, I don't know yet whether I want you to apply or not. I don't know anything about you. Don't worry about the snake, it has nothing to do with the job."

"Thank you, Miss."

"Now then. Are you in employment now?"

"No."

"I see. Where have you worked before?"

Billy told her about the chip shop and being a paper boy. Miss Palmerston made vaguely sympathetic noises, her responses vacillating between the non-committal and the unconvinced.

"And why did you leave the fish shop, Billy? Is it all right if I call you Billy?"

"Yes, Miss."

"Billy, my name is Miss Palmerston."

"Yes, I know. It was in the window."

"Quite. So about the fish shop?"

"Mr Wu, he asked me to leave."

"Did he now."

"Not exactly now. It was about a week ago."

"Yes, very well, I understand. Billy, why were you dismissed?"

"What?"

"I'm asking you why Mr Wu told you to go."

"Because – he said I was late. Mainly when Denzil escaped."

"Who's Denzil?"

"Denzil, he's my pet python."

"Ah yes. I think I'm getting the picture now. You were late for work because you had to look for your snake. Is that right?"

"That's right."

"So did you tell this Mr Wu why you were late?"

"Well, actually, I didn't go in that day."

"Right. Did you explain the problem to Mr Wu?"

"Yes, but he sort of didn't want to listen."

"Hmm. Why was that, do you think?"

"I suppose because, well, I'd been late once or twice before."

Miss Palmerston sighed heavily and moved the phone to her other hand. "Billy, are you telling me, when you worked at the fish shop, you were habitually late? Is that what you're saying?"

"I'm sorry about it, Miss – Miss Palmerston."

"Yes, well, you should have apologized to Mr Wu rather than to me – don't you think?"

"I did apologize. Then he sacked me."

"Okay. Look, Billy, I'm willing to give you a chance. I'd like you to attend for an interview. Then we can get to know each other better."

"You don't mind about me being late, then?"

His mother rolled her eyes to the ceiling, shaking her

head.

"On the contrary, Mr Smart, I mind very much about lateness, but I'm prepared to discuss this problem with you at interview. Umm…can you come along on Friday at eleven? You'll be meeting Mr Priddle and myself."

"Is that eleven o'clock in the morning?"

Miss Palmerston paused to draw breath. "No, Billy, I mean eleven o'clock at night, when it's pitch-dark and we've all gone home. Of course, eleven in the morning. Is that confirmed?"

"Yes, right. I'll be on time. I only live across the road."

"That, Billy, will stand you in good stead."

He switched off the phone and swallowed hard, tasting a nervous bile on his tongue. His mother was cracking eggs and layering bacon in a pan, the heartening smell of cooking already drifting across the table.

"Done it, Mum."

She turned to face him, a spatula in her hand. "I heard. Well done. So you've got an interview."

"Friday at eleven in the morning."

"You be ready to leave here at quarter to. People are impressed by punctuality."

"Can I have a sausage?"

"I'll put you one in. A good boy sausage," she added, with a smile.

Billy's stomach was still fluttering. He seldom used the telephone. He had never had a job where he was required to answer the phone or ring anybody. If he got the job at the waterworks, they would probably expect him to be familiar with the phone. Perhaps that would form part of his training. The more he thought about the job, and particularly the interview, the more nervous he became. Even eating his breakfast would be difficult. He wished he had just asked for cornflakes.

He fiddled with the phone to make sure he had switched it off. Then he sat on his hands and pulled them free again. Leila wrapped a hot plate in a teacloth and placed it in front of him.

"There. That's a working man's breakfast," she said.

"Mum, I haven't got the job yet."

She flipped the cloth over her shoulder and came to stand beside him. With a warm, fragrant hand, she brushed the hair from his brow. "You will," she said, "you will."

# Chapter 41

## *Number 30: Stephen J. Kettering-Barclay*

Mr Kettering-Barclay was sitting in a lightweight canvas chair on the front lawn, bare-footed but for his carpet slippers, wearing a bottle-green cable-knit sweater over a pair of knee-length khaki shorts, supporting his feet on the tub of an upturned wheelbarrow. The early sun highlighted the stark frailty of his lower legs, one white as a whittled stick, the other almost gruesomely mechanical, its sun-polished metalwork reflecting the light in blinking silver sparks.

Mrs Stirrup paused at the gate, staring. "Why are you sitting in the front garden?"

"Because it's a nice day," he replied, frowning.

"Most people sit round the back."

"Yes, well, most people can do what they like. I like to sit at the front, where I can watch the world go by."

Mrs Stirrup turned to scan the street, as if looking for the world. "Strikes me folks are more likely to be looking at you than you looking at them."

"Let them look. It's my garden and a free country."

"It's quite unusual, that's all – to see someone sat in their front garden."

Mr Kettering-Barclay curled his lip thoughtfully. "Yes, I suppose you're right. Why is that, do you think?"

"I dunno. I expect people like to be private."

"Indeed. And so, dear lady, this morning I have graciously consented to be placed on public display."

He allowed himself the self-satisfied glimmer of a surreptitious smile as Mrs Stirrup moved away, vanishing behind next-door's hedge. Adjusting the position of his ankles on the wheelbarrow, he reached down for the flask of strong tea he had propped against the leg of the chair and carefully unscrewed the cap. Perhaps, he thought, he should have brought a hat with him, for the sun was finding uncomfortable access through his thinning hair. There being not the slightest whisper of a breeze, he pulled a handkerchief from his pocket and laid it over the top of his head. It was a black handkerchief and he imagined himself scowling under beetling brows at a doomed convict, solemnly informing him that he would be taken away and hanged by the neck until he was dead.

He took a generous swig of hot tea. This was living. This was revival. A sudden itch in his shorts required scratching, so he plunged his free hand under his waistband and let his fingers scrabble in his pubic hair. Ah, such relief, such tactile beauty! And this small act, inevitably, brought him to recall yesterday's visit to the pale and pulchritudinous Miss McIver, and the way she had massaged lilac-scented gel into his groin and eased him into a glorious other place. It was the most exciting experience he had known since being torpedoed.

He had asked to see her again. She had nodded and helped him re-attach his prosthesis. He wondered if she would ask him about the war, but then he realized that it was ancient history to her and he decided not to initiate a discussion on the subject, for fear of seeming a bore. She had looked after him and brought him pleasure, so she deserved better than to be stifling yawns beneath the stultifying tide of an old man's tedious ramblings.

Stephen, with no shirt under his sweater, lifted the crew neck and inhaled the lingering aroma of aloe vera from the girl's shower tray. Not in months had he been so clean. A mat of white hair overlaid his ribs and his good leg, too, was furred with a snowy down that gleamed softly in the sunlight. Irish Willow, eh? Well, she was Irish, for sure, though not so very willowy. The instantaneous elation he felt as he recalled her was quickly tempered with a more sobering reflection, for he was an old man with part of one leg missing and a cadaverous, wrinkled body, hardly an enticing prospect for a young woman contemplating intimacy with a mature gentleman. All he had to offer her was money, of which fortunately he had more than enough, for there was little in his orbit to spend it on. Occasionally, in port from the *Daedalus*, he had joined his shipmates in search of female company, but these exploits were invariably tinged with a murky sense of the carelessly sordid; whereas in the house with Irish Willow he had found himself bathed in a glowing, rapturous rejuvenation, a personal rediscovery at once enthralling and overpowering. It was as if, that afternoon, Miss McIver had thrown open the door not only to her modest home but also to another, brighter corridor in the old man's life.

Disconnecting his prosthesis, he let the appendage fall into the grass and, leaning back, studied his pink stump. In that moment, he thought about courage. As the *Daedalus* rolled on to her side, mortally wounded, bravery burst in the blood in a desperate fight for survival. It was that, or go down before the ship, a frothing, jibbering wreck, stripped naked of reason or decency. It was courage forced upon each man in the face of death. Though he had not spoken to Irish Willow about his past, he had divined enough of her own situation to identify a particular brand of courage in that secretive endeavour, a resolve fuelled not by a wild hope of survival but by the measured need of it. She would, of bleak necessity, open the door to a total stranger and entrust her body to him, knowing the risks entailed, in order to protect her child and pursue an uncertain salvation. Very well, she could choose to expel a client who proved himself unwelcome, but there was always the risk that he might take offence and resort to violence. Of that likelihood, she could make no prior assessment. In her line of work, the newcomer's position was offered without preliminary meeting or interview, while his scheduled dismissal, though hardly peremptory, lay in similarly uncharted territory. Stephen thought it a brave world.

"See you've taken your leg off." Mrs Stirrup was back at the gate.

"It itches when it gets hot," he told her sullenly.

She nodded sympathetically. "I expect."

They stared at each other.

"Do you want something?" he asked.

"Sorry?"

"I asked if you wanted something."

"Such as?"

He blinked. "It's me asking the question."

"You're a funny old chap, and no mistake. Here." She reached into her shopping bag and withdrew a small package folded in brown paper. "I got you this."

She opened the gate and walked on to the lawn. "Before it melts." She handed him the cool, damp parcel.

Stephen unwrapped the gift and found a choc-ice inside. Mrs Stirrup put down her bag and stood with her hands on her hips.

"This is – you're very kind," he said. "I shall eat it now."

"Well, either that or I'll put it in your fridge for you. It won't keep in the sun."

He pulled the ice-cream wrapper off and bit into the chocolate. "Delicious. Very kind. Much appreciated."

Mrs Stirrup was studying his wounded leg. "Was that wartime?"

Stephen glanced at his stump, thumbing his nose reflectively. "Merchant Navy," he said. "I was a lucky one. I didn't get killed."

His inquisitor nodded. "That's one way of looking at it. Sort of puts a different perspective on kindness, though, doesn't it? I gave you an ice-cream and you gave away half your leg. But for that, reckon we'd have all starved." She picked up her bag. "Saved our lives, you lot. Don't let no-one forget it."

Chocolate dribbled down Stephen's chin. He squinted in the sunlight and his eyes grew glassy with tears. He thought of all the lives he was supposed to have saved, most of a lifetime ago, and then he thought about good men like Glaister and the stoker and the others whose

235

names he couldn't remember or had never known, men whose lives he had beaten into nothingness, whose families and loved-ones he had robbed. The war had spared him then to crush him afterwards. He lowered his head and wept silently in the sunshine.

The grass beneath him seemed to float, seen through his shimmering eyes, like the undulating waves of a green sea, and the vision bloomed in his brain, imprinting scenes from the past, the barnacled hulk of the *Daedalus* on her side in the depths with her cargo of sleeping, fish-nibbled souls, ghostly-white in the darkness, their silent world webbed with the tissue-thin music of the current stirring the pale planets of plankton beads drifting in black space. Stephen moved his damaged leg and squeezed the blood in his thighs. He asked himself: Why? Why, when he had fed fine, honest men to the ocean and the sharks? Why this small physical impairment, a thing of so little consequence? Was this, perhaps, a mere down-payment, a blemish for him to think about while he waited for a greater punishment, a mortal debt to be called in? Now he felt that such an event might be his moment of supreme closure, his manner of escape from a terrible haunting.

He would need someone to help him, of course. He could not do it alone. Somehow it would seem right and just only if another person were to send him on that final journey, as though that agent might fittingly represent the lives of those whose loss could yet be avenged. There was still time to pay. Then, for sure, the ghosts would pass on and he would be at peace. In this world, that resolution could never happen; but in the next place, surely. Stephen licked the ice-cream stick until it was clean and drying in the sun and then he thought of how the task might be achieved and at what time and in what place. He dried his tears and smiled and steeled himself in every fibre and sinew to prepare for the journey.

# Chapter 42

## *Number 15: Aisling McIver*

A day later, she heard from RobRoy 51 again. He telephoned her, saying he hoped he hadn't woken the baby.

"That's all right, my love. She's dead to the world, bless her. So what can I do for you?"

"It's Aisling, isn't it?"

"That's my name, yes."

"Aisling, can I sleep with you?"

She hesitated, uncertain what he was asking. "How do you mean, exactly?"

"Well, we got on fine, I think."

"Surely."

"So – uh – I wanted to know if you ever see guys overnight and, if so, what you'd be charging. Your Profile doesn't mention overnight."

"No, well, see, I have the baby, as you know."

"I know. We don't have to wake the baby. If you need to get up to see to her, that'd be fine, of course. It's only what I'd expect."

Such a fair, reasonable man, she thought. She remembered his manly gentleness, his neatly trimmed nails and sweetly minty breath. If only they were all like that.

"When would you be wanting to come?"

"Would tonight be too soon? If I came about nine and maybe brought us a take-away. Then I'd stay until about seven and just slip quietly away. You wouldn't even have to get up."

She laughed. "I'm always up before seven. I'm a mother, remember."

"Well, yes, I understand. Of course I understand."

"I'm sure you do. It's Robert, isn't it?"

237

"You remembered."

She was expecting someone at twelve-thirty, then she was free. To sleep with a man again, actually sleep with him, might be something she'd enjoy, the glorious protective warmth of it, the *thereness,* which could only come from intimate closeness to another human being. In all the world, she knew no sensation remotely like it. If the experience did not cure all ills, it at least seemed to render them inconsequentially manageable. Neamh's daddy had been the last. Bad memories, good riddance. Here, now, was a man who wanted something more than half an hour's fumble on a rumpled towel on the bed, something better than a slippery, selfish path to gratification while he checked his watch and tried not to fart.

"This is not something I normally do, Robert."

"Is that a no?"

"No. I mean, no, it's not a no."

"So you'll consider it?"

"I'm considering it now. If it's what you want."

"Oh, it's absolutely what I want. All you have to do is say yes and tell me how much you'd ask."

He heard her small, submissive sigh.

"Five hundred," she said. She had plucked the figure out of the air. Five hundred pounds to go to bed and get up again. It sounded like a fortune.

"Five hundred? That's cheap."

"You calling me cheap?" she asked, poking her tongue in her cheek.

"Most certainly not. If that's your price…"

"It is. Do we have a deal?"

"We do. I'll come at nine. We shall dine at nine with wine."

"Robert, you don't have to do that. Just turn up."

"I'd like to do this properly. Please. Do you like Indian?"

"I like anything. I like nice men. So come round and be a nice man."

"Aisling, put the oven on. Ten minutes to you from the

238

restaurant, the food'll cool. Okay?"

He was punctual, of course. From a plastic bag he unloaded a chilled bottle of New Zealand Sauvignon Blanc together with an aromatic pack of onion bhajees, lamb dansak, mixed biryani, pilau rice and a huge flap of nan bread. A black leather bag hung from his shoulder.

She pulled the nan from its envelope, grinning. "Like an elephant's ear," she said.

"And how's Neamh?" he asked her, wiping moisture from the wine bottle.

"Well, she won't be having curry, that's for sure."

"I know. I was just asking."

He carried the bag to the kitchen and returned with two glasses.

"She's fine. Thank you, by the way, for leaving the money on her cot. That was kind."

He shrugged. The food was in the oven, warming up. Already the spicy smell was making her hungry. She had never entertained a client this late before. This felt strange. She wondered about this man. Was he all he seemed? *Looking for Mr Goodbar.* She remembered the movie, its jarring, desperate finale. How could anybody ever truly know another human being? For that, even a lifetime was too brief. She had known this man for an hour. In exchange for a pile of cash, she would pay him with her trust.

Robert produced a white envelope from his jacket pocket and placed it on the table next to the bottle. "For you," he said quietly. "And thank you."

She opened the envelope and flicked her thumb over the notes. "You don't have to thank me. I've done nothing yet."

"You're entertaining me. You're giving up your time for me." He poured the wine. "You should count it."

"I'm sure it's all there."

"You can't be sure. You should count it."

She withdrew the wad and counted it, twenty-five twenty-pound notes in an elastic band.

"Now put it somewhere safe," he told her.

She stood up and took it to the kitchen to put with the other money. In the morning, she would need to go to the bank, just leave a hundred in the jar.

Aisling brought warmed plates and conversation was suspended while they gorged themselves on the food until the last morsel, pausing now and then to drain the wine to the dregs. In her cot by the window, Neamh slept, snuffling like a puppy.

Robert mopped his plate with a last corner of nan bread. "That was good. And yours?"

"Loved it. Thank you. And the wine's made me feel relaxed, maybe a little sleepy."

"Okay. So what do you want to do?" He pulled back his chair. "I can wash up if you like."

"Robert, please. You're not here to do that."

"Meaning?"

"You've given me dinner and wine and a stack of money. I don't expect you to be washing dishes as well."

"I know you don't expect it. It's just I – "

"Why don't you just tell me what you'd like to do, eh? In the circumstances, it's not me calling the shots."

He rested his elbows on the table, nodded and looked into her eyes. She met his gaze for a moment, then turned away.

"What time do you usually go to bed?" he asked.

"Oh, any time. Probably about now. You know, early to bed, early to rise."

"Do you have a dishwasher?"

She shook her head, laughing. "You're impossible."

"We can't leave these," he said, waving a hand over the plates.

"Right." She stood up. "I guess you can help me rinse them and stack them in the dishwasher. If it makes you happy."

"Just being here makes me happy," he said. "You make me happy."

"Really? Most of the guys I see, they want more than

sitting at the table and doing the washing up to make them happy."

"Point taken. And do you see a lot of guys?"

"Robert, I think that's my business. Let's say I'm cautiously selective." She took the plates as he rinsed them and loaded them in the machine. "I see who I think I might like. Sometimes I get it wrong. When that happens, I don't see them again, my call."

"Then I'm glad to have been selected."

"My pleasure."

As she bent down to straighten a bowl at the back of the rack, he ran his hand lightly over her bottom, letting it linger there for a few warm seconds.

Rising, she turned to face him, linking her arms around his neck. "Now that's more like it," she said. "That tells me it's time."

"Time?"

"Time for a little organic pleasure, my friend. That's really why you're here, isn't it? Or have I completely misjudged you, RobRoy? Don't tell me – you get off on chicken biryani."

He laughed and kissed her moistly on the lips, feeling her hand stray down from his shoulder to brush the front of his trousers. "Let's go up," he said.

Robert picked up his shoulder bag and took it upstairs with him. Probably some toiletries, she thought, and perhaps a change of underwear. She had men's toilet items in the bathroom, anyway, but he need not have known that. She saw him as composed, *together,* but not worldly. He still wore a wedding ring, she noticed, and she wondered how much he must miss his departed wife. Occasionally, when married men came to her, they removed their rings before sex, as though by that device they were somehow making their behaviour less of an infidelity. One man even left his ring behind on the bedside table and had sheepishly to come back for it.

He put his bag on the floor under the window and crouched to empty it. Her eyes widened in amused amazement, as he pulled out an immaculate pair of pyjama trousers and tossed them nonchalantly to the foot of the bed.

"Now will you be needing those?" she asked him, suppressing a smile.

He made a doubtful, nervous face, and she hoped she had not embarrassed him.

"I'm not too comfortable sleeping naked," he said. "An age-old habit, I suppose. I may put them on after… well, I could put them on later, you see."

She touched his cheek. "Robert, you just do whatever you like. You're buying my time and my understanding."

Perhaps, she thought, that assurance was a little disingenuous. He was buying her body, surely. How could she leave that element out of the equation? It would be ridiculous for either of them to pretend that this was merely a social visit, two friends enjoying a sleep-over. The meaning of this, the objective, was itself as naked as their bodies were soon to be.

Though not surprised, Aisling was moved by his gentleness, reminding her that for a few of those who came to play with her, intimacy and sex were not synonymous, sensuality not to be confused with the rawness of sexuality. As Robert lay beside her, enjoying her fragrant warmth, so the all-pervading aura of intimacy was itself a kind of conquest, a life-force strata layered alongside the lesser dimension of mechanical sex. For Robert Jamieson, it was the human closeness, the feeling of *oneness,* he craved.

Slowly, tenderly, he helped her undress, quietly patient as he unfastened buttons and clips and helped her fold her clothes into a neat pile. He would allow nothing of hers to be thrown on the floor or left tangled in the bedclothes.

"Leave the light on for a while," he said. "I want to see you."

"You want to see me?"

"Yes. Is that so wrong?"

"Of course it's not wrong. If this - us – is not wrong,

then nothing is wrong."

"We are not wrong," he said, "we are beautiful. You are beautiful."

They kissed and lay facing each other on top of the duvet, their arms and legs entwined. She waited for him to pleasure her, but he lay quite still and let himself grow against her and moved hardly at all, while she held him tightly and inhaled the scent of him like an ether.

"Just tell me," she said, after a while.

"Tell you what?"

"Tell me what you'd like to do." She nuzzled his neck. "Anything."

"Aisling, I would like to lie next to you naked and be close and warm and full of contentment. That's what I would like to do."

"I think perhaps you're a strange man," she told him.

"Oh? Why strange?"

"Because – because you've paid me five hundred pounds for sex and yet you aren't asking me for what everyone expects. You aren't asking me for anything."

"Maybe because I'm not everyone. I'm my own man." He rolled over and sank his head in the pillow. "In any case, we have all night. We can make this moment last until the dawn, if we want."

Aisling stroked the inside of his thigh. "Until the dawn. Sure, I like the idea of that."

Before midnight, they slept. The curtains were parted and a silver shaft of moonlight sliced across the bed, painting them in a still-life chiaroscuro. Aisling woke once, lifting her head to listen for any sound from Neamh, but the child lay silent, and the only sounds in the room were the faint humming of the fridge from downstairs and the gentle cadence of Robert's breathing. She smiled as she saw that he had put on his pyjama pants, as though the privacy of sleep required some modest degree of propriety. The top button of his waistband was undone and she slipped her hand inside and curled her fingers lightly around him, but all she felt was a moist softness and he did not wake. She planted a feather-light kiss on his bare chest.

At five she was fully awake, lying on her back, staring at the ceiling. When she threw out a lazy arm, she felt only a cooling space. Digging both elbows into the mattress, she levered herself upright and saw Robert's silhouette at the brightening window. He was bending over Neamh's cot.

"What on earth are you doing?" she called.

He turned and raised a languid hand to her. "It's all right. I heard her make a little noise, so I got up to see if she was comfortable."

"You should have woken me, if you were worried. I'm her mother."

"I know that. I was only – concerned."

Aisling sat up with her legs folded against her. "Robert, please. You're not here to do that. You don't have to be anxious for my baby."

"I didn't mean any harm."

"Of course not. But don't you see – this is not part of the arrangement?"

He came to perch on the edge of the bed. "So, am I exceeding my authority? Is that it?"

"It's not a matter of authority. It's simply – well, I'm not comfortable with you looking out for my child, that's all. This, this whole thing, has to be about you and me, we need to narrow it down. D'you get me?"

He sat there, nodding slowly, rhythmically, absorbing her admonishment, assessing the extent of his transgression. His pyjama pants had slid down over his hips, revealing a tangle of hair.

"Oh God! Now I've upset you." She leaned towards him and reached out a hand. "Don't take it the wrong way. You're a lovely man, a real nice guy. We mustn't spoil this."

"I was just looking out for you. I didn't want to wake you."

"No, I understand." She patted the bed where his

indentation still creased the duvet. "Come back to bed now. We still have time."

He swung round to meet her, pulling off his pyjamas.

"God love you," she murmured.

They still had an hour left before she needed to get up, which was all the time she normally gave her clients, anyway. Calmly, she accepted his weight and lay in a starfish shape, watching the way his lips pulsed as he moved, as if he were sucking something.

"I know we don't love each other," he said, panting, "but I'd like to think we are making love, not just having sex. That's how I think of you."

She gripped his shoulders. Her eyes were very wide. "Yes," she said.

Afterwards he wore a patina of perspiration on his face and brow. Aisling dabbed him with a damp baby wipe, caring for him as if he were a child.

Downstairs, clad only in her dressing gown, she made him bacon, eggs and toast.

"You're good to me," he said, rubbing his hands together.

"Neamh thanks you for your generous donation," she told him, as she stroked the back of his hand.

At the door, she kissed him on the lips and made it last a while. A taste of bacon lingered there. Grinning artfully, he slid a hand inside her gown and eased two fingers between her thighs.

"Go on with you," she said, slapping him playfully on the arm.

"Aisling, can I see you again?"

"Oh, I'll think about it," she said, smiling.

From the window, she watched him walking slowly down the road, hitching the leather bag on to his shoulder. Over her head, Neamh began to cry.

# Chapter 43

## *Number 33: Minnie Starling*

Minnie ran her hand over the patch where Raj had filled the hole and applied new plaster. The colour was a good match and the finish was smooth. He seemed to have done a decent job. He had even put the towels and sheets back and tidied them up. Maybe he wasn't such a bad man. It was a pity he smelled of curry, but that wasn't really his fault; in his house, that might be all they had. Minnie wondered whether the surprise she had in store for Raj at the party was quite the one he deserved, but it was too late to change her plans now. She imagined the shock on that mahogany-coloured face when she revealed her specialty.

She was feeling rather stiff this morning and it took her several minutes to totter into the bedroom, where the contents of the battered box lay loosely in her handbag by the dressing table. There were five drawers in the dressing table: a wide central drawer and two square ones at either side. She opened the top left drawer and took out a pink velvet bag with a drawstring neck. Unpicking the top, she carefully drew out a sparkling necklace and laid it on a soft mat in front of her. The jewellery had belonged to her mother, a wedding love token from Minnie's father, so it was more than a hundred years old. As the story went, the groom had presented his bride with this glittering gift on their wedding night, soon after he had returned from a secretive courier commission in Vienna. He did not enlighten his wife as to the true value of the necklace, and this reticence had led her to believe that the stones embedded in it were, as she put it, 'simple but attractive jube-jubes'. Not until Minnie had shown the necklace to Charlie, half a lifetime later, a disclosure encouraging him to take it to a London valuer, was the item's actual worth made known. The inset stones were diamonds and amethysts, arranged in silver, and the valuer's estimate was approximately twenty-eight thousand pounds. In Minnie's house, there was nothing remotely as valuable.

For now, the beautiful necklace would have to reside outside its bag. Minnie scooped up the pieces from her handbag and secreted them in the bag, pulling the neck tight. That would do. She would not go to the party without her handbag. Smiling mysteriously, she replaced the necklace in the drawer beneath a pile of handkerchiefs.

Once Charlie has asked her: "Gran, would you ever consider selling this?" The necklace lay in his hand, the stones draped over his fingers.

"Selling it? Now what would I want to do that for?"

"Ages ago they valued it. What's it worth today? Forty grand, maybe?"

"Don't talk to me about money, Charlie. If it's worth that much, that's your inheritance."

"I just thought – you could get out of here, put the money down on a nice house."

"Charlie, don't be ridiculous. I won't get a house for forty thousand, and who'll give me a mortgage at my age?"

"You could afford to move into a residential place where someone would look after you and you'd have no worries about maintenance."

"Yes, and all that money would be gone in a year. Charlie, Charlie, use your head."

"I just thought…"

"No doubt you did. Take my advice, stop thinking, Charlie. You'll soon feel all the better for it."

The conversation about money came back to her when the letterbox rattled and she stooped to pick up an envelope from the mat. Inside was a letter from Roland James, curtly informing her that, with effect from 1st October, he was to increase her rent by 15 per cent. She put on her glasses, sat at the kitchen table and read the letter twice. Then she reached for the phone.

"It's Mrs Starling here. I've received your letter about

theft."

"I'm sorry?"

"You're telling me you're about to steal more of my pension."

"Ah. You see, Mrs Starling, like you, I have to make ends meet. Last year's increase was only six per cent."

"And what am I getting for the money, Mr James? Cupboard doors falling off, back door not fitting properly, gutter hanging loose. Shall I go on?"

"Surely Raj fixed the gutter when he mended the hole?"

"You called him back, remember, before he had time. There's still water running down the window."

"He had to stop a leak, Mrs Starling."

"A leak? What about my leak? I've got a leak all down my window. And a bigger leak in my purse, if you have anything to do with it."

She heard him sigh and draw breath. What was he supposed to do? How could he argue with a 99-year-old woman? He would check Raj's worksheet for the day and see if that gutter could be repaired this afternoon. He clawed at his face with his fingers, enlarging his tired eyes.

"Mrs Starling, all my tenants are receiving the same letter. You're not being singled out."

"So you're robbing everyone."

"I'm not robbing anyone, my dear."

"Oh, I am not your dear, Mr James, believe me. I could just become your nemesis."

Roland James suspected that the position had already been confirmed. His eyes were smarting in frustration. There had to be better ways of earning a living. Saints preserve us, he thought, from sweet old ladies. Age had the unfortunate habit of casting a protective shield around them, just when the popular misconception was that they were terminally vulnerable.

"Tell you what, Mrs Starling."

"What?"

"I'll have a look at Raj's schedule this week and see if I can move him round to you for a full day, so he can mend the gutter and whatever else. Okay? Anything more you can think of while he's there, any small jobs, you can get him to do them as well. How does that sound?"

Minnie rolled her head wearily from side to side. "Mr James, what does it matter how it sounds? All that counts is seeing it done. That's what I never see. I don't care what the work sounds like."

"Figure of speech, Mrs Starling, figure of speech. On this, you have to trust me."

"Yes, I'm at your mercy, aren't I? So you'll get him to spend the day here?"

"I will."

"Will he want lunch?"

"Raj likes his sandwiches. He'll bring his box. Half an hour and he'll be back on the job. If you can maybe make him a drink…"

"Hasn't he got a flask?"

"Hasn't he - ?" James ground his teeth until they hurt. "I don't know, Mrs Starling, really. Let's not get bogged down in the detail, eh? I'm going to speak to him and come back to you with a date. It'll be soon. Trust me."

Minnie gave due consideration to trusting Roland James and, for that matter, Raj the fixer. There was no precedent for such a concession, since neither of them had ever demonstrated any trustworthiness before. This was a late stage for breaking new ground.

"So my rent rise is inevitable, it's non-negotiable?"

"I'm afraid so. I'm not trying to get rich, I'm trying to survive. Costs are going up all the time and the least I must do is keep pace."

"Yes, I'm hoping to achieve much the same, Mr James, but you're racing me."

"Mrs Starling, honestly, I can only – "

"Never mind, Mr James. I'm tired now. I'm ringing off. Just do what you said and do it soon."

So Roland James was attempting to survive. She thought about that: survival. She had survived very nearly one hundred years. Two world wars had been fought in

249

that time and there had been wars fought in this house as well. Her marriage to Henry had been menaced, and finally aborted, by his war with dementia and a swift, powerful bout of pneumonia, dispatching him to the cottage hospital from which he never returned. Daughter Maisie, once the rosy-cheeked apple of Henry's eye, had fallen headlong down the stairs, unsighted while carrying a tea tray, when visiting her mother at Christmas, whacking her skull into three pieces on the hall coatstand. In Intensive Care, she battled to keep her bruised brain messaging the neural and orthopaedic dislocations of her mangled body, but blood and pulp alone were not fuel enough. Compared with these disasters, of course, her tedious *contretemps* with the landlord and his Mister Fixit were small distractions, but still they irked her, rendering her a woman maligned and malignant. Now Minnie Starling was too old to be forgiving, burdened with too much to forgive. On the near horizon she could see her own history in the making.

No doubt they would invite her to make a short speech on her special day. Well, no matter, she would make one anyway. Perhaps she would scribble a few notes to cue her as the babble subsided and the hush of expectation settled. For sure, there were things to be said, people to thank and unthank, reminiscences to be aired upon the breath of a lifetime. It would be a day such as Paradise had never known.

Half an hour later, Roland James telephoned.

"Mr James, don't tell me, you're reducing my rent by forty per cent."

"Umm…no, Mrs Starling, I'm afraid not. Unfortunately that won't be possible."

"I see. You know, I was always told you shouldn't express regret for your own regulations."

"Maybe not. But look – I'm getting Raj over to you tomorrow, nine o'clock on the dot. He'll be with you all day."

"I can hardly wait. I'm all a-shiver, Mr James."

"So let's hope we can see an end to these prevarications, eh? We'll do the work and you pay the rent."

Minnie rolled her eyes and put the phone down. She could not convince herself that a miracle was about to happen. She did not have the confidence. She was not even confident enough to sustain the hope. In that regard, age had indeed wearied her. In the fragile realm of trust, she could no long trust herself to be trusting.

# Chapter 44

## *Number 22: Mr and Mrs Slocombe*

Arthur Slocombe sat by the back door, preening. In a deftly circular motion, he rubbed one paw over his white nose, conscientiously taking his time. He had eaten his breakfast nuts and taken a few sips of water, but his hunger was not entirely appeased and he fancied some greens. The square flap in the door allowed him easy access to and from the garden, although if he waited patiently on the mat, his mother would often open the door to let him out, warning him, as she did so, to be careful in that uncontrolled space, where there was no-one to protect him from danger. Danger meant foxes, sneaking in from the fields beyond the bottom fence. Foxes had the uncharitable habit of eating rabbits like Arthur, or at least clamping them in their jaws and carrying them away to some dark, feral oblivion. There was also the hazard presented by next-door's cat, Charlemagne, who liked to play with mice and birds and had once expressed an interest in a romping altercation with Arthur under the hedge. On that occasion, Arthur had declined the invitation and escaped by a rapid burst of acceleration towards the rabbit-flap. Back in the kitchen, panting wildly, he had watched as the cat's paw appeared through the aperture, ineffectually swishing the air. Arthur's mother, standing at the sink, had observed the incident and quickly thrown a plastic cup at the offending part of Charlemagne, who had immediately retreated. Since the cat had never again sought access by that route, it was to be assumed that the message had been received and understood.

Arthur hopped into the garden and felt the sun's warmth on his back. The dewy lawn moistened his feet and made his nostrils tingle. A tapping sound stopped him in his tracks and he looked up to see his father knocking on the shed window. Straining to discern the man's face, he saw that the face was mobile, the mouth opening and closing, but through the glass it was not possible to hear what was being said and, in any case, Arthur would not have been able to comprehend the words, even had they not been soundless, for he was a rabbit, hopelessly handicapped by limited intelligence.

It occurred to Arthur that his father, having seen his young son loose in the garden, was anxious lest an attack should be mounted on his vegetables. Alf Slocombe was very proud of his vegetable patch, which the man who cut the grass and tended the plants had dutifully cultivated into a rectangular bed sufficiently well stocked with cabbages, lettuces, onions and carrots for Alf and his lady to avoid the purchase of supermarket vegetables. Regrettably for them, it was not possible to avoid the incursion into the same area of Arthur Slocombe, whose appetite for fresh carrots and lettuce leaves was enormous and insatiable.

Arthur hopped out of sight of the window, hoping that his father would not bother to follow him. He seldom saw Alf in the garden nowadays, though that lady who lived with him in the shed did sometimes come out and pick some flowers or peer at a cabbage. Quite why his mother and father no longer lived together in the big house, he could not fathom. He had heard some kind of argument a long time ago and his dinner had been unusually late that day, after which the two people had seemed not to like each other much any more and there had been a lot of coming and going and crashing and banging in the shed and the strange lady spending more and more time around the garden. One day, he remembered, he was munching grass in the garden when he noticed the shed door open, so he decided to investigate, and peeped over the sill of the wooden door to see what was happening inside. The strange lady was in there on her own, sitting on the bed, and she didn't have any clothes on, none at all, and up between her legs she was doing something funny with a carrot, and when she looked down and saw Arthur in the doorway she squealed and threw a brush at him and he scampered away. That was the only time he tried to go in the shed.

Against the tall hedge at the bottom of the garden, the vegetable patch was still in morning shade and Arthur hoped that once he had moved out of the sun his activities would be inconspicuous. He ran down behind the shed and jumped over a row of onions, landing beside a large, pale green cabbage with ragged holes in its leaves. He crouched low and began nibbling a cabbage leaf, but it was leathery and tasted unpleasant. A few feet away, a long line of vivid green lettuces sparkled with dewdrops, beckoning him like jewelled bouquets. He darted over the soft earth and settled in a hollow next to a plump lettuce, baring his teeth in readiness. The lettuce was cold and crisp and delicious. One of the leaves was decorated with yellowish worm things, which Arthur would take care to avoid, for he had inadvertently eaten one of these before and found it mushy and disgusting. He paused occasionally to look over his shoulder, in case the strange lady might be about to shoo him away, then resumed his breakfast, selecting a second leaf and drinking the chilled water from the stem. Lettuce was Arthur's favourite. Carrots were good, too, but not as good as lettuces. He thought he should leave plenty of carrots for the strange lady to put between her legs. He wondered if she and his father possibly ate the carrots as well, though probably not if they had been up the lady's legs.

Before moving on, Arthur left a pile of dark pellets in the soil. Then he realized that by this act his intrusion would be revealed, so he leaned forward and scooted his hind legs vigorously backwards until the evidence was covered with earth. Disliking mud on his feet, he hopped on to the grass again and scuttled round and round in rapid circles, cleaning himself. It was time, then, to find a sheltered place in the garden to sit quietly and twitch his nose, scenting for danger. He chose a spot facing the big hedge, so that he would instantly see an approaching fox or farm cat. Arthur enjoyed breakfast, but he knew he would not enjoy *being* breakfast. Arthur liked the idea of breakfast on the inside, but not breakfast on the outside. He would rest a while and then go back to the house for a sleep, because in the house he was protected from danger. For now, he stretched out his front paws and back legs and settled down with his nose just touching the grass, but he would not sleep, not here in the open, because he needed to remain on his guard. When you were a rabbit, you could never be too careful.

When Arthur returned to the house, Janice Collins had arrived to see her client. She and Hettie were sitting in the kitchen, checking a file of care notes. Janice watched, peering over the rim of her spectacles, as Arthur hopped into view, clattering the flap.

"Your rabbit goes out on his own then?" Janice said.

"Well, I don't take him for walks," said Hettie.

"I mean, is it safe? Might he not run away?"

"Run away? Why would he do that? He's got a warm home and nice food. He'd have to be daft."

Janice pondered the logic of this assertion. Arthur hid under the table and lifted his hind quarters to urinate on the floor.

"Does he not have a hutch?" Janice asked.

"He had one when we first got him," Hettie said, "but he didn't like it. We used to shut him in and he stamped his feet and pounded the door to come out again."

"Perhaps you should have ignored him. He's a rabbit."

"I know he's a rabbit," Hettie said. "Did you ever have a rabbit?"

Janice chewed her top lip thoughtfully. "My mother, I remember she sometimes made us a nice rabbit stew. Carrots, onions, celery and little chunks of rabbit meat."

Hettie screwed up her eyes and tightened her lips.

"Course, rabbit can be a bit salty. But it's not unlike chicken. You have to be careful about small bones."

Sneaking a look under the table, Hettie hoped Arthur wasn't listening. She didn't want him running away in fear. "Me, I'd never eat a rabbit."

Janice sighed and placed a hand lightly on Hettie's damaged arm. "You're keeping your plaster nice and clean."

"I thought I might draw a picture of Arthur on it, only I'm not much of an artist. I could get some signatures, except I don't see anybody. When I was a girl up north, me and my friend Sylvia, we went to a concert and Sylvia had a broken arm, so after the show we had to wait in the cold at the stage door, and after about fifteen minutes, well, Cliff Richard came out and signed his autograph on her plaster. She was that pleased."

"I always liked Cliff Richard," Janice said. "Here, do you know his real name?"

"No, dear. Isn't it Cliff Richard?"

"It's Harry Webb."

"Fancy," Hettie said. "Are we having some tea?"

Janice checked her watch. "Just a quick one." She stood up and filled the kettle. Over her shoulder, she enquired, "Would you ever think of another man?"

"Think of another man? What do you mean, dear?"

Janice switched the kettle on, turned and leaned against the sink. "I mean, if your Alf's taken another woman, you could take a replacement man, then you wouldn't be on your own."

"But I'm not on my own, am I? I've got Arthur."

"Arthur's a rabbit," Janice pointed out.

"Well, I know he's a rabbit, dear. I'm not stupid."

"It's just – I was thinking, if you had a man here, he could look after you – do things a rabbit can't do."

"Oh, me and Arthur, we look after each other." She peeped under the table. "Don't we, Arthur?"

Arthur looked at her and nibbled his paw. Janice Collins made the tea. A movement beyond the window drew their attention and they saw the shed door swing open and Gloria Glenister come out with a scarf wound round her neck and the lower half of her face.

"Blonde tart's on the prowl," Hettie scowled.

"Is that her idea of travelling incognito?" Janice muttered darkly.

Hettie sniffed contemptuously.

Janice wrapped both hands around her cup. "Mrs Slocombe, did you ever consider forgiving him – giving him a second chance?"

"Oh, I considered it for five minutes, dear. Then I wised up."

"How do you mean?"

"Like I told you, I love him with all my heart. But once the bond's been broken." She spread her hands over the table. "Tell me, have you ever been broken into, dear? In your home, I mean."

"I don't think so, no."

"No? Well, I have, see. In our old house, when we lived in town, we were burgled. It wasn't so much what they took, it was that feeling when you know someone's been going through your home and messing with your things. Sort of an unclean feeling."

"I can understand."

"Course you can. And that's how I felt with him, afterwards. This stranger had – plundered him. She'd been in a place that belonged to me and soiled it. I just couldn't get over that."

"Do you think he still loves you?"

"Lord, I couldn't say, dear. I don't much mind either way. Sounds like a cliché, I know, but you have to move on – isn't that right? Dwelling on it's just too painful."

"Hmm. They do say men are easily led."

"Well, men are the weaker sex, dear, and that's a fact. Trouble is, they never lose their whatsit – their libido. They can be mooching along all quiet, then suddenly it pops up out of nowhere and says, 'Hey, look at me! Here I am!' Just like a bad friend you'd tried to forget."

"So in a way, you aren't really blaming him."

Hettie sighed, gazing through the window. "I suppose not. I blame her. She's the burglar, he's the victim of crime."

"I think that might be a harsh judgment," Janice said.

"Yes, dear, I expect it is. Now finish your tea and go. You've people to take care of. You don't want to be dilly-dallying with daft old widows like me. Only don't forget to come back, eh?"

Janice stood up and stuffed papers into her bag. She glanced at the floor in front of her chair. "Your rabbit's done a poo under the table," she said.

"Yes, dear, he does that."

"I'll let myself out, Mrs Slocombe. It's always nice talking to you."

Hettie sprang from her chair with unexpected energy and threw her good arm round Janice's back, her crinkled lips clumsily nuzzling the carer's neck.

As she opened the back door, she found herself staring into Alf Slocombe's face, framed in the shed doorway. Alf's mouth hung wide open, as in a surprised and wordless greeting.

Janice Collins turned and felt the sun leaning on her back. She shook her head and took a deep breath as she fumbled for her car keys. For a while she sat at the wheel, staring emptily through the windscreen. Then she turned on the radio and twiddled the knob until she found some music she liked. Pulling down the sun visor, she studied her face in the mirror on the back. She looked worried, tired. She stuck out her tongue and peered at it. Then she tugged down each lower eyelid to examine the whites of her eyes.

Flipping the visor up, she started the engine and revved it fiercely. "Nothing new under the sun," she murmured, "but this comes close."

# Chapter 45

## *Number 25: Joan Descours*

She had expected the hallway to feel warmly welcoming after the chill of the suspended cradle, but somehow, with its tan-coloured paint and sparse, drab furniture, the entrance felt coolly clammy, offering a meagre relief.

"Shut the door, Barry." She shuddered. "I'll get some heat on."

"But it's summer."

"I know that. Reckon that ride's chilled me to the marrow." She pushed open the front room door. "Go in there and sit down. I'll be right back."

Barry Brown sat awkwardly on the sofa, gazing idly around the room. He heard Joan striding about, opening and shutting doors, muttering to herself. Yesterday's *Times* lay on a low table in front of him; he picked it up, flicked through a few pages and put it down again. Apart from Joan's movements, the house was very quiet. Something drummed in his ears, the rhythm of his heartbeat.

"Now then." She was in the doorway, rubbing her hands.

"Are you all right?" he asked her.

"Me? Yes, I'm fine." She craned her neck, peering at him. "Barry, you look puzzled."

He shrugged, not looking at her. "I'm sort of confused, that's all."

"Confused? Why confused?"

"I thought you were running me home. Now I'm back here."

"Are you in a hurry? You said they weren't worried."

"I'm not in a hurry."

"Good. Then I shall make us some tea. Nothing fancy. I'll bring it on a tray." Her eyes travelled from his face, down his chest and stiffly parted legs, and back up again.

"Why don't you relax, eh?"

She brought tea in a pot, Oreos on a floral plate and a pile of toasted teacakes with butter and jam. "Just a little something," she said brightly. "Damn!"

"What's wrong?"

"Cups and saucers. Not thinking straight."

He bit into an Oreo, waiting for her to fetch what she had forgotten. The biscuit stuck to his dry mouth, gritty and tasteless. He would try to make sense of this.

She sat down heavily beside him and he felt her warmth and caught a drift of perfume he had not noticed before.

"Okay, ready to go. More if you want it." She poured the tea. "Got to look after you."

He could feel her thigh transmitting heat through his trousers. His hand trembled as he lifted his cup and saucer and he hoped she hadn't noticed. He took a plate and a teacake and spread butter thinly on the tawny surface.

"My sister made the jam," she told him, pointing with her little finger.

"I don't care for jam much, Joan."

"Really?" She turned towards him. "And what do you care for, Barry, hmm?"

"What do you mean?"

"I should have thought that was a clear enough question. What sort of things do you like, Barry?"

"You mean food?"

"Food, activities, anything. I don't know nearly enough about you, Barry."

"Not sure where to start," Barry said.

"Oh, I bet you do, Barry. You're not so lost for ideas." She squeezed his thigh. "You seemed to know where to start when we were up in the sky."

"I suppose."

"No suppose about it."

Barry smiled quickly, nervously, clenching his hands in his lap. Though he stared straight ahead, he could feel Joan's eyes searching his face.

"You should let yourself go more, Barry. Try to relax."

"Yes, Joan."

"Barry?"

"Yes, Joan?"

"I suppose, really, you want to kiss me. Unless I'm reading you wrong, of course. I could be making a mistake about – "

"Yes," he interrupted, staring morosely at his feet.

"And is that 'yes, you want to kiss me' or 'yes I'm making a mistake'? Which is it, Barry?"

"I – I really like you, Joan. You're not making a mistake."

She sat back, nodding reflectively. "Trouble is, Barry, if you think about it, I could actually be making a very big mistake. I wonder if you realise that."

Barry carried on staring at his shoes without comment. Joan allowed her gaze to wander over the boy's face, his flawless, downy skin, his full lips and long, apprehensively fluttering eyelashes. He was a beautiful young man, she thought.

She patted his thigh to draw his attention. "Barry, listen, this is important. I have a worthwhile profession to safeguard. I've been a teacher for twenty-five years and in that time I've not merely learned my craft, but earned the respect and approval of my peers, engendering a self-respect which lends me confidence and a sense of well-being. My work is of vital importance to me, both as self-definition and as a lifeline. I've worked hard to get where I am today. There is no way I can contemplate abandoning my position, throwing all my security away. I'm sure you understand that."

Barry, head still bowed, nodded gently. "Yes," he said quietly.

"Good, Barry, that's good. It's only right we understand each other."

"Yes, Joan."

"So what I'm saying is, anything that happens, aside from your studies, is a private matter between us and it stays strictly within these four walls. You have my solemn word on that, and I hope I have yours."

Barry sat up and looked gravely into her eyes. Then, like the sun coming out, a warm smile spread over his face, flushing his cheeks. "Of course," he whispered.

She reached down to squeeze his hand. "Funny, you weren't so backward when we were a hundred feet up in the air. Remember?"

"Yes, I know."

"So now we need to establish how we feel here, down on the ground."

"I feel – I think you're a lovely person, Joan. I sort of get this funny feeling when I'm close to you."

"Do you, Barry? Well, maybe that's good. Maybe that means we were meant to be more than just teacher and pupil. What do you think about that?"

"I like the thought of it, Joan. Only…"

"Only what, Barry? It's all right, you can tell me."

"It's just, I'm not used to this, see. I suppose I don't know where to begin."

"Where to begin," she repeated slowly. "Where, indeed?" She took his hand and pulled it gently. "Come on, come with me."

He seemed to resist, averting his eyes.

"Barry, look. All you need do is say the word, and I'll get my keys and put you in the car and run you home. I promise you that. Because, well, perhaps you aren't ready to be encouraged. I don't know you well enough to make a reliable judgment on that. But one thing I will tell you now is, if you convince me you want to walk away from this, fine, and so far as our college interaction is concerned, nothing but nothing will change, but I won't be left hanging on a string, Barry. That means, I won't let us tease each other again, because it'll only lead to more disappointment."

"Is that what you're doing, then – teasing me?"

"Only as a prelude, Barry. I can offer you so much more than mind games, truly I can."

The boy stood up and let her draw him to her. "We'll be more comfortable upstairs," she said.

Joan drew back the curtains to admit more daylight, for the bedroom was not overlooked. "So you can see me properly," she said.

Barry responded with a scarcely visible, tight-lipped smile, saying nothing, for there had been no question asked. For the moment, nothing was expected of him, except an amenable compliance.

She sat on the side of the bed and patted the space next to her. "Sit," she said, as to a willing dog.

He settled himself beside her, clasping his hands submissively between his knees.

"You look as if you're awaiting some form of punishment," she told him. Kneading his shoulder with strong fingers, she added, "That's not what I had in mind."

He raised his hands hesitantly, as if wondering what to do with them. "I'm sorry."

"Nothing to be sorry about. Just try to let yourself go. Close your eyes, imagine you're floating."

"Floating?"

"Yes. I'll close mine too. Let's imagine we're together on a desert island in the middle of the ocean. Mind you, I don't know why they insist on calling them desert islands. You wouldn't have a desert in the middle of an ocean, that's absurd. Anyway...we're totally naked and we're sitting in a little patch of shade under a palm tree. Our feet are in the sun and the sand is really hot round our ankles. Our legs are sticky with salt off the sea and sand is getting into the cracks of our bums. In a minute we'll run down to the water's edge and fall into the waves, that'll cool us down and wash the sand out of our bottoms. There's sand in my – my other part as well, but the tide will rinse it all away. When we come up for air, the sky is so blue, it's almost purple. There's nobody else in sight and the only sound around us is the surging of the sea."

"That would be so wonderful," Barry said.

"Don't open your eyes, not yet."

He sat quite still, waiting, wondering, the ocean and the sand and the palm tree disintegrating into fragments in his head, tumbling in pieces like exploding planets. Joan seemed to be moving, making the bed rock, tugging something with a kind of swishing sound.

"You can open your eyes now, Barry."

He straightened up, blinking. Joan sat with one hand on his far shoulder, holding him in a loose embrace.

"Oh, Joan."

"So, Barry. Do you like what you see?"

He nodded, swallowing hard.

"Give me your hand, Barry."

His hand was limp and moist, quivering as if an electric current pulsed through it. He licked his lips and let her guide his hand, which seemed no longer to be a part of him. The hand felt as if it belonged to her, an accessory.

"I don't normally wear red," she said, "but I saw this underwear set in this lovely shop in town and I couldn't resist it. Do you like it, Barry? I think the bra flatters my figure, hmm?"

"I really like it," he said hoarsely.

"Well, I certainly like the look of it with your hand there. And it's such a warm hand."

"I – I feel a bit like Benjamin Braddock," he said. "You remember?"

"I remember, Barry." She laughed, a small, happy exhalation. "I can be your Mrs Robinson. Except I don't think I look much like Anne Bancroft."

"You do, a bit," he said.

"Really? Well, you are certainly a lot better looking than Dustin Hoffman. But every bit as vulnerable."

His hand dropped and lay trembling in her lap. She picked it up and kissed it, holding it to her mouth, touching the fingers to her lips. The telephone rang.

"I shall leave it," she said.

"What if it's important?"

"I shall leave it. There's an answerphone."

"It could be important."

"This is important, Barry. We are important. You and me, we are important people. The only two people on a desert island. We can't hear the phone for the sound of the sea."

# Chapter 46

## *Number 35: Mrs Leila Smart and Billy Smart*

Leila Smart had fought back her revulsion to join her son in the pungent bedroom, where the smells could be tasted on the tongue and the scraping and skittering of small animals felt like itches to be scratched.

"Mum, what are you doing?"

"Doing?"

"You don't come in here, like normally."

"Important day, Billy. I want to be sure you're ready for your interview."

"I'm getting ready."

"Have you had a shower? You don't want to go in there smelling of animals."

"I've had a good wash, all over."

"Hmm. Okay. Did you have a shave?"

Billy rubbed his face, jutting his jaw. "Don't really need one today."

She sighed. "Right. Get dressed, no jeans or trainers."

"Do I have to wear a tie?"

"You're not going to be Managing Director. Smart casual, I think. Billy, it stinks in here. You sure something hasn't died?"

"Go downstairs, Mum. Leave me alone."

"Did they send you a job description?"

"No."

"Well, ask to see one. Have a quick look at it before committing yourself. You need to understand what you're applying for."

"What if they think I'm being awkward?"

"On the contrary, they will probably think you're organized and professional by asking for information. Then, when the interview is finished, they'll almost certainly ask you if you have any questions. So ask them something, something sensible and relevant. Do you understand?"

"Sensible and irrelevant," Billy intoned.

"Sensible and *relevant*. Trust me, it always looks good if you ask questions. They're impressed if you ask questions."

Billy nodded, looking bemused. "Do you think I'll get the job, Mum?"

"I can't say, Billy. It depends on lots of things: what they're looking for, how you conduct yourself, what they think about your background…"

"What if they ask me something I don't know?"

"Then just say you don't know, be honest, and explain to them why you can't answer. They'll accept that. Oh, and remember to look them in the eye, not under the desk or out the window. You're not good at eye contact, Billy. Make a conscious effort."

Leila found a clothes brush in the hall and waited for Billy to come downstairs. His trousers were always furred with animal hair and she wanted him to be as tidy as possible this morning. She brushed him vigorously at the door and gave him a hug, detecting only the merest feral tang about him. She smiled anxiously. The boy would do.

He crossed the street, looking carefully both ways, and she watched his back receding along the pavement, jogged by the small steps he habitually took, the unworldly child's gait he exhibited outdoors.

"Oh, Billy."

The words were hardly more than a breath, the fluttering of a candle flame. *"Do you think I'll get the job, Mum?"* Well, there could be small miracles. Billy was good with animals and loved them dearly. In his curriculum vitae there was little else. He was honest and possessed nothing of deceit or guile, but neither did he naturally accept responsibility. Leila could not recall that he had ever been interviewed before, by anyone for anything. Sometimes, even as he frustrated her, her heart, a mother's heart, ached for him. She thought about the hours he spent shut in that dreadful room, a refugee from life, eating with animals, sleeping with animals, absorbing their sourness into his very skin. The clean duvet cover she had given him this week was already dotted with the black whorls of python faeces and there were rat droppings on the window sill next to the bed. Billy did not need a bedroom; he would happily live in a barn with animals, clucking and grunting and crawling with them. They were his *alter ego*, his awareness.

Miss Palmerston and Mr Priddle were aware of their candidate's domestic involvements from the local news story, but they had agreed not to discuss the matter today, reasoning that the young man would have enough to think about without being reminded of the mishap. They would focus on the job and expect Mr Smart to do likewise.

Billy arrived five minutes early and a receptionist told him to wait. He sat on an uncomfortable plastic chair, wringing his hands and staring at the floor. A drinks machine stood nearby, but although his mouth was parched from nervousness, Billy was too unsettled to want refreshments. He tried to remember what his mother had told him to say, but her words kept tumbling about in his head in an unintelligible jumble.

"Billy Smart?" A door clicked open and a woman's face appeared. "Would you like to come in?"

Billy would not exactly like to come in, but he stood up and allowed the woman to usher him through the door into a large, airy room, brightened by a tall, uncurtained window, the light accentuated by its reflection from a large mirror above a marble mantelpiece. A heavy wooden table occupied the centre of the room, with four chairs evenly distributed around it. In the two chairs along one side of the table sat a portly man with a grey moustache and matching suit and the woman who had invited him in, now folding her skirt under her as she took her position and bent to pick up a wallet of papers from a briefcase at her feet.

Billy stood awkwardly behind an empty chair, hands

hanging.

"Do sit down, Billy." The woman indicated the chair with an upturned hand. "Is it all right if we call you Billy?"

Billy scraped the chair across the floor and sat down. "Yes, Miss."

"Good. Well now, I am Evelyn Palmerston and this gentleman" – she used the same flattened hand to point out her colleague – "is Eric Priddle, one of our directors."

Billy nodded and pulled his chair closer to the table. His mouth felt dry as a bone. He wished he could be anywhere but here. Miss Palmerston and Mr Priddle glanced at each other, presumably to establish who was to initiate proceedings. Billy's stomach rumbled, making a noise like the bath water running away.

Someone knocked on the door. "Interview!" Miss Palmerston shouted and shook her head.

Billy wished he had used the five minutes to go to the toilet. The grumbling seemed to have gravitated down to his bowels.

Miss Palmerston rested her clasped hands on the table and offered Billy a pleasant smile. "Regrettably we didn't have time to send you a job description." She withdrew an A4 sheet from the wallet and pushed it across the table. "You may read it now, it's only a single page."

Billy drew the paper towards him with his fingertips, looking perplexed.

"Is something the matter, Billy?" asked Miss Palmerston. "Billy, you can read, can't you?"

"Yes, course I can. Only I – " Billy lifted the page and put it down again.

Mr Priddle wiped a stubby forefinger across his moustache and peered sideways at Miss Palmerston. "Perhaps you should read it out to him," he suggested, his voice a gravelly growl.

"Good idea," Miss Palmerston said brightly.

Billy sat upright and immobile while she recited the twelve numbered paragraphs printed on the sheet. Her words clattered into his ears and jostled for some

269

semblance of order in his brain.

"Now, Billy. Please keep the document for reference."

"Thank you, Miss."

"This is essentially an outline, of course. There may be some *ad hoc* duties in addition."

"Yes, Miss."

Miss Palmerston and Mr Priddle exchanged glances and shifted in their chairs. Billy's stomach gurgled.

Mr Priddle leaned forward, tugging at the lapels of his jacket. "Tell me, young sir, is there any task in that schedule which you feel you may be ill-suited to undertake?"

"Pardon, sir?"

"Mr Priddle means anything in the list you don't like."

"Quite so," Mr Priddle grunted.

"I'm willing to give it a try," Billy said.

"Well, that would be a useful first step." Miss Palmerston thumbed her thin nose and rummaged among her other papers. "There is also an application form we would ask you to fill in – or fill out, as our American friends say."

Billy nodded unhappily.

"Tell us a little about your last job," said Miss Palmerston, leaning back and making a church and steeple out of her fingers.

"It was at the chip shop."

"Yes, you told me that on the phone. Did you enjoy the work?"

"I enjoyed the chips," Billy said.

"The chips. Right. Billy, I always believe, in life, there are late people and early people. Which would you say you are, hmm?"

Billy frowned. "Isn't late people when you're dead?"

"When – yes, indeed, though that's not quite what I meant. What we need to establish, so far as is possible, is the likelihood of you – assuming for the present that we were to offer you a position here – regularly reporting for work at the correct time. Is that clear?"

"I can come any time, Miss."

"Billy, my name is Miss Palmerston, if you please."

"Yes, you already told me that, Miss."

"Yes, I thought I did. So can we take it you could be relied upon to turn up for work on time each day? I ask because, as I understand it, this is something you were unable to achieve at the chip shop."

"It was that Mr Wu," Billy said.

"How do you mean?"

"He had it in for me, Miss."

"Well, if you kept coming in late, I suggest he had some justification."

"I got on all right with the others, see."

"Yes, well. That was easy for them if they didn't have the business to run."

"I suppose."

"And did you have any clerical duties at the shop?"

"No. I helped out. I did the chips and that."

Mr Priddle leaned conspiratorially towards Miss Palmerston. "Err...where are we going with this?"

She flapped her hand, waving his enquiry aside with an irritable toss of her head. "Tell me, Billy, what prompted you to apply for this job?"

"My mum," Billy replied sullenly.

"Your mum? Was it your mum who saw the notice?"

Billy nodded.

"Perhaps your mum should have applied," said Mr Priddle.

Miss Palmerston sucked in her cheeks and fixed Billy with a penetrating gaze. "Does Mrs Smart have a job, Billy?"

"Yes, she looks after me."

"She doesn't go out to work?"

"No, she works in the 'ouse."

"To the best of my recollection, Billy, you haven't answered my question about punctuality." Miss Palmerston tugged her ear as though this might better enable her to hear Billy's muted voice. "It's important, you

271

see, that whoever we appoint is willing and able to be here on time, and that means each day."

"I only live over the road, Miss – Miss Pasterman."

"The name is Palmerston, Billy."

"Sorry, Miss."

Mr Priddle fingered his moustache pensively. "In my experience," he growled, "proximity and punctuality are not necessarily the same thing. The latter is not an automatic consequence of the former."

Miss Palmerston blinked rapidly, suspecting that the observation may have gone over Billy's head. It had not escaped her notice that her original question had still not been satisfactorily answered, but she sensed that the moment had now arrived when it was no longer prudent or productive to labour the point.

She leaned forward, resting her arms on the file of papers. "Would you describe yourself as a methodical person, Billy?"

"Miss?"

"When you have a job to do, do you like to have a system or some kind of order in approaching the task?"

"Well, when I feed all my animals or clean them out, I always do it right, I mean, I always do them in the same order and I don't start the next one till I've done the one I was doing, see. That would get confusing."

"Have lots of animals, do you?" Mr Priddle asked.

"Twelve," Billy said.

"Where do they all live?" asked Mr Priddle.

"In my bedroom, sir."

Miss Palmerston's face shrivelled up in distaste.

"You don't have a pony, I take it," said Mr Priddle.

"I don't much care for 'orses, sir."

Miss Palmerston sighed extravagantly, perhaps as a signal to her colleague that, in her view, a critical point in the proceedings had been reached. The bull was stamping its hooves impatiently and demanded to be taken by the horns.

"Billy," she asked, "do you have any questions for us –

about the job or the conditions?"

"When would I be starting, Miss?"

"Hmm. A good question, Billy, if perhaps a shade presumptive. The fact is, we do – "

"Can I say something, Miss?"

"Of course you can, Billy. I've already offered you that opportunity."

Billy sat up straight in his chair and clenched both fists on the edge of the table. "The thing is, I don't want this job for me, see, I want it for my mum. I know sometimes she gets cross with me when I do stuff, but really she loves me and that's why she gets upset if she thinks I'm not trying hard enough about things. So I want to show her I can be, like, responsible and I can bring her home some money to help her and then we can buy that old lady a present to make up for her cat and p'raps when we go to the party we can be all nice to her, the old lady I mean, and give her a nice present and my mum won't have to put all the money in if I can earn a bit towards it by working at the water place and I'll be sure to get up quick in the morning and get here on time, not like when I was at Mr Wu's and I done it wrong, I know that, only this time I promise you, Miss, I'll show you can trust me and you'll do the right thing by giving me the job, which I really and truly want. Please, Miss."

Miss Palmerston puffed out her cheeks and exchanged another, more lingering glance with Mr Priddle.

"Please, sir."

"So that's the essence of your application," Mr Priddle said gravely.

Billy gripped the table as tears flooded his eyes.

"Billy, listen." Miss Palmerston stroked her temple with a slowly rotating finger, as though by this device a clearer train of thought might be released from within. "Billy, we appreciate what you've told us and we are grateful for your honesty. You haven't tried to hide anything from us and that's to your credit." She turned momentarily to her colleague.

273

"It's in your hands, Evelyn," Mr Priddle said, without moving his lips.

"We're going to give you a chance, Billy. Okay? Mr Priddle and I have a few – reservations, but we are prepared to set them aside for the moment and grant you the benefit of any doubt. A formal letter of appointment will be sent to you today, setting out terms and conditions, and we will expect you to commence work here next Monday at nine o'clock. That's nine in the morning, Billy. Do you understand?"

Billy nodded, grinding his teeth together. "Thank you," he whispered. "And you, Mr Piddle, sir."

Mr Priddle rearranged his moustache with a thumb and forefinger. Miss Palmerston shuffled her papers, allowing herself the vestige of a self-satisfied smile. For the first time that day, there was a twinkle in her eye.

# Chapter 47

## *Number 30: Stephen J. Kettering-Barclay*

He sat stiffly on a plain wooden chair in front of the full-length wardrobe mirror, studying his pale reflection. His prosthesis lay on the bed behind him. He lifted one leg and then what remained of the other leg, hearing the chair creak as he moved. Breathing slowly in and out, he inflated his almost concave chest until the furrows of his ribs disappeared under the downy mat of white hair. Lowering his head, he rolled up his eyes to see the brownish crusts and speckles that lived on his scalp beneath a floating white cloud. Parting his thighs, he peered at the small bundle curled there, like a baby bird resting in a nest of bleached grasses.

"Look at you," he said to the man in the mirror. "It's not a pretty sight."

He brought his legs together, opened them and closed them again. As he did this, he thought of the Irish girl, the young woman with the eyes that were strangely neither blue nor green, more a fusion of the two, according to the light, and he thought also of the way the sepia freckles over the bridge of her nose were perfectly repeated on the upper curve of her right breast, as though each peppery spillage had occurred at the same time, by the same hand. Then, too, he wanted to look with his mind's eye at the other parts of her which he remembered because they were unforgettable; but he administered to himself a mental slap, acknowledging that such devious ruminations would do him no good and merely stir the onset of an old man's futile frustrations.

"Will you just look at yourself," he said to the man in the mirror. "You're some kind of joke."

He got up from the chair and sat at the foot of the bed, next to his false leg, so he could still see himself in the mirror. His male parts were hardly visible here, lost in the depression in the bedclothes.

"You look vulgar without your clothes," he told himself. "In fact, Stephen, you look obscene. White, hairy, scrawny, sinewy, scabby…I reckon it's a miracle that girl would even look at you, even for ready money. Reckon she has the worst job in the world."

He looked at the alarm clock on the bedside table. Nine fifteen. He was booked to see Irish Willow at four in the afternoon. That was a long time to wait. Time to bolster courage. Time to lose heart. Time to ask searching questions about the point of it all, about his fitness for the task.

"Perhaps you should just go round and keep your clothes on," he said. "Give the girl a break, for God's sake. There's no reason for you to be naked. Beauty and the beast."

He picked up the prosthesis and inspected the fittings. The thing could do with a clean. Swinging himself round, he slid open the drawer in the bedside table, took out the white packet and checked the foils inside. *Sildenafil 100mg.* They seemed to work quite well and the branded *Viagra* was a lot more expensive. Funny how the first thing to happen was that the tablet gave his face a hot flush, like warm water coursing under his skin, a not unpleasant sensation. So long as his heart didn't give out before he got there, or worse, while he was halfway into the procedure. He wondered if she would be strong enough to drag him out to the landing and toboggan him down the stairs by his feet.

"I wonder if she gets many like me," he said over his bony shoulder to the old man in the mirror. "I mean, does she need the money that badly?" He replaced the tablets in the drawer. "About time you got dressed, made yourself respectable – if you can still expect to be respected."

His clothes for the day lay on a chair by the window, trousers draped over the back, shoes underneath. He had chosen a crew-neck sweatshirt and a pair of slip-on loafers, for these items could be slipped off and on again with the minimum of fuss, obviating the need to fumble with buttons or laces at a time when a feeling of self-conscious awkwardness attended any arthritic attempt to remove or replace his clothing. Last time, he remembered, Aisling had helped him button his shirt before he left, her face held sweetly close to his as she worked her fingers down his chest.

In the bathroom, he used the toilet and shaved and washed perfunctorily, finally spraying deodorant in various places. He would brush his teeth after breakfast. 'A tad unfresh', she had called him before, words chosen to minimize the hurt to his feelings. The shower had been refreshing and she had washed him with great care and a semblance of affection, revealing another aspect of her nature. Not since Francine had any woman run her hands over his body. Now, staring into the steam-fringed bathroom mirror, so positioned on the wall that thankfully the bottom frame cut off too high to reflect his dangler, Stephen examined his sunken chest and the ridges of his ribs and tried to imagine what Irish Willow must think when he turned to her, apologetic in his nakedness, resembling an unspent Swan Vestas with his white-stick body and that flaring pink face, inflamed by the blue bean he'd swallowed in the hope of making his old friend stand. *What the hell, we won't be long, he's paid me the money, get over it.*

"Hello again," he said to the cadaverous spectre in the mirror. "I just saw your twin brother in the other room. He's in as bad a state as you."

There was surely a simple solution: he should be eating better, more fat, more carbohydrate. Those brown bread sandwiches in triangular boxes, filled with wet lettuce and slivers of chicken, were not a satisfactory diet; he ought to be wolfing down good, hot, solid food to build himself up, put some flesh on those spooky bones. Once, when Francine came to cut his hair, she brought him a home-made chicken pie, still warm from her oven, a creation not to be confused with the puny articles supplied in cardboard boxes at the supermarket, shreds of chicken drowned in grey slop, so unappetizing you could as well eat the box instead. A Francine Kessler chicken pie, bulging with prime bird, was to die for. Where was she now, he wondered. Who was she now?

He pummelled his chest, pretending to be Tarzan. It made him laugh, and the laughter made him cry. Gasping, he wiped his eyes with his knuckles. "Stop blubbing, old man," he admonished himself.

Behind his back, the bathtub, spotlessly unused, appeared in the glass, and Stephen let his focus adjust and lock on to the rim's curvature. In that moment he came to understand what he must do to bring his torment to an end. In considering the mechanism, he realized that while what he proposed would allow those men he had wronged so many decades ago to avenge their murders, that unburdening could come only by exposing someone else to another form of destruction, an act which would surely send him from the world with no honourable discharge, but shouldering the dark cloak of one final disgrace. He would go down a bad man, which was all that he deserved, in the manner of a final absolution. He could not believe in his right to be a good man lost.

Stephen sat naked on a chair and allowed his gaze to slip to the floor while he turned these dark prospects over in his mind. Two more innocent people would suffer at his hands, pawns in his dreadful game. Then, as he lay in eternal darkness, their faces, too, would rise up to haunt him, so there would be no pure release and no escape. Yet he would find the strength to smile in his torture, knowing that at last a terrible justice had been gifted him.

He stomped, half-legless, back to the bedroom, clutching the banister rail for support, and began to dress. When he had put on everything but his shoes, he sat on the bed and attached his metal leg, rocking slowly backwards and forwards to make himself comfortable. Half a day remained before he could go to Irish Willow, time enough to reflect upon his plan, to hone and polish its components and ramifications in his mind. Would he really go through with this? Would the shame of backing away exceed the pain of execution? In any case, it could all go wrong; there was no guarantee of consummation. If it entailed a risk, it was perhaps the final risk he would take in his life. For that, he was ready.

Closing his eyes, he saw the girl sitting cross-legged in front of him on the bed. Her blonde hair curled softly over her shoulders and, beneath the upswept tresses, her cream-white breasts, cherry-capped, were poised in perfect harmony. He blinked, glimpsed the light, and closed his eyes again, exhaling deeply in his reverie. She had kept her white knickers on, cut high around her slender thighs, and the line of his sight drew him along the shadowy tunnel that ended at the lace-edged V compacted between her legs.

Stephen reached out a hand and the girl disappeared. He was back in his room again. There was a glaze of sweat heating his brow. Yes, very well, he would do this thing. It was the right way. He smiled. The blood pounded like percussion in his head. Yes. Oh yes.

# Chapter 48

## *Number 15: Aisling McIver*

She had a new man coming this morning, young-sounding by his telephone voice, called himself Blade Runner. That was a film by Ridley Scott, she knew, though she hadn't seen it. She wasn't into science fiction. By half past nine she was getting herself ready, a simple blue cotton dress, quite short, that buttoned up the front, pale blue panties underneath and dark grey stockings. She didn't like to greet them in just her underwear, though any number of the girls did, judging this to be kind of tarty. Being an escort didn't have to make you a tart; you could call yourself a courtesan and introduce yourself respectably.

She wondered about the young guys. If they were in their twenties or thirties and not bad looking, why would they need to pay good money for their pleasure? The old punters, she could better understand – *crinklywinkles*, Rona called them – as they would have more of a problem finding physically appealing, and willing, girlfriends within their normal social circles. But the young men puzzled her a little, not that it mattered, so long as they behaved themselves. Blade Runner wanted an hour and a half for a hundred and thirty, half ten until twelve. That, too, she wondered about. Doing it in the middle of the morning seemed out of the zone, somehow, like you'd hardly got started in the day and already you had the urge, without any emotional input to engender it. She liked men right enough, but she didn't always understand them. Some of them, she supposed, must wander about all the time just gagging for it, as if it were all they thought about from dawn till bedtime. They needed to get out more, see the world.

There would be plenty of time after this man had gone to prepare for her second visitor of the day. That old chap was coming round again. What was his name? Seadog, yes, that was it. Seadog was due at four o'clock. That was all right, he was polite and harmless. This time she might have another try at getting him down in the bath for a proper scrub, which he needed, for sure. He'd agreed to the shower last time, but it hadn't exactly worked as thoroughly as she'd anticipated. In a manner of speaking, he was a dirty old man. Inevitably, some of them did turn up less than clean, that was a risk you took, and then it was no insult to tell them so and make them jump in the shower or go home and play with themselves. She always smelled sweet for them and expected the reciprocation. Of course, she never put on strong perfume or wore lipstick, in case the guy lying next to her absorbed her scent and carried it home to a partner or waltzed in the family front door with red smudges on his face. Not that she minded kissing them, even French kissing, if they were clean-shaven and had fresh breath. After all, some of them only wanted hugs and kisses, something they were starved of, and maybe a nice little rub at the end to seal the deal.

She had expressed some milk last night and now she sat Neamh on her lap and fed her from a bottle, wanting to keep baby stuff off her breasts with the man coming soon. There'd be a face suckling her nipples shortly anyway, most of them wanted that. Sometimes it was all they asked for and she could almost have kept her clothes on. You never knew. It was always a guessing game.

Blade Runner was running late. At a quarter to eleven there was no sign of him in the street and no phone call. She sat with the phone in her hand, gazing at her knees in the sheer stockings. Five more minutes passed and the phone rang. Aisling gave the man the house number and went down to open the door. It wasn't a good idea to leave a client standing on the step.

He put his hand on her bottom as he followed her upstairs, which she didn't like. Even in this situation, there was a protocol to be observed, and she expected each visitor to be mature enough to respect it. She could see he was young, perhaps in his twenties, but age was not an acceptable excuse at either end of the spectrum.

Upstairs, she shut the door and leaned against it. "You're late."

"Traffic," he said.

"Okay, well, you're here now. Can I get you a drink?"

"Some water. Tap water."

When she brought the water he was sitting at the table with his legs splayed. "So what'll I call you?" she asked him.

"Michael."

"Then hello, Michael."

He nodded expressionlessly and drank the water in one go, thrusting the empty glass under her nose. She took it to the kitchen and came back fingering the buttons on her dress.

"Irish Willow, eh? And what's your real name?"

She told him, then held out her hand. "Have you forgotten something?"

"What?"

"Look, Michael, I don't know what you want to do this afternoon, but there'll be nothing happening without you pay me first. Right?"

Whereupon Blade Runner leaned back, stretching out one leg, and delved into his pocket to withdraw a wad of notes, which he placed in Aisling's hand. Backing away from him, she counted the money with a flicking thumb.

"Hundred and thirty. It's all there," he said.

"You may know that, but I don't," she muttered. "I always check. In my position, you'd do the same."

She hid the cash in the kitchen, sighing, wondering about this man. He didn't connect, somehow. At a first meeting, it normally took her only three minutes to intuit a level of rapport with her client; Michael had had longer than that and although she had divined a reading from his signals, it did not put her at her ease. On the meter of her empathy with this charmless young man, the needle had not risen from the stop.

"Well now, Michael." She clasped her hands, beaming artificially into his upturned face. "Tell me what it is you like."

"How d'you mean?"

"What I mean is, the things you enjoy doing."

"Like, my hobbies?"

Aisling blinked rapidly in disbelief. "Michael, this is not an interview. Why do you think you've paid me all that money? I'm talking about sex."

Michael nodded and scratched his head. His eyes were dark, almost black, and he had allowed his eyebrows to grow together over the bridge of his nose, lending him a vaguely sinister aspect. Aisling felt that she would like to take an electric razor and quickly shave a half-inch gap between the hairy caterpillars.

Swivelling round in the chair, he grabbed her hand and pressed it against the front of his trousers with a leering grin.

Snatching back her hand, "Let's go upstairs," she said.

In the bedroom he began peeling off his clothes and tossing them to the floor.

"Don't make my room untidy." She scowled at the littered carpet. "Look, there's a chair and a hanger. Pick your stuff up."

Michael frowned. "You're not my mum."

"Sure, if I were your mum this would be illegal and we wouldn't be doing it."

He bent to scoop up his clothes, muttering under his breath.

"And your shoes. Don't leave them there for me to trip over."

He kicked the shoes under the bed. "You don't like me much, do you?"

Aisling sat down at the end of the bed, sweeping a hand through her hair. "Mister Blade Runner, I don't have to like you. This is a business arrangement. We don't have to be friends."

Shrugging, he tugged himself briefly and scratched

beneath his navel. "Better get down to business, then."

"Sure. Want me to take my dress off?"

"Course I do. Why wouldn't I?"

"Some guys like to do it themselves. Gets the adrenalin going."

"Okay." He sat beside her, naked, still limp, and began unfastening her buttons, his breath warming her face. "Hey, you're nice."

"You don't know if I'm nice or not. You don't know me."

"I know some girls aren't nice," he said.

"Oh? So do you go to many girls, Michael?"

"Not many. Depends if I have the money."

"Ah, sure. It can be an expensive hobby. Some guys I've seen, they spend five grand a year."

"Yeah? Could buy a car for that."

"You could, you could. Then you could give up on the women, just sit in the car and have a wank."

Blade Runner attempted a laugh. Aisling helped him slide her dress off, lying next to him in her bra and pants. She reached out and took hold of him, feeling a pulse.

"Careful," he said.

"Something the matter?"

"I've paid for an hour and a half."

"You have, so."

"Just – I don't want to, you know, too quick."

"And is that a problem you have, Michael?"

"There's nothing wrong with me," he said.

"I didn't say there was. Okay, so I'll be gentle with you."

As a rule – and she did aspire to play this game according to her printed rules – she did not mind kissing them, mindful of Rona's inclusion of French Kissing in Aisling's profile column, though she accepted this condition as discretionary. If the man turned up with halitosis, beer breath, the morning's full English stuck in his teeth or in obvious need of dental care, she refused to kiss him or be kissed. Blade Runner seemed safe and enthusiastic, leaning into her to kiss her lips, her cheeks, the side of her nose and her neck with a passion she had not expected.

"Mind my neck, Michael, I don't want any purple bites."

She kissed his mouth obligingly.

"God, you're lovely," he whispered hoarsely. "Oh, this is…oh."

She looked down at him. "I think you're kind of ready."

"I don't know."

"You don't know?"

"Oh, my God!"

"Wait a moment, Michael. Let's make this safe."

He rolled on to his back, stomach pumping as he drew deep breaths. Aisling reached in the bedside drawer, ripped the foil in her teeth and teased him with the trick she had learned and perfected, trapping the condom bulb in encircling lips and bobbing her head to seal the sleeve over his erection.

"There now."

For Michael, the magic moment was all too much. He groaned and cried out, convulsing to a premature finish. "Damn!"

Aisling sighed, propped on one elbow. "Short and sweet," she said.

"You – you shouldn't have done that," he whined.

"Done what? Put a condom on you?"

"Done it – like that."

"Your problem, Michael. Your call."

"Waste," he said, struggling to sit up.

"Right, let's get you tidied up."

"Damned waste."

"It happens, Michael. Guys come too fast or maybe they don't get there at all, then sometimes they sit outside in the car, going home, and finish themselves off from memory. It's not a perfect science. Sure, I wish it was."

He had slid to the edge of the bed, where she reached

over him and cleaned him up with a tissue from the box she kept at hand.

"Try not to let it upset you. Okay?"

"Upset me? Of course it upsets me. I've wasted a load of money."

"Well, you've wasted a load all right," she quipped.

"It's not funny."

"And I'm not laughing."

They dressed in silence, avoiding eye contact. Hovering by the window, animation suspended by a toxic uncertainty, he waited to follow her downstairs.

His jacket hung on the back of the chair and he shrugged himself into it, solemn-faced, working his mouth in suppressed frustration. "So what are we gonna do?"

"Do? What's to do? You're on your way."

The jacket zip was halfway up and he seemed to freeze with both hands in the air.

"What, are you playing statues now?"

"Miss, I've only had half my time."

"So?"

"So what happens about the money?"

"The money? Nothing happens about the money." She screwed up her eyes in mock incredulity. "Are you wanting a discount?"

"I did pay you for an hour and a half."

"You did. Then you gave up early and put your clothes back on. What's it to me?"

"I said, I paid you for an hour and a half!"

"Please don't be raising your voice to me. Remember I have neighbours and the baby's sleeping."

He banged a fist on the table, glaring. "You can't do this. I've paid you for something I haven't had."

She put out a warning hand. "Don't go hitting my furniture! You, you're Mister Bad Behaviour!"

Michael's hands were balled into knuckle-whitening fists now and he was trembling with incipient rage. Aisling felt her mouth turning dry, her face chilling as if iced water suffused the blood. This was something else, a creeping awareness that a mere absence of spontaneous warmth had degraded into a situation darkly unstable. If the argument were spawned by money, there was a miasma more sinister spreading from it like a livid stain.

He banged the table again, open-mouthed, no words coming out, only a snake-like gasp of mindless anger. Aisling heard Neamh blurt a disorientated cry of fright.

"Okay, okay, so you're a madman. If I give you some money, will you just go, please!"

Michael wiped his knuckles across his lips. "You're a thief!"

"And you're a wanker!"

Before he could respond, she hurried into the kitchen and pulled some cash from the jar. It was full, anyway. She would go to the bank later.

"Here, forty quid! So you've just paid me for the normal hour. That's all you're getting."

He snatched the money and stuffed it in his pocket.

"A few words of friendly advice, Michael. Get out of here and don't ever come back."

"Or what?"

"Don't make me lower myself to threats."

Blade Runner hunched down in his jacket, as if protecting himself. "You women, you're all the same underneath. You wouldn't be doing this, otherwise. You're just dregs."

"Is that so, my friend?" She squared up to him, glaring icily into his narrowed eyes. "Well, I'll tell you a fact of life. You and me, we're no different when we're in this house. I need it and so do you. If we're bad, we're as bad as each other. And remember – I only need this to care for my child. You, you need it to feed your weakness."

She stood rooted to the spot, shaking, as the door slammed. Then a yelping wail from Neamh obliterated her indignation, and she went to the cot and scooped the child into her arms with a soothing sigh.

"There, there, Neamh my darling. Did that awful man scare you? Well, I guess he scared me, too, for just a while, but he's gone away now and he won't be coming back."

She rocked the baby gently, one hand under her tiny back, the other cupping her head. A shaft of sunlight fell through the window where she sat, finding Neamh's face, and in the baby's left eye gleamed the golden cataract of a sunbeam.

"See, there's a jewel in your eye, my love. Is that a gift or a promise?"

Neamh looked up at her mother's face and bowed her lips in a smile.

"God love you, I don't want you should ever be afraid. See, your mammy's only doing this for you. Soon as all the bills are paid and you've got all the nice things I've promised you, then there's to be no more strange men walking in here, emptying their pockets and wanting to be putting their hands in private places. Neamh, you have to trust me. Wait till you're a wee bit older and see the world, and you'll find out the truth of it, how it's a sad, bad old place where you need your friends and some money and maybe an idea or two to get you by, like the one your Auntie Rona had, bless her. I shall have you Christened soon, love, and Auntie Rona will be your Godmother and swear she'll help me to keep you safe for all your life. For all your life."

A single tear trickled down Aisling's cheek and dropped on to her daughter's chin. Aisling wiped it away with her thumb. "So help me, I'd weep you my very blood if it were a better comfort to you."

Through the fog of her tears, she saw Neamh's pink mouth open like a flower under the sea.

"Are you hungry, darling?"

She lifted the warm bundle against her, unbuttoning her dress, letting her left breast slide out into the light.

"Come on then, little one."

The telephone rang.

"We'll leave that. We're busy loving."

The answerphone cut in. Abstractedly, she angled her

head to hear the message.

"Hello, this is Aquaboy 5 calling Irish Willow. My real name is Gareth. I wonder if I could come and see you for an hour at one o'clock today. I've read your profile and would really like to meet you. I'm a mature man and I'm in your area right now. Please ring or text me with your answer. Thanks."

She gave Neamh a reassuring hug. "Aquaboy, he calls himself. Is he a round-the-world yachtsman or he just fancies the watersports? Never gone in for that, darling. I don't mind you weeing on me, little poppet, but I don't know as I'd care much for a grown man doing it. Rona says it's popular enough. Can you imagine it, Neamh? Sure, it can be one way, so you send them home to the missis stinking of pee, well, whatever turns you on, like they say. Reckon I should put in my profile I won't do the kinky stuff, so's we know where we stand. Still, maybe your mam's a mite boring, after all. Maybe the truth of it is, she's not cut out for this, even after…Jesus, I don't know, I've lost count of them, and that's a fact."

Neamh gurgled softly and blew the pearl of a silver bubble from one nostril.

"I'll hold you a while longer and then I'll ring him, tell him, not today, Aquaboy, I'm playing all right, but I'm playing with my baby."

The sun was warm on their faces, spilling into her lap like buttermilk.

# Chapter 49

## *Number 33: Minnie Starling*

Raj had been busy. By lunch-time he had dismantled the broken guttering and fitted a shiny new length in its place, then come down to the kitchen and replaced the damaged hinges on the cabinets under the sink. When Minnie plodded into the kitchen to see what he was doing, she found him surrounded by a glinting array of chrome collars and spigots, industriously set about with spanners and wrenches.

"What are you doing, Raj?"

"Ah, Miss Starling. Now I fix the tap."

"It's Mrs Starling. What's wrong with the tap?"

"Water coming out."

"That's what happens. Water comes out of taps."

"Ah, but here is your water emerging when it is not bidden."

"You mean, it leaks?"

"Yes, yes, is a leak. I repair."

"It's dripped for ages," Minnie told him, evincing little interest. "I hardly notice it."

"Ah, soon you will notice it is no longer dripping. I am fixing right now. I think, a new washer."

"I'm sure you know best, Raj."

"When I am finish, the water comes only when is asked. Excellent."

Minnie looked up at the clock with the red rooster on the face. "Isn't it time for your lunch?"

He pointed to a plastic box on the worktop. "I have sandwiches, very soon."

"That's good. I can offer you some cake for afterwards. I'm afraid I have nothing Indian in the house."

Raj turned down his lip. "I am not always eating Indian. English very nice, mostly."

"I can make you a hot drink."

"Maybe later, a nice cup of tea. Then I go upstairs."

"To do what?"

"Mend tap in bathroom. Not screwed tight."

"Have a rest first, Raj." She tamped the floor with her stick. "Let me know when you want your tea."

Minnie wondered idly whether Roland James had given Raj a list of tasks, or if the young man had worked it out for himself. She manoeuvred herself on to the stairlift and rode upstairs to wobble the tap on the bathroom sink. Watching her through the banisters, Raj waved politely as she ascended from view. At heart, she thought, Raj was a good man. It was a shame, but his decency did not make him invulnerable.

She balanced with one hand on her stick and the other on the loose tap. Once, a long time ago, she had mentioned it to Roland James, and he had mumbled something about it getting a lot of use, as if the explanation were tantamount to a resolution of the matter. No, surely Raj must have noticed the problem when he was plastering the bathroom wall. She would give no credit to the landlord. Sighing, wearily nodding her head, she lowered herself on to the scuffed and steam-blotched wooden chair she kept there and let her gaze fall dreamily to the floor. The beat of blood in her ear sounded as the scrunch of boots in wet snow before the squeak came. In the corridors of her brain a thin wind whistled, seeking the right of redemption. But the young man's efforts on a single day, even his innate goodness, somehow did not redeem him after years of slapdash work, after all the frustration and disappointment he had caused her. She grappled with the realisation that Raj's inefficiency was not entirely his fault, for he could only approach each allotted task armed with the capability at his disposal. If his training and instruction had been inadequate, proficiency would surely elude him. No matter how resolutely he did his best, the result would always be unsatisfactory.

"I'm sorry, Raj," Minnie said quietly to the floor.

The winds in her brain had not absolved him from liability, because she would not allow so much gnawing dejection to pass unpunished. The same applied, of course, to Roland James, fiddling in his office while her indignation burned, counting the pennies he might save by employing the cheaply unsuitable.

"You too, Mr James," Minnie said to the four walls, shaking her head.

In any case, her mind had been made up months ago and she would not change it now. She would not change anything now. She would go forward with her head held high and do what was necessary and face the consequences. In her world there was nothing to be afraid of except, perhaps, the frailty of her judgment. Sometimes, if doubts cannot be resolved, they can simply be cast aside into a kind of emotional blackness, a place where reason cannot penetrate, a door slammed on what is good and fair. Minnie had slammed the door and rested her soul against it.

She waited until Raj had gone, bidding her a sparkling-toothed farewell, before she began carrying her party clothes into the spare room to be laid out on the bed. A dark blue two-piece suit, comprising a broad-collared, three-button jacket and a tulip-flared skirt, would look just slightly formal worn with navy blue stockings and low-heeled black shoes. Under the jacket, softening the effect, she would wear a round-necked pale pink silk blouse, set off with a modest string of cultured pearls. In her left lapel glinted the silver-and-ruby seahorse brooch she had inherited from her mother. She would look smart but not unapproachable, mature but not frowsty, elegant but always feminine. Next to the suit and blouse she placed the shoes, resting on sheets of tissue paper, and alongside the shoes, her handbag, from which everything had been removed except a small hairbrush, a square pack of moist wipes and the pink velvet drawstring bag which had once held the priceless Viennese necklace, now misshapen by its vital contents.

Minnie clipped the handbag shut and sighed in satisfaction. There was no chair in the spare room, only a quilted stool under an unused dressing table. She pulled out the stool and sat down, leaning forward, hands folded on the knob of her stick.

She glanced up only briefly at the sound of a blackbird fluttering on the window sill, tapping his beak on the glass.

"You're lucky," she told the bird, without looking at him, "you know nothing about commitment or consequence. Yes, you're fortunate." She bowed her head and closed her eyes, rocking slightly from side to side, pinioned on the stick.

"Thanks, God," she murmured. "Most people don't see as much of life as I have, and I suppose that's down to you. I haven't kept faith with you these past years, or maybe it's just you've not kept close to me. What I ask now is, in a few days' time, you won't bring down your wrath upon me for my transgression. I mean, I don't want to wake up blind or paralysed or look in the mirror and see myself grotesquely disfigured by some awful pestilence, a plague of boils or worms living in my nose, because you in your *finite* mercy have visited some savage retribution upon me. I am not, at heart, a bad person – although, of course, that can only be my somewhat prejudiced estimation. How much can I truly damage myself in the span of a day? One day, that is, out of – wait a minute – I make it something over thirty-six thousand. All that honourable, weightless light and dark. Oh, I won't expect you to smile down benignly on me and issue wondrous platitudes of forgiveness – because, after all, this is really a measure of my own limited forgiveness. Perhaps I simply need to be better at forgetting. And then, well, if you ignore my prayer for leniency, at least I shan't have to endure the pain for long, for there can't be many years left to me. Wherever I'm going, wherever you send me, I'm almost there already. They will all tell me I have a distorted idea of what's right and wrong, that I'm a daft old woman who's finally lost her reason, become of diseased mind. Maybe they'll even castigate themselves for not noticing it beforehand. *We should have seen the signs. We could have saved her.* People do that; it's eternally fashionable for folk to blame themselves. Yes, well, I can't be worrying over all that now. There's no time. So I'm not insulting your munificence by asking for forgiveness in the days to come. I have no right to expect that. The only right I have, and hold fast to, is the right to do what I believe is right for me, because then I will rest in peace, embalmed in my own private justice. The risk I run, I understand, is for my name to be sullied ever after by a poisonous epitaph. For sure, I won't be around to read it. I will be resident in the great elsewhere, blissfully exempt from further judgment. Thanks be to God."

Minnie raised her head, stretching the tired tendons in her neck. Contentment coursed through her, warm as her blood. Everything she required herself to do had now been done; everything except the last detail. She looked forward to her birthday party, where friends and neighbours would circle around the faltering sun of her smile like orbiting planets. Standing, she turned again to inspect the clothes she had arranged on the bed, touching them, straightening them, rolling the shoes on to their sides so that the soles and heels would not mark the tissue paper. This was a good time for her, this quiet moment. She was happy in the waiting.

She thought the blackbird had returned when she heard more tapping at the window. This time, though, the sound seemed of a lower register, more solid than before. She stared at the window and then she nodded and her smile was full of a terrible wisdom.

Black against the grey of the sky, a long spar of guttering hung in space, its broken bracket thumping the glass.

# Chapter 50

## *Number 25: Joan Descours*

Barry Brown waited. There was an odd taste in his mouth, rather like the tang of salt and vinegar. He wasn't sure what he should do right now, so he did nothing. In the pit of his stomach, a balloon seemed to be inflating and deflating, transmitting a seeping chill to his bowels. Joan was in the bathroom, running water, opening and shutting cupboards, sounding busy. The boy took a deep breath, held it for a count of thirty and let it go again. He smiled vacantly as the bathroom door opened.

Red and black bra and matching knickers. He glimpsed them only briefly as she tied the sash of her lilac-coloured dressing gown and moved towards him. The bed dipped under him as she settled herself by his side.

"You look nice," he said, not looking at her.

"Why, thank you, Barry."

"I think…"

"Yes, Barry, I would like to know what you think. Perhaps there are some little secret thoughts tied up in that head of yours."

"I think we could get into trouble," he said.

"Oh? And who's this 'we'?"

"Us."

"Barry, listen." She placed one hand on top of his. "You aren't doing anything wrong, so you can't get into trouble. Youth and inexperience conveniently absolve you from liability."

Barry wasn't sure about the liability. He thought it was a worrisome choice of word. "But you could get found out," he said. "You could lose your job."

"Do you think I don't know that? Do you think I'm not processing that risk?"

"It's just – I don't want to be the one who gets you into

295

trouble. I'm not ready for that responsibility."

"Oh, I don't think you're responsible for anything, Barry. I mean – are you seducing me, for God's sake?"

"Course not."

"Well then. You see, I just want us to be friends. Intimate friends, perhaps, but friends."

"Intimate, like how?"

"Like however we want. Like however we feel."

Barry nodded once. His eyes were clouded with doubt. "Tell me some more about the desert island," he said.

"Oh yes, the desert island. Our desert island."

"Yes. I like the sound of it."

"I wouldn't want you to feel lonely there, Barry. There'd only be the two of us, you and me, together for ever."

"Unless we get rescued."

"Who wants to be rescued from an idyllic paradise? Who wants to be hauled out of there and dumped back in the rowdy old world? Eh?"

Joan undid the dressing gown sash and massaged her stomach. The patch of red caught Barry's eye, accelerating his breath.

"Where would we sleep, Joan?"

"We'd probably sleep on the beach or near it. Inland there could be unseen hazards. I think I'd feel safer by the ocean. Animals prowl under cover."

"I suppose. And what would we do about going to the toilet?"

She laughed shortly. "No toilet, Barry. This is not the Isle of Wight. No, we'd pee in the sea and the tide would wash it away. For the other thing, well, we'd dig a hole and squat, cover it up afterwards. Easy."

Barry looked impressed. "You've got it all worked out, haven't you."

"I like a plan, Barry. I like to think ahead." She eased her shoulders out of the gown and let it fall loosely on to the bed behind her. "It's warmer in here now. I don't need this."

"What are we going to do, Joan?"

"On the island?"

"No, not on the island. I mean here, now, in this room. What do you expect?"

"What do I expect? I expect you to tell me of your expectations, that's what I expect."

"But you brought me here. You must have had a reason."

"Yes. To find out your expectation. Remember when we were on that ride and you – "

"I remember." He bit his lip, blinking his smarting eyes. "Somehow it's different now."

"Different? How is it different, Barry? Tell me."

"I've got the temptation and no excuse. Before, the situation protected me."

She scratched her head with a fingernail. "Yes, I suppose it did. Funny, we're more exposed in here than we were up in the air."

"We're kind of exposed to our instincts," Barry admitted. He placed a trembling hand on the fabric covering Joan's left breast. "We're – we're dangerous."

"Dangerous? Are we dangerous?"

"We're in a dangerous situation."

"And what's the danger, Barry, hmm? The danger we might find out about each other? The danger we might enjoy ourselves? The danger we could experience a little harmless pleasure?"

He moved his hand away. "But it wouldn't be harmless, would it? If anyone found out."

"Found out what? Found out how?" She swept a hand irritably through her hair. "Oh, please, Barry, tell me you're not about to go squealing to the authorities on me. I really thought you were more manly than that."

"Course I won't. I'd never do that. I like you too much."

"Well then." She leaned over and kissed him on the lips. "Let's not get neurotic about it." Grabbing his wrist, she dragged his hand on to the soft flesh below her navel.

"Does that feel good, Barry? Does it feel good to you?"

Barry nodded, licking his lips.

"Can you hear the sound of the sea, Barry? Remember, we'll be naked on the island. You won't be bundled up in your clothes and I won't bother with a dressing gown or underwear. We'll be dressed in each other."

Barry turned his head away, one hand clasping the side of his face.

"Have you got toothache?"

"No."

"How much do you like me, Barry? Do you just like me, or do you want me?"

"Joan."

"That's my name, Barry." She reached behind her and unfastened her bra, tossing it across the bed. "And do you like me any better now, Barry?"

"You – you're braver than me," he said.

"Oh, I don't know about that. I'm more experienced, yes."

"You're brave. You have the courage of your convictions."

She eyed him levelly. "Conviction, Barry, is something I am naturally anxious to avoid."

He smiled and shook his head, meeting her gaze with honesty. She closed her eyes when she felt his hand cupping her breast. Neither of them spoke. They leaned together, quietly bumping heads. Barry could see the island shore quite clearly now. He could see Joan lying naked on the wet sand, one leg extended, the other drawn back, flexed at the knee. The high sun sparkled in the water droplets jewelling the nest of her pubic hair. With her back flattened against the beach, her breasts had lost their fullness and diminished. Brown scuds of sand decorated her toes. He was walking down from the undergrowth behind her, probably she didn't know he was there, his soft footsteps inaudible in the sea's susurration. Seconds later, he knelt down and kissed the side of her neck. There was no need for either of them to say anything. The language was in the scene. Talking meant nothing. There was only the sun and the sand and the sky and the sea, and their bodies were safely enfolded within that small, magical world.

Joan lifted her hands to Barry's shoulders and moved him to arms' length. "I don't know what to make of you," she said.

"What?"

"The biggest difference between us is, I know what I want and you don't. I've arrived and you're still travelling."

"Perhaps that's because I'm not sure where I'm going."

"You only have to follow me, Barry. Look, I'm not in love with you and I mean you no harm, but the last thing I want is for you to feel scared of me."

"I'm not scared of you."

"Scared of the situation, maybe. If you're not scared of me, you could be scared of *us*."

"Us? What's us? I'm a pupil, you're the teacher. That's us."

"And that's all you're interested in? So I'm just making a complete fool of myself?"

She stood up and walked to the window. Barry, watching her, saw her small, slightly triangular breasts darkly silhouetted against the light. She bent to lean on the sill, looking out, and his eyes roamed over the curvature of her bottom, the sculpting of her upper thighs pinkly imprinted by the folds of the bedclothes.

"Joan, what are you doing?"

"Nothing. Looking. Nothing. Nothing for you to worry about."

"Please come here. Come and sit by me."

"What for?" She spoke over her shoulder. "What is it you want?"

"I want you to like me."

"You know I like you. We wouldn't be here otherwise."

"I disappoint you, don't I?"

"No, as a matter of fact, you don't. This – I suppose it's

pretty much how I expected it would be."

"Please come and sit with me."

She came back and sat with one arm looped loosely around his shoulders. He touched her breast again.

"I sort of feel we could be here a long time," she said.

He put his forefinger in her navel. "I like that," he said.

"It's a start," she laughed. "I don't know as I'd call it penetration."

"I like your tummy."

"Barry."

"What?"

"Will you please take your clothes off and lie down on the bed."

He was silent for a moment. "And then what?"

"And then – whatever happens, happens. There's no script, Barry, no rules or regulations. Nothing for you to worry about, and I won't judge or measure you. Understand?"

"I understand," he said.

She kissed him. "Would you like me to help you?"

He nodded.

Joan slid from the bed and knelt on the floor at his feet. Barry's hands reached down to balance her breasts while she unbuttoned him. Their eyes met. She stopped moving.

"What's wrong?" he asked.

"Oh, there's nothing wrong, Barry." She sighed and smiled mysteriously. "Nothing in the whole wide world."

# Chapter 51

## *Number 35: Mrs Leila Smart and Billy Smart*

Billy's favourite white and tan guinea pig trotted to the front of his cage and stood on his hind legs with his miniature front paws clutching the metal bars.

"Hello, Aubrey," Billy said.

Aubrey made no audible reply but ground his tiny incisors on a convenient bar, twitching his whiskers. A small pile of droppings, resembling Lilliputian rugby balls, spontaneously appeared on the sawdust behind him. Releasing his grip on the metal, the little animal tucked his head neatly under his belly and gobbled up a gleaming pellet.

"I'll feed you in a minute," Billy told him, but Aubrey didn't hear the offer as he had gone back for a second helping.

"Now I've got something important to tell you." Billy stood stiffly before the cage and raised both fists as though clutching invisible lapels. "This is how people stand in offices," he said, rather proudly. "That's when they're making a delegation – a declaration. Are you listening to me, Aub? You got to take this in. I need you to tell the others later, only some of them's asleep. The thing is, I'm going away, see. That is, I'm not going to live somewhere else, no, but I've got a job now and so you'll all have to manage on your own some days. Course I'll feed you in the morning and I'll ask Mum to look in, see you're all right. I don't really want to be doing this, only Mum wants me to be useful and help her and earn some money, so. It won't make no difference, not really, when you think about it, cos I'll still be here in the evening and at night when it's dark, so I don't want you getting scared or nothing. We'll still all be friends like it's always been, promise you. Yeah."

His mother tapped on the door. "Billy, who are you talking to?"

"Who do you think? No-one comes in my room."

The door clicked ajar and Leila's face appeared. "You spend too much time yakking to those animals."

"I'm not yakking, I'm talking."

"Are you now? Can I come in?"

"No."

"I just want to help you, Billy. I want to be sure you're ready for tomorrow."

"I'll be ready. I'll set my alarm."

"And what about your clothes?"

"What about them?"

"Do you need anything ironing? Are your shoes clean?"

"Mum!"

"Billy, you don't seem to understand. It's very important you make a good impression. I mean, from the outset. It's so important."

"Mum, they're not going to think I'm a good employee just because I've got shiny shoes."

"No, but if you attend to the details, Billy, you'll find the bigger factors often take care of themselves. It's called being conscientious." She pushed the door wider. "Billy, I can't talk to you like this."

"Like what?"

"Round the side of the door. Look, I'm coming in just for – oh, Billy, for Christ's sake! Why haven't you got any clothes on?"

"It's Sunday," Billy replied, placing one hand over his penis.

Leila let out a long, laboured breath. "I've got a son who stands around naked, talking to animals. I despair of you, Billy."

"I said not to come in."

"My being in here's not the point. You've been up for hours and you're still not dressed. What are you going to do tomorrow morning? Are you going to work in the nude?"

Billy turned aside and showed her his white bottom. Close to his ankles, Denzil's scaly, chiselled head appeared from the darkness under the bed.

Leila swallowed, restraining her disgust. "I'll thank you not to wave your arse at me when I'm talking to you, Billy Smart. You'd think we were dogs in the park, socialising by sniffing each other's bums. I'm your mother, for God's sake!"

"Mum, please. Just leave it." He turned to face her again, grabbing a pair of discarded pants to cover his crotch. "I know what I gotta do."

"Then see you do it. Get some clothes on. I'm shutting this door before that bloody snake gets out."

She sat at the kitchen table with one hand over her eyes, inhaling the sweetness of her wrist. Billy was everywhere, bumping around upstairs, fuelling her anxiety, blundering through every space in her head. Her son was a migraine that never went away, a dull ache in her stomach that could not be vomited to oblivion. Even as she cajoled and encouraged him, she knew that her support was wasted on him, for he had failed at the paper shop and at the chip shop because that inadequacy was all he was capable of, an inertia that irredeemably defined him. She could weep not only for this recognition of hopelessness but also at the stark spectre of her own betrayal, the bankruptcy of her capacity to believe in the worthiness of her own son.

He stood beside her, hastily dressed in tracksuit bottoms and a T-shirt. "I was going to ask you."

"Ask me what?"

"As I'm going away, you might keep an eye on the animals."

She shook her head as if to clear her mind. "Keep an eye? Billy, what's with this 'going away'? You're crossing the road to do a bit of work. You're not emigrating or walking to the scaffold."

"I know. Just if I'm late or anything."

"Billy, that rather depends on how late you mean. If it's winter, say, and you're wanting me to walk into a dark room and meet a python…"

"I'll put Denzil in the wardrobe when I leave."

She sighed. "When you get the chance, start writing your life story: 'The Python in the Wardrobe'."

"Honest, it'll be all right, Mum."

"Will it, Billy? Will it really? Will any of this, anything in your life, ever be all right? Convince me, Billy."

"Mum?"

"Billy, you've no shoes on. Put something on your feet."

"I like being barefoot."

"Yes, and last week you trod on a drawing pin in the hall. Have a try at being sensible, Billy. Surprise me."

"Mum, why are you always having a go at me? You've always got it in for me."

Leila ground her teeth, balancing her fists on the table top. "No, Billy, it's not me that's got it in for you. It's you that's got it in for you. Can't you see that?"

"I don't know what you mean."

She didn't quite know why, but tears began to blur her vision, stinging like ants crawling in her eyes. "Sit down," she told Billy.

Huffing, pouting, he moved past her and subsided into the opposite chair. "What is it?"

"Billy, do you think I've let you down? With your father and all that stuff?"

"What? All what stuff?"

"I've tried hard to be a good mother to you ever since your dad left. It's not been easy."

"It's all right, Mum."

"But it could be better, I know. I never thought I'd be bringing you up on my own."

"It's all right, Mum."

She wiped her eyes with her fingers. "How can it be, though? You could have had a better life. Your dad would have taken you places, helped you to make friends, do

304

other things with boys your own age."

"It's all right, Mum, honest."

"That's why I want you to promise me something."

"I promise, Mum."

"Don't be daft, I haven't told you what it is yet. Now, I want you to promise me you'll do your very best in your new job to get on and make a success of it, so they'll appreciate you and grow to like you. In time, you could be promoted and earn more money, or maybe move on to something different, something more important that would challenge you. Do you understand what I'm saying, Billy?"

"I told them at the interview, Mum. I told them I would do my best. That's why they gave me the job."

"Of course. And if you want to make them happy, and make me happy, then you just stick with it and show them how determined you are." She reached across the table and stroked the back of his hand. "No doubt you'll meet lots of new people, maybe make some good friends. You won't have to talk to animals all the time. Could be you'll find a girl-friend there, you never know."

Billy pulled a deprecating face. "I'm not looking for a girl-friend."

"No, well, shut in your room with a bunch of rodents, you wouldn't be. My point is, there's a whole wide world out there, Billy, and some of it's for you. So you need to get out and claim your share."

The boy looked doubtful, glumly inspecting his fingernails, their undersides rimmed with greyish crescents of animal dirt from tanks and cages.

"You'll soon see I'm right, Billy. Just give it a little time."

"I know."

She gazed at him with her head inquisitively on one side. "Billy, do you miss your dad?"

"Why are you asking me that?"

"Because I'd like to know, that's all."

He shrugged. "A bit."

"Is that a big bit or a little bit?"

"Does it matter?"

"Yes, I think it matters. He's still your father. Do you know it's his birthday today?"

Billy shook his head.

"I've got his address and phone number. You could send him a card or else ring him, wish him a happy birthday. He'd like that. Then you could tell him about your new job."

"I suppose."

"Or…or you could wait till you've worked, say, a week and then go and see him and tell him how you got on at the water company. I bet he'd be proud."

Billy flattened his hands on the table and stared at her. "Mum, that's not important. I don't care if he's proud. He doesn't know me now. It's you I want to be proud of me."

"But I am, Billy. I am proud of you."

He shot to his feet, scraping the chair noisily on the floor. "Why?" he blurted, tears glinting in his eyes. "How? What have I ever done to make you proud of me? In my whole life, what have I ever done?"

He ran from the room. She heard his footsteps on the stairs and the bedroom door slamming. Tilting back her head, she heard a strangled cry, a staccato yelp of despair.

She could go to him, but certainly he would not want to see her, would not let her in. She remained quite still, eyes wearily roaming the table top, as if in vain search of some guidance or inspiration. For several minutes she sat quietly, moulding her hands in her lap, and then she stood up and reached for the phone.

"Hello," was all he said.

"Roger? It's me, Leila."

A dismissive click of the lips. "What the fuck do you want?"

"A nice greeting, when I've rung to wish you a happy birthday."

"Come off it, Leila, you haven't bothered previous years."

"No, well, all right. Happy birthday, anyway. How are you?"

"Leila, what is this? What's going on?"

"Me. Us. We're going on."

"I tell you, I'm putting the phone down if you don't make sense."

"Roger – "

"You ring me up out of the blue and all you can say is you're going on. Look, I'm not an academic, Leila, but it seems to me this is one of your mad conversations starting up, which I don't need to be a party to, not no more. In case you hadn't noticed, I'm out of it."

"Your son, Roger." She was shouting now, gripping the phone fiercely in her trembling hand. "Billy, your son!"

"What about him," came the quiet response.

"Roger, Billy needs you. He's upset and confused. I do my best for him, but sometimes…sometimes it's not enough. He's going through a difficult time and he's not getting the support he needs. I don't know, I even wonder if I'm not up to it."

There was only silence on the line, overlaid with his reflective breathing.

"Roger, are you there?"

"Course I'm here. Leila, I'm not coming back."

"I'm not asking you to – not in that way."

"So what is it you want? Why are you ringing me?"

"I thought you might be interested," she said meekly. "I thought you might like to know about your son."

"And what about him? Is he ill? Is he in trouble?"

"No."

"What then?"

She took a deep breath and brushed back her hair. "Roger, please will you come and see him, talk to him, even if it's just for an hour or two."

"What, come to the house?"

"Yes, come to the house, come to where he lives."

"What's happened?"

"Actually, Billy's got himself a new job, starting

Monday."

"The age of miracles."

"Roger, he's nervous and mixed up and worried and…"
Her voice broke, trailing off into inaudible fragments.

"Jeez. What's the name of that pub up the road?"

"The Rifleman."

"Tomorrow, seven o'clock. Tell him I'll meet him
there, buy him a pint. Might even buy him two."

"I don't want you to get him drunk."

"For goodness' sake, woman!"

"Okay, Roger. Thanks. I'm sorry I phoned you like
this."

"Don't worry about it."

"I'm only worried about him. If you could see him…"

"I've said."

"Happy birthday, Roger."

"Get lost, you silly cow."

# Chapter 52

## *Number 15: Aisling McIver is Re-acquainted With Stephen J. Kettering-Barclay*

The grit in his hair was nothing more than tiny specks, almost microscopic, but clearly visible. It resembled greyish-white seeds or maybe grains of dust. Aisling frowned, testing the texture of his peppered scalp with her fingertips. It put her in mind of those poor, terrified New Yorkers, ash-cloaked, looming out of the fog like gaping ghosts as the Trade Centers telescoped to the ground behind them. But this was fourteen years later and they were not in New York. Could the gritty stuff be eggs? She shuddered, wiping her fingers on her sleeve.

"Mister, do you ever wash your hair?" she asked him.

"What? Why are you fiddling with my hair?"

"I'm not fiddling. I just noticed."

"Noticed what?" he growled.

"Your hair is very dirty. Surely it must itch."

"I don't notice it. I don't worry about it."

"Well, I do. In fact, my friend, you are not clean."

"You said that the last time."

"You weren't clean the last time." She put her hands on his shoulders to ease him away from her. "When did you last have a bath?"

"I'm not good with baths. I wash, up and down. That does me."

Not for the first time, she recoiled at the prospect of being close to this man. She would be naked, or very nearly. He would be naked, a bundle of white sticks, redolent of decay. This would not do.

She had greeted him with her normal clothes on. Whoever was coming, she nowadays did this anyway. Rona was explicit in the matter of the introduction, the manner of it. "Don't open the door to them with nothing on. Don't meet them just in your scarlet underwear. Makes you look like a slut. They won't come to the door naked and neither should you."

Without Rona, where would she be? Stuffing envelopes, perhaps. Beavering grimly for a pittance. Dear Rona. Sometimes it seemed the wisdom fairly poured out of her. As for old Seadog, well, she'd hardly come to the door for him stark naked, he might have a bloody heart attack, then they'd both have some serious explaining to do.

He was waving a folded wad of cash at her. She took the money and counted it, looked puzzled and counted it again.

"Stephen, hey, this is too much. There's a hundred and fifty here."

His response was a desultory wave of his skeletal hand. "Don't worry, my dear. I had the money in the house."

"And now it's in my house. I only want ninety."

"Why is it a problem? I can afford to pay it. Can you afford to refuse it?"

"I can't take more than the right money. I can't."

He rocked his head, seeking conciliation. "Very well. Give me the extra time, then we're all square."

"It still feels wrong, Stephen. I've insulted you and now you're rewarding me."

"No, you haven't insulted me. You told the truth, that's all."

She took the money to the kitchen and returned. "You need to start looking after yourself, you know. Why are you not doing that?"

"Does it matter, really?"

"Sure, it matters to me. If I'm to be spending time with you."

Nodding, expressionless, he looked her up and down. She was wearing an old denim dress in two-tone blue with a faded collar and patch pockets. Rona, she suspected, would not approve of the bare legs and flat shoes. Stockings, preferably dark, were considered *de rigeur,* whatever the state of your legs. Sorry, Rona.

"Stephen, do you want to come upstairs now or sit a while, eh?"

They sat on the sofa. Neamh cried in her sleep, bleating lamb-like, and was quiet again. Seadog sighed and put his hand under Aisling's skirt. The phone rang but she made no move to answer it.

The old man's hand clawed at her thigh. "Aren't you going to – "

"I don't answer it when I'm working. Bad practice."

"You're a good girl," he said. "You look lovely."

"What, in this? How can you tell?"

"I can imagine."

"You don't have to imagine. You've seen me before. You can see me again – only first…"

"First?"

"Stephen, dear man, I really think I should start by putting you in a nice warm bubble bath. What do you say? And take your hand off my leg, your nails need cutting."

That was Rona again. "Always check their fingernails. Clip them yourself if you feel the need. Imagine, if they want to touch you up there and you get scratched. Unpleasant is hardly the word." Yes, Rona. Tell me, in all the world, is there anything you don't know?

Stephen stared morosely at his knees. "I told you, I'm not good with baths."

"Sure, I heard you. And, you know, I'm not good with grubby people." She took his arm. "Come on, I'll look after you."

Seadog knew in that moment that he must yield. If in that breath of clarity there was something less than an apocalypse, still it was more than a turning point and he was left with nowhere to go but the fragile platform from which he would confront his resolution. He accepted the invitation, quietly and with a thoughtful grace.

Aisling, leading him upstairs by the hand, wondered briefly at his calm compliance. "Undress and put your things on the chair," she told him. "I'll run you a bath. I'll help you in, of course."

"Thank you. You are a wonderful woman." He sat to unfasten his leg. "Your child…"

"What about her?"

"She is fortunate. She is loved. You have bequeathed her the world."

"I surely hope so," Aisling said.

He sat naked on the chair with his clothes draped over the back. The bath water hissed as Aisling swished the foam, steam coiling against the wall. She turned to look at him, flicking the wet from her hands. *You poor man*, she thought. Where had his brave world gone? Where now was his pride, his self-esteem, his confidence? Could it really be that a small, pale hand laid upon him gave him all that he could expect? This was surely an appalling truth.

"I'm ready to be helped," he said. "You – last time there was a stool in the bath for me to sit on."

"No stool, Stephen. I want you sitting down in the water, the nice clean water."

"That's not right. I'm not comfortable with that."

"I'm here. I shan't leave you. You'll be safe."

He remembered. He remembered what he had to do. He let himself subside into the moment of arrival. "Dear God," he whispered. "Bless this woman."

She marvelled at her own strength as she manoeuvred him into the bath. "You're ungainly but not heavy," she said.

He slipped down into the surging water, the fragrant tide lapping halfway up his chest. She steadied him with one arm against his back, then cautiously released him, heaving a sigh of relief as the bath scents rose to mask his odour. Taking a sponge, she knelt beside him and tended him. She worked silently, patiently, until he was clean, almost as clean as he had ever been. Small beards of foam dangled from the clumps of hair on his chest. Lowering her hand into the darkening water, she felt between his legs, teasing him lightly.

Dropping the sponge, she unbuttoned the front of her

312

denim dress. "Do you want this now? Or would you rather wait till you're out, till we're in the bedroom? Just tell me."

Tears gleamed in his eyes. "Later," he said. His breathing had altered, his chest flexing erratically.

"Are you okay, Stephen?"

"Get me out," he told her.

"Not yet, Stephen, not yet. We're not done yet. Roll over a tad and I'll do your bottom."

"No."

"Sure, I've got you this far. We'll finish now, come on."

He lunged towards her, gripping the bath rim. His jaw was set and suddenly the wetness in his eyes was a glaze of anger. An electric tremor blurred his face.

"Stephen, what's the matter?"

"Get back!" A creamy spittle streaked his chin. "You'll have us over!"

"Stephen!"

"Get back! Go!"

His forehead butted her nose.

"All right, all right, I'll get you out, if you just stay still!"

"Get back! You'll tip us over!"

"Stephen, please!"

The water whooshed as he threw himself forward again. Aisling saw the punch coming and ducked aside, but in the next instant Stephen's hands had grabbed her throat in a vice-like grip, dragging her tightly against the side of the tub. His ferocious strength dismayed her, as she felt the grating pressure in her windpipe and heard the blood roaring in her ears.

"Yaaah!" The old man rocked her madly back and forth, spitting from twisted lips. "I – told – you!"

Scratching the side of her face with her nails, Aisling seized Seadog's wrists and flung his hands desperately upwards, ripping his clawed and whitened fingers from her neck. She struggled to her feet, bent over the bath, choking, and punched the old man violently on the back of his neck with the base of a bunched fist, smacking his head against the taps. A trickle of blood smoked the scummy water under his chin. His left hand lashed out, catching her beneath the eye, and in her defensive rage she clamped her hand over his head and drove it down into the crashing water with all her might, closing her eyes, gritting her teeth, holding his head there until her arm sang with the pain of it, the quivering ache of it.

The bubbles spiralled up from Seadog's mouth. A hollow warbling issued from the bottom of the bath, but the gurgling stopped when the bubbles stopped. Aisling, gasping, let go of the man's head and stood back, hands shaking uncontrollably. She stumbled back and sat on the chair, staring at the slumped form heaped like a white island in the water. She waited quietly for the splashing to subside.

Slowly, her breath returned. She rubbed her bruised throat with trembling fingers. The thin wisp of a groan filtered out of the tub. From Seadog's exposed bottom, a burbling fart rippled. Aisling sat quite still, staring at the old man in the bath, the swarthy hump of his arched back, the white mat of his drenched hair jammed under the taps. She was very still. She could not move. She could not speak. In her head, she counted to one hundred, just moving her lips. Nothing else in the room moved. The old man did not move. She reached one hundred, but the old man had not moved. In the room was a deafening silence.

With both hands clasping the underside of the chair, she shuffled herself forward until she could see into the bath. Seadog's face was still immersed in the grey water. His arms seemed to be crushed under him. His scrawny thighs protruded in the air and a caramel-coloured ooze of faeces smeared one cheek of his buttocks. Aisling tore off a square of toilet paper and wiped him. She touched his cold back, pressing the bony nodules. Nothing happened. The torrent of a wild pulse pounded in her ears. She lowered her head and waited, and slowly, surely, inexorably, the tears came. She tasted the salt on her lips. She tasted a terrible despair.

"Stephen?" Her voice was hardly more than a whisper. "Stephen!"

She crept forward to look at him. Soaking her arms in the cooling water, she heaved his body over so that he lay on his side with his legs drawn up. Then, no longer requiring the buoyancy, she pulled out the plug and watched the tub empty. The old man's eyes were open, cold pebbles staring, and they would not respond when she tried with her fingers to probe them shut, so she walked stiffly to the bedroom, found a grey wool hat in the drawer and took it to the bathroom, pulling it down over Seadog's forehead to cover his eyes. From the airing cupboard she removed a blanket, draped it over her arm and carried it to the bath, where she laid it loosely over his folded body. Then she left the room and closed the door quietly behind her.

Downstairs she lifted Neamh from her cot and cradled the child warmly in her arms. She held her very closely, tightly, as if she might crush the breath from her. Her tears dripped from her chin and spattered the baby's blanket. Neamh slept. Her mouth was a small pink flower. She was perfect. Aisling held her for what felt like a lifetime passing, and it was as though that sweet pain would go on for ever.

"God bless you, little one," she murmured. "May He always bless and keep you."

# Chapter 53

## Saturday 13*th* June
## The Rifleman Public House

A mellow evening sun bronzed the brick front walls of The Rifleman, tinting with freshly resplendent colour the luxuriant planted baskets hanging at the windows. Polly, the landlord's wife, had even managed to suspend them by the first floor windows, doubling the display's glorious impact. Her baskets glowed with blooms of pink and red and yellow, trailing fuchsia caressing dense begonia, the brightness perfectly balanced and enhanced by the subtler fronds of tradescantia, some striped, some purple, in which the flowers were cradled. Even those who passed The Rifleman without entering to drink would often pause there and admire the beauty of Polly Broome's window displays and perhaps take photographs to capture the gorgeous colours.

Mervyn Broome's sole contribution to the imposing frontal aspect of the pub of which he and Polly had been owners and landlords for the past ten years was a large rectangular sign board above the doorway. *The Rifleman* was picked out in gold lettering on an olive-green background over the glinting gold outline of a marksman in a beret, depicted in head and shoulders profile, aiming a rifle at some distant quarry. As the sun inflamed the brilliance of Polly's floral bouquets, so did it send streaks of gold fire through Mervyn's arresting name board, and it was small wonder that many locals referred to the landlord as The Man with the Golden Gun.

Inside the pub, as afternoon waned into evening, Mervyn Broome was busy preparing the function room for a special party. While his wife climbed a ladder outside to water the plants, Mervyn strode purposefully to and fro carrying plastic banners, packets of balloons, paper tableware and a small toolbox. Dragging aside the ruby-red curtain separating the room from the main bars, he began pushing chairs and tables in a line towards the wall and laying out the decorations neatly at one end. Shortly the caterers, Nick and Patricia of *QuinQuisine,* would arrive to arrange the buffet food, and their daughter Sally was to help Mervyn hang the celebratory bunting. Then there was Charlie Dixon, Minnie Starling's grandson: he was coming early to hang over the tables a photo montage of scenes from his grandmother's long and remarkable life. Mervyn paused for a moment and smiled; everything was in hand and this would surely be a memorable evening.

The band arrived at six. Albert Thirlwell was helped in by his daughter. His grey hair, still luxuriant, was tied into the tuft of a ponytail, secured with an elastic band. In his lapel, a tin badge, printed black on yellow, read 'Rock On, Teddy', a tribute to violinist Teddy Baverstock, who had recently died. In his place Albert had employed a bald man with a ginger beard, who carried a white violin case from which he produced a battle-scarred white violin. Painted on the case was the ginger man's name: Pat de Ville. These two were followed in by a fat trumpeter, a thin percussionist and a tall youth, apparently more than a generation younger than the others, carrying an electric guitar. The young man propped his guitar against the wall and went outside again to fetch his amp and soundbox from the group's van. On the front of the box the silvered plastic script read 'Wayne Laine'.

Mervyn stood in the middle of the floor, appraising the assembled musicians. "When you're ready," he said.

Albert Thirlwell stared at him blankly. "There's nobody here. You want us to play?"

"Just something easy. Best if people can be serenaded as they come in. That way they don't feel so exposed."

Albert shrugged and unzipped his clarinet from a leather bag. "Suit yourself."

"I'll get me kit," the thin percussionist muttered, placing his pint of lager on the floor.

"Go easy on the drums," Mervyn told them. "We don't want anyone scared off at the start."

The trumpeter blew one shrieking blast, worked his lips and gazed around in apparent confusion.

"Do you want chairs?" Mervyn asked.

"Got mine in the van," said the drummer.

"I'm eighty-four," Albert pointed out. "I can't stand up all night."

"I'll get four chairs," Mervyn said. He turned and walked away, wondering if they should have had some flashing lights and a DJ. He reckoned the combined ages of the Albert Thirlwell Combo came to nearly three hundred. Even if people wanted to dance, he would have to give the band a rest.

Polly Broome came in and looked around, fiddling nervously with the tables. Gazing up at the dark beams, she *tutted* crossly at the yellow and orange tufts of paper left over from the Christmas streamers.

"Evening, Molly," Albert called, one foot on the raised platform where the band would play.

"It's Polly," she reminded him sullenly.

"Good Golly, it's Polly," exclaimed Pat de Ville, grinning artfully.

Polly Broome stared at him until he looked away, stuffing his violin under his beard. She stood and surveyed the group, wondering why Mervyn hadn't gone for Ricky Rascal and the Trailblazers. This lot didn't look as if they would last the evening.

Mervyn appeared, placing a hand on her shoulder. "The *QuinQuisine* van's here."

She turned. "Let's hope the food's better than the music's likely to be."

"Come on, Poll, give them a chance. At least they're cheap – cheap and cheerful, eh?"

"Cheerful? Albert Thirlwell gave up being cheerful forty years ago. And what's with the ponytail? Looks like he's replaced his head with an onion."

The fat man brushed past her, carrying his trumpet in

one hand and zipping his fly with the other. "That's better," he croaked.

They exchanged brief nods and launched into 'Moon River'.

Polly pulled a knowledgeable face. "Yeah, best place for them," she said, "the river."

She need not have worried about the buffet. The catering staff made countless journeys between their van and the party room, bringing multi-coloured armfuls of film-covered food to distribute along the brightly dressed tables. Flaps of white and gold chicken the size of a man's hand were displayed alongside bowls of creamy potato salad flecked with chives, next to them broad platters of cocktail sausages impaled on plastic sticks, mounds of triangular sandwiches tiered like the Sydney Opera House, vegetable samosas still warm from the oven, heaped flaky pastry sausage rolls, green salad tossed in sweet dressing, sliced beef artistically arranged in a russet fan, tiger bread loaves with assorted cheeses, a whole side of honey-roast ham, a filleted and carved salmon, a tureen of garlic mushrooms...no-one would go hungry this special evening.

"There are desserts, gateaux, trifles, that sort of thing," Pat the caterer informed Polly. "We'll bring them in so you can put them in your fridge for later."

The landlord's wife surveyed the tables open-mouthed. "I'm amazed," she gasped. "The Residents' Association – they've paid for all this?"

"They had a collection as well," Pat allowed. "Mrs Starling is obviously a very well-respected lady." She took off her plastic apron and folded it neatly. "I'm sorry I can't stay. Best wishes from us at *QuinQuisine.*"

The catering van reversed and pulled away. The Albert Thirlwell Combo eased into 'Strangers in the Night'. At the open pub doorway, people began to arrive in small, huddled groups, chattering amiably. Some of them had dogs on leads. Some of them brought children. Some of them carried cards and gifts or bunches of flowers. All of them smiled and moved their hands in cheerful animation. Charlie Dixon came in, looking flustered, and began hastily tacking up a frieze of photographs showing Minnie through the century, Minnie in her baby's bonnet, Minnie astride her tricycle, in uniform on a school trip, windblown on a cruise steamer, grinning with friends in Times Square, poised nervously on a camel, on a picnic with Charlie beside a glinting river.

The Albert Thirlwell Combo slid unsteadily into 'Smoke Gets in Your Eyes'. Charlie left to go to Paradise Park to collect his grandmother and bring her to the party. Someone furtively prised a sausage from under the cling film and fed it to a slavering German Shepherd.

The people came. They came from each of the three Paradise roads, old and young, fit and frail, and though many had not known one another before, they mingled warmly and conversed agreeably about the weather and the price of a pint and the Arabs and Israelis and how the postman had got knocked off his bike at the roundabout. They separated into small, beaming clusters and found themselves comfortable corners, where they were not too near the band and could keep a watchful eye on the status of the food. Quite soon the talk was of the old man from number 30, who had been found, so it was rumoured, dead in the bath.

"I heard he slipped and drowned," someone said.

"Well, I heard that, only..."

"Only what, dear?"

"It was a bit funny. Well, no, I don't mean it was funny. More sort of peculiar."

"How peculiar?"

"See, I saw the police and the ambulance, and they were parked outside another house on the opposite side of the road."

"What, he wasn't in his own place?"

"Seems not. Very peculiar."

A woman with blue hair and a red gash of lipstick cut in. "Oh, that's a mistake, surely. I mean, why would he go for a bath at someone else's house? It makes no sense."

"Maybe his own bath wasn't working. Maybe – I don't know."

"People do funny things," said a florid-faced man in a tweed jacket.

"You talking about that old chap?" The young girl wore a purple T-shirt over tracksuit bottoms. The sequinned legend on the T-shirt said 'Kiss Me Slow'. The girl smiled at the man in tweed, revealing braces on her teeth that gleamed like a radiator grille. "I think he done himself in deliberate."

Tweed man supplied a watery smile and wondered vaguely about *kissing her slow.* She was a bit young for him, he thought, and he might get his lips stapled together. This was a small community; you had to be careful.

Polly Broome shouldered her way in amongst them. "Just waiting for Minnie to arrive," she explained. "Should be any minute now. Then we'll unwrap the food and get some dancing music going."

The Albert Thirlwell Combo were playing something slow which no-one had ever heard before. Albert Thirlwell lowered his clarinet and shouted "One of my own compositions. It's called 'Springtime in Sienna'. Hope you like it."

"Not so's you'd notice," declared Polly Broome, to no-one in particular.

A fat man in a vest, bulging arms tattooed, dropped his full pint glass on the floor, sending a dozen bystanders leaping backwards.

"I'll fetch a broom," said Polly Broome. "Don't step in that broken glass. We don't want any nasty accidents."

At 6.45 by the station clock over the bar, Charlie Dixon arrived with Minnie Starling. "I'd like a drink first," Minnie told Charlie, waving her stick precariously.

"Can you manage a bar stool, Gran?"

"No. Get me a chair."

"They all seem to be taken, Gran."

"Move someone. I'm a hundred, for God's sake." She

321

cast her eyes round the saloon. "There's no-one sitting here over forty-five. This is my party."

Charlie smiled apologetically at a young man with pink hair and took his chair from under him, dragging it to the bar. "Sorry, mate."

"I'd like a large Campari and soda, no ice, with a twist of lemon," Minnie announced, lowering herself carefully into the chair. "You got my handbag, Charlie?"

Charlie Dixon gave his grandmother her handbag. "Why's it so heavy, Gran?"

"Mind your own business," came the reply.

People began gathering around Minnie's chair, wishing her a happy birthday, expressing their amazement at her great age.

"Suppose you all expected me to be dead," Minnie said. "Sorry to have disappointed you, to have confounded all your theories."

The people shook their heads and laughed sycophantically. Polly appeared and hugged the old lady, whispering in her ear. Beyond the curtain, the Albert Thirlwell Combo upped their tempo with a battering of percussion.

"What's that dreadful racket?" Minnie protested.

"Albert Thirlwell," Charlie said.

"Huh. He's another one as should be dead."

"Gran!"

"Where's that Campari?"

Charlie peered anxiously along the bar. He suspected this could be a long evening. A man with bad breath pressed close to Charlie's ear, hustling to get served. "Move up, mate."

"Wait your turn," Charlie told him, without looking round. "Mrs Starling was here first."

"Who's Mrs Starling, when she's at home?"

There was nothing wrong with Minnie's hearing. "I am Mrs Starling," she said, and she elbowed the man in the thigh. "I am one hundred today and this is my party. You'll get served well before you reach my age."

322

In the function room, people were allocating themselves space on the floor to facilitate dancing. Extra bar staff had turned up for work, anticipating more customers than usual, releasing Mervyn Broome from his duties as barman. He stood parting the curtain, watching the dancers' antics as they fought for room in which to gyrate. The Thirlwell band began massacring some of the latest chart hits, Albert and the fat trumpeter already glowing red in the face as their lungs struggled to compete with the demands of the accelerating rhythm.

Mervyn stood aside, nodding a greeting, as Leila Smart and her son brushed his arm, followed by a crocodile of Minnie's friends and neighbours, keen to be in position for the unveiling of the buffet. Hettie Slocombe was accompanied by Mrs Stirrup, while Joan Descours, the college teacher, had brought along a young man surely less than half her age, appearing politely bewildered as he clutched his Coke. A few minutes later the landlord's back was nudged again as Roland James and his workman Raj peered into the room and sidled round the walls towards the groaning tables. The scene reverberated with pulsating music and raucous shouts and the careless stamping of feet.

Mervyn wondered what this spectacle was all about. It made no sense to him, if he really thought about it. Here were people throwing themselves at the walls, idiotically contorted like puppets with their strings cut. They were sweating, grim-faced, lunging at one another in a desperate defiance of the laws of gravity, hypnotised in a crazed belief that they were enjoying this ugly, spasmic outbreak of convulsions. Few of them, if any, were actually dancing, because that was a skill they did not have. In his lifetime Mervyn had been invited to innumerable parties, but he could not recall any at which a magician had stood up to pull a rabbit from a hat, for no-one with such a talent was present, just as no party-goer, to the best of his recollection, had ever sung a medley of songs or recited his latest anthology of poems. Neither had these variety acts been expected by the assembled multitude or their absence from the party repertoire lamented as a deficiency in the entertainment. There were simply no magicians, no singers, no poets available. More often than not, there were no dancers, either. Tonight was much the same; there were no dancers to be seen, however hard he looked for them.

"It's murder tonight," he said to himself. "The murder of music. The murder of artistry."

Polly Broome wound her way through the maelstrom of jerking bodies and deftly stripped the film from the plates of food. Blending with the smell of perspiration, a fresher, more palatable aroma began to rise on the air. On a table set aside in the corner by the exit doors, a growing pile of cards and gifts attracted attention. Someone had left a home-made pie, its constituents undivulged, wrapped in foil, next to it a plastic bag containing two pairs of warm socks in different sizes. A stylish blue box tied with a pink bow came from Leila and Billy Smart, inside it a Waterford crystal glass fruit bowl, towards the cost of which Billy had proudly contributed a pound from the reluctant sale of an irascible gerbil called Ralph.

Charlie intercepted Polly as she crossed the room, weaving and ducking to avoid the dancers' flailing arms and jabbing elbows. Amid the frenzy, Polly looked reassuringly calm.

"Mrs Broome, my grandmother – "

"Please, it's Polly. We're all friends here."

He nodded with a tight-lipped smile. "Polly, Minnie would like to speak to everyone for a few minutes, to thank them for coming. Only there's the music. It would have to be – paused for a while?"

"Of course, of course." Polly pinched the bridge of her nose thoughtfully and leaned into Charlie's ear. "I don't know about music, though. There's a loud noise coming from those old blokes on the stage. I could tell them to shut up."

"That would be – uh – yes, ideal."

"Shall I do it now?"

"Yes. I'm bringing her in."

When the band stopped, the crowd melted to the sides of the room, breaking into applause as Minnie Starling, with Charlie's hand in the small of her back, crept slowly through the parted curtain. A row of chairs stood along one wall and Charlie pulled one out for his grandmother to sit on and make herself comfortable. The applause continued for several minutes, interspersed with random cheers from the older men, beaming at Minnie over their beer mugs.

A baby squawked and someone yelled "Ssshh!"

"Don't you shush my baby!" retorted the child's mother.

Albert Thirlwell made a mental note to compose a new number entitled 'Shush my Baby'. It would be a big hit at the forthcoming Little Glandings Agricultural Show Ball. How would it go? He took advantage of the relative silence to hum a few experimental bars in his head. Yes, he could be on to something.

Bending to murmur in Minnie's ear, Charlie indicated the gift-laden table across the room. The old lady nodded in satisfaction, lifting her handbag on to her lap. At a signal from Charlie, Albert Thirlwell and his trumpeter blew a tinny fanfare to introduce the guest of honour's address to the multitude. There was a scattering of renewed applause, then a respectful silence. Minnie pulled a pink handkerchief from her bag, coughed quietly into it and tucked the hanky under her sleeve.

"Well now. Well, well. What a splendid gathering. I am most touched. You need to know that. I need to say thank you three times this evening: thank you for coming here to help me celebrate my birthday; thank you for the lovely presents so many of you have brought; and, most importantly of all, my thanks for being such good friends and neighbours down through the years. That's the thing I appreciate the most, the feature of my life I shall always remember. And now I want not only to express my appreciation, but also to make sure that all of you will long

325

remember this special event. I really intend that this party – well, that it goes with a bit of a bang."

She paused to allow a brief moment of dutiful laughter.

"Fifty-five years I've lived in the village. Well, it was hardly even a village when I first came here. Since then, and certainly in my long life, I've seen a lot of changes. Oh, I know people always say that, it's quite a cliché, but it does happen to be true. Think about it: one hundred years, a whole century. It's a very long time. I can't say as all the changes I've seen in that time are what I'd consider changes for the better. Let's see how many young people we have here this evening – put your hands up so I can spot you."

Slowly a desultory show of hands rose from the jumble of shoulders.

"Right you are, quite a few. You know, when I was your age we didn't have any of the luxuries and advantages you take for granted today. We had to show respect for our parents and we had to maintain that respect even when we got a clout round the ear for misbehaving. Back then, that wasn't considered child abuse, it was called responsible parenting. Respect, too, for authority, for your teachers and guardians of the law. I remember I used to run around out of school-time with a little lad called, called – what was his name? – ah, Jackie Jepson, yes, and Jackie Jepson, he often had these white pants showing below his short trousers, yes, and he would always stop and salute, real grown-up like, whenever he saw a police car, salute the policemen in the car, to show he thought they were important people and how maybe he was even a little afraid of them. Huh, can't imagine any youngsters doing that now. Nowadays it's the policemen as sometimes has to run away in fear. These are bad times. I remember, clear as day, when we first got the wireless – you call it the radio now – and the telephone and the television in black and white and nobody had a fridge or a washing machine. How did we manage? We made do, that's what happened, we made do. You know, it's funny,

I look out of my window some days and I see all the kids plodding down the road with these confounded gizmos in their hands – startphones or whatever it is you call them – and it makes me want to laugh, seeing them going along with their heads down like they was war criminals on their way to trial. Course, you don't view it that way, you call it progress."

The monologue was interrupted by a loud clatter as Albert Thirlwell dropped his clarinet on the floor.

Minnie squinted into the distance. "Ah, yes, that reminds me. I forgot a vote of thanks – to my old mate Albert Thirlwell for coming along tonight to entertain us with his attempts. They tell me young Albert is eighty-four. Glad to see you've still got the wind, Albert."

Albert Thirlwell brandished his instrument in acknowledgement, while the onlookers chuckled politely. Charlie Dixon, standing with one hand on Minnie's chair, glanced surreptitiously at his watch.

"Of course, when you've been around as long as I have, you know you can't look back and see just the good stuff. Sometimes it's a fair trick just to be able to notice the good stuff. My husband Jack got dementia, only they didn't call it that back then. The Good Lord took him from me and he died a drooling nutter who had not the slightest notion who I was, staggering about bow-legged in his wet trousers with his eyes gone blank as two aniseed balls. Thanks be to the Good Lord."

A few people coughed quietly and shuffled their feet, momentarily examining the floor.

"I had a sweet daughter, Maisie, her name was. Maisie-Daisy, I used to call her. I called upon the Lord to protect her, for she was a simple soul but full of goodness, and he threw her down the stairs and broke her neck, so I had no-one, nothing. I saw the Reverend Paulson when I came in, and I expect he wondered why, in all my long years, I've never once attended his church. Well, I think by now I've answered that question. Put simply, I can't afford the humility. Oh, right, I can see some of you looking a bit peeved now, like I'm not quite saying what you wanted to hear. Well, I'm sorry if I'm making you feel uncomfortable, but this is my final opportunity to say my piece, to tell you how relieved I am to be anticipating my departure from this tainted world. God help us all, eh?"

The band were inspecting their instruments, turning them this way and that, eyes downcast. Some people had returned to the buffet for light relief. Charlie felt his hand perspiring on the back of the chair.

"It's all right, I'm nearly done. We're nearly done. Now I don't like to name names, to single folk out and place them in an invidious position. It's not the done thing. But there's three people here I particularly want to mention, in fact, if you'll all just bear with me a few more minutes, I'd like to call them forward – for a specific reason." She turned to look at her grandson. "Charlie, will you do something for me? Will you please fetch another three of those chairs and put them here in front of me? I've something to give my friends and I can't be doing it if they're standing up."

Charlie carried three chairs to the space in front of his grandmother. She told him to push them close together.

"Go and stand behind me again, Charlie. I don't want you to be in the way."

Charlie did as he was told.

"Now then, let's get this finished. You've heard enough of an old woman droning on. You didn't come here for that." She heaved a deep sigh and rested both hands on top of her handbag. "I want Roland James and Raj and young Billy Smart to come out and sit in front of me. Please, don't be shy."

Looking at one another awkwardly, almost tripping over their feet, the three people she had called for stepped forward and sat down to face her. The other people smiled at them benevolently. Aware of a different mood in the room, Polly and Mervyn Broome had moved to peer round the curtain, waiting to see what was about to happen.

"Hello, special people," Minnie said, facing each of the

three in turn. "Well, it's come to this. Billy Smart, you live next door to me and though I've always known you're not the brightest, I had thought that really didn't matter, that you were a perfectly harmless lad. That is, until you let your bloody python slither through the wall and kill my dear cat. That was careless, wasn't it? Trouble is, you see, I never made a big fuss about it and so you thought you'd been forgiven. Well, funny how you make these mistakes, isn't it?" She shuffled round in her chair. "And here we have my landlord, Mr Roland James and his useless sidekick, Raj from India. Mr James wants to fleece me for more money. Raj wants a lesson or two in how to do his job. Or maybe it's a bit late for that."

Charlie Dixon knelt down and whispered harshly. "Gran, I think that's enough. Don't spoil your own party."

Billy, Roland and Raj sat quite still, as if transfixed. Behind them, Leila Smart was thrusting her way through the crowd.

"Don't move!" Minnie shouted at her. "One more minute and I'll be done!"

Standing at the back of the room, Polly and Mervyn Broome had Minnie in plain view. They saw her slip one hand into her handbag and withdraw something black, a soft-boned bat's wing perhaps, becoming three slim blindfolds, one of each she handed to the puzzled men who faced her.

"I have a present for each of you," she told them. "It's a surprise and I won't ask you to close your eyes in case you cheat and peep and spoil the fun. That's why I've brought these blindfolds. You must put them on and only remove them when I tell you."

Billy Smart and Roland James and Raj fitted the blindfolds over their eyes.

"Now you're all getting exactly the same surprise, which is quite fair. Sit up straight."

A breathless hush settled over the room. The friends and neighbours stood still as statues, watching the small group of four seated before them.

"That's good," Minnie said, "that's very good. Just give me a minute."

The people saw Minnie reach inside her bag with both hands. She used one hand to grip the pink velvet drawstring bag and the other to prise open the neck. Her right hand was quite steady as she drew out the gun and pointed it two feet from Billy Smart's forehead. Then she pulled the trigger and swung the barrel round with chilling accuracy to fire again at the bridge of Roland James' nose and once more into Raj's throat. The first bullet catapulted blood and cerebral matter across the room, splattering the nearest bowl of salad. Billy jolted backwards and crashed to the floor, still in his chair, with his splayed legs hooked over the chair seat. Roland James slumped forward like a dummy, blood pouring from a gaping hole beneath his brow. Raj toppled sideways to the red-slicked floor, clutching his throat as the escaping monster of his blood pumped through his fingers.

Charlie Dixon was shaking his grandmother by both shoulders, trying to grab the gun. With an icy, steel-eyed smile, she let him take it.

"You know, even at the last minute, I wasn't sure I could do it," she said, but her words were lost in the chaos of leaping and screaming.

Charlie dragged her frail frame out into the fading daylight and sat her on a wooden bench beneath a panic-shadowed window. The screams seemed to rattle the glass, tearing, guttural screams, unearthly, endless.

"You see, Charlie dear, they can't do anything to me. I'm a hundred. I am not without sin, but I am without fear."

Charlie Dixon could not know if he would live to be a hundred. But what he did know was that, for however long he lived, he would never forget the screaming.

# Chapter 54

## *Eight Years Later*

I told Sasha, when I thanked him for my book, that I was calling it my journal, and he laughed – well, sort of – but not in bad way, and said that sounded very grand. I told him I loved the soft, red leather cover and the way, because of the spiral binding, it opens flat and is easy to write in. Sasha got the book from work. I hope he didn't steal it. Well, he is quite important there, so I don't think it would be a problem for him to take a nice book from the office without getting into trouble. I have decided to make an entry in my journal at least twice a week and at the end of the year I will show what I have written to Sasha and Louise.

Perhaps I will even draw some pictures.

I like living in this house. It's big and bright and I have my own big room with two windows. You always know a room is big if it has more than one window. The main window looks out on the garden with the woods at the end. The garden path leads you to a blue wooden gate which lets you into the woods, and if you walk through the woods you come to the park. The other, smaller window looks on to a kind of paddock with grass and a fence and not much there. I said to Sasha that maybe there ought to be a horse there, but Sasha made a face and said he didn't like horses because they bite you and they were expensive to buy and keep and a car was loads better because you don't have to keep feeding a car. Then he looked worried and asked if I wanted to have a horse, so I made him feel better by telling him, no, I really didn't want a horse or even a pony. I wouldn't mind a rabbit, though. I would look after it very well and call it Hopscotch.

My favourite colour is orange. In my room I have three papered walls and one painted wall – painted a tangerine colour. Louise painted it herself. Louise is good at painting. The wallpaper is orange, too, with a sort of woodland scene on it, brown squirrels and brown birds and curly green leaves. It's a bit like I've got the woods in my room. I'm quite lucky, I think. Anyway, that's what my friends say when they come here.

I go to school at Saint Peter's. It's about three miles, but there is a school bus. Some days, if the bus doesn't run, Louise drives me to school in the Range Rover and we have the radio on loud and we sing along together and it's really fun. I quite like it when the bus doesn't run. Louise is very pretty. She tells me when I grow up I will be pretty, too, pale and pretty.

We have a nice dog, a black and white border collie called Bossy. He's called that because he likes to get his own way, though Louise says we mustn't encourage that. We don't want Bossy to become too bossy. One day I saw Sasha smack Bossy on the head with the newspaper and I didn't like him doing that, because Bossy doesn't mean any harm. So I told Sasha off and he pulled a funny face and looked a bit sorry. I really love Bossy. I'm not allowed to take him for walks on my own yet, but I go out with him and Sasha quite often and mostly we go through the woods to the park and let Bossy run off the lead. If we go in the early morning and the sun comes up, it's like magic in the woods, and the sunshine comes through the trees like silver swords and you can't look at it, it's so dazzling.

My two best friends from school are Rebecca and Samantha. I haven't got a boyfriend yet. Probably I'll get one when I get pretty, whenever that is. I like Rebecca best of all. Samantha is all right, but she is a little older than us and just wants to talk about boys all the time, which gets quite boring. She says she wants to marry the boy from the supermarket who delivers their food, but that seems rather mad, because he's about fourteen years older than her, so it wouldn't be an ideal match, and in any case Samantha is too young to get married and I bet when she's old enough she will have found someone else and the boy from the

Co-Op will have got married to another girl by then anyway. I wonder sometimes if Samantha is a bit crazy.

We went to the park yesterday, me and Sasha and Bossy, and we stopped for a while to watch some boys playing football. It was a proper match with a referee and everything and parents in their coats standing by the field. Sasha kept chuckling and shaking his head. When I asked him about this, he said it always amused him, because the boys playing football looked tired and had glum faces and the dads watching and shouting at them were jumping up and down and getting all excited, which just showed that the dads took their sons to football because they – I mean, the dads – were failed footballers who only wanted to see their boys doing stuff they weren't ever good enough to do when they were little. Sasha said the boys doing the football would mostly much rather be at home in the warm eating buttered toast and playing with their X-boxes and phones, if their dads hadn't dragged them out to the cold park to run about in short trousers while everyone else was wrapped up in hats and coats. Sasha knows about these things. Sasha is clever.

I must stop now and do my homework. Tonight I have Biology and an English essay to do. I love writing essays because they give me the chance to invent things and imagine people living in a different world. Whatever you write, it can never be wrong. I will try to write another page of my journal at the weekend. Sasha says he will find me a calligraphy pen so I can write my name beautifully in the front of this book where there is a square with a red border for the owner to fill in.

I will simply write:

*Neamh Anne McIver*
*Aged 9*


Finally, I can make a wish. One day soon, when I look out of the window at the woods, I hope, instead of the silver words flashing, I see my mother walking towards me through the trees.

Printed by BoD"in Norderstedt, Germany

9 781787 192676